H...s
Baby

**DELORES
FOSSEN**

**DONNA
YOUNG**

**CINDY
GERARD**

MILLS &
BOON

Mills & Boon, an imprint of Harlequin (UK) Limited, Eton House, 18-24 Paradise Road, Richmond, Surrey TW9 1SR

HER HERO'S BABY © Harlequin Enterprises II B.V./S.à.r.l 2013

Undercover Daddy © Delores Fossen 2007
Secret Agent, Secret Father © Donna Young 2008
A Convenient Proposition © Cindy Gerard 2006

ISBN: 978 0 263 90682 0

011-0713

Harlequin (UK) policy is to use papers that are natural, renewable and recyclable products and made from wood grown in sustainable forests. The logging and manufacturing processes conform to the legal environmental regulations of the country of origin.

Printed and bound in Spain
by Blackprint CPI, Barcelona

UNDERCOVER DADDY

DELORES
FOSSEN

THE BABY COLLECTION

May 2013

June 2013

July 2013

August 2013

Imagine a family tree that includes Texas cowboys, Choctaw and Cherokee Indians, a Louisiana pirate and a Scottish rebel who battled side by side with William Wallace. With ancestors like that, it's easy to understand why Texas author and former air force captain **Delores Fossen** feels as if she was genetically predisposed to writing romances. Along the way to fulfilling her DNA destiny, Delores married an air force top gun who just happens to be of Viking descent. With all those romantic bases covered, she doesn't have to look too far for inspiration.

To Daphne Betterton. You're the best.

Chapter One

Crystal Creek, Texas

"Elaina, your husband is…alive."

The eight-by-ten piece of amber glass that Elaina Allen had been examining slipped from her hand and crashed onto her desk. It didn't break but smashed right into a paper plate containing a half eaten slice of cherry pie. The red sugary filling spattered in every direction.

"Excuse me?" Elaina asked her assistant, Carrie. "What did you say?"

"Your husband is alive," Carrie repeated, nodding frantically. She bobbled up and down on her tiptoes and gave an excited squeal. "He's in Crystal Creek and on the way to the shop. He should be here any minute."

Elaina's heart dropped to her knees.

"There must be some mistake. Daniel's missing in action in the Middle East," Elaina lied. "If he'd been found, the air force would have told me."

Carrie grinned. "Well, they obviously didn't. A snafu maybe, or Daniel probably just wanted to surprise you. Anyway, he stopped by the gas station, and when he got ready to pay, the attendant, Jay, saw your picture in Daniel's wallet. That's when Jay figured out who he was. Jay said after Daniel filled up, he headed in this direction." Carrie's crystal blue eyes widened. "Oh, God. I blew the surprise by telling you, didn't I?"

Elaina couldn't answer. She could only shake her head. No. This couldn't be happening. It just couldn't be.

"Are you all right?" Carrie asked. "You look like you're about to be sick."

There was a reason for that. Elaina knew that the comfortable, safe life she'd created was *over*. Her house and her stained-glass shop were as good as gone. She'd have to go on the run again.

"You're happy about this, right?" Carrie asked. "I mean, this is what you wanted—for Daniel to come home to Christopher and you. You're always saying how much you miss him."

She stared at her shop assistant. They were more than employer and employee. The eternally optimistic Carrie had become her friend. Well, as much of a friend as Elaina could have considering she'd lied to Carrie from day one.

Elaina wasn't immune to the guilt she felt about that, either. She'd never quite come to terms with the pretense.

But she had a more pressing problem.

Daniel Allen was on the way to her shop.

Because that took her to the brink of panic, Elaina almost came clean about everything to Carrie. She almost explained all the lies. And, sweet heaven, there was a mound of lies. But she stopped her near confession and tried to make some sense of all of this.

"Jay said this man had my picture in his wallet?" Elaina clarified, praying for an out.

There had to be an out.

Carrie nodded, and the concern deepened in her eyes. "But he didn't just have your picture. When Jay asked, he told him that he was Daniel Allen."

Then, he was lying. No doubt about it.

Because there was *no* Daniel Allen.

He was the biggest lie of all.

Daniel Allen was an idea that Elaina had concocted to explain why she'd moved to the sleepy Texas town of Crystal Creek. An MIA husband. A grieving heart. The desire to start a new life while keeping hope that her *husband* might be alive and that he might return someday.

Elaine had purposely kept the personal details sketchy, because details could be examined too closely. So, she'd had no picture of her fake husband in case someone compared his looks to her son's. Instead, she'd told everyone that all her photos had been destroyed in a house fire.

The façade had kept some nosey questions from being asked, had given her space and privacy and it had allowed her and her baby, Christopher, to be accepted in a town where newcomers were often treated as outsiders.

That acceptance wouldn't continue once the townsfolk had learned that she was a liar. And this man, this imposter claiming to be Daniel Allen, would expose her.

But why?

Better yet—who was this imposter, and what the heck did he want?

Unfortunately, an answer immediately came to mind. A really bad answer. He might be linked to her late fiancé—the slimy, cheating con man who'd nearly gotten Christopher and Elaina killed.

"Well, don't just sit there," Carrie insisted. She latched on to Elaina's arm to lift her from the chair. "You haven't seen Daniel in over a year. Comb your hair. Put on some makeup. You have to do *something* to get ready for him."

The full impact of that hit her like a heavyweight's fist. Elaina got to her feet somehow. She had to do *something* all right.

She had to get out of there.

Fast.

She'd have to pick up Christopher from the sitter and drive out of town. There probably wouldn't be time to pack or stop for cash. She'd literally have to leave everything behind.

However, before she could even shake off Carrie's grip, Elaina heard the cheerful jingle of the brass and crystal bells that she'd installed over the front door of her shop. It caused her pulse to pound out of control.

Because it no doubt signaled her fake husband's arrival.

This was her own personal version of judgment day.

"Since you don't seem too steady on your feet, I'll bring him in here," Carrie volunteered.

"No!" Elaina caught on to her as she turned to leave.

What remained of Carrie's gleeful expression melted away. "What's wrong?"

"Nothing," Elaina assured her. Yet another lie. "I just need a minute to compose myself. I thought he was dead." Elaina didn't have to fake an over-whelmed expression. She was sure it was there all over her overwhelmed face.

"I'll be right there," Carrie called out to their *visitor*. It was something she would have done for any ordinary customer, but this time there was excitement and anticipation in her voice.

Elaina nodded her thanks for the brief reprieve, and she went to the door that separated her office from the stained-glass shop. With Carrie right behind her, she opened the door just a fraction and peeked out.

His back was to her, and he appeared to be exam-ining a Victorian window panel that Elaina had restored just days earlier.

Whoever he was, he was tall. Six-three at least. Not lanky, either. Solid and formidable. He wore jeans and a brown leather bomber jacket that was nearly the same color as his short, efficiently cut hair.

He turned to the side, and Elaina got a good look of him in profile. That good look was more than enough for her to realize that he was a complete stranger. If he was somehow connected to her late fiancé, Kevin, then she'd never seen him before.

That didn't mean she was safe.

She still had to leave with Christopher and find a new hiding place. Because if this man had found her, *they* could find her.

Elaina blinked back the hot tears that instantly sprang into her eyes, and she silently cursed. Kevin had been dead for over a year, and he was still casting shadows over her life.

"Well?" Carrie prompted in an anxious whisper when Elaina shut the door. "Daniel's here. Aren't you going to run out there, jump into his arms and haul him off to bed?"

Not a chance. The only thing Elaina planned to do was avoid him. "I need you to do me a favor, Carrie. Stall him."

Carrie shook her head. "W-hat? This is the extremely hot husband that you haven't seen in months and months, and you want me to stall him?"

Good point. The next lie came easily. "I need some time to make myself look presentable. I don't want him to see me with pie filling all over me and without a stitch of makeup. I'll only be a minute."

Carrie nodded, eventually, but judging from her bunched up forehead, she didn't understand.

How could she?

And better yet, how would Christopher?

Her son was barely three months past his first birthday. He wouldn't know why his mommy was dragging him away from the only home, bed and toys he'd ever known. One day, she'd have to tell him the truth.

If she remembered the truth by then.

Elaina had lived with the lies for so long that she had to wonder what exactly the truth was. Unfortunately, she might never know.

"Don't keep Daniel waiting too long," Carrie insisted. "And by the way—*he* is hot, just like I figured he'd be." She gave Elaina a wink and then headed back into the shop.

Elaina didn't waste a second. She locked the door behind Carrie and grabbed her purse from beneath her desk. She also took the picture of her son from the top of the filing cabinet. It was her favorite, taken on his first birthday. She stuffed it in her purse, and while she fumbled around the bottom of the shoulder bag for her car keys, she headed to the back exit that led directly to the parking lot.

She estimated that it would take her ten minutes to get to Christopher. She'd call on the way to tell Theresa, the sitter, that Christopher had an appointment with the pediatrician in nearby Luling. An appointment that had slipped her mind until the last minute. Though it would be a first for her to forget something like that, she hoped it'd be a believable lie. She didn't have time for questions.

Elaina located her keys and threw open the exit door. She heard someone trying to get into her office. Carrie maybe. Or maybe the imposter. Elaina ignored the frantic knocks and raced out of the shop.

The winter air was a little more brisk than she'd figured, and a chilly gust temporarily robbed her of her breath. Goose bumps rifled over her arms. The cotton shirt she wore wasn't much of a barrier. It didn't stop her. She ducked her head against the wind and made a beeline toward her car.

"Going somewhere?" she heard someone ask.

It was a man's voice.

Oh, mercy.

His voice, no doubt.

She didn't freeze, though she had to fight her instincts to prevent that from happening. Instead, Elaina began to run toward her car. Even though her heart was pounding and her shoes were slapping on the concrete, she could still hear his footsteps behind her.

Elaina made it all the way to her car before she felt the beefy hand clamp around her arm. She struggled against the grip and slammed her purse into the man's chest.

It didn't help.

As if she weighed nothing, he caught on to her, whirled her around to face him, and he pinned her against the hood of her car.

She screamed. Or rather tried to do that, but he pressed his hand over her mouth.

No profile view of him this time. She caught the full brunt of those lethal looking granite-gray eyes. In fact, lethal described every part of him from his hard body to the expression on his face.

Because he used his body to restrain her, she had no trouble determining that he was strong. No extra body fat on this guy. She also had no trouble spotting the shoulder holster and gun that was only partially concealed beneath his leather jacket.

Still, it didn't matter that she was outsized, out-maneuvered and outgunned. She wouldn't give up without a fight. Especially since this man might go after Christopher. Thankfully, the Crystal Creek police station was just up the block from the shop. She'd yell for help and deal with the inevitable questions later.

First though, she had to get free.

She managed to grab on to his wrist, and she ripped his grip from her mouth. "What do you want?" she snarled.

"Elaina Allen, I presume?" He didn't wait for her to confirm or deny it. "Let me introduce myself. I'm your long-lost husband, Captain Daniel Allen."

Oh, there was some cockiness in that voice tinged with a hint of a Texas drawl, but there were also questions. And accusations.

She forced herself to meet him eye to eye. "You're lying, and you know it."

"Yeah. I guess I do know it. But the way I see it, both of us have told some big fish stories, and both of us have some explaining to do. You start first."

Elaina was about to tell him that she owed him no such explanation and that he'd better let go of her at once or she'd scream, but then she heard Carrie. She peered over the man's shoulder and spotted Carrie in the doorway of the exit.

Elaina cursed under her breath.

So did the man.

She met his gaze to try to figure out what he was about to do. It was entirely possible he might try to kill Carrie so there wouldn't be any witnesses to Elaina's own murder. If that's what he had planned.

Elaina didn't have to wait long to find out.

Much to her shock, the imposter lowered his head and kissed her.

Chapter Two

Luke Buchanan had to keep reminding himself that the woman he was kissing was a liar. Maybe even worse. But just the fact he had to remind himself of that riled him to the core.

Why?

Because he didn't need a reminder that she tasted almost as good as she looked. And she *did* look good, far better than she had from the other end of long range surveillance equipment.

"Play along," Luke warned her, pulling back only slightly.

His warning earned him a nasty little glare. Those ice-blue eyes tapered to slits; and he could have sworn she hissed at him. But maybe that was the brutal November wind that was assaulting them.

"Oh, good," the skinny blond sales clerk said from behind them. "You found each other."

Luke didn't look back at her. He kept his gaze staked to the liar he'd just kissed.

The liar who tasted remarkably like cherry pie.

"Who are you?" the liar demanded.

"Your husband," he lied back. "Trust me, you'll want to go along with that for now. It's in your best interest."

Since his body was still against hers, he felt her go board stiff. She no doubt would have questioned him, or slugged him so she could escape, if the sales clerk hadn't stopped right next to them.

"This is so exciting," the clerk declared. She walked closer and grinned from ear to ear. "I'm a sucker for happy endings."

Well, this wasn't one of them.

Luke knew the clerk was Carrie Saunders. Age twenty-four. Born and raised in Crystal Creek. He was reasonably sure that Ms. Saunders didn't have a clue that she was working for a woman who'd fabricated an entire life. So, in a sense Carrie Saunders was a nonplayer. Or at least she would be once Luke got away from her. He definitely didn't want her or the local police to get suspicious, and he needed to get his *wife* alone so they could have a little chat.

"You wouldn't mind if Elaina left for the day, would you?" Luke asked the other woman. He kept his tone playful and needy, as if he truly were the long-lost husband who'd returned to his loving family.

"Take as much time as you want," Carrie insisted. She wagged her finger at Elaina. "I don't want to see you anywhere near this shop for at least a week. Oh, and if you need someone to babysit Christopher, just give me a call."

Luke assured her that they would, and he slid his arm around Elaina's waist to get her moving. She had that deer-caught-in-the-headlights look, and for a second, he wondered if she was going to try to run away.

"Don't even think about it," Luke mumbled. "You're leaving with me."

He took her keys from her trembling hand and practically pushed her inside her economy-size car. To keep the loving couple façade intact, he pressed a kiss on Elaina's gaping cherry-scented mouth, gave a friendly wave to Carrie and then drove away.

But he didn't breathe any easier now that the first part of his plan had worked. Because there were a lot of steps to this particular plan, and there were pitfalls with every one of them.

"Who are you and what do you want?" she demanded the second they were out of the parking lot.

Since this would no doubt be the beginning of many questions, Luke decided to give her the ground rules. "Here's how things are going to work. I'll ask the questions, and you'll provide the *truthful* answers. We'll start with why you're living this lie."

Her chin came up. "That's none of your business."

"I beg to differ."

It wasn't just his business.

It was his *life.*

"Why the lies?" he pressed.

She stayed a quiet a moment though she continued to stare at him. What she didn't do was answer him. "Are you here because of Kevin?"

Luke figured that name would come up soon enough. "Kevin Arneson, your late fiancé. I never met the man. And that's the only information you're going to get until you start talking. Oh, and remember that part about being truthful. I figure that'll be difficult for you, so try very hard."

No more deer-in-the-headlight look. She aimed her index finger at him. "Let's get something straight. I knew nothing about Kevin's illegal activities. *Nothing.* And I've already paid enough for his stupidity and deception."

"I'll be the judge of that."

She frowned and angled her body back slightly. "What's that supposed to mean?"

"That's another question and still no answer to mine. You're not good at following the rules, so let me clarify the information you're going to tell me. Why all the lies? And why are you in hiding?"

"I have my reasons, and you probably know what they are as well I do." She paused only long enough to draw breath. "I covered my tracks. I haven't used any of the money from Kevin's and my bank accounts or investments. And I haven't contacted a single person that I knew in my former life. So, how in the name of heaven did you find me?"

Luke huffed. Yet another question. This was turning into an annoying interrogation, and his intimidating scowl wasn't working.

Odd.

It usually did.

"Okay. A modification of the rules. Tit for tat, we'll call it. I'll give you a little info, and you'll do the same. I found you through your glass," he informed her.

That gave a moment of hesitation. "You what?"

"When I realized I was looking for Laina McLemore and that you'd disappeared, I started digging for clues. You were a successful stained-glass artist when you lived in San Antonio. I figured that's the line of work you'd fall back on, so I studied your designs, and I started scouring shops and Internet sites until I finally found pieces that I could attribute to your artistic style. People always leave trails when they try to hide." He glanced at her. "Your turn. Start answering my questions."

"Oh, God." But she didn't just say it once. She strung them together and plowed her hands through the sides of her short, spiky, honey-brown hair. "Is that why you're here? Are you one of those men, or did they send you?"

Luke had already geared up to remind her that it was her turn to provide information, but that stopped him cold. "What men?"

"The ones who followed me after Kevin was murdered." Anger fired through her eyes. "Well, if you're one of them, you've wasted your time."

Luke ignored her outburst. "Back up—who are these *men?*"

"They didn't exactly introduce themselves to me, but they did try to run me off the road." Her voice was clipped with anger, and the words came at him like bullets. "There were two of them. Both probably in their early thirties. One had very pale blond hair, and the other had a deep scar on the left side of his face. He wore an eye patch."

Luke wasn't sure what to make of that. Just retelling the event seemed to shake her, but then, this was a woman who was very good at telling believable lies. Still…

"What did these guys want?" he asked.

"I don't know. But I think it had something to do with some computer software that Kevin was modifying for someone he only ever referred to as T. Maybe those men were associated with this T, or maybe they thought I had the modifications or Kevin's research notes. I didn't." She snagged his gaze. "I really don't know anything about my late fiancé's criminal activity, okay? But I've paid for it. I've paid dearly by losing my home, my friends and by having to recreate a life among strangers."

Luke wasn't unaffected by the weariness and pain he heard in her voice, but he pushed aside any sympathy he was feeling by reminding himself of what this woman had done.

She'd robbed him of his life.

"What about the illegal adoption?" he asked. Not easily. It was almost impossible to keep the emotion out of it. "Have you paid for that, too?"

She blinked and pulled in her breath. "How did you know about the adoption?"

"I know a lot about you, Laina Marie McLemore. You're twenty-eight. Born in Bulverde, Texas. A rancher's daughter, though both your parents are dead. I can tell you the name of your third-grade teacher and what you had for dinner last night. What I'm trying to figure out if you were the mastermind behind Arneson's illegal ventures, or were you just along for the very lucrative ride?"

"I knew nothing about Kevin's business dealings or the legality of the adoption." And she was adamant about it, too.

Luke continued to push. "But you went along with it?"

"*Unknowingly* went along with it," she corrected.

When she didn't say more, he made a circular motion with his hand for her to continue.

She started with a huff. "Kevin was sterile, we wanted a baby, and he didn't want me to use donor sperm to get pregnant. He's the one who arranged for the adoption through an attorney in San Antonio. I didn't know it was illegal, not until months after Kevin was murdered, when I read about the illegal adoption ring in the paper. Even then, I didn't know that's how Kevin had gotten Christopher."

"But you suspected it," he accused her.

"No, I didn't. Not until I saw the name of the attorney who'd been arrested. By then, it was too late. I was already in hiding. I'd already established a life here in Crystal Creek. And I knew if I didn't stay hidden, those men would come after me—"

"Ah, the men again," he mocked. "They're getting a lot of playtime in this fantasy world of yours. And it's because of *these men* that you fled San Antonio and went into hiding."

"Yes." She paused. "You don't believe me?"

"No, but that's not important. The important thing is that after a year of digging, I found you."

"Lucky me," she grumbled. She turned in the seat so she was facing him. Her loose, well-worn jeans and dark red cotton shirt whispered against the vinyl seat. Her breath whispered, too. There was more weariness in it, but Luke could see her fighting it off. "Now, it's your turn to answer some questions. Who are you and what do you want?"

"I'm Luke Buchanan." Since the truth would no doubt speed this along, he added, "I'm a federal agent with the Department of Justice."

She put her hand over her heart as if to steady it. "Prove it."

The crisp demand had him doing a double take. For a weary lying woman, she certainly had a lot of resolve left. "Prove what?"

"Show me a badge or some kind of ID."

Jeez. Why couldn't she just confess all?

Irked, Luke reached into his jacket pocket and pulled out his badge. She took it, stared it and even scraped her thumbnail over the picture. Not just once. But twice.

"It's real," he assured her.

She must have agreed because she thrust it back at him. What he wouldn't tell her, yet, was that while the badge was real, this wasn't official Justice Department business.

No.

This was as personal as personal could get.

"I suppose you're here to arrest me for the illegal adoption?" she asked.

"That all depends."

"On what?" Finally, there was slip in her resolve. Her voice cracked.

"You." He came to stop in front of the house, turned off the engine and stared at her.

Probably because she hadn't taken her eyes off him, she hadn't realized where he'd taken her. She glanced out the window for a second before she snapped her head back in his direction. "This is my babysitter's house. What are we doing here?"

He turned toward her so he could see every nuance of her reaction. "Why do you think I'm here?"

"Oh, no." She began to shake her head. "I can't let you do this. You can't arrest me. You don't understand—he's my son. I've raised him since he was three days old. I'm the only mother he's ever known."

"Believe me, I know that."

And that was the only reason he hadn't had Laina McLemore arrested.

"I won't let you take him from me," she insisted.

"You have no choice." And he was just as adamant.

"But you do." Her bottom lip began to tremble,

and she gripped the sides of his leather jacket. "You can walk away from this. You can pretend you never found me."

Luke had thought he would be immune to a reaction like that, but he wasn't. "I can't do that."

The grip she had on his jacket melted away, and she touched her fingers to her mouth. Tears sprang to her eyes. "Oh, God. The birth parents know about Christopher, and they want him back."

"His birth mother is dead." Luke had to take a deep breath after saying that. And another deep breath before he could continue. "But his birth father does indeed want him back."

Twin tears spilled down her cheeks. "Then, I need to talk to him. I need to make him understand how much Christopher means to me."

"You're already talking to him, and there's nothing you can say or do to make me change my mind. Christopher is *my* son."

Chapter Three

Elaina's breath vanished. And her heart. God, her heart. It was pounding so fast and hard that she thought her ribs might crack.

This was her nightmare come true. Well, one of them anyway. The only thing worse than this would be another attack from those men. But this was an attack of a different kind.

Luke Buchanan was Christopher's birth father.

Or was he?

On the surface it seemed stupid to challenge him, but she was desperate. "Why should I believe you?" she asked. "Show me some proof that he's your son."

She figured that might buy her some time. It didn't. As if he'd anticipated the question, he calmly reached inside his leather jacket and produced a manila envelope. Elaina also noticed the gun tucked in a leather shoulder holster. It looked as authentic and official as his badge. Luke Buchanan seemed to be the real deal.

"Let me start with how I found out that you had my son. A woman named Collena Drake, a former cop, has been digging through the hundreds of files left by the criminals who orchestrated the adoptions, among other things. She got in touch with me and was able to tell me the names of the couple who'd illegally adopted Christopher."

"Collena Drake could have been wrong," Elaina offered. "And the records could have been wrong, too. After all, the people who put them together were criminals. You just said so yourself."

He ignored her, opened the envelope and extracted a picture. "That's Taylor, my late wife."

Elaina took the photo from him, dreading what she might see. It was the picture of a couple on their wedding day. The bride, dressed in white, was a beautiful brunette. The groom, Luke Buchanan, wore a tux.

"That's still not proof," Elaina insisted.

Luke Buchanan's calm demeanor remained in place. From the envelope, he produced a marriage license. He placed it on the seat between them. Elaina was about to repeat her doubt, but the next document kept her quiet.

It was a lab slip indicating a positive pregnancy test.

The date on the slip was eight months prior to Christopher's birth.

"In addition to the lab results, this is a report that details how I learned about what happened to Taylor and our baby." He plopped the stapled pages onto the stack. "There's an eyewitness account of Taylor arriving at the Brighton Birthing Center just outside San Antonio. She was in labor. The eyewitness helped her into the E.R. section of the building and then left. All of this happened August eleventh of last year."

That information hit her hard. Because August eleventh was Christopher's birthday. And his place of birth was indeed the Brighton Birthing Center. Still, Elaina wasn't going to accept this blindly.

"Eyewitness accounts can be falsified," she countered.

"Not this one. It came from the cab driver who took Taylor from our house to the birthing center. He has absolutely no reason to lie."

She swallowed hard. "Maybe not, but that still doesn't prove Christopher is your son. There were probably dozens of babies born that day."

"Three." He paused a heartbeat and snagged her gaze. "But only one boy. Seven pounds, four ounces. Twenty-one inches long. Sound familiar?"

Oh, mercy. It did.

Elaina felt the tears burn hot in her eyes, and she didn't even try to fight them back.

"Take a good look at that photo," he said, fishing out the wedding picture from the pile. "You'll see that Taylor and I are Christopher's birth parents."

Though it was nearly impossible to see clearly through the thick tears, Elaina did study the photo he handed her. Luke and Taylor Buchanan were both brunettes. As was Christopher. And though she hadn't made the connection when she first met Agent Buchanan, she could see it now.

Christopher had his eyes.

Except on her son, the color seemed softer. Kinder. Rainy-cloud-gray, she'd whimsically called them. It was ironic to see those same eyes on this man who could destroy her.

And there was no doubt about it—losing Christopher *would* destroy her.

That's why Elaina didn't give up. She couldn't. He'd made a good case, but other than the similar eyes, he certainly hadn't proven anything.

"Why did your wife have to take a taxi to the Brighton Birthing Center?" she asked. "Where were you during all of this?"

"I was on a deep-cover assignment trying to stop a terrorist attack." A muscle flickered in his jaw. "Taylor and I were having problems, and we'd gotten a legal separation right before I left. I didn't know she was pregnant until after I returned. Then, I learned she'd died of complications from a C-section. I also learned that the baby, our son, had been adopted, but the records had supposedly been destroyed. The records didn't surface until the police busted the illegal operation and Collena Drake decided to devote all her time to locating the missing kids. That's why it took me this long to find you."

Each word added dead weight to her heart. Because this was unfortunately all starting to make sense.

"I found you eight days ago," he continued. The

calm façade seemed to slip a little. There was a touch of hot, raw emotion in his voice. "And I put you under surveillance."

She shook her head. "I didn't know."

"Of course, you didn't. I do a lot of surveillance in my job, and I'm very good at it."

No doubt. It riled her that someone had been able to intrude into her life without her even realizing it. That gave her the resolve she'd been searching for. "So, you watched me and decided to step into my fake life and pretend you're my husband?"

He nodded. "You made it easy for me to do that. I had a fellow agent ask around town. He pretended to be interested in having some church windows repaired. And he learned there were no photos of your fake spouse. No specific physical accounts or descriptions. No one around here seemed to know what Daniel Allen looks like."

"I didn't want anyone comparing the photo to Christopher. Since he doesn't look like me, I just told people that he took after his father." Elaina paused and tried to fight off the dark reality she felt closing in around her. "And maybe he does."

"*Maybe?* You still have doubts after everything I've shown you?"

"I have to have doubts." She slapped her hand on the documents he'd shown her. "Doubts are the only thing that prevents me from screaming and running inside to hide my son from you. Besides, you have no DNA proof—"

"I do have proof. I got back the results about two hours ago. That's why I'm here."

There was no way Elaina could have braced herself for the final paper that he took from the envelope. She shook her head when he tried to hand it to her, but he finally dropped it onto her lap.

She had no choice. Even though she didn't want to look at it, her eyes refused to cooperate. It was indeed a DNA test, and it identified Luke Buchanan as the father of one Christopher Allen.

That put another fracture in her heart.

"This can't be accurate," she challenged. "You don't have Christopher's DNA so you had nothing to make the comparison."

But his expression said differently. "After I found you, I took a pacifier that Christopher had left in his car seat. And before you accuse me of breaking and entering, I didn't. I had a warrant."

She hadn't thought it possible, but her heart pounded even faster. Elaina frantically searched for holes in his case and found one. "If you have this proof," she said picking up the DNA test, "then, why pretend to be my long-lost husband?"

"Because there's something I need from you."

He let that hang between them for several moments before he scooped up all the papers and put them back into the envelope. "Here's what's going to happen—we'll go inside and you'll make introductions. To the sitter and especially to my son. For the next few days, I'll pretend to be the husband that you've so cleverly created."

But once they were inside, he could take Christopher. "And if I don't agree?"

He lifted his shoulder and slipped the envelope back into his jacket. "Then, I call the FBI, and have you arrested for participating in an illegal adoption. Then, I take Christopher from Crystal Creek, and you'll never see him again."

Mercy, he was indeed holding all the cards. "And if I cooperate?" She held her breath, praying for some good news in all of this.

"I'll still take Christopher, eventually. After he's gotten to know me." More of that calm reserve slipped away. He scrubbed his hand over his face. "Look, I know you've been a good mother to my son, but he's mine, and I have no intentions of giving him up. We might even be able to work out visitation rights for you—if you can ever convince me that you didn't do anything illegal to get him."

Elaina was about to ask how she could ever prove that, but she caught some movement out of the corner of her eye. She looked out the window. Theresa, the sitter, was making her way across the yard toward the car.

Elaina groaned. She didn't need this visit. Not now. She still somehow had to convince Luke Buchanan to leave and never come back.

A smiling Theresa tapped on the window, and Elaina reluctantly lowered it. The elderly woman had sugar-white hair and smelled of ginger cookies. Christopher's favorite. Theresa had no doubt been baking them for him.

Theresa's attention went straight to Luke Buchanan. "Daniel, it's so good to meet you," Theresa said before Elaina could offer any explanation. "I'm Theresa Gafford. I babysit your precious son."

Luke nodded and even flashed a smile. The facial gesture seemed stiff as if it'd been a while since he'd done that. "Good to meet you, too, Theresa."

There were tears in Theresa's eyes and a smile on her face. "Thank goodness you're home. You're the answer to so many prayers."

More like the answer to a nightmare. "Carrie called you to tell you that Daniel was here," Elaina said to Theresa.

"Yes. And Jay from the gas station, too," Theresa verified. "It's impossible to keep secrets around here."

It was a comment that caused Elaina to cough.

Theresa motioned toward the house. "Christopher's taking a nap, but I can wake him. I suspect you're anxious to see him." She smiled. "Or maybe you two should just head home and I can bring him after he's awake."

"No." Elaina quickly vetoed that. She wanted to spend no more time alone with this man. Of course, she didn't want him around Christopher, either. "We'll come back later."

Much later.

"Darling," Luke said. The term of endearment

seemed as foreign as his smile. "If you don't mind, I'd love to see my son. Now."

Those stormy eyes warned her to defy him.

Elaina cast him her own warning, but she knew his carried far more weight. He could have her arrested. He could legally remove Christopher from her life.

Because she had no choice, Elaina reached for the door handle. She would cooperate, for now. But there was no way she could let him take Christopher.

Luke got out of the car at the same time she did, and he quickly went to her and slid his arm around her waist. Since Theresa was ahead of them and couldn't see, Elaina tossed him a scowl and pushed her elbow against his ribs to keep some distance between them.

"Daniel, the three of you will have to come for dinner once you're settled," Theresa said.

"Thank you," Luke answered. "I'd like that."

Elaina mumbled the same fake gratitude under her breath, knowing that there'd be no dinner. If she couldn't talk Luke into leaving, she'd have to consult an attorney about what her rights were.

If she even had rights.

It was entirely possible that she didn't.

"Oh, I nearly forgot," Theresa said, stopping on the top porch step. The wind rifled through her hair when she turned around to face Elaina. "About two hours ago I went over to your house to get Christopher his bunny. You forgot to bring it this morning.

Anyway, while I was there, two men drove up in a black car and asked to speak to you."

Elaina stopped, too, and stared up at the woman. "Who were they?"

"Census takers, they said." Theresa's forehead bunched up. "I thought it was a little early for that, but they said they needed to ask you some questions. I told them you might be at your shop and let them know that it was easy to find since it was on Main Street just up from the police station."

Elaina was more than a little concerned. In the entire year she'd been in Crystal Creek, no one had come looking for her. It seemed too much of a coincidence that she'd have three visitors in the same day.

"Did these men show you any ID?" Luke wanted to know.

Theresa shook her head. "No. I didn't ask for it. Oh, dear. Should I have?"

"No," he assured her. "It's just they might have been from the air force, to give Elaina official notification that I was coming home."

"They definitely said they were census takers." Theresa paused. "But to be honest with you, they made me a little uncomfortable. Especially the one with the eye patch."

"Eye patch?" Elaina repeated, her voice barely making a sound.

Theresa nodded. "You just don't see many eye patches these days, and this guy had a scar to go with it. Anyway, he didn't talk much, but the tall blond man with him said they'd come back later to discuss things with you."

Elaina looked at Luke, and would have given him an I-told-you-so glare if she hadn't been so terrified.

Luke reacted. And his reaction terrified her even more.

He shoved his hand inside his jacket so he could grip his weapon, and his gaze fired around them.

"Get inside," he ordered. *"Now."*

Chapter Four

"What's wrong?" Theresa, asked. "What's happening?"

Luke didn't answer her. Instead, he hooked his arms around both women, hurried them inside and locked the door. He did a quick visual scan of the interior of the place. It was clean and homey with the smell of freshly made cookies. But the main thing he wanted to establish was that there were no gunmen inside.

There weren't any signs of them. Hopefully, it would stay that way.

"Are the other doors locked?" he asked Theresa.

Her eyes widened. "Yes. I did that before I drove over to Elaina's. I haven't been out back since then, so I'm sure they're still locked."

Good. A locked door wouldn't stop pros, but it might slow them down. "Check, just to make sure."

Theresa didn't question him. She hurried to do what he'd asked.

Luke automatically went through a mental checklist. According to the sitter, the baby was asleep. The men were likely only minutes away. Maybe less. And basically, once he'd verified that the doors were locked, Theresa's house was about as secure as he was going to be able to make it without equipment and assistance.

"I can't believe this is happening," Elaina mumbled. She rubbed her hands up and down her arms and paced.

Yeah. Luke was having a hard time believing it, as well. "You're sure these guys are a real threat?"

She stopped in midpace. "Oh, they're real. I'm just wondering why they didn't go to the shop after Theresa told them that's where I was."

Probably because the shop was so close to the police station. If the men were up to no good, that's the last place they'd want to confront Elaina. More likely scenarios were that they'd either hang around her house. Or they'd come here.

"Everything's locked up," Theresa said, returning to the room.

Luke took out his gun and pulled back a lacy white curtain so he could see outside.

"Please tell me what's wrong," Theresa said. She sounded on the verge of tears.

Elaina answered before he could. "There are war protestors who might have followed Daniel to Crystal Creek. You know how some people are opposed to the military being overseas. Daniel just doesn't want to take any chances that these protestors might be fanatics."

Luke wasn't surprised that Elaina's lie had come so easily, but this time, he was thankful for it. He needed to focus on what had to be done. Because, simply put, his son could be in danger.

"Go to Christopher," he instructed Theresa. "If the windows aren't locked, then lock them. Close the curtains, turn off any lights and stay with him until we're certain these *protestors* are gone."

Theresa nodded. "Should I call the sheriff?"

Luke didn't really want to have to deal with the locals on this. Not until he was certain what he was dealing with. "No. Don't call him yet. This might turn out to be nothing."

The sitter rushed away again, headed toward one of the side rooms of the house, and Luke turned his attention to the street. Would the men arrive in a car, as they'd apparently done at Elaina's, or were they on foot? Luke had to be prepared for either.

He took out his cell phone and pressed in the number for his backup: a friend and fellow agent, Rusty Kaplan. He was waiting just a few miles away.

"I need your help," Luke told Rusty. "Look for two men driving around town in a black car. One is blond. The other is wearing an eye patch. If you find them, take them in for questioning."

Rusty assured Luke that he would, and Luke hung up, slipping the phone back into his jacket pocket.

"I blame you for this," Elaina snarled in a hoarse whisper. She frantically looked around the room and extracted an umbrella from a tall reed basket by the door. Presumably, she planned to use it as a weapon.

Luke moved to another window in the living room where he had a better view of the street and the side of the yard. He kept his gun ready.

"How do you figure?" he asked.

"Those men must have followed you to Crystal Creek."

Luke couldn't completely rule it out, but that scenario wasn't very likely. "If someone followed me, I would have noticed."

"Maybe not," she fired back.

"*I would have noticed*," he insisted.

Maybe someone hadn't followed him per se, but they might have gotten the information from Collena Drake and backtracked until they found Elaina.

Now the question was—what the hell did they want?

Luke didn't want to get into a lengthy discussion, or argument with Elaina to try to figure all of that out. Later, he would have to learn what kind of hornet's nest her dead fiancé had left her to deal with. Because according to what Elaina had said, these men were almost certainly connected to Kevin.

Unless…

There was an outside shot that they were connected to him. Oh, man. He hoped that wasn't the case.

Elaina moved to the window next to him and stared out. "Do you see them?"

"No." In fact, no one seemed to be around.

Except Elaina, of course.

She moved so close to him that he caught her scent. Something fresh, floral and feminine. Something that he didn't want to smell or notice. Luke stepped away from her and moved to a window in the adjoining dining room.

Of course, she and her feminine scent quickly followed him. "How long before you hear something from your partner?"

"Soon. He'll be as thorough and as fast as he can possibly be." Luke only hoped that it wouldn't be hard to spot two strangers in the small town. Thankfully, there wouldn't be many guys with an eye patch.

"This is a nightmare," she mumbled. "And this is what I've been trying to avoid for over a year."

Luke spared her a glance to see how she was physically reacting to the situation. Elaina had a white-knuckled grip on the perky yellow umbrella, but other than that, she seemed to be holding up.

"You sure that's all you were trying to avoid?" he asked.

Elaina's grip tightened even more. "What's that supposed to mean?"

"Maybe you were trying to avoid me because I'm Christopher's father."

She probably would have pounced on that accusation if Luke hadn't noticed the car driving toward the house. He held up his left hand to cut off anything she might have said, and then raced back to the front door so he'd have a direct shot if it became necessary.

Luke waited, his heart in his throat, as the black

four-door car slowly approached and stopped in front
of the house. A blond man was driving. The guy with
the eye patch was riding shotgun.

This didn't look good.

He took out his phone and called Rusty Kaplan
again. "The suspects are at the sitter's house. Get
here ASAP."

He put his phone away so he could focus on keeping his weapon aimed and ready. Beside him, Elaina
did the same. She lifted her umbrella.

Luke rolled his eyes at her attempt to defend
herself. "Get down on the floor," he ordered.

"I want to protect Christopher," she countered.

"Well, it won't happen with an umbrella. Get on
the floor in case they fire shots."

"Oh, God," she mumbled.

She was obviously terrified at the thought of
bullets flying.

So was Luke.

But it wouldn't help matters if Elaina got hurt. In
fact, it was his responsibility to keep everyone in the
house safe. He might not have been the one to bring
these men to Crystal Creek, but there was too much
at stake for him to not make sure they did no harm—
especially to his son.

Instead of getting on the floor, she stooped down
next to him and put her shoulder against the door so
she could peek out the stained-glass sidelights. "I
can't just hide. I have to do something to stop them."

Luke knew how she felt.

"For now, the best way to help is stay put. Backup in on the way."

The men didn't leave their parked car. They just sat there, watching the house, occasionally saying something to each other.

More than anything, Luke wanted to go out there to confront them. But that was too big of a risk. If he got shot or hurt, then that would leave Christopher, Elaina and Theresa without protection. He couldn't do that. But he could try to make sense of all of this while they were waiting.

"If these guys are looking for Kevin's software modifications, what do you think they'll do to you if they can't get them?" he asked.

"They'll kill me." Her voice wasn't shaky or trembling. Nor was she hesitant.

Luke didn't take his eyes off the car or the men inside. "And these guys didn't show up until after you'd adopted Christopher?"

"That's right." Now, there was some hesitation. "Why do you ask?"

"Because they might not be associated with software but with the adoption itself. Maybe they're working for someone who wanted to cover their tracks."

"Maybe. But the people involved with the adoption ring have already been arrested."

"That's why they'd need to hire someone on the outside to do it for them," Luke pointed out.

Especially if their crimes included murder.

There, Luke had finally made a connection that he

didn't want to make. A connection that linked him with these goons in the car. And it also might link them to his estranged wife's suspicious death. "What did this so-called adoption agency tell you about Christopher's birth mother? Specifically, what did they say about her death?"

"Nothing."

"They didn't even tell you that she was dead?"

Elaina's eyes widened, and she shook her head. "I didn't know. The paperwork was sketchy at best, and I never dealt directly with them. Only Kevin spoke to them."

Great. One crook dealing with a bunch of others who were making a fortune in the baby-selling business. The police had estimated that Kevin had paid nearly fifty thousand dollars for his son.

"You think they killed your wife?" Elaina asked.

The woman was certainly good at connecting the dots. "Someone did," Luke mumbled.

He heard Elaina suck in her breath. Luke had a similar mental reaction. Just thinking about Taylor's death affected him that way. Even though Taylor and he had fallen out of love long before their separation, he would always blame himself for not being there to protect her.

"I had Taylor's body exhumed," Luke explained. "They're doing the autopsy in a day or two, but it looks as if she had help dying from complications from a C-section."

That was all Luke had time to say.

Because the two men stepped from the car and started walking toward the house.

ELAINA LIFTED HER umbrella, knowing it was probably futile and borderline stupid, but also knowing that she wouldn't let these men get to her son.

If that's what they intended.

It was entirely possible they'd come just to kill her. She wasn't ready to die, but she preferred that to any attempt they might make to harm Christopher.

The two men stopped at the end of the walk and stared at the house. The blonde said something to the other and then glanced over his shoulder at Elaina's car. They obviously knew she was there.

Would they just try to break in?

Would they storm the place?

Maybe. But with Luke there, she was betting they wouldn't be successful. For the first time since she'd laid eyes on the man who could destroy her, she was thankful Luke was with her. Protecting Christopher was everything now, and though Elaina had plenty of doubts about Luke Buchanan, she didn't doubt his ability to keep her baby safe.

But safe from what?

Were these men connected to Kevin, or as Luke had suggested, were they connected to the adoption? If so, had they already murdered Luke's wife?

That chilled her to the bone. Because if this was linked to the adoption, then they might plan to go after Christopher. Maybe they'd do that to eliminate a connection to a murdered woman. But if that was true, then Luke would be a target, as well.

The men began walking again. Beside her, she was aware that Luke tensed his muscles. But that was only reaction. He aimed his weapon directly at them.

"Move away from the door," Luke whispered. And even though it was a whisper, it was still an order.

This time, Elaina obeyed, because she knew that bullets could easily go through the wood. Theresa's fifty-something-year-old home wasn't designed to block intruders.

Elaina crawled to the side. Not far. She wanted to be near that door if the men tried to break it down.

"There's my backup," she heard Luke say.

Elaina scrambled to the window to see what he meant, and she saw the other car approach. But it didn't just *approach.* The dark blue SUV came screeching around the corner and came to a jerky stop right behind the men's vehicle. And that wasn't all. The agent who got out was armed. He pointed a huge gun right at the men.

"Stay put," Luke warned her.

Luke barreled out the door, probably to give back up to the backup. Elaina didn't mind. She wanted those two men arrested and away from Christopher and her.

She couldn't hear what Luke said to them, but both men lifted their hands into the air. Luke kept his gun trained on them while Luke's partner, a tall brown-haired man, rushed to handcuff the two men.

The agent also searched them. Both men had not just one weapon but two each.

Luke and the agent didn't waste any time. They ushered the men into the backseat of the agent's SUV. Elaina sat there, her face glued to the sidelight window, and she watched as Luke said something else to them. The men didn't respond. A few moments later, the agent drove away with the men.

Elaina got to her feet, though the adrenaline made her jittery. Later, when all of this sank in, she was certain she'd be furious at those imbeciles for putting her through this.

Luke came through the door, and he tucked his gun back into his shoulder holster. "Agent Kaplan is taking them to the local jail. As soon as they're processed, I'll go there and assist with the interview."

"So, they didn't admit to any guilt when you arrested them?"

He shook his head and blew out a weary breath. "No. But unless they have permits to carry concealed weapons, we can hold them on that for a while."

For a while didn't sound nearly long enough.

"Why would those men have killed your wife?" Elaina asked. She shoved the umbrella back into the basket and made sure that Theresa was still in the nursery. She didn't want the woman overhearing any of this. "You think they did it to get Christopher from her so they could hand him over to the lawyers running the adoption ring?"

Luke adjusted his leather jacket so the weapon wouldn't be visible. "That's one theory."

She snapped toward him. "There's more than one?"

He nodded. Raked his fingers over his eyebrow. "Right before I went on the deep cover-up last year, I arrested a man named George Devereux. He was slime, into too many different crimes to name. Devereux vowed revenge because I arrested him. I haven't been able to prove it, but it's possible that Devereux murdered Taylor shortly after she gave birth. It's also possible that he or one of his henchmen sold or gave Christopher to the adoption ring."

Elaina felt as if someone had punched her in the stomach. It took several seconds to regain her breath and some semblance of composure. It took her slightly longer than that to manage to think his theory through. On the one hand, it would make her feel marginally better to put the blame on Luke. But on the other hand, she didn't want a heavy-duty criminal like Devereux to be involved in this.

"So then, why would Devereux's men come after me?" she demanded to know. "I certainly can't link him to Christopher's adoption or to Taylor's death."

"Maybe Devereux didn't want to stop with Taylor." Luke paused and met her gaze. "Maybe he's had time to stew while sitting in prison and wants to continue his revenge."

"Oh, God." Elaina dropped back a step. "You mean Christopher?"

"Yeah," he confirmed.

Elaina groaned and felt the sickening knot form in her stomach. "So, either George Devereux or Kevin might have spawned this?"

"There's only one way to find out which one. Those two men will provide the answers."

Yes. The men. With all the talk about Devereux and revenge, she'd nearly forgotten that they might be very close to learning what this was really about. In fact, if the men confessed to trying to kill her, then they'd be off the streets for a long, long time. Their confession and incarceration could give her the safety she'd been praying for and the freedom to resume a normal life.

For all the good it'd do her now.

Luke Buchanan's arrival had changed everything, and Elaina didn't think they would agree on what she considered a *normal life*. Heck, he could still try to have her arrested for the illegal adoption.

Elaina felt sick. That feeling didn't go away when she heard Theresa call out. "I hope those protestors are gone. Christopher's up from his nap. Is it okay if I bring him out there?"

She was on the verge of saying no, but the word stuck in her throat. Luke, however, seemed to have no trouble responding. Obviously following the sound of Theresa's voice, he headed straight for Christopher.

Elaina rushed after him. It was like a train wreck about to happen.

Luke paused in the doorway of the nursery, and

since he took up nearly the entire space, Elaina had to stand on her tiptoes to see what had stopped the agent in his tracks.

Christopher was there. He wore the denim overalls and long-sleeved knit blue shirt that she'd dressed him in that morning. He was standing, holding on to the arm of the rocking chair where Theresa was seated.

"The protestors are gone?" Theresa asked.

"They're gone," Luke assured her, but his attention was focused solely Christopher.

Luke stepped toward the baby. Elaina's instincts screamed to stop him. But she couldn't. She could only stand there and watch as Luke reached down and gently lifted her son into his arms.

Chapter Five

Luke forgot to breathe.

In fact, he forgot everything when he picked up his son. He'd never thought anything could feel like this. It was magic. Pure magic. And the weight of the world slipped off Luke's shoulders.

Well, in one way it did.

In another, he knew instantly that he would do whatever it took to protect—and claim—his son.

Christopher whimpered a little and tossed a questioning glance at Elaina before turning those suspicious gray eyes back on Luke. Eyes that were a perfect replica of Luke's own.

The genetics didn't stop there. Luke had seen baby pictures of himself, and Christopher was a little DNA copy, right down to his chocolate-brown hair.

His son's bottom lip quivered, and judging from his expression he was about to cry.

"It's okay," Theresa said, her voice soothing. "It's Da Da. Remember, we talk about Da Da. Well, Da Da's come home to be with you."

Even more skepticism came into Christopher's eyes, but he tested out the syllables he'd heard his sitter say. "Da Da."

Behind him, Luke heard Elaina's breath shatter, and he looked back to see the tears streaming down her cheeks. Theresa was crying, too, but Luke was almost positive that the sitter's tears were of the happy variety.

He couldn't say the same for Elaina.

Those were real tears of pain and anguish. Luke understood them. Though he hadn't cried, he'd felt those same raw emotions from the moment that he learned he had a son. It'd ripped his heart into pieces. Now, just holding his baby, just hearing him say those precious sounds, made all the pain and anguish melt away.

"I'll give the three of you some privacy," Theresa insisted. She stood and left the room, closing the door behind her.

His son smelled like baby powder and cookies. Luke brushed a kiss on Christopher's forehead, and because he suddenly wasn't feeling too steady on his feet, he sat down in the rocker. Elaina sat, as well. Groaning softly, she sank down onto the floor and buried her face in her hands.

That seemed to be Christopher's cue to get moving. The little boy squirmed to get out of his arms, and though Luke hated to let go of him, his son was insistent. Fearing that he might drop him, Luke finally deposited him onto the floor. He held on to him until Christopher plopped into a sitting position and then immediately crawled toward Elaina.

The only mother his son had ever known.

Christopher used her knees to pull himself up to a rather precarious standing position. He slapped at her hands until she lowered them. Despite her tear-stained face, the little boy smiled at her. It wasn't an ordinary smile, either. It was a smile of joy and love.

Seeing that love aimed at Elaina put a fist around Luke's heart. On the one hand, he despised the woman who'd perhaps robbed him of months with his son. On the other hand, she was the center of his baby's world.

For now, anyway.

She reached out and pulled Christopher to her. "You can't take him away from me."

Maybe not right away he couldn't, but if she was innocent Luke couldn't see including her permanently in his life. Except for perhaps visitation rights. He only hoped that was enough.

"Concentrate on the here and now," Luke told her. "I will raise my son, and that'll be a lot easier to do with your *cooperation*."

That sent her gaze slicing to his. "And what do you consider cooperation?"

"Help Christopher through this adjustment."

She huffed. "You're talking about your plan. You want me to pretend to be your loving wife until you're comfortable enough to take Christopher."

"I don't want him to have too many changes at once," Luke clarified. "I want this to be the easiest possible transition for him. If we're in the house that he considers home, if you're there, and if we can create a safe, nurturing environment for him, then—"

"Then you'll wait until he gets to know you and then take him."

Yes. But Luke couldn't say that to her, not with those tears in her eyes. "We'll see what we can work out," he offered.

And under the circumstances, it was the best he could give her.

They sat there, both looking at the little boy they loved and wanted. And there was no doubt about it. Luke did love this child. Unconditional, total love. Even though he'd just met him for the first time, he couldn't imagine a life without his son.

Christopher babbled something indistinguishable and dropped back to the floor so he could crawl to his toys. Luke got down there with him, but before the playtime could start, his cell phone rang.

Hating the interruption but knowing it could be critical, Luke answered the call. "Agent Buchanan."

"It's me, Rusty," he heard his friend say. "We made it to the jail without incident. The sheriff is booking the guys now. This is all just preliminary, but I checked their IDs. Their names are Damien Weathers and Simon Foster. Neither have a permit to carry concealed weapons so we can hold them. I ran their priors. Both also have records for burglary and some outstanding traffic tickets, but that's it."

That didn't mean the two were innocent of this

particular count. Whatever this *count* was. And it didn't mean they weren't the ones who'd tried to hurt Elaina a year ago.

"I'll come down for the interviews," Luke insisted.

"There won't be any, not for a while at least. Both lawyered up, and both are giving us the silent treatment. You're not getting anything out of these guys."

Luke mentally cursed. "When will the lawyer be there?"

"Not until morning. No interviews, no interrogations until then."

He mentally cursed even more. It wasn't what he wanted to hear. But on the upside, as long as the men were behind bars, then Christopher was probably safe. Still, Luke wasn't about to take any chances.

"You take care of things there with your little boy," Rusty insisted. "I'll arrange to install the security equipment we discussed."

Luke had nearly forgotten about that. Not good. He needed to be totally focused because that equipment was a necessity. He wanted it installed in the wooded area behind Elaina's house. With a motion-activated silent alarm, it would warn in advance if someone tried to sneak onto her property.

"I can get one of the agents from the Austin office to install it," Rusty explained. "We'll connect it to your cell phone signal so we won't need to put any equipment inside Elaina's house."

"That'd be a big help," Luke assured him.

"No problem. I'll spend the night here at the

sheriff's office. In the mean time, I'll keep digging and see if I can find any outstanding warrants on them. I'll have their car impounded, as well. Something might turn up that we can use to put these guys away for a long, long time."

"Thanks, Rusty."

Elaina was staring at him when he ended the call. "What happened?"

"The men are in jail. I'll interrogate them tomorrow after their lawyer shows up." But no lawyer was going to stop him from getting answers.

"So, what do we do until then?" she asked.

It would not be an answer she liked, but it was the only answer Luke was going to give her.

"We take Christopher to your house," he said. "*Together.* I'll start getting acquainted with my son."

She swallowed hard. "Does that mean you'll be staying the night?"

It was yet another answer she wouldn't like. Actually, Luke didn't like it much, either. "Of course. That's been my plan all along," he reminded her.

But he'd come up with that plan before he'd ever met Elaina face-to-face. Before he'd had these stupid lustful thoughts about her.

Luke definitely hadn't counted on the attraction.

Now, he had to figure out how to get past it. Because if he didn't, it was going to be a very long night.

SHE COULD RUN AGAIN.

That was the one thought that kept going through

Elaina's mind. She could wait until Luke was asleep and try to sneak out with Christopher. Yes, she'd probably be breaking the law, but she couldn't bear the thought of losing her son.

Elaina unlocked the front door of her house, and as she always did, reset the security system. She motioned for Luke to walk in ahead of her while she aimed a few daggers his way. Not that it would do any good. He obviously wasn't going to change his mind about this asinine plan.

Luke had a sleeping Christopher cradled in his arms. The baby obviously hadn't finished his nap because he'd fallen sound asleep on the short drive from Theresa's to the house. It wasn't unusual for him to do that, but because Christopher wasn't awake, that meant she'd have to spend time *alone* with Luke. Elaina was not looking forward to that.

"His bedroom is at the end of the hall," Elaina explained. She showed Luke the way, but she didn't give him a tour or even a friendly expression. She simply opened the door to the nursery and pointed to the crib.

Luke gently lay the baby down and covered him with a pale blue quilt. What he didn't do was leave. He stayed right there, looking down at Christopher.

Elaina didn't want to speculate about what he was thinking, but she couldn't help herself. Luke was no doubt realizing how much he loved this child. That love would only make him more adamant about taking Christopher.

Unless she did something to stop it.

She had to either sneak away with Christopher, or convince Luke to give up his plan.

"How long will you be staying in my house?" she demanded in a whisper.

He turned, frowned and walked toward her. Elaina automatically backed up to keep some distance between them, but he closed that distance.

Luke leaned in and practically put his mouth right against her ear. "First things first—how good is your security system?" he asked.

She'd anticipated that he might say a lot of things, but that wasn't one of them. Though she should have anticipated it. Because after what'd just happened with those men, it was relevant.

"It's an excellent system," she explained. Elaina whispered, too, and then she inched back away from him. "I had it installed right after I moved here. It's monitored through the sheriff's office and covers all the windows and doors."

"What about the backyard and those thick trees that divide your house from your neighbor's property?"

That'd been her concern when she moved in, as well. The lots were huge, at least an acre each, so there was plenty of space in between the individual homes. "There are motion-activated lights that come on in the front and back porches if someone approaches at night."

He nodded, and it seemed to be an approval. "Make sure the system is on at all times. A fellow agent will be adding some extra equipment in the wooded area. If someone trips the system, I'll be alerted through my cell phone."

That hiked up her blood pressure. "You think those men are going to get out of jail tomorrow?"

He whispered again and closed the already narrow space between them. "Not if I can help it. I just need you to be cautious."

For some reason, that riled her. Maybe it was the comment. Or maybe it was the closeness. Elaina definitely didn't like being close to Luke. It was too much of a reminder that he was a man.

A man that she was stupidly attracted to.

"Oh, I'm cautious all right," Elaina insisted. "Remember, I didn't move to Crystal Creek for the beautiful scenery. I moved here because those two men tried to run me off the road."

Their gazes met and held.

For way too long.

Something happened. The air changed, maybe. The curl of heat returned. Her body seemed to suggest things that it should never have suggested. She warned her body to knock it off because it wasn't going to get Luke Buchanan.

Elaina folded her arms over her chest and looked away. "How long will you be here?" she repeated. Best to get her mind back on business.

He glanced back at the crib. "Originally, I'd planned a week or two."

After the reaction she'd just had to him, that sounded like a lifetime. "And now?"

"It'll depend on what happens with that interrogation tomorrow. I want to get to know my son, but first, I have to make sure he's safe."

"Trust me, that's my priority, too. What I don't get is why we have to pretend to be a couple."

He moved closer still, and some frustration crept into his whisper. "I've already told you that I want Christopher to get to know me here, in the place he considers home. I'd rather do that without a lot of questions from your friends and neighbors. Besides, it's only a temporary arrangement. I'll be out of your life soon enough."

That improved her posture. "I don't want you out of my life, not if that means that you take Christopher with you."

Another glance at the crib, and he caught her arm to move her in the hall. She welcomed it. No more whispered, cheek-to-cheek conversations.

"I'm trying to be fair about this," he said, huffing. "Why don't we call a truce? Just let me get to know my son. Let me take care of these possible security issues. And in a few days, we'll assess the situation."

Elaina didn't like the sound of that last comment. "What does that mean?"

He lifted his shoulder. "My job is in San Antonio. If the security threat is removed, if you're free to leave Crystal Creek, then maybe you can move back into the city so you can see Christopher more often."

Her heart sank. That arrangement wasn't nearly enough. "I don't want to just be able to see him. I want to be his mother."

"Trust me, this isn't easy for me to say. You *are* his mother."

Elaina couldn't imagine being more shocked. She stood there. Speechless. It was a huge concession coming from a man who just an hour earlier had accused her of participating in an illegal adoption.

Luke groaned and leaned his back against the wall. "When we were at the sitter's, Christopher went right to you. He smiled at you. It's obvious he loves you, and I can't completely discount that." His eyes met hers. The gray color turned to steel, and his expression hardened. "Just don't give me a reason to."

Elaina hoped she didn't look too guilty, because, after all, she had been thinking about leaving that night. But that was before she saw how much Luke already loved Christopher. If she took the little boy, Luke would come after her. With his contacts and experience, he'd no doubt find her, too. And he'd have her arrested. She wouldn't stand a chance of being part of Christopher's life if she was behind bars.

"I won't give you a reason to cut me out of Christopher's life," she promised.

Elaina hoped it was a promise she could keep.

The doorbell rang, and that had Luke reaching for his gun again. It also had her heart racing out of control. Before Luke had stormed into her life, she'd managed to find a small sense of security.

That was all gone now.

Feeling safe might be a thing she'd never experience again. His gun and mere presence were reminders of that.

"Are you expecting anyone?" Luke asked.

She shook her head, and Luke followed her when she went to see who it was. Elaina looked out the door scope. The person on the other side certainly wasn't the threat that her body had prepared itself for. She recognized the lanky man with the mop of unruly ginger-colored hair.

"It's Gary Simpson. My neighbor."

That didn't cause Luke to relax one bit. He still kept a firm grip on his gun. "He comes by often?"

"Yes." Elaina refrained from adding *too often.* "He probably saw my car and is checking on me because I'm not usually home this time of day. Or else he heard about the men who were arrested in front of Theresa's house. If I don't answer the door, he'll get suspicious."

Luke waited a moment, as if deciding what to do with that information, and then reholstered his gun. He tipped his head to the door, an indication for her to open it.

Elaina did, after she temporarily deactivated the security system. She wanted to do everything possible to make certain this wasn't a long visit. Her goal was to put Gary's concerns and questions to rest so she could get rid of him.

Gary was about to ring the bell again, but he stopped when he saw her. "Elaina."

That was the only greeting her neighbor provided,

but his cautious blue eyes immediately landed on Luke. He didn't have to look far to see him because Luke quickly joined her. Side-by-side. He even slipped his arm around her waist, a reminder that this was showtime. He wanted them to go into their couple routine.

"It's true then," Gary said. "Your husband came home."

"I did," Luke volunteered.

And there was definitely something territorial about the way Luke said it. The embrace was territorial, as well, and he pulled her even closer to him.

Gary's reaction wasn't exactly passive, either. His too-full mouth tightened, and he shoved his hands into the pockets of jeans, but not before Elaina noticed that his hands had fisted.

She knew that Gary was attracted to her. After all, he'd asked her out several times. Not for real dates, he'd said, but invitations to join him for steaks that he was barbecuing. Or for a swim in his pool. Elaina had always declined and then flashed her fake wedding ring to remind him that she wasn't available. But judging from his expression, Gary wanted to believe differently.

"Elaina, are you…okay?" Gary asked.

His hesitant question had more than a tinge of suspicion to it. Maybe because despite the embrace with Luke, she didn't look like a loving wife whose missing husband had just returned to her.

Her lack of sincerity would no doubt rile Luke if

he thought she wasn't doing her best to play her part, so she immediately tried to do just that. Elaina looked up at Luke and hoped she had love in her eyes. Fake love, of course.

Luke looked down at her at the same moment that Elaina looked up. He was doing the fake love act, too, but he was obviously a lot better at it than she was. His eyes softened. The corner of his mouth lifted. And he smiled. He probably didn't know that his smile was his best feature. He was handsome with the stone face, but with that smile, he was in whole different category of handsome.

Okay, he was hot.

Elaina hated that she had to admit that, especially since she was doing her best to forget anything remotely positive about him. But it didn't matter. In the grand scheme of things, good looks meant nothing.

"Elaina?" she heard Gary say.

She forced her attention away from Luke. "I'm fine," she answering, trying to smile. It didn't come as easily for her as it did Luke.

"Are you sure, because you—"

"She's fine," Luke interrupted. He leaned in and brushed that smiling mouth over hers.

It was a simple gesture. An act. But Elaina felt herself go all tingly and warm. Heck, she even felt it all the way to her toes. Furious at her reaction, she dismissed it as fatigue and fear. Or at least that's what she tried to do, but Luke didn't take his mouth from hers. The tingling and warmth soon began to skyrocket.

She pinched his back and would have pinched herself if she hadn't thought it would make Gary even more wary.

Luke reacted to the pinch. He pulled away and stared down at her. He looked stunned. Or something. And he shook his head as if he couldn't believe what had just happened. Maybe that's because he might have experienced it, too.

"I'm fine," Elaina repeated to Gary. "Really. Couldn't be better." And she put an unspoken "goodbye" at the end of that.

"Good. That's good." Gary nodded awkwardly. He obviously didn't catch the goodbye part because he continued. "I heard about the protestors. The sheriff's holding them for questioning or something. There's also a federal agent of some kind down at the jail, but the sheriff sure isn't saying anything about why he's there."

Well, it'd taken less than an hour for that information to make it to Gary, which meant it was all over town. Hopefully, it would keep most folks from visiting because they'd probably think she wanted to spend some time alone with her *husband*. Being alone with Luke was no piece of cake. Her body couldn't take much more of this.

Elaina decided to go for the direct approach. "I'll see you soon," she said to Gary. She waited until he issued an unenthusiastic goodbye before she shut the door.

Luke didn't let go of her.

She didn't let go of him.

They just stood there with his arm still curved around her waist.

"This is a lot harder than I thought it'd be," Luke mumbled.

"Welcome to the club."

She paused, trying to figure out how to say what she needed to say. Elaina finally decided to heck with it. This was something that had to be said. But Elaina didn't continue until she stepped from his embrace and put some distance between them. "We dislike each other. But you're still a man, and I'm a woman. Our bodies aren't reacting as if we're enemies."

He nodded. "Our bodies were reacting to the adrenaline."

Elaina toyed with that explanation and figured it was a good one. She only wished she'd thought of it first.

Even more, she wished it were totally true.

"Just in case it's a little more than that," she added, "I'm going to suggest no more kisses."

His eyebrow came up. "You're probably right. Besides, we have enough to deal with without adding adrenaline reactions to the mix."

Elaina had no trouble agreeing with that.

Luke reached over and reactivated the security system. Since he pressed in the correct code, he must have watched her before she opened the door for Gary.

"Do you think your neighbor is suspicious that I'm not your husband?" Luke asked.

"No. He's jealous. I don't think anyone in town

suspects that you aren't Daniel Allen. If they did, we would have already heard about it."

"Good. Let's keep it that way." He propped his hands on his hips and glanced around the room. "We need to make sure all the windows and doors are locked. And close the blinds."

He didn't wait for her to comply; he started the task by checking the windows in the living room. "After we're done, stay away from the windows and don't go back outside."

All of his activity got her heart racing. "Wait a minute. Those men are still in jail, aren't they?"

Luke snared her gaze, and Elaina saw it then. Not the attraction. Not the cockiness. Definitely not the "loving husband" he'd been just moments earlier.

She saw the concern.

"Those men are in jail," Luke confirmed. He turned toward Christopher's room and said the rest of what he had to say over his shoulder as he walked away. "But that doesn't mean they're working alone."

Chapter Six

Luke was practically soaking wet, but he didn't care. He wasn't about to leave his son's bath time just so he could dry off.

Christopher was enjoying himself in what was left of the two inches of warm water inside his little yellow plastic tub. Elaina had placed that tub inside the regular porcelain one in the bathroom. At first, Luke hadn't understood why she did that. But after watching Christopher splash water over Elaina, Luke, himself and most of the entire room, he knew this was the best place for his son.

He wondered how long it would take him to learn all the little things that made Christopher's life happier and safer. Feeding him dinner had been an enjoyable challenge, but those challenges were just starting.

Luke smiled at that.

Then, frowned.

He'd never felt more incompetent at anything in his life. And yet, he'd never looked so forward to anything, either. Through the baths, feedings and playtimes, he'd get to know his baby, they'd form a bond, and he'd no longer be a father in name only.

"He's a special little boy, isn't he?" Luke heard Elaina say.

Luke turned toward her. She was watching him watch Christopher, and the pain and doubts were there all over her face. A huge contrast to the laughing, splashing baby in the tub.

"He's usually happy like this?" he asked.

She smiled, just a brief one, before she clamped it off. "Most of the time. But he'll get sleepy soon, and then he's likely to be cranky."

Luke checked his watch. It was nearly 8:00 p.m., which meant his son would soon be going to bed. That would leave Luke alone with Elaina. When he'd come up with this plan, he certainly hadn't realized that the hardest part wouldn't be dealing with his son, but with the woman who'd raised him.

"You won't change his name, will you?" Elaina asked.

It seemed an odd question, but after giving it some thought, maybe it wasn't so odd. He certainly hadn't had any say in anything to do with Christopher—including something this important. "You named him?"

"Yes. Christopher Sean. He's not named after anyone. It's just something I liked. So, there's no baggage or relatives attached to it if that's what you thought."

He hadn't thought that at all. Luke had done a

thorough background check on Elaina, and neither of those names had come up.

"Christopher suits him," Luke concluded. "The only thing that'll change is his surname."

"That doesn't matter," she mumbled. "It's fake anyway. As you pointed out, my entire life is fake."

That wasn't true. What his son felt for her was real, and even Luke couldn't dismiss that.

Christopher reached for her, batting her hand with the rubber duck he was clutching. She smiled and tickled him on his belly. Christopher giggled and splashed some more.

Elaina caught the brunt of the water this time. Christopher doused the front of her clingy, garnet-red top. The water made it even more clingy, and that was Luke's cue to get his attention off her clothes and the way they fit her body.

"Just to let you know," Luke said, going over the ground rules. "We'll be sleeping in the nursery tonight with Christopher."

She froze a moment, shook her head as if ready to disagree with that, but then her eyes widened. "You mean because of the danger? Well, I'd planned on sleeping next to him anyway. I figured you'd take the sofa in the living room."

"Not a chance of that." He caught on to one of Christopher toes and played a silent game of Little Piggy. Christopher grinned from ear to ear.

Elaina didn't grin. She frowned. "Then, I'll take the sofa. You can stay with Christopher."

She obviously didn't understand that these were rules, not suggestions. "No one is going to take the sofa. We're all going to sleep in the same room because it's the only way I can make sure both of you are safe."

That improved her posture. Her shoulders went back, and he got a better view of what the water had done to her top, the way it clung to her breasts. Man, he could see the outline of nipples.

"You think gunmen are going to storm the house?" Elaina asked.

It took a second to gather his breath. Nipples! "I think I don't want to take a chance like that," he countered.

She handed Christopher his toy duck when it floated out of his reach. "You've seen the nursery, and you know it's not big enough for both of us."

He wasn't sure a shopping mall was big enough for both of them. "You're wasting your time with this argument. We're staying in the nursery. I'm doing this for your own good. For your *safety.*"

"But who'll protect us from each other?" she mumbled. But then, Elaina immediately waved that off. "Don't answer that. I don't want to know."

Too bad. It suddenly seemed like a critical subject. Or at least an interesting one. "Maybe we should address it. The attraction," he clarified just to make sure they were on the same page.

"The only reason to address it is to dismiss it. I'm not getting involved with another man. Especially a man who has the power to destroy me."

He found her honesty refreshing, and his attitude had nothing to do with her top. Or her nipples. Or her snug jeans. Or her bare feet with their peach painted toenails. Or even her scent.

Okay, maybe it did have something to do with those things. But Luke vowed that he wouldn't let his stupid male body make bad decisions for him.

"Kevin left you with a bitter taste in your mouth," he commented to keep the conversation going. It was better than the silence. He did a second round of the Little Piggy game with Christopher.

"Oh, yes. But then, you can probably say the same thing. After all, you were separated when your wife died."

Touché. "It'd gone beyond that," he confessed. Why, he didn't know. He just suddenly felt the need to spill his guts to the one woman who didn't care one iota about what he'd been through. "Taylor had filed for a divorce."

She studied him, and he could almost see the wheels working in her head. "Yet she didn't tell you that she was pregnant."

"Nope. She didn't. But then, Taylor never wanted kids. That's one of the reasons we decided to go our separate ways."

Her stare softened a bit. No more visual accusations. "You wanted to have children?"

"For as long as I can remember." For some reason, he wanted to blather on about this part, too. Maybe the bath water had soaked his brain. "My parents died in a car accident when I was three, and I was raised in foster care. *Bad* foster care," he added. "I always wanted a chance to experience a good family life. Taylor, though, wanted the opposite. She'd had a rough childhood, too, and felt she couldn't be a good mother."

Elaina stayed quiet a moment. "Do you think she was planning to give up Christopher for adoption?"

He wanted to shout a resounding no, but he couldn't. Because Luke honestly didn't know the answer to that. "Maybe. Another of our big areas of disagreement was my job. She said it was too dangerous, but she didn't want me to quit because she liked all the traveling I did. It gave her some space, as she used to like to say."

"So, maybe she was planning on giving up her baby to keep that *space?*" she asked.

"Either that, or she reasoned that because of my dangerous job, I wouldn't make a good father." This time, Luke retrieved Christopher's duck. "What Taylor didn't know was that I was up for a promotion that would essentially mean a desk job. I got that promotion, but within the same hour I learned that Taylor was dead."

Elaina made a soft sound of sympathy. "If Taylor planned to give up your baby, then the adoption might have been legal."

Ah, so that's where this was going. Luke didn't let it go far. So much for pouring out his heart and spilling his guts. Elaina had taken all those bits of info so she could try to clear her conscience.

"Taylor's intentions might have made that part of it legal, but the paperwork and the process weren't." He stared at her. "Do you have any doubts that your late fiancé was capable of an illegal adoption?"

"No," she said, but the admission was laced with frustration. "In hindsight, I think Kevin was capable of just about anything." She aimed her finger at him. "I won't go through that again, and that's why this attraction thing between us won't go any further."

Luke didn't doubt the smoldering glances he'd been giving Elaina, but he hadn't noticed Elaina sending any his way. Of course, he was aware of the uncomfortable tension between them.

"How do I know the attraction is real on your part?" he asked. "You could be faking it."

She looked genuinely surprised and offended. "And why would I do that?"

"Because you think it'll help your cause."

"My *cause?*"

Luke figured he was about to put his foot directly into his big mouth. "You must be trying to figure a way to keep custody of Christopher."

Yep. Definitely foot in mouth. Her eyes narrowed, and her mouth tightened. "I'm so glad you said that, because it reminds me of why I dislike you. Not everyone has ulterior motives for what they do, Luke Buchanan. Trust me, I had my fill of that kind of stuff when I was with Kevin."

Christopher started to make fussing noises, and he rubbed his eyes. Elaina jumped to her feet, grabbed a towel and scooped him up in it. "Bed time," she announced.

Well, there were definitely no more smoldering looks between them, and the air had chilled. She turned her back on him and went into the nursery.

"He won't like this part," she grumbled as she placed Christopher on the dressing table.

Learning from his mistake, Luke shut up and watched her diaper the baby. Though he considered himself a smart man, he figured that would take a while to master the technique and all the steps. Christopher wiggled, squirmed, fussed and generally did everything but cooperate. Yet, Elaina managed to get the baby dressed for bed in only a couple of minutes.

She kissed Christopher on both of his chubby cheeks and lay him in the bed. She covered him with the quilt and began to hum softly. Luke recognized the tune: "Lullaby and Goodnight." While she hummed it, she lightly rubbed the baby's stomach. Like the dressing routine, it only took a couple of minutes before Christopher closed his eyes.

Since there was a night light in the corner of the room, Luke turned off the overhead light. He made his way to the window to look out, to check the yard one more time. He'd lost count of just how many times he'd done that in the course of the afternoon and the evening.

He'd check many more times throughout the night.

"See anything?" Elaina whispered.

"No. It's all clear."

Christopher was no doubt asleep because she moved away from the crib. "I'm exhausted. I'm going to try to get some sleep."

It was early, but Luke knew how she felt. It'd been a long day, and even with the extreme fatigue, neither of them would get much sleep.

She walked toward the hall. "I'll get some pillows and blankets for us."

She disappeared into her bedroom, and because that didn't seem an appropriate place for him to be, Luke stayed put and looked down at his now sleeping son. It was hard to imagine that the little boy who'd been a ball of energy just minutes earlier was now sleeping so peacefully. Luke wanted to make sure things stayed peaceful.

Elaina returned to the nursery and deposited an armful of bedding on the carpeted floor. With her arms free, Luke could see that she'd changed her clothes. Nothing provocative. She wore cream-colored flannel pajamas. But it was still somehow intimate to be in the same room with her while she was preparing for bed.

With the uncomfortable silence, Luke had time to go over everything they'd discussed, and the one thing he kept returning to was Kevin. Was Elaina's ex the reason those men had come to Crystal Creek? If so, what was the way to make the connection, especially if the two men weren't in a talkative mood during the interviews?

"You said that Kevin was doing some kind of

software modification," Luke whispered. "Was it legal?"

"Probably not." She spread out the covers and tossed him a pillow. "In fact, I'd be shocked if it was."

Luke placed the pillow on the floor, but since the room was indeed small, his pillow was less than two feet from where Elaina's was. "If Kevin was that bad, then why'd you get involved with him in the first place?"

"We were college sweethearts. I didn't learn about his criminal activities until he was dead and I started going through his things." She settled into her make-shift bed. "It was like he was two different people. Despite bouts of manic depression, he was usually kind and generous with me. But to the rest of the world, well, he was a scumbag."

Luke made a mental note to learn just how much of a scumbag Kevin was.

"Who hired Kevin to do these software modifications?" Luke asked.

"I don't know. He only referred to his boss as T. I don't know if T was a man or a woman, and I certainly have no idea what the person's real name is. But I do know that the modifications were important. Kevin spent a lot of time doing them, and he said it was a project that would make us millionaires several times over."

Interesting. A big project worth a lot of money. "You believed him?"

"Yes. He'd never said anything like that before.

And before he was killed, he made some rather large deposits into our investment accounts."

Well, that added some credence to Kevin's claims. "How was he doing these modifications?"

"He put everything on a miniature memory card."

That wasn't something Luke wanted to hear. There were memory cards half the size of a dime and just as thin. "Did you bring anything with you when you left San Antonio?"

She turned slightly to make eye contact. "Just some files, investment account statements and the adoption papers. I brought some of Christopher's toys, of course. And his car seat. Oh, and I also brought the clothes and blanket he was wrapped in the day I first saw him."

"That was the day Kevin brought Christopher home to you?" Luke asked.

She nodded.

And here he had been on a case while another man was essentially stealing his child. Luke knew he'd never forgive himself for that. All he could do was make the world a little safer for Christopher.

"Kevin was killed only hours after he handed me the baby," Elaina added.

Yeah. Luke knew that, and he'd come to the conclusion that Kevin hadn't had the miniature disk with him. If he had, those men likely wouldn't have come after Elaina.

"How about a computer?" Luke pressed. "Did you bring one to Crystal Creek with you?"

"My laptop, but Kevin never used it."

Perhaps not when she was around, but Luke knew Kevin still could have used it. "I'd like to see the files, the clothing and the laptop."

She stared at him, and for a moment he thought she might refuse. But then Elaina huffed, got up and indicated for him to follow her. Where did they go?

Her bedroom.

The last place on earth he should be.

Luke wanted to hit himself in the head with a rock for such a blunder, but he needed to see what Elaina had brought with her to Crystal Creek. It could help them figure out what was going on.

The room had been painted the color of fresh butter, and the bedding was a floral print with that same yellow and some mint green. There was very little furniture. Sparse but comfortable. In the short months that she'd been in the house, she'd turned it into a home.

"There's the computer," she said, pointing to the laptop on the small desk tucked in the corner.

Luke glanced at it while Elaina went to the walk-in closet. There was a small attic space just above the top shelf, and she stood on a footstool to reach the hatch door. When she reached up, her pajama top rose, and he got a great look at her bare midriff.

He forced himself to look elsewhere.

Unfortunately, elsewhere turned out to be her butt. Lifting her arms and standing on her tiptoes adjusted the fabric, as well, and he got an intimate view of the outline of her derriere. Great. He hoped that was the last of the torturing peepshow.

His body laughed at him for hoping that and begged to see more. Luke didn't fulfill that wish. He nailed his attention to Elaina's hands, figuring he couldn't get in mental trouble with those.

He watched as she took out a small cardboard box. It definitely wasn't in plain view, and she'd likely done that on purpose. She probably hadn't wanted anyone to learn of Christopher's adoption or Kevin's activities.

She deposited the box on the desk next to him. When she didn't say anything, Luke looked up at her to see if anything was wrong.

"Your shirt," she said. "I hadn't realized it was so wet."

Luke glanced down and verified the wetness on his white button-down shirt. It was like her own top in the bathroom. Clingy. "I'll change it in a few minutes."

And then he remembered, he'd left his suitcase in his car at the parking lot of Elaina's shop. Her expression said that she remembered even if he hadn't.

"This shirt will dry," he grumbled.

He made a mental note to get his suitcase when he went to the jail for the interviews. For that, Rusty and he would have to trade places, with his fellow agent staying with Christopher and Elaina. Luke didn't want either of them anywhere near that jail with those two men.

Of course, Luke's presence at the jail would mean

a lot of questions from the locals, but he'd have to deal with it somehow. He couldn't miss those interviews.

"These are the clothes Christopher was wearing when he came from the adoption agency," Elaina said, taking a blue gown, a knit pom-pom cap and satin-rimmed blanket from the box. The gown and hat were tiny, and he couldn't help but wonder how his son had ever fit into them.

Luke sat down at the desk and turned on her laptop. While it was booting up, he looked at what she handed him. Yeah, they were baby clothes all right. He put them closer to his nose and inhaled. It was probably his imagination, but he thought he could still detect his son's scent.

He also suddenly became aware that Elaina was staring at him. Luke looked at her, figuring she would have a good laugh about a grown man sniffing baby clothes, but she didn't. In fact, her eyes got a little misty.

"There's more," she said, clearing her throat.

She handed him the adoption papers. Unlike the clothes, he had no desire to sniff these. In fact, they made his blood boil. Because these were the documents the criminals had used to sell his son to the highest bidder.

The papers looked perfectly legal, right down to the official gold seal on the top document, but Luke knew they were phony. The documents had basically been created by an attorney who wanted to get rich. No rules had been followed, and no legal official had given it that seal of approval.

Luke thumbed through the papers, and the only signature he saw was Kevin's. "You weren't there when these papers were signed?"

She shook her head. "No. In fact, I didn't really know what Kevin was up to. He'd mentioned an adoption, of course, but I figured it'd take months or even years. Then, just a few days later, he showed up with Christopher."

"You weren't suspicious?" he asked.

"Of course. But Kevin said that adoption happened faster because it was private and he was willing to pay more to expedite the paperwork."

Yet more proof that it was illegal.

Not that Luke needed more.

While Elaina sat on the edge of her bed, Luke surfed through her computer. He didn't immediately find anything out of place, but then, he wasn't a computer expert.

"How did you get the money to buy this house and pay the lease for your shop?" Luke asked when he didn't find any financial records. In fact, the only thing he did find was art software that she'd obviously been using to create her stained-glass designs.

"I had some money in an investment account that I set up when I sold my condo in San Antonio," she explained. "I also sold some jewelry. None of the pieces were distinctive or unique enough so I didn't think anyone who saw them would associate them with me. I didn't touch the joint accounts I had with

Kevin because I thought it'd create a paper trail that would lead those men to me."

"It would have," Luke mumbled. "I'd like to send this laptop to the Justice Department."

"Okay. I use it to keep track of my Internet orders, but if you think it'll help, send it. I've already got my files backed up on my jump drive." She tipped her head to the thumb-size memory stick and then paused. In fact, she paused so long that Luke looked at her to see what was wrong. "We'll be safe here, right?"

He certainly couldn't doubt the sincerity of that question. Nor could he doubt that concern in her voice. "As long as those men are in jail."

She wadded up the quilt in her hands, squeezed hard and then got up to pace. "But if you can't keep them there, then what?"

There was no way to sugarcoat this. "We'll have to leave. I'm trying to avoid that, of course. For Christopher's sake."

Elaina nodded. A shaky nod. "I'm tired. You can send any of the things in that box to the Justice Department, but when they're finished with them, I'd like to have the clothes back." She walked away.

That was obviously a good-night, and Elaina probably thought he'd sit in her room and pore over the papers. But he wouldn't. He didn't want to leave Christopher or her alone while he did that. So, he followed her.

She glanced over her shoulder, and even though the hall was dark, he was pretty sure she rolled her eyes.

"We can't avoid this," he whispered as they entered the nursery. "I'm sleeping in here with you."

She turned around so quickly that he bumped right into her. In fact, his hands were suddenly filled with her. She was soft. And warm. And she smelled damn good. Not like cherries, this time. It was mix of baby shampoo and the spicy pasta dish she'd fixed for dinner. Normally, he wouldn't have found that combination erotic, but he certainly thought so now.

Of course, he also thought he was acting like a fool.

Elaina didn't stay in his arms long. Mere seconds. The night light provided the only illumination in the room, but he had no trouble seeing her expression. She was frowning and nibbling on her lip at the same time.

"I'm warning you, I snore," she snarled.

If that was the worst thing he had to face, then that would suit him just fine. But Luke wasn't very hopeful.

There were way too many things that could go wrong tonight.

Chapter Seven

Elaina dreamed. It was the nightmare again. A race against time, armed men and other terrifying shadowy things that could harm her baby. She would dodge one shadow, only to be faced with another.

One of those shadows was Luke Buchanan.

Even in the depth of the dream, she knew he was the greatest threat of all. She could run from the men. She could hide. But she couldn't escape a biological father who wanted to raise his son.

She stirred, trying to force that painful thought aside, and she opened her eyes. The first thing she saw and felt was Luke. He was there. Right next to her. In fact, they were on their sides facing each other. Well, rather she had her face right against his bare chest. Sometime during the night, he'd obviously removed his shirt.

And she'd cuddled right up to him.

And there was no mistake about it, this was cuddling. Body against body.

Just as she'd expected, his body was toned and perfect. He was all strength and muscles, and he smelled warm, musky and male. It was a dangerous combination that had her pushing aside the nightmare and remembering things that she hadn't even realized she missed.

Like French kisses and sex.

Things that weren't going to happen between Luke Buchanan and her.

Elaina scrambled away from him and winced when she banged her foot on the baby bed. It was loud, and maybe because the room had been so quiet, the noise seemed to echo.

The noise created a simple chain reaction. Luke woke up. Not a slow, drowsy wake up, either. His eyes shot open, and in the same motion he reached for his gun on the floor next to him. His attention sliced around the room, and he relaxed when he realized there was no threat.

Christopher woke up, too. Not quietly, either. He let out a baby howl, and he sat up. He used the bed railings to pull himself to a standing position.

Luke and she got up at the same time to reach for the baby. She won, only because she was closer. She scooped Christopher into her arms and tried to soothe him with a kiss which didn't work.

Elaina checked the clock and realized why. It was well past 8:00 a.m., which meant it was well past his breakfast time.

How could she have possibly overslept with Luke

in the room? And then she remembered. It'd been the wee hours of the morning before she'd been able to fall asleep. She knew for a fact that it was the same for Luke, because he was still awake when she'd finally drifted off.

"He's hungry," she grumbled.

Normally, she would have put Christopher in his high chair while she fixed his breakfast. But then, normally her baby wasn't crying. The late start had thrown everything off schedule.

"I'll take him," Luke said obviously sensing her dilemma.

"I figured you'd need to get dressed and go the sheriff's office for the interrogations." In other words—*leave,* Elaina tried to convey.

"There's no need to go in until the lawyer arrives. Rusty will call when that happens." Luke reached for Christopher again.

"He'll need to have his diaper changed first," Elaina informed him.

Luke blinked, but the hesitation didn't last long. "I'll do it."

Elaina hesitated, as well, but Christopher's tears helped her with a quick decision. She handed the baby to Luke and headed for the kitchen.

While she fixed baby oatmeal in the microwave, she listened for any sounds that Luke was in over his head. Christopher stopped crying, and it was because of the near silence that she heard Luke make an odd sound. Elaina raced back toward the nursery.

By the time she made it there, her mind was already ripe with possibilities as to what had caused Luke to make that noise. Bad possibilities. But all she saw was Christopher on the changing table. He was smiling and kicking his legs. Luke's chest, however, was wet.

"He's got good aim," Luke mumbled.

Elaina couldn't help it, she laughed. "I should have warned you about the hazards of diapering a baby boy. He's peed on me more than a time or two."

The corner of Luke's mouth lifted, and they shared a smile. Along with Christopher's happy gurglings, the moment turned a little weird. It was too intimate. As if they were a family. Which they weren't.

The happy moment ended as quickly as it'd come.

"I'll get back to making breakfast," she told Luke. "You might want to use the baby wipes to clean yourself."

Feeling awkward and warm at the same time, Elaina made her way back to the kitchen to finish the oatmeal. What was wrong with her anyway? She'd started the morning thinking about French kisses and sex. Now, she was thinking about family. Talk about insane notions.

Or was it?

She was almost afraid to let the thought fully materialize in her head, but she couldn't seem to stop it, either. After all, it was Luke who wanted to pretend to be a loving, happy couple. For Christopher's sake. But what was wrong with continuing that pretense until they could figure out what to do about shared custody and such?

Plus, there were the men in jail. Having Luke around would mean that Christopher would be safe, because Elaina knew he would protect his son.

Of course, the downside to having Luke around was that she was starting to feel things that she thought she'd never feel again. Feelings she'd buried with Kevin.

Feelings that Luke would never be able to feel for her in return.

To him, she was the enemy. She was the woman who'd robbed him of all these months with his son. The only feelings that Luke would ever have for her would be part of this pretense.

And that was okay.

Elaina repeated that to herself.

She already had enough to deal with without adding feelings and emotions to the mix.

By the time Luke and Christopher joined her in the kitchen, Elaina was reasonably sure that her little talk with herself was working. She was getting her mind back on the right things. Then, she saw Luke's bare chest, watched him lovingly put Christopher in his high chair and she needed another attitude adjustment.

It was going to be a *long* day.

Luke had just sat down to start feeding Christopher the oatmeal when his cell phone rang. Elaina took over the feeding duties while he took the call.

"Hello, Rusty," he answered after glancing at his Caller ID.

Elaina divided her attention between feeding Christopher and watching Luke's reaction. She knew the call could be important, but judging from Luke's tight jaw, something had gone wrong. Unfortunately, she couldn't tell what.

Other than simple yes and no responses, she did hear Luke request a "safe house" which sent a shiver of panic through her. Did he honestly think they needed something like that? Unfortunately, Elaina had to wait until he'd finished the call before she could get an explanation.

"That was Rusty who's down at the sheriff's office," Luke relayed to her. "He said he'll drop off my suitcase this morning so I won't have to leave you to drive over there."

She studied him. "Then, why are you scowling?"

"Well, it's not because of the suitcase. The lawyer's been delayed. He won't be in Crystal Creek until tomorrow afternoon at the earliest. That means the interviews aren't going to happen until then."

She scowled then, too. She wanted this over and done, and that couldn't happen until the men gave up some information.

"And the safe house?" Elaina asked. "What was that all about?"

"A precaution. I asked Rusty to request a safe house just in case we have to release those men tomorrow. I don't want Christopher or you here with them loose."

Neither did Elaina. But then, a safe house seemed a little extreme. Unless… "Does this mean you think the men will be released?"

Luke shrugged. "We have reason to hold them, so I don't think they're going anywhere, but we have to be prepared, just in case." He leaned against the counter and watched her feed Christopher. "There's also the likelihood that these men aren't working alone."

"Yes," she said, feeling that panic again. "They could be working for T."

"It's also possible that one of the men could be T," Luke quickly pointed out.

Elaina prayed that was true, because if so, that meant the threat was contained. Too bad she didn't know how long that would last.

There was a soft knock at the door. Because she'd been deep in thought about the threat, she embarrassed herself by gasping.

Luke took the knock seriously, too. He hurried to the bedroom and retrieved his shirt and gun before he went to the front door and looked out the peephole.

"It's not my neighbor, Gary, is it?" Elaina whispered.

"No. It's two women." He slipped on his shirt. "One of them is your assistant, Carrie."

No more panicked feeling, but Elaina was a little concerned. Carrie wasn't in the habit of dropping by for an early morning visit. That was especially true since her assistant no doubt thought she was on what was essentially a second honeymoon.

Elaina sprinkled some dry cereal bits onto Christopher's tray so that it would keep him occupied, and she joined Luke at the door. She glanced out and saw not only Carrie but Brenda McQueen, a frequent visitor to the shop. Both women looked apprehensive.

"The other woman is a customer," Elaina explained.

"You know her well?"

Elaina shrugged. "Not really. Her name is Brenda McQueen. She moved here a couple of months ago, and she works out of her home as the editor of a children's magazine."

"I didn't run a background check on her," he mumbled. "But I will."

Her first instinct was to say that wasn't necessary, but Elaina no longer knew what was necessary or not.

"I'll see what they want," Elaina told Luke. She disengaged the security system so that it wouldn't go off when she opened the door.

Luke tucked his gun in the back waist of his pants and stepped to the side so she could face their visitors.

"Elaina," Carrie greeted. Her voice was strained, as was her expression.

Both women stood there. Carrie, in a pair of jeans and a blue hoodie. Brenda wore black sweatpants and a Duke sweatshirt that brought out the blue in her eyes. The winter wind whipped at Brenda's midnight-black hair that she'd gathered into a loose ponytail, and it would have done the same for Carrie's if she hadn't been wearing a French braid.

Carrie glanced at Luke who was standing just behind Elaina. "I'm so sorry to bother you—"

"I insisted that we come," Brenda interjected. "I was out for my morning jog and saw that the front door of your shop was open."

Sweet heaven. What else could go wrong?

"I locked it before I left work," Carrie insisted.

"Why don't you come in," Luke offered.

Elaina followed Luke's gaze to see why he'd said that, and she quickly noticed that he had his attention fastened on Gary, her neighbor. Gary had his Golden Retriever on a leash and was walking the dog on the sidewalk just in front of Elaina's house.

Or rather, Gary was lingering with the dog.

Luke obviously didn't trust the man. Elaina knew how he felt. She was beginning to not trust *anyone*.

"Nothing is missing from the shop," Carrie volunteered as they stepped inside. Luke shut the door and buttoned his shirt. But not before both visitors eyed his chest.

Elaina knew how they felt.

She'd done some eyeing herself.

"The lock wasn't broken, either," Carrie continued. She went to Christopher and gave his cheek a pinch, but the cheerfulness of the gesture wasn't present in any part of her body language. "I guess it's possible that I didn't fully close the door when I locked up, but I could have sworn I did."

"We were going to report it to the sheriff," Brenda added. "But since nothing appears to be stolen, we wanted to check with you first, just to make sure you weren't the one who'd left it open."

"I'll take care of it," Luke insisted before Elaina could say anything.

Brenda stared at him, and that's when Elaina realized that she'd failed to make introductions. "Brenda, this is, uh, my husband, Daniel."

"Obviously," the woman said, her mouth bending into a smile. She directed her comments to Luke. "I'll bet you're not so happy about us bursting in here like this. I hope we didn't interrupt anything too personal."

"We were just feeding Christopher," Elaina said because she didn't know what else to say.

That seemed to be Luke's cue to slip his arm around her waist. Elaina didn't fight it. In fact, she felt herself leaning into the embrace.

Carrie leaned down and kissed Christopher on the top of his head. "Brenda, we should be going."

"Absolutely." But the woman didn't head for the door. Instead, she pulled Elaina aside and whispered in her ear. "I think I might have started my period, and I don't have anything with me."

Oh. So, it wasn't anything huge. Elaina was getting weary of the huge stuff. "You'll find some *supplies* in the master bathroom," Elaina whispered back. "Under the sink."

Brenda thanked her and disappeared down the hall. Elaina welcomed the reprieve. She liked Brenda, but she wanted a minute with Carrie. Obviously, so did Luke.

"Did it look as if someone had picked the lock on the shop door?" he asked Carrie.

"No. I checked for scratches or some kind of marks but nothing. I'm so sorry this happened, Elaina—"

"You don't have to apologize. That shop door is old, and I should have had it checked months ago."

And she hoped that was all there was to it. An old door with an old lock. Elaina didn't want to think about an intruder. Or what an intruder might have been looking for inside her place of business.

"Would you like me to take Christopher today? I could drive him to the sitter's or take him to the shop." Carrie asked. "You two must want some alone time."

"We'll get our alone time," Elaina insisted. Besides, she didn't want Christopher anywhere outside until Luke had been able to confirm that there'd been no break-in.

"Were you with Brenda when she discovered the shop door open?" Luke continued.

"No. She called me on her cell phone. I was still at home. She knew you had gone home, and Brenda wasn't sure if she should interrupt you guys."

That sounded plausible, but Luke didn't look as if he totally bought the explanation. Of course, they were both suspicious of almost everyone.

"I noticed Gary outside," Carrie commented. She blinked and lightly rubbed her right eye.

Elaina nodded. "He came by yesterday afternoon."

Carrie offered a flat, dry smile. "Let me guess. He wasn't that enthusiastic to see Daniel here."

"No, he wasn't," Luke provided.

"He'll get over it. I swear, Elaina never gave him any encouragement. Just the opposite. She was always telling everyone how much she was in love with you."

It was another of those awkward moments.

Because Christopher started to fuss, Elaina moved out of Luke's embrace so she could finish feeding him his oatmeal. It was a welcome reprieve.

Carrie checked her watch. "Brenda needs to hurry. I have to get to the shop. The woman from Luling is coming by this morning to pick up that Victorian panel."

"Do you need me there for that?" Elaina asked.

"Not on your life. You're staying here with your husband. I insist. Remember, I don't want to see your face in that shop for at least a week."

Elaina had no intentions of being gone that long. But then, it wasn't easy to think of the future, mainly because she had no idea what her future held.

Brenda came back into the room and she immediately grabbed Carrie's hand. "Let's get out of here and leave these two lovebirds alone."

But Carrie pulled out of her grip. She blinked hard again. "There's something underneath my contact, and it's bothering me. I won't be long." And she rushed off to the bathroom.

Brenda looked at Luke and smiled nervously. "The whole town is talking about you, you know. Everyone is anxious to meet you. Don't worry though, they'll stay away for another day or two. Will you stay in the military?" Brenda asked.

It wasn't something Luke and she had rehearsed, though thankfully he had an answer. "No. I'm on what they call terminal leave right now. I should receive papers soon that'll release me from active duty."

Brenda studied him. "I don't guess you want to talk about being held captive?"

"No," Elaina and Luke said in unison.

"I understand." Brenda paused. "I know you're just trying to get your footing, but I hope you won't take Elaina and Christopher away from us."

"We haven't made a decision about where we'll live," Elaina provided. And she kept her tone a little cool so that it would hopefully prevent any more questions.

It worked. Well, that and the fact that Carrie came back into the room. Carrie gave Christopher another kiss and then followed Brenda out the door. Luke didn't waste any time locking it and resetting the security system.

"If someone really did break into my shop, then it must be connected to those two men," Elaina suggested.

"Maybe. I need to check the lock myself and have the sheriff dust for prints." He glanced down at his rumpled shirt. "I also need a change of clothes."

"Will Christopher and I stay here while you get your things?"

"Not a chance. You're coming with me." He took the oatmeal bowl from her hand. "I'll finish feeding Christopher while you get dressed."

Since she, too, wanted to get a look at that lock, she hurried into her bedroom and went to the closet. She reached for an ivory-colored sweater and jeans, and then turned back.

And that's when she noticed that her window was open, just a fraction.

She wasn't in the habit of leaving it open, but she wondered if Luke had done it while checking the security system. Elaina closed it and glanced around the room.

Something else wasn't right.

The box that'd contained the adoption papers. The night before she'd taken the box from the attic space above the closet and had put it on the corner desk. It was still there, but it'd been moved, practically to the edge.

She looked inside, at the meager files. Nothing seemed to be missing, but things were out of place. Specifically, the adoption papers with Kevin's signature. Elaina was certain she'd left them on top of the other files, but they'd been tucked inside.

With her clothes clutched in a death grip, Elaina returned to the kitchen. "Did you leave the window open or get anything from the box in my bedroom?"

"No to both." He stopped feeding Christopher and looked at her. "Why?"

"The files have been moved around."

Slowly, he stood. "As if someone had rummaged through them?"

Elaina nodded. "God, did Brenda do this? Or

maybe someone sneaked through the window and did it," she said, thinking out loud. "After all, the security system wasn't on while Carrie and Brenda were inside. Someone watching the house, like Gary for instance, might have known that."

But why would someone do this? Idle curiosity, maybe? After all, the box of papers had been just sitting there in plain sight. Maybe Brenda just wanted to see what they were. And maybe Gary had sneaked in because he was suspicious of Luke.

But Elaina couldn't be sure of that.

Obviously, neither could Luke.

He took out his phone. "I'll have a background check run on both. Within an hour, we should know who they really are and what one or both of them were really doing in your bedroom."

Chapter Eight

When Luke finished his call to headquarters, everything was official. He'd requested a full background check on Brenda McQueen and more extensive ones on Gary Simpson and Carrie Saunders. Hopefully, those checks would provide him with much needed answers to an ever-growing list of questions. He'd also informed his boss that he intended to work "this case" until everything was resolved.

His mind was racing, and he forced himself to slow down so he could think things through. He certainly hadn't counted on all these issues when he'd come up with the plan to get acquainted with his son.

First, there were the two now-jailed men. Once their lawyer showed up, he needed to figure out what part they had in all of this. Now, he could add Brenda to his list of persons of interest. He really didn't like the possibility that the woman or Carrie had rummaged through Elaina's files.

"You said that Brenda moved to Crystal Creek a few months ago?" Luke asked Elaina.

"Yes." She wiped the oatmeal from Christopher's face and took him from the high chair. "I think that's why we became friendly. Because we were both outsiders."

And maybe they'd become friends because Brenda had orchestrated it.

"Brenda's visited you here at the house before?" Luke wanted to know.

"Of course, but I don't think anything was out of place after she left." She kissed Christopher's hand when he patted her mouth and babbled Ma Ma. "But I can't be sure. I just wasn't looking for something like that."

Well, they'd be on the lookout for it now. If he let Brenda return, that is. Until he knew everything there was to know about her, Brenda wouldn't be making another visit.

The doorbell rang again, and like before, Luke reached for his gun. That reach put another look of near panic on Elaina's face, and he hated what all of this was doing to her. Thankfully, Christopher seemed oblivious to it. He continued to babble and make happy sounds.

Luke went to the door and looked out. He instantly relaxed. "It's Rusty."

Elaina blew out a long breath and probably because she still wore pj's, she took Christopher and headed for her bedroom. Luke disengaged the security system and greeted the one man he did want to see.

"Your suitcase," Rusty said, depositing the case inside the small foyer. He eyed Luke's rumpled clothes. "Hey, you really do look like a guy on his honeymoon."

Unfortunately, Luke felt that way sometimes, but he kept that to himself.

"What about the security equipment?" Luke asked, going straight for business. It'd lessen the chances of Rusty making any more honeymoon comments. Maybe it'd also lessen Luke's thoughts about such amorous activity.

"I have it with me. It shouldn't take me more than ten or fifteen minutes to install. Don't worry. I'll be discreet. I don't want Elaina's neighbors wondering what the heck I'm doing."

"Believe me, I appreciate that. Her neighbors and friends seem overly curious. One of them might have even rummaged through her things. I've already requested a background check," Luke added.

"Good. I guess it's too much to hope for a quick in and out for all of this."

Luke shook his head. "It doesn't look like it."

That brought on a few under-the-breath grumbles from Rusty. "I'll get that equipment installed. My advice? Take a shower. You look like you just climbed out of bed after several long rounds of really good sex."

Luke aimed some obligatory profanity at his fellow agent. "Wait right here a second. I want to give you Elaina's laptop so the lab can check it out. Her late fiancé might have left something about his illegal projects on it."

He left Rusty in the foyer while he went to Elaina's bedroom. The door was open just a fraction, and he fully opened it when he spotted Christopher sitting on the floor. His son was pounding the carpet with a small plastic hammer.

But Elaina was nowhere in sight.

Luke's reaction was immediate. A slam of adrenaline. His heart kicked into overdrive, and Luke raced across the room to see if she was in the adjoining bathroom. She wasn't.

He heard the movement in the closet and hurried there. Luke found her.

She was naked.

Well, practically naked, anyway. She wore just her underwear. Sheer pink panties and a matching bra. She quickly grabbed her robe to cover herself but not before he got an eyeful.

"I was dressing," she said. She sounded startled and out of breath.

Luke knew how she felt. He was having trouble breathing, too. Where the hell had the air gone? Better yet, where was his head? He obviously wasn't using it to think straight.

He finally looked away.

"I, um, needed to get your laptop. I didn't know you were changing. Sorry."

"No problem."

Oh, but it was a problem. A huge one. Despite all the crud going on around them, Luke didn't think he would be able to forget the sight of her in her pink panties.

He gave Christopher a quick kiss, and nearly got playfully bammed in the face with the plastic hammer. Luke grabbed the laptop from the desk, and took it to Rusty, who was still waiting for him by the front door.

"Let's hope we find something on this that we can use," Rusty commented. "And I'll call you if and when that lawyer shows up."

"Thanks."

Rusty turned to leave but then stopped. "Say, are you okay?"

"Why do you ask?" Luke countered, wondering just how poleaxed he really looked.

Rusty studied him a moment. "It's just that before you got to Crystal Creek, you were so riled that Elaina had taken your son."

Oh, that. Luke shrugged. "I don't think she had any part in the illegal adoption."

Rusty flexed his eyebrows. "Any reason for that change of heart?"

No logical one. "Gut instinct."

That caused Rusty to curse under his breath. "Elaina's a beautiful woman."

Luke stared. Nope, he glared. And hoped this wasn't going where he thought it might be going. "What the hell is that supposed to mean?"

Rusty aimed his index finger at him. "It means that you need to forget that she's beautiful. She loves that baby. We saw that when we had her under surveillance."

Luke's glare worsened. "And your point would be?"

Rusty's index finger landed against Luke's chest. "Elaina would do anything to keep your son. *Anything.* Just remember that."

Luke didn't need any help remembering that particular detail. He could say the same for the attraction he felt for her. And it was time to put an end to this finger-pointing visit. "Call me when that security equipment's installed," Luke grumbled, and he shut the door.

When he turned around, Elaina was standing there with Christopher in her arms. She was fully dressed, thank goodness. In addition to wearing an ivory-colored sweater and jeans, she was also wearing a scowl.

"I'm not faking this attraction," she volunteered. "In fact, I'm doing everything to nip it in the bud, understand? I wouldn't use sex to keep custody of Christopher."

He held up his hand in a mock act of surrender. "Rusty was wrong."

She made a yeah-right sound. "You suggested the same thing last night."

"And I was wrong." It was time to eat a little crow. All right, a *lot* of crow. "I was wrong about a lot of things. Your involvement, or lack thereof, in the adoption. About us being able to live together, pretending to be a loving couple, without it leaking into reality. We're both human. It's only natural to be attracted. Especially after seeing you in that pink underwear."

She looked ready to argue some more, but then the fight dimmed. Christopher might have had something to do with that. He began to kiss her cheek. It was difficult to stay angry with a cute kid showering you with sloppy kisses.

Elaina smiled at the baby's antics. Man, she glowed when she looked at Christopher. Luke stood there, watching them. And wanting to be part of it.

Well, he felt that way until Elaina looked at him.

"Is something wrong?" she asked.

"No." And he left it at that. "Rusty's in your backyard installing security equipment," he let her know. "I'd like to take a shower while he's in the area."

She combed her gaze over him. It took a while. She lingered on his unbuttoned shirt. "You can use my bathroom."

Luke's idiotic body wanted to watch her visual appraisal, but he forced himself to pick up his suitcase. Unfortunately, he felt uneasy with Elaina being out of earshot. Elaina likely felt the same.

That didn't mean she was going to like his suggestion.

"Considering what we just talked about, this is going to seem like a really dumb idea, but I need you to stay close to the bathroom while I'm showering," he insisted. "I want to be able to hear you if something goes wrong."

She nodded, picked up Christopher, and led him toward her bedroom. "I've been giving a lot of thought to things that could go wrong. I'm not anxious to experience whatever that might be. Not while Christopher is here, anyway. So, while watching you shower might be a little, uh, awkward, it's better than the alternative."

Luke couldn't agree more.

Elaina sank down onto the floor with Christopher. He immediately crawled out of her arms and lay belly first on the carpet. He jammed his right thumb into his mouth and began sucking it.

She pointed to her bathroom. "The shower curtain is opaque. And I won't peek."

For some reason, Luke found that amusing. "I peeked at your underwear," he pointed out because he thought they could use some levity.

It didn't have the effect Luke intended. Maybe it was the threat of danger or the intensity of the moment. Or maybe it was both. But Elaina didn't smile. Her mouth tightened, and she glanced away.

"You can leave the bathroom door open," she said, taking the plastic hammer from the baby. "And I can sit right here with Christopher."

Right here. In other words, very close to where he'd be naked and showering. Thankfully, his son would act as the ultimate chaperone. Nothing remotely sexual was going to happen with Christopher around.

Except Luke immediately had to rethink that when he looked down at his little boy.

Who had fallen asleep on the floor.

Oh, man.

So much for his chaperone.

Luke reached inside the shower stall, turned on the water and started to undress. His body apparently thought it was about to get lucky because he started to react in a totally male kind of way.

Frustrated with himself and this burning need for Elaina, he tossed his shirt into the sink. The jeans followed. Then his boxers. He turned to step into the shower, but the noise alerted him.

He turned around. Fast. A gut reaction to possible danger. But there was no danger. Well, not the ordinary kind anyway. There was just Elaina reaching for Christopher's plastic hammer that she'd apparently dropped on the floor beside her.

Elaina reacted, too. Her gaze flew in Luke's direction, probably so she could see what had caused his own reaction.

She froze.

Luke didn't exactly move, either. He just stood there. Naked. Elaina just sat there. Staring. And looking very interested in what she was seeing.

Chapter Nine

Elaina had several *oh-mercy* reactions at once. Luke had a hot body. A body so hot that it made her hot. But she was also aware that she shouldn't be looking at him and that she should be trying to hide what she suddenly wanted.

And what she suddenly wanted was Luke.

"The water will get cold," she mumbled, saying the first thing that came to mind. It was absurd because nothing had the potential to be cold in that room. Everything was sizzling.

Luke snared her gaze and waited a moment before he cursed and stepped into the shower.

Elaina didn't breathe a sigh of relief. She leaned her head against the doorframe and tried to stop the *sizzling* from getting any hotter.

Her body was acting insanely. She felt desperate and needy. Her, needy! She hadn't experienced those sensations in years. Which made her think about the whole crazy notion of attraction. It was making her feel like a hormone-crazed teenager. That had to stop. And she would make it stop, somehow.

Elaina's pep talk lasted mere seconds. She caught a glimpse of the outline of Luke's body behind that shower curtain. That obstruction was useless when up against her overly active imagination.

She could almost see him. Naked and wet. Heck, she could almost see herself in the shower with him. Doing things. Having shower sex.

What would it feel like to have him take her right then, right there?

Would he be gentle? No, she decided. Not with his intensity. But Elaina was positive that it would be one of the most pleasurable experiences of her life.

Elaina was imagining the pleasure of such a coupling when Luke's phone rang. Before going into the bathroom, he'd left it on her desk. Where he probably couldn't hear it. Since there was no way she was going to go tapping on that shower curtain, she answered the call.

"Hello," she said.

And she heard a long pause.

"This is Agent Rusty Kaplan. Is Luke there?"

Oh, Elaina really hated to say this. "He's in the shower."

Another pause. She could have sworn Agent Kaplan was filling in the blanks with naughty scenarios that involved Luke and her. But then, Elaina had done the same thing just seconds earlier.

"Get him please," Rusty insisted. "It's important."

Elaina glanced at the shower. Oh, mercy. The agent would want her to do that.

"Is this about Brenda McQueen?" she asked, making her way into the bathroom. She was certain that snails had moved faster than she was moving.

"Part of it is. I *really* need to talk to Luke."

Of course he did.

Turning her head, she tapped her fingers on the shower curtain. "You have a call from Agent Kaplan. He says it's important."

Maybe because she'd practically shouted, Luke turned off the water. Elaina grabbed a towel and had it ready for him when he pulled back the shower curtain. He tried to be discrete by using the curtain to cover himself.

It didn't work.

In fact, it made things worse.

Elaina got another glimpse that was only slightly concealed with the opaque vinyl material. She felt herself go warm and damp, and she knew that, coupled with the preshower incidents she had more than enough visual information about Luke to inspire a whole lot of fantasies.

He took the phone and the towel and managed to cover himself. But not before she got yet another glimpse of something she shouldn't be glimpsing at. Oh, mercy.

She had to fan herself.

With the water streaming down his body, he

stepped from the shower tub and onto the mat. "What's the problem, Rusty?" Luke asked.

Elaina watched his expression so she could try to gauge what the call was about, but there was no change in his demeanor. She started to step from the room, but Luke caught on to her arm. "I'll put the phone on speaker so Elaina can hear this."

"She's right there with you?" she heard Rusty ask the moment Luke pressed the speaker function.

"You said it was important," Elaina countered. "That's why I got him out of the shower."

"It *is* important," Rusty verified after pausing. "Don't trust Gary Simpson or Brenda McQueen. At least not until I can clear some things up. Let's start with Brenda. She's clean. Maybe a little too clean."

Elaina moved closer to the phone so she could hear him better. Unfortunately, that meant moving closer to Luke. He smelled good, and she hadn't remembered her soap smelling like that on her own skin.

"Brenda McQueen doesn't have a driver's license," Rusty continued. "No loans, no credit cards."

Elaina didn't have to ask if that was unusual. She knew it was. Heck, she was in hiding, living a lie and she still had a driver's license and credit card.

"You think Brenda assumed a fake identity or something?" Luke asked.

"Could be. Elaina might have a gut feel about this. Is she sort of recluse?"

"I guess you could say that. She doesn't get out much, and when she does, she either jogs or rides her bike. I remember her saying something about having a fear of cars because of a bad accident when she was a child."

"Dig deeper," Luke advised the other agent. "What about Gary Simpson?"

"One thing popped up. He recently had a rather large amount of money deposited into his bank account. I can't find a source for it."

"Maybe a payoff," Luke suggested.

"That's what I thought, too. He's certainly one to watch, especially since he's a former Army Ranger. He was discharged because he failed a personal reliability exam. In others words, he had some issues that made the army think he was no longer a suitable candidate to carry combat weapons."

Elaina knew none of that about Gary. Odd. Why wouldn't he have mentioned his military career, especially since he believed she had an MIA husband? Or maybe Gary hadn't bought her lie at all.

"See if you can access his military records," Luke continued. "And while you're at it, do a more thorough background on Carrie Saunders. It's possible one of them is working for a person known only as T. This T was involved with Elaina's ex-fiancé."

Well, that got her mind off his body. Luke actually suspected Carrie of something so devious? Elaina might be able to believe that about the other two, especially Gary, but not Carrie.

"The exterior security equipment is installed," Rusty continued. "It basically works like this. If anyone comes into the wooded area behind Elaina's house, then the motion detector will trigger a silent alarm, which will then send a signal to your cell phone. It'll sound as if you're getting a text message, and on your phone screen, you'll see the numbers 911. In this case, 911 means a trespasser."

"Thanks, Rusty. Let me know as soon as you have those background checks."

Luke ended the call and he placed his phone on the sink so he could give his towel a much needed adjustment. It was a little towel, and Luke was a big guy. Not a good combination. Well, not good unless she wanted another cheap thrill. She didn't.

Really.

Disgusted with herself, Elaina forced her snail-pace feet to get out of there. She went back into her room and sat on the edge of the bed. Luke closed the door, but not all the way, while he dressed. Unfortunately, she could see his reflection in the bathroom mirror.

Sheez. She didn't think her body could handle more of this, so Elaina forced herself to look away. She also forced her attention back on the issue at hand. And there was a huge issue at hand.

"Carrie isn't behind any of this," she informed him.

"*Everyone* is a suspect," Luke countered. "If T wants the software modifications badly enough, then he or she would have paid big bucks for someone to find them."

Elaina couldn't argue with that, but she could argue with the overall logic. "Then why wait until now? If it's Brenda, Gary or Carrie, why wouldn't they have started looking months ago?"

"Maybe they've been doing just that."

That sent a chill through her blood, but she couldn't completely discount it. Gary had been inside her house dozens of times, and she remembered that he'd used her bathroom once or twice. He'd also replaced a burned-out bulb when she'd mentioned that she didn't have a step ladder. Elaina hadn't stayed with him while he did it, and he could have easily gone through the things in her room. Or worse. With his training, he might have been able to sneak in while she wasn't even there.

"Okay, suppose one of them is our culprit," Elaina said. "Why step up the search now? Why risk rummaging through the house while both of us are here?"

"Maybe your security system prevented other searches when you were away from the house. And as for the timing, maybe that has something to do with me. The person could have gotten suspicious of my arrival. If he or she has some computer expertise, it wouldn't be that hard to figure out that I'm a federal agent."

Elaina gave that some thought and couldn't argue with it, either. "Especially if this person already knew that I didn't have a husband."

"You bet." He opened the door and faced her. Not naked this time. He wore jeans and black long-sleeve pullover. Both items of clothing hugged his body. "That means we need to find out who T is because he or she might do something stupid to get those modifications."

"Modifications I don't have," Elaina mumbled. But she wouldn't stand much of a chance of convincing T's hired guns of that. And then she thought of something else.

"What about this criminal you mentioned—George Devereux? The one you think had something to do with your wife's death. Do you still think he might have something to do with the two jailed men?"

"It's possible," Luke said. "I'd planned to visit Devereux tomorrow. He's in a federal prison not too far from here. But that visit's probably not going to happen. With any luck, I'll be doing the two interrogations at the local jail instead of seeing Devereux."

Yes, *that*. It suddenly seemed like too much to do, and all of it was important, if not critical. Elaina groaned and scrubbed her hands over her face. "So, we have Gary, Carrie, Brenda, George Devereux and heaven knows who else who might do something dangerous and crazy to get their hands on Kevin's final project?"

He lifted his shoulder. "And as you pointed out, it might not even be related to Kevin."

She'd known that, of course. But it was *not* knowing which was the truth that was getting to her.

"What I worry about most is Christopher," Elaina continued. "Greedy, desperate people often do greedy, desperate things, and I don't want there to be any possibility for Christopher to be hurt."

"Trust me." Luke eased down next to her on the bed. "I want the same thing."

"But how do we make sure it happens?" Her voice broke on the last word, and she thought for a moment that she might break, too. "There's so much coming at me. I'm not weak, I swear. But it scares me that I might not be able to protect him."

Her voice did more than break that time. It was a mess of quiver and nerves. Exactly the way she felt.

"My emotions are all over the place," Elaina admitted. "Like I have a nasty mix of ADD, PMS and adrenaline." She wouldn't mention the lustful urges, but they were there. It was like there was an alley-cat war going on inside her body.

Luke gave a heavy sigh. One with undertones of frustration and perhaps even disbelief at what he was about to do. He slipped his arm around Elaina and pulled her to him.

Elaina wanted to reject the gesture. She wanted to move away to regain her composure. But she didn't. She stayed put and took everything he was offering.

It felt like heaven.

It'd been so long since Elaina had relied on or trusted anyone other than herself. So long since she'd felt anything but lots of fear. But this wasn't fear. Luke was warm, solid, strong, and, if only for a few seconds, he made her believe that all was right with the world.

"I'm not weak," she repeated.

He chuckled. It was husky and low. Very manly. "You're not weak," he agreed. "Actually, you've handled this far better than most people would have."

Alarms went off in her head. Big ones. Elaina

pulled back and met Luke's gaze. "That sounds, um, friendly and compassionate."

He looked a little puzzled. "It was meant to be."

"Then, this isn't good." Elaina groaned.

"Probably not," he readily agreed. "This won't be a good idea, either."

"*This*?" she questioned.

He lowered his head. Slipped his hand around the back of her neck. And hauled her to him.

Luke kissed her.

His mouth was solid and warm, like the rest of him. That was her first thought. Her second, was that he was very good at this. He was at least a thirty on a scale of one to ten. He pressed his mouth against hers. Moving. Just a little. Touching the seam of her lips with his tongue. Again, just a little. But it was just enough to make her want so much more.

Giving into the need, Elaina lifted her arms, first one and then the other, and slid them around his neck. Her heartbeat slowed. Her breath became thin. Everything slowed, and the dreamy sensation of pleasure and heat washed over her. Like warm water on a tropical beach.

Luke pulled her closer to him. Until her breasts were against his chest. Until they seemed to be touching everywhere. Well, touching everywhere except in the place that wanted to be touched most. Elaina tried to push that urge aside so she could just concentrate on the pleasure of his mouth.

Long, slow French kisses. They were her passion.

And Luke was very good at satisfying that particular passion. He kissed and tasted, savoring her as she was savoring him.

Elaina knew she should stop. This wasn't a rocket science decision that required a lot of analysis. They were two aroused adults who shouldn't be aroused even after seeing each other practically naked. Yet, that logic didn't stop her when she slid her hand down his chest and had the pleasure of feeling all those muscles react and tense at her touch.

Luke touched, too. He never stopped the barrage of delicious kisses, but he escalated things in his own way. His hand left her neck, and he slid his fingers over her throat. Touching. Lighting little fires along the way.

His touch was weightless. Barely there. And yet, like his gentle kisses, it was enough. Thorough was the word that came to mind.

Luke was *thorough*.

The thoroughness went up a notch when those clever fingers made it to her breasts. He found her right nipple. It was puckered and tight from arousal and probably not hard to locate under her thin bra. He gently pinched her.

The hunger shot through her.

And the need. Mercy, the need. She could feel those stroking fingers on every part of her body. Here they were on her bed. Christopher was asleep. There was nothing to stop her from letting this lead to what would no doubt be the hottest sex she'd ever had.

But it couldn't happen.

Elaina repeated that to herself.

Her body tried to veto her decision, but she somehow managed to break the kiss. She had no idea that she had that much willpower, and after she looked at Luke, she wasn't sure that willpower would last more than a second or two.

"I didn't fake that kiss," she said, just to make sure he understood. And to make sure she could speak.

"I know." He leaned back slightly, and he reached out. He ran his thumb over her bottom lip, gathering up the moisture from their kiss. He then touched his thumb to his tongue and made a low sound of pleasure.

That simple gesture ignited her body again, and Elaina actually had to get up so that she wouldn't throw herself right back in his arms. Thankfully, she didn't have to put her failing willpower to the test because Luke's phone rang again. Not a normal ring. It was a series of beeps.

"You have a call," she said, forcing herself out of her lusty trance.

Even though her eyes were still blurry, she could see that he no longer had that look of lust. "It's not a call," he let her know. "That's a text message."

Luke hurried off the bed and picked up his phone from her dresser. He cursed when he glanced at the screen. "Someone or something tripped the exterior security system."

Elaina couldn't say anything. Before that mind-numbing kiss, she'd just been thinking of the danger.

And now, it might be here. Not some vague sense of unease. The danger might be right outside her door.

Luke took something from his suitcase that was still sitting on the bathroom floor. It was a small black gun. He removed what appeared to be a safety lock from it, and he pressed it into her hands.

"Wait here with Christopher," he instructed.

She didn't want to wait. She didn't want to move, either. And she definitely didn't want to panic. But that's what she seemed to be on the verge of doing.

Elaina forced herself to breathe and spring into action. She got down on the floor to shelter Christopher's body, and she prayed that the security equipment had malfunctioned. Maybe that was all there was to it. But her out-of-control heart and mind were screaming differently.

Moments later, she heard Luke's hurried footsteps in the hall. "There's a fire out back."

"A fire?" A dozen things went through her mind, and none of them were good.

"I've already called the fire department," Luke told her. "Lock this door and stay inside."

Her out-of-control feeling soared. "You're going out there?" she asked, instantly alarmed.

"I have to. I need to use the hose to try to put out the fire, or the flames might make it to the house."

Oh, God. Now, she was ready to panic. "My house might burn down?"

"Not if I can stop it. If the fire gets out of hand, you'll hear me shout for you to take the baby and evacuate. Don't leave unless you hear me say differently. Try not to worry. This could be nothing."

One brief glance passed between them, and in that glance, she could tell that Luke was trying to reassure her before he rushed away. She heard the back door close, and she heard the clicks to indicate he'd locked it. Elaina got up, as well, and went to the window. She didn't open the blinds, but she peeked out.

There was black smoke billowing from the woods.

The fire wasn't close, at least twenty yards away, but it was close enough for Elaina to catch a whiff of the smoke and feel the horrible threat that seemed to be closing in around her house. Worse, the ground was winter dry, and there was a cold wind blowing. That fire could easily get out of control.

She saw Luke. He had his gun in one hand, and the hose in the other. He was spraying the water on the fire. Unfortunately, the flames were large, and the water pressure wasn't any match for them.

Elaina wanted to run out and help him, but one glance at Christopher, and she knew she couldn't. She couldn't leave her baby alone. So, she waited with her heart in her throat, and with her concerns and questions growing.

She put a halt to some of those concerns by reminding herself that all of this could have been an accident. This could have been caused by a spark from Gary's barbecue grill. It didn't matter that it was still morning and in the dead of winter. Elaina had seen him using that grill at all times of the day and in all kinds of weather.

And then she heard a sound.

It was something coming not from the fire area but from the front of the house. It sounded as if someone were testing the doorknob.

Oh, mercy.

Elaina hadn't thought things could get worse, but she was obviously wrong.

She glanced at the gun and hoped she could shoot straight. Since she'd never tried, she doubted she could, but the gun made her feel marginally safer.

The doorknob jiggled again.

She tried not to make a sound because she didn't want to give away her position in the house, but she tiptoed to her bedroom door and unlocked it. She stepped into the hall. This time, Elaina didn't just hear the knob move, she saw it.

The motion was almost frantic as if someone were desperately trying to pick the lock. Which in all likelihood, that's exactly what was happening.

She couldn't go to the door and look out the peephole. Too risky. This person might have a gun, as well. Worse, the person might know how to use it. Unlike her. But she couldn't just stand there and let someone break in, either. She couldn't risk Christopher being hurt.

"Get away from the door now, or I'll shoot," Elaina shouted.

The jiggling immediately stopped.

She heard footsteps, and she wanted to run and see who was responsible for them, but again, she raced back to Christopher in case the intruder tried to come through a window or another door.

Then, a terrifying thought hit her.

What if this would-be intruder went after Luke? Oh, God. What if something happened to him?

Elaina had never felt more helpless in her life. She couldn't leave the house, and she had no way to help him. So, she stood there, her hands aching from the grip she had on the gun.

More seconds ticked off the clock. It seemed to take an eternity, but Elaina finally heard something that she wanted to hear.

The siren.

That meant the fire engine was approaching her house. She hurried to the blinds and looked out. It wasn't long before she saw the two firemen running across her lawn.

She said a quick prayer of thanks, but that prayer got a lot longer when she heard the key in the back door. She waited, just in case, but then she heard the security system being reengaged.

It was Luke.

Elaina raced out into the hall and saw him in the kitchen.

"Are you okay?" She couldn't help herself. Elaina ran into his arms and held on tight.

"I'm fine." He sounded out of breath, and he

smelled of the scorched wood and smoke. There were smears of black ash on his face and clothes.

Elaina wasn't sure she believed him. "Someone tried to get in through the front door. I was afraid he'd go after you."

Alarmed, Luke shook his head. "No one came after me."

"Thank God." She brushed some soot off his chin. "What about the fire?"

"It should be out in no time. The house isn't in danger."

That was good news, but there wasn't happiness in his eyes. He eased back and looked down at her.

"I smelled accelerant while I was out there," he whispered. "I'm almost certain it was gasoline."

Elaina held her breath and waited for him to finish what she already knew he was going to say.

"Someone intentionally set that fire. It was arson."

Chapter Ten

Luke was mad as hell.

He didn't like the speed with which things were moving. He didn't like the evidence, or lack thereof, in what was now officially an arson investigation. And he didn't like feeling as if he were spinning his wheels at one of the most crucial times in his life.

"We have the car packed and ready to go. What do you mean the safe house isn't ready yet?" Luke demanded. He made that demand of the agent in San Antonio who was handling his request. A delay wasn't an option, not after dealing with that fire.

Luke had to get Elaina and Christopher some place safe.

"We're working as fast as we can," the agent on the other end of the line insisted.

"Then, work faster." Luke stabbed the End Call button and got up to pace. It didn't help. But then, not much would help at this point. Well, not much other than a call to say the safe house was ready and that the arsonist had been caught and was behind bars.

"It's already getting dark," Elaina commented. She was in the kitchen feeding Christopher dinner. Mushy peas and some other food item that Luke couldn't readily identify. It looked disgusting, but Christopher was wolfing it down. "Does that mean we'll stay the night here?"

"No. Absolutely not." He softened his tone when he heard the harshness. "The safe house will be ready soon."

"And then what?" she asked.

It wasn't an easy question for him to answer. "Once I have Christopher and you settled in, and once I'm sure that you'll be okay there, then I need to find out who's playing these games."

"You think the fire was a *game?*"

"More like a ruse. I think the arsonist wanted us out of the house and was willing to create a diversionary tactic to make that happen."

Elaina gave that some thought. "The arsonist did this so he or she could get inside and search while we were out there battling flames."

Luke nodded. "I think that was the plan. But this idiot obviously didn't realize that there was no way I would let you outside like that with Christopher."

"True. But Rusty said there weren't any useable prints on the doorknob. Only smears." She met his gaze. There was so much weariness in her eyes. "So, maybe this person isn't as stupid as we'd like to believe he or she is. Maybe he or she wiped down the knob. Or wore gloves."

"Could have. But anyone who's ever watched a crime show would have done that. What it does tell me is that this person is under some kind of pressure to come up with something—*fast*. Probably those modifications to Kevin's software."

"Or it could be the adoption papers," she offered cautiously.

Luke couldn't rule that out. And if it was the papers that had precipitated it, then this was his fault. He'd literally brought this right to Elaina's door. Either way, no matter what this person wanted, Luke would have to find a way to stop him or her.

He had his list of suspects, and while technically anyone in town could be guilty, his primary ones included: Carrie, Brenda, Gary and his old nemesis, George Devereux. Carrie was least suspect of those four, but Luke wasn't about to take her off the list. He'd learned the hard way that people would do all sorts of things for money. Besides, Carrie had had just as much opportunity to set that fire as Brenda and Gary. Devereux was the unknown factor here.

And Luke was soon going to remedy that.

Elaina took Christopher out of the high chair. "So, we go to the safe house, what will happen then?"

She eyed him suspiciously. It made Luke wonder if he was that transparent or if she'd managed to figure him out. Odd, because most people accused him of being hard to read. That kiss had probably broken down some barriers and created an intimacy and familiarity that shouldn't exist between them. Those kinds of connections could cause him to lose focus. That couldn't happen.

"There'll be an agent at the safe house," Luke explained after he cleared his throat. "Someone I trust. He'll stay with you and Christopher."

"And where will you be?" Judging from her expression, she'd already guessed the answer.

"Here."

Yep. Elaina had guessed, and she wasn't happy about it. *"Here?"*

"I need to search the place, and I can't do that if I'm worried about Christopher." He almost added Elaina's name in there, because he would worry about her, too, but it was best not to add any more of that familiarity to this already dangerous mix.

She shifted Christopher to her hip, and both of them gave him an accusing stare. "So, you're going to put yourself in danger and possibly make yourself a target?"

That about summed it up. "I'm a federal agent, Elaina. This is what I do. Besides, I wouldn't be any more of a target than I am right now."

She didn't say anything for several moments. "Maybe," Elaina finally mumbled.

He knew what she was thinking and what terrified her. He also knew that her semicalmness was a façade. "Christopher and you are targets, too." And it was hard as hell to admit the rest it aloud. "You can blame me for that."

Her gaze whipped to his. Elaina stared at him. But she didn't deny it. She couldn't.

When she rubbed her fingers over her forehead, he noticed she was trembling. The façade was crumbling fast. "Sometimes I just want to run and hide again." Her voice was trembling, too. "I want Christopher to be safe."

Luke wanted that, as well. It hurt to know that he couldn't make that promise.

He reached for her, but Elaina moved away. She sank down onto the sofa and placed Christopher on the floor so he could play with his toys. "I'm scared," she admitted.

Those two words encompassed a lot. Elaina was scared of this arsonist-intruder who'd come into her life. She was scared of another attack. Scared of her uncertain future. But that wasn't all.

"You're scared of *me*," Luke said. He sat down in the chair directly across from her.

When she lifter her head and met his gaze, he could see that Elaina was blinking back tears. She stared at him. Then, she nodded. "I *am* scared of you."

Even though he'd braced himself, it was still difficult to hear. "Your fears are justified."

She shook her head. "I don't want to make the same mistakes I made with Kevin—"

"I'm not Kevin."

"I know." Every part of her was filled with emotion. Her voice. Her body. Her eyes. "But I've let that kiss and my feelings for you get in the way. I can't see you objectively. I can't see myself objectively. And things are moving so fast. That can't be good because I have to think beyond this day and this week. I have to look at the future, and I have to wonder where we'll be if and when this attraction fizzles out."

Luke knew exactly how she felt. In less than two days, he'd gone from despising Elaina to kissing her.

And worse, he wanted to kiss her again.

So that he wouldn't do just that, he got up and moved away from her. Elaina took the cue. She picked up Christopher and headed for her bedroom. Luke followed them because he didn't want her to be anywhere in the house without him.

He wanted to do something to ease her fear, but the only thing that would accomplish that would be to identify the person after them. So, that's the direction Luke took.

"I have an idea," he said. "Why don't you get out everything else you brought with you from San Antonio? Clothes, toys, everything. I have to go through all of that anyway, and this way, it'll save some time."

As if it were the most natural thing in the world, she handed Christopher to him. His son went willingly and didn't give Luke that disapproving look that he sometimes did. In fact, Christopher snuggled against him and gave him a sloppy kiss on the cheek.

The whole situation suddenly seemed so intimate. They seemed like a family. But they weren't. Still, that didn't stop Luke from playing what-if.

Could he possibly make this work with Elaina?

He quickly came to his senses and decided he didn't want to know. It wasn't the right time to try to work through all of this. Truth was, it might never be the right time. Elaina could be correct—this attraction could all fizzle out and leave them both with bad tastes in their mouths.

Which made him think of her mouth, again.

He was in danger of developing a case of obsession.

"I had on these clothes the day I left." She deposited a pair of dark gray pants, a top in a lighter shade and a pair of shoes. Another reach into the closet, and she added a purse to the pile. It was empty, Luke soon learned, after Christopher and he had a look inside. Christopher didn't stop with a look, he began to slap at the purse and laugh. He even tried to put it on his head.

Luke smiled and kissed him.

Despite the wonderful moment, Luke knew he should be concentrating. His precious son was yet another distraction. The sooner he had him in a safe house, the better.

Elaina put the box of files on the bed, and then she went into the nursery. When she returned she had several items in her hands. "These are the toys I brought with me." She put those next to the other things.

There were two small stuffed animals. A purple

bear and a yellow bunny that drew Christopher's attention. He ditched the purse for it.

"Kevin had these with him the night he brought Christopher home," Elaina explained. "He called Christopher our little bunny."

Luke didn't care much for a criminal giving his son a pet name. "This is everything?" he asked.

She shook her head. "I honestly don't know. There could be other things."

Luke was afraid she'd say that. "When you get to the safe house, sit down and write a list. That way, I know what to look for when I come back."

"Suit yourself, but it'd be easier if I just went through everything in person."

"It wouldn't be *safer,*" he reminded her. That earned him an eye roll. "You said Kevin used a miniature memory card. So, we're looking for something very small, just as thin as a dime."

"Something Kevin might have had on him the night he was killed," Elaina pointed out.

"No. If it'd been on him, then someone wouldn't still be looking for it. They would have found it. I read the police report of Kevin's death, and he'd been stripped and searched—thoroughly. So had his car."

Luke sat on the bed so he could better examine all the items. The most obvious things were the purse and toys. He squeezed all three and looked closely at the small details. The bunny's glassy eyes. The bear's padded black nose. The strap of Elaina's purse. There were no obvious signs of the memory card, but these things needed to be checked and double-checked.

"I'm going to put this stuff in the car," he let her know, passing Christopher back to her. "I can take it to my office in San Antonio once you're settled into the safe house."

Elaina opened her mouth, probably to argue about him returning here, but his cell phone rang. Finally! That safe house had to be ready. But the person who spoke to him on the other end of the line wasn't from the Justice Department.

"Luke, it's Collena Drake," the woman greeted.

He certainly hadn't expected to hear her voice, and it brought back a barrage of memories. The search for his son. The frustration of not being able to find him. And then, Collena's help. If it hadn't been for her, he'd no doubt still be looking for Christopher. Luke owed her a lot that he'd never be able to repay.

"I had to call," Collena continued, her voice rusty and thick as if laced with too much emotion and fatigue. "Did you connect with your son?"

"I found him, yes. I can't thank you enough."

"You don't have to thank me. In fact, it's my guess that the adoptive mother would want to do the opposite. If she's a good loving mother, then having you learn the truth must have turned her world upside-down."

"It has." Luke wasn't immune to the guilt he was feeling over that, either.

"Well, it might take time, but you'll work through this. I'm sorry it took so long to get you the information to find your son. The files were a mess. Little bits of info in one place. Other bits in other places. It took time to put the pieces together."

That opened the door for something that Luke had wanted to ask from day one. "Why did you help me?"

She chuckled. It was rusty like her voice. "Penance, of sorts."

"Yours or mine?"

"Mostly mine. I was the undercover cop investigating the Brighton Birthing Center. If I'd been able to identify the culprits sooner, then some of those babies would have never been illegally adopted."

There was no mistaking the pain in that. "Something tells me you paid hard for that."

"I have. I'm still paying," she added in a mumble. "I found something else in the files, and I thought you should know. First of all, the leaders of the adoption ring have all been arrested. The police are now in the process of rounding up the investors."

"There were investors?" This was the first Luke had heard of it.

"Lots of them. I don't believe that most knew they were providing funds for illegal activities. And in some cases, the activities weren't illegal at all. Which brings me to the point of this call. Before I gave you the information about how to find your son's adoptive mother, I checked your background. I wanted to make sure you were a suitable father."

Luke wasn't surprised by that. He'd checked her background, too. "And what did you find?"

"You're suitable. But I also learned that you're the one responsible for putting George Devereux behind bars."

Luke's stomach knotted. He did not like hearing that connection. "Didn't you have a minor role in that, too? You were on one of the surveillance teams when you were still with San Antonio PD. It's a small world." He paused. "Some things have been happening here. A suspicious fire. And someone might have rummaged through Elaina's bedroom. Do you think Devereux could be behind what's going on here?"

"I don't know. But I've learned that he's connected to the Brighton Birthing Center where your son was born. Luke, George Devereux was one of their investors."

Chapter Eleven

Elaina had to sit back down on the bed after hearing what Collena Drake had just told Luke.

Mercy.

She didn't want a man like Devereux involved in this. Now, the question was—how involved was he? Being an investor in a birthing center didn't mean he had a hand in Taylor's death or Christopher's adoption. It also didn't mean he had a part in what was happening now.

But then, it didn't mean he was innocent, either.

Luke obviously felt the same because the moment he finished giving her the news, he began to make phone calls. The first was to Rusty to brief him on what Collena Drake had told him. The second call was to the Justice Department office in San Antonio. With both calls, he requested the status of the safe house and a thorough check on Devereux's recent activities.

However, that wasn't all.

Elaina listened as he made some comments laced with frustration and anger. Then he set up an appointment with Devereux for the following day.

"You think meeting with George Devereux is a wise thing to do?" she asked the moment Luke finished the call and put his phone into his pocket.

Christopher fussed, and she picked him up from the floor. Elaina rocked him gently to soothe him. She only wished it had a soothing effect on her, but that wasn't going to happen. Not with Luke less than twenty-four hours from meeting with a convicted felon.

"I have to find out if Devereux is part of this," Luke answered.

"I understand that. But what if the meeting only upsets him even more? What if seeing you makes him want to come after you?"

"It's a risk I have to take. I won't meet with him until Christopher and you are in the safe house. So, if Devereux wants to retaliate against anyone, then I'll be the only one he can come after."

Elaina couldn't believe what she'd just heard him say. "Well, that's just great. He'll come after you and only you. Is that supposed to make me feel better?" She couldn't sit still any longer. She stood and began to rock back and forth. Christopher must have liked the motion because he put his head on her shoulder, and she felt him relax.

"You're angry."

"You're right." But then, she heard herself and groaned softly.

"See, this is the problem with having feelings for someone," he concluded. "Now, instead of thinking of the best way to approach this case, you're thinking about the possibility that I might be in danger."

Since that was dead-on accurate, she didn't bother to respond.

"I'm dealing with the same thing," he admitted. "What I should do is turn all of this over to another agent. One who isn't personally involved. That's by-the-book." He put his hands on his hips. "But I can't do that, and that means this isn't fair to you or Christopher."

"It's fair," she insisted.

He walked closer, and he lightly touched Christopher's back. "He's asleep."

That didn't surprise her. He'd had a very short afternoon nap, so she wasn't going to wake him even if she hadn't had a chance to bathe him yet. Elaina took him into the nursery and put him in the bed.

Luke followed her, of course, and stood in the doorway waiting.

"I'll get him up when it's time to leave for the safe house," she whispered.

He got that concerned look again. Luke reached out, touched her arm, and rubbed softly. It was soothing, or at least it would have been if she hadn't been waiting to hear what would no doubt be bad news.

"The safe house probably isn't going to be ready tonight," Luke confessed.

That didn't do a thing to steady Elaina's raw

nerves. "Well, that explains why you got so angry while you were on the phone."

"Anger is too mild a word for what I was feeling when I found out." Luke took a deep breath. "We're going to plan B. Just for tonight, we'll stay here, and Rusty will sit outside in his car and make sure no one gets near the place."

It wasn't ideal, but then nothing about this situation was. She could only hope that the culprit wasn't stupid enough to return with a federal agent standing guard. Plus, they had the security systems to give them warning if someone did try to approach the house or break in.

"I don't want you to turn this case over to another agent," Elaina told him. "This will probably sound maudlin, but you would do everything possible to protect Christopher. I can't say the same about another agent, and that's too big of a risk to take."

He stared down at her, and Elaina could have sworn he was fighting a smile. It didn't last long before the concern returned. "I don't have a good track record when it comes to a personal life."

Now, she fought a smile. It seemed an odd change of subject. "Is that meant to be some kind of warning?"

"Yeah," he readily admitted.

She shrugged. "You don't have to be good at it, Luke. Not when it comes to us. Just a few minutes ago, we admitted that this isn't personal." That hadn't sounded as good as it had while still in her head. "What I mean is that it's simply an attraction between two adults who haven't had sex in a long time." She winced. That didn't sound right, either. "Well, that's true in my case."

"My case, too. For months I've been obsessed with finding Christopher. That hasn't given me much time for anything else."

"So." And she wasn't sure what to add to that. Maybe she could say something along the lines of *there, we've established an out for us, again.*

But it was beginning to feel like a situation where the lady doth protest too much.

He was close enough for her to touch him. Close enough to see the swirls of gray in his eyes. Close enough to feel his breath brush against her face. It stirred her blood. Stirred her body.

And the heat rolled through her.

His touch didn't help things, either. He slid his fingers along the outside of her arm. A sensual, slow caress.

"Talking about sex probably isn't a good idea," he commented.

But he didn't move.

"Just remember all the anger you feel toward me." She didn't move, either.

"The anger," he repeated. He nodded. Nodded again. And for a moment, she really thought that was going to do the trick. Elaina expected him to back away. To put up those shields and barriers that were in both of their arsenals of relationship avoidance.

He didn't.

Luke latched on to her hair with one hand, the back of her neck with the other, and he hauled her to him.

LUKE DIDN'T EVEN try to hold anything back. He would have failed anyway. He knew it. His body knew it. And his brain just surrendered to the inevitable.

Elaina surrendered, too.

She melted against him, and she let him take her mouth as if he owned her. Ironic, because even with the heat and the need slamming through him, he knew that she was not his for the taking. This was temporary. A lull before the storm of a custody battle. He'd deal with that when the time came. For now, he intended to take everything she was offering, even if it was a really bad idea.

Luke maneuvered her so that her back was against the wall and kissed her, deeper and harder. The kiss didn't stop, it escalated. Elaina's mouth was suddenly just as hungry, just as demanding as his. Not a good combination for a couple who had any hopes of trying to maintain a hold on their feelings.

She came up on her tiptoes and coiled her arms around him. Luke reacted to the intimate contact. Man, did he ever react. He pressed his body against hers. Tightly against her. Until they were perfectly aligned. His chest against her breasts. The front of her pants against his jeans.

Elaina reacted, too.

She made a throaty moan of pleasure and

deepened the kiss. The taste of her fired through him, as did the feel of her in his arms. She fit. *They* fit. A thought that had him doing a mental double take.

Luke might have stepped away from her to consider why he shouldn't be thinking that way, but their midsections brushed against each other. Specifically, her soft feminine body brushed against his erection. And all doubts and coherent thoughts went straight out the window.

The kissing session became a different kind of battle—they fought to get closer to each other. They fought for the intimate contact. The connection of man and woman. Each touch, each brush of her hips fanned the flames higher, and Luke knew he was lost.

She slid her leg along the outside of his, creating even deeper contact between them. Luke let go of her hair so he could shove up her stretchy top. Thankfully, the top cooperated, and he suddenly had her bra-covered breast in his hand. He shoved down the bra, as well, though it was hardly more than a swatch of lace, and she spilled into his hand.

He broke the kiss long enough to go down her body and take her nipple into his mouth. She moaned with desire. And she grabbed on to him and pulled him closer.

Luke didn't stop there. He kissed her stomach, circling her navel with his tongue, and he sucked her. Not gently, either.

She said something. Something incoherent because his pulse was pounding in his ears. Elaina didn't need words, however, to make herself clear. She slid down, as well, and eased her palm over his erection.

Luke damn near lost his breath.

The sensation was so intense that he knew this couldn't last long. He considered carrying her to the bed. Or maybe the floor. Taking her. In some hard, fast, frantic coupling that would exhaust this maddening need for release.

But he also knew this was definitely not the time for full-blown sex.

After all, his sleeping son was only a few yards away from them. And if they had sex, he certainly wouldn't be thinking about protecting Christopher and Elaina. His brainless body would take over, and he'd only one thought on his mind. *Take Elaina now.*

She obviously had the same thought in her mind, too, because she tried to unzip his jeans. Luke put his hand over hers to stop her. He had to distract her before she made a second attempt because he didn't think he could resist her if she got his zipper down.

Luke shoved his hand down her stomach, past her pants, and into her panties. His fingers found her. Wet and hot. He made his way through the slick moisture. A few strokes, and she gave up the zipper quest.

One touch, and he heard her breath break.

She slid her hand into her own hair, her eyelids fluttered down, and she rocked against his fingers. He could feel her already so close to release, and he took her mouth so he could taste her when she shattered.

But Elaina obviously had something else in mind.

While he was distracted, she went in for the kill. She was fast, too. Damn fast. One deft move, and she had his zipper down, and her hand was inside his jeans.

She didn't fumble or hesitate. Those agile fingers bypassed his boxers and slid right over his erection. She proved that she was just as adept at stroking and touching as he was. A rather skillful swipe of her thumb, and she had him close to begging for the sex that he already knew they couldn't have.

It became a war of will, and Luke fell back on his combat training. He couldn't lose concentration because it would simply be too dangerous.

On many levels.

Including a personal one.

Luke gritted his teeth and dragged her to the carpeted floor. He landed on her. Between her legs. All in all, it wasn't a bad place to be. For a moment, anyway. But he had to gain even more control of the situation. He caught both her hands in one of his. Imprisoning her.

It worked…for a few seconds.

And then there was another round of jockeying for position. She didn't have use of her hands, but she made use of her body. She lifted her hips, thrust them forward, and the friction nearly caused them both to shatter.

The second phase of the battle began. He wedged his knee between her legs and eased his fingers back inside her. Just like that, Elaina stopped struggling. Thank goodness. She gave into the moment.

Luke practically cheered. This was a battle he couldn't lose. Somehow, someway, he had to keep his wits and sanity, even if it required multiple cold showers later.

A long, deliberate sigh left her mouth. Once again she moved into the strokes. And she moved against him. Deeper this time. Against his fingers, against his body. A slow, sensual slide that brought out every basic, every carnal instinct inside him.

"We can do this," Elaina whispered, her voice threaded with the heat. "Together." But it was the passion talking. Later, she'd thank him for holding back.

Even if he wouldn't be thanking himself.

"I don't have a condom," Luke lied. "We'll have to do it this way."

He snagged her gaze, because he wanted to see her face. Luke fought through the clawing primal need to claim and possess so he could see exactly what this did to her. Elaina shook her head, as if she wanted to pull back, as if she wanted to wait for him.

But Luke deepened the strokes inside her. He kissed her, hard. He added some pressure with the leg still wedged between hers. He touched and touched and kept on touching until she no longer shook her head. Until she couldn't catch her breath. Elaina could only do one thing.

Surrender.

He felt her go over. Tasted her mouth as the pleasure rushed through her body. And when she melted, he gathered her into his arms and held her.

Elaina's eyes stayed closed for several seconds. Her body stayed limp. Then, she opened her eyes and looked at him. She looked on the verge of saying something—what exactly, he didn't have a clue. But whatever was on her mind, she didn't have a chance to tell him.

His phone beeped.

That soft little sound tore through his body like a bullet.

"Text message," he managed to say. Hoping he wouldn't see the numbers on the screen, he pulled his phone from his pocket and looked down.

The numbers were there. Nine-one-one.

"Someone tripped the security equipment out back," he told Elaina.

He didn't watch her reaction, but he didn't have to do that to know it wouldn't be good. She quickly got to her feet and fixed her clothes.

Luke did the same, and he called Rusty. It took him two rings to answer, and with each ring, Luke's adrenaline skyrocketed. "We might have an intruder in the backyard," he relayed when Rusty finally answered. "The security equipment just went off."

"I don't see anything out there. Stay put. I'll have a look around."

"Be careful."

Luke ended the call and waited. While Elaina stood directly across from him. She smelled like sex. Looked like it, too. But his brain had already kicked into protection mode. He reached over and turned off the overhead light in the nursery.

"Deer sometimes feed out there at night," she said. There was no more heat and passion in her voice. Only concern.

He nodded. Prayed that's all there was to it. And waited some more. He stared down at the screen, willing Rusty to phone back with a good report.

That didn't happen.

There was a crash. The sound of breaking glass. And it came from the nursery.

Because Luke knew what it was, he automatically pulled Elaina back to the floor. But he didn't stop there. He scrambled toward the crib in the nursery so he could get Christopher.

Christopher was alone, thank God. His son woke up and started to fuss. Luke ignored him and dropped with him to the floor. He sheltered Christopher with his body so the baby wouldn't be hurt. Then, Luke started the mad scramble back to Elaina's bedroom so he could turn off the light there and get his gun.

"We have an intruder," Elaina said. She sounded terrified. And no doubt was.

Luke knew what he was about to tell her would terrify her even more.

"That wasn't an intruder. That was a gun rigged with a silencer. Someone just fired a shot into the house."

Chapter Twelve

Elaina took Christopher from Luke so that he could grab his gun from her dresser. Within the span of a few seconds, she'd gone from postorgasmic bliss to sheer terror.

Someone had fired a shot into the house.

A shot that could have hurt Christopher.

There was another crash of glass, and Elaina knew another round had been fired.

But where?

The first had obviously been fired into the nursery, but this one appeared to have come from the direction of the living room. In other words, the front of the house. The gunman wasn't standing still.

He was on the move.

Or there was more than one.

With the overhead lights off, she had to rely on the meager light filtering into the hall from the kitchen. It was literally the only interior light still left on. She checked the baby for any signs of an injury, but he was fine. Well, except for the fact that he was crying at the top of his lungs. Christopher had no doubt been startled when Luke pulled him from the crib. But thank God Luke had reacted so quickly. Elaina didn't want to think about what might have happened if Luke hadn't done what he did.

"Stay on the floor," Luke ordered.

Elaina did, and she sheltered Christopher with her own body. She tried to soothe him by humming, but she failed miserably. But then, Christopher could likely feel the fear and concern in her.

Luke crawled forward so that he was between her and the door so he could fire if someone stormed into the house and tried to get into the bedroom.

"Press redial," he said passing his cell phone to her. "Ask Rusty what the hell is going on out there."

Somehow, she managed to do that, though she had to struggle with Christopher who was trying to wiggle out of her arms. "Someone fired a bullet into the house," she relayed to Rusty the moment he answered.

Silence.

Even over Christopher's sobs, Elaina could hear breathing so she knew someone was there on the other end of the line. God, was he hurt, unable to speak?

Or had something much worse happened?

And if so, if Rusty had been killed or incapacitated, then who was this on the phone?

Elaina snared Luke's gaze and passed the phone to him. He pressed the phone to his ear, listened.

Waited. "Agent Foley, if you can hear me, we're inside, in the kitchen. Can you get to us?"

"Did he answer?" Elaina mouthed.

Luke shook his head. He listened several more seconds and then ended the call.

Since Luke had obviously lied to the caller, that meant he probably didn't think this was his fellow agent.

Did that mean that Rusty was dead?

Who was this SOB who'd put her son in danger? She only wished she could get her hands around his throat.

Thinking of the danger reminded her that someone might be lurking around the house. So, he would know where to fire the next shot. Christopher's crying would make them much easier to find. It could make them targets.

Elaina tried again to soothe the baby. She kissed him, forced herself to hum a lullaby and she began to move in a rocking motion. Thankfully, Christopher cooperated, and his sobs tapered off to soft whimpers. He finally hushed, and Elaina prayed that he'd gone back to sleep. She didn't want him to have to experience any of this.

Luke jabbed in more numbers on his phone. "Sheriff Dawson," she heard him say. "This is Elaina's husband. Someone is firing shots into the house. Agent Foley is somewhere on the grounds, but he's not responding. We need assistance immediately."

But how soon would that be? Elaina calculated the distance between the sheriff's office and her house.

With luck, he could be there in five minutes if he came alone. Ten minutes, if he waited for backup from the deputy. That wasn't an eternity, but she was certain it would feel that way before this was over.

With his gun aimed and ready, Luke stayed in a crouching position and made his way to the hall. He looked out and lifted his head, listening. Elaina listened, as well, but she didn't hear anything.

That thought had no sooner formed in her mind, when there was another crash.

From the kitchen.

"Stay put," Luke whispered. "Keep Christopher quiet if you can."

Alarmed, Elaina frantically shook her head. "What are you going to do?"

"Create a diversion."

Elaina definitely didn't like the sound of that, but then she didn't care much for the crash of more breaking glass. It was still coming from the kitchen. Why hadn't the security alarm gone off? Someone must have disarmed it.

Luke backtracked toward her and dragged the mattress from her bed. He shoved it in front of the window and then hurried back to the hall.

"Be careful," Elaina whispered, but she said it so softly that she doubted he heard her.

A few seconds later, the light came on in the nursery. She craned her neck and saw Luke crouched down just outside the nursery door. He was waiting for another round bullet, probably so he could return fire.

Christopher stirred, and she began to hum to him again. Her breath was all over the place, and she wasn't sure she could produce enough sound to keep Christopher quiet. But her lullaby was interrupted by another crash.

Another bullet.

This one in the nursery again. So, the gunman was watching for any sign of activity and had fallen for Luke's diversion. Elaina only prayed that the shots stayed in the room and didn't stray into the hall where Luke was. He'd put himself in the line of fire to save them. She hadn't doubted he would do that, but that didn't stop her fears from soaring.

Luke couldn't be hurt.

He had to stay safe.

She didn't care if she felt that way because of what had happened earlier in the hall. She didn't care if lust and attraction were part of this. Elaina just wanted the shots to stop and for Christopher, Luke and her to be unharmed.

There was a slash of light in the front of the house. She thought of the earlier fire, but there weren't any flames. She heard the slam of a car door, and hoped that signaled the arrival of the sheriff.

There were more shots.

All the bullets came spewing through the nursery windows. One right after another. She counted four, and she had no doubt that they'd gone through the wall, perhaps even into the kitchen.

Then, it stopped.

"This is Sheriff Dawson," he called out.

Elaina recognized the voice and knew that help had arrived. But at what cost? The sheriff likely hadn't heard the silenced shots from the front of the house, and the man could be ambushed if he got near the shooter.

"The gunman's out back," Luke shouted to the sheriff. "Take cover. I'm going to return fire."

"No!" Elaina whispered. She didn't dare say it any louder because she couldn't alarm Christopher. Nor could she move closer to Luke. It would put the baby at risk.

But Luke took all the risks. He levered himself up, aimed his gun at what was left of the back nursery window and fired. These were not muffled shots but thick, deafening blasts. Elaina hugged Christopher even closer to her and prayed that he wouldn't wake up. While she was at it, she added a prayer that Luke would be okay.

"Halt your fire," the sheriff called out. "I see the shooter. I'm in pursuit."

Luke scrambled into the nursery. Elaina could no longer see him, but she figured he'd moved to the window so he could provide backup for the sheriff if necessary.

She sat there, holding the baby and waiting for all of this to end. She could hear the hum of her clock and Christopher's soft rhythmic breathing. She tried to let that calm her so that she wouldn't be tempted to call out to Luke to make sure he was okay.

"He got away," she heard the sheriff say. He sounded close, perhaps by the nursery window. But just the fact that he was nearby made her breathe easier. The sheriff probably wouldn't be standing in the open if he thought the gunman was still a threat.

"*He?*" Luke questioned. Elaina moved closer to the door so she could better hear the conversation. Thankfully, Luke asked the question that was foremost on her mind. "You're sure it was a man?"

"I'm not sure of that at all. The person was wearing dark clothes. You have a suspect in mind, or any idea why someone would want to do this?"

"I'll go over that with you just as soon as I've checked on Agent Foley."

"I'll do it. You stay put," the sheriff insisted. "Just in case our shooter returns."

So much for breathing easier. And at least from this angle she could see Luke. He wasn't hurt. But he was angry. His jaw muscles were iron stiff, and he seemed primed and ready for a fight. Elaina understood that. Someone had endangered Christopher. Neither Luke nor she would forget that anytime soon.

Luke didn't look back at her. He kept his gun and attention focused on the gaping hole in what was left of the window and the plantation blinds. The gauzy pale blue curtains fluttered around him like ghosts. And beneath his shoes was a thick layer of broken glass. It looked like carnage and chaos.

"This won't go unpunished," she heard Luke say.

And she didn't doubt him. What Elaina did doubt

was that Luke could catch this shooter and come out of it unharmed.

He would die to protect them.

Two days ago, that would have made her feel safe. Right now, it made her sick to her stomach. She didn't want to deal with the thought of losing him, which was ironic, because Luke Buchanan wasn't hers to lose.

There was a heavy-handed knock at the door. The sound shot through her and made Elaina gasp. Her body prepared for a second round of deadly threats, but she soon realized that wasn't necessary.

"I found Agent Foley," the sheriff shouted. Luke hurried to the front door and opened it. "He's been shot."

Luke cursed. Silently, Elaina did the same thing.

"How bad?" Luke asked.

"He's alive, and I've already called for an ambulance. I'll wait with him."

So, this wasn't over. A federal agent had been shot. If Rusty didn't make it, then they had a killer on their hands. A killer who'd tried his best to murder them tonight.

Why?

Was this really about that damned software? Or Devereux's retaliation? How could anyone risk a baby's life for the sake of money or reprisal?

"Don't come out just yet," Luke instructed. His voice was level, but there was raw emotion in it. He was no doubt thinking of his fellow agent, a man who'd been shot while trying to protect them. "How's Christopher?"

She looked down at him. "Sleeping."

Luke made a sound of approval. "I swear I won't let this happen again."

"You didn't *let* it happen this time," Elaina countered.

She would have said more, probably something sappy and emotional. She no doubt would have gushed her thanks. Gratitude that Luke would have resented because he wouldn't have seen his actions as an option.

But there was another knock at the front door.

"It's Sheriff Dawson," the man said. She heard Luke open the door again. "More bad news."

Chapter Thirteen

Luke waited until he was alone in the bedroom of the safe house before he cursed. He cursed the situation that Elaina and he were in and he cursed the list of things that just kept going wrong.

Most of all he cursed himself.

He should have pushed to get this safe house in San Antonio sooner. That way, Rusty wouldn't have been sitting in front of Elaina's house, he wouldn't have been shot in the chest and he wouldn't now be in the hospital fighting for his life. If they'd been in a safe house, Elaina and Christopher wouldn't have had to go through an attack that could have easily gotten them killed.

Those things were massive mistakes, but there was another by-product of Luke's failure to speed up the safe house process. Because Sheriff Dawson had had to respond to the shooting, that left the jail manned only by a bank security guard who occasionally did duty as an auxiliary deputy. The sheriff estimated there was a half-hour window of time while he and his real deputy were dealing with the aftermath of the shooting that the two prisoners were alone with the security guard.

The two men—the blonde and the guy with the eye patch—had managed to knock out the guard and escape.

Now, they were at large, and that meant in addition to keeping Elaina and Christopher safe, Luke had two more culprits that he had to be on the lookout for.

Yeah. He'd made a mess of things.

Luke was trying to remedy that. He now had Elaina, Christopher and even the sitter, Theresa, settled into a safe house in San Antonio. But that didn't mean they were *safe*. As long as the two escapees and their boss were out there, Elaina and Christopher would be in danger.

He glanced at the computer he'd set up on a fold-up card table. The screen was still blank, which meant the audio feed wasn't coming through yet. But it would. And then Luke would get a chance to do something else that he should have done before he ever visited Elaina…have a chat with George Devereux. And thanks to computer technology that should happen within the next half hour.

There was a soft tap at the door, and he peered over his shoulder as Elaina came in. She'd showered and changed into jeans and a shirt the same honey color as her hair, but she didn't look refreshed. Her eyes were sleep starved, and she looked as stressed out as Luke felt.

Elaina glanced at the computer screen, saw that it was blank and she walked in. But she didn't walk in too far. She kept her distance.

"How's Christopher?" Luke asked.

"He's fine. Theresa's feeding him breakfast. It was a really a good idea to bring her here with us. It's nice to have the extra pair of hands."

Well, that was one reason Luke included Theresa in their rushed evacuation of Crystal Creek. The other reason was that he was concerned that the escapees would go to the sitter's house and try to get her to tell them where Elaina was. Theresa was likely in as much danger as the rest of them. Maybe more since she wouldn't be able to defend herself.

"The hospital just called Agent Culpepper," Elaina told him.

That got Luke's attention. Agent Culpepper was the guard assigned to the safe house. A man that Luke trusted. Thankfully, Culpepper was in the living room and would stay there throughout this ordeal. "Is Rusty—"

"He made it through surgery and is in stable condition," Elaina interrupted. "The doctors think he'll make a full recovery."

Luke released the breath he didn't even know he'd been holding. That was one thing knocked off his mental list of concerns. Still, Rusty shouldn't have been put through this.

"What about the escapees?" Luke wanted to know. "Has anyone called Agent Culpepper about them?"

She shook her head and walked to the window where he was standing. Like him, she peered out at the morning sun and the empty sidewalk of the sleepy middle-class neighborhood. "But Culpepper did say that the Justice Department was involved in the search. Maybe that'll speed things up and get them back behind bars where they belong."

"That can't happen soon enough. These are the men who tried to kill you last year."

"But it wasn't them last night," she commented. She turned, faced him and raked her fingers through the side of her hair. "I've been trying to piece it together, and I think we're back to square one."

Luke nodded. Frowned. Cursed. Because he'd come to the same god-awful conclusion. "Gary, Brenda, Carrie or George Devereux. Any one of them could be behind what happened. Maybe none of them was the actual shooter, but they could have hired someone to do it."

"True. But were they merely trying to create a diversion so the prisoners could escape?" Elaina asked.

Luke wished that were the only reason, but he suspected something much more sinister. "With you and me out of the way, it would be much easier to search your house."

"Of course." She waited a moment, obviously trying to grasp and get past that. "What about the background checks you did on the suspects? Any news?"

He shook his head. "I talked to the investigator early this morning before you got up." At least he thought it was before that. Elaina and Christopher had stayed in one room. Theresa, in another. Luke had ended up in the third bedroom, where he'd spent the night mentally kicking himself.

"And?" she prompted.

"Gary has those mysterious funds in his account, but he claims it was repayment of an old loan from a college buddy. Nothing financial has popped up in Brenda's files yet, but the investigator can't rule her out, especially since Brenda moved to Crystal Creek just a few months ago."

"They didn't find anything on Carrie, either." It wasn't exactly a question.

Unfortunately, Luke had an answer that Elaina wouldn't be pleased to hear. He certainly hadn't been thrilled about it. "Were you aware that Carrie recently started using one of those prepaid cell phones that aren't traceable?"

Elaina shrugged. "That's not a crime. She's always on a tight budget. She probably ran up too big of a bill on her last phone and had to switch to something cheaper."

"Maybe. But the Justice Department isn't quite as trusting as you are. Carrie left the cell phone behind in the Crystal Creek diner yesterday, Rusty spotted it, and he sent it to the crime lab to see if we can retrieve any of the numbers she called."

"I'm sure you won't find anything incriminating," she insisted.

Luke didn't give up. He continued with the next bit of info he'd learned about her assistant. "Two weeks ago, Carrie applied to Rice University in Houston for their summer term. Did you know about that?"

She blinked, and it took a moment for her to answer. "No. Well, I knew she wanted to take art classes, but she said that she couldn't afford them."

"Well, she can apparently afford it now, which means that Carrie might be on the verge of a big payoff for locating that miniature memory chip that Kevin used to store his modifications."

Elaina folded her arms over her chest and stepped back. "I just can't believe she'd do something like this."

Luke understood that skepticism, but he wasn't about to cut Elaina's shop assistant any slack. Carrie was a suspect, and he would treat her as such.

Behind them, Luke heard a voice, and he turned to see the image of an agent on the screen. "The video interview has been set up," the agent informed Luke. "Are you ready to speak with inmate George Devereux?"

"Give me a second." Luke caught on to Elaina's arm and moved her to the corner of the room so that she'd be out of camera range. "I need you to stay quiet." He didn't want Devereux to know that Elaina was with him. It was best to give his old nemesis as little information as possible.

Luke sat down at the computer, glanced over the

notes he'd made earlier and he gave the nod to the agent. There was a flicker on the screen, mere seconds passed, and he saw the face of a man that Luke had hoped he'd never see again. It wasn't easy, but Luke put a chokehold on his anger. However, if he learned that Devereux had had some part in the shooting, that chokehold would snap.

Devereux didn't look like a beaten man. In fact, he looked pampered. He had a good haircut. No signs of aging, even though the man was in his early sixties. Luke hoped that didn't mean that Devereux had used part of his multimillion dollar estate to bribe a guard or two.

"Agent Buchanan," Devereux greeted. "I'm missing my midmorning workout."

Luke considered some smart-mouth response, but he held back. "I've been going over a list of your visitors and call sheets. Your daughter, Genevieve, has phoned the prison six times in the past month. Your conversations were unsupervised."

Devereux shrugged. "Because she's acting as my legal counsel."

Yes, that's what the guard's note had said. "But she's not a lawyer."

"I can designate anyone to legally represent me." His cobalt-blue eyes seemed to pierce right through the screen. "Agent Buchanan, if you have plans to go after my daughter—"

"Has she done anything that warrants an arrest?" Luke quipped.

"No. And I won't have you try to use her to get back at me. What happened between us is finished."

Luke was more than a little surprised with that comment. He'd expected Devereux to be defensive. Irate, even. But the man seemed to be protecting his daughter.

Now that he had Christopher, Luke totally understood that reaction. He glanced at Elaina who was nibbling on her bottom lip. Yep. She understood it, too. It gave people a bond that might not always be a good bond to have, but that was a thought for another time, another place.

"I just wanted to make sure you weren't using your daughter for more than legal council," Luke continued.

Devereux's reaction was mild, a slight tilt of the head. "Such as?"

"Perhaps Genevieve is doing your dirty work. There was a shooting last night. What do you know about that?"

Devereux sat there amid the dust-gray walls and stared at him. "I know nothing about it. Neither does Genevieve. My daughter is trying to start a family, Agent Buchanan. The only thing she has on her mind is motherhood. I want it to stay that way. Under no circumstance will you bring any of this to her, understand?"

"Fine. Then, give me the answers I'm looking for, and I won't have to go to her."

"What answers?" Devereux snapped.

"Have you been in the market for some software modifications?"

Devereux paused as if absorbing that, smiled and shook his head. "No. I'm not a computer person. I hire people to do that sort of thing for me."

That wasn't the answer Luke was looking for. "Are you saying one of your employees was in the market?"

"I'm not saying that all, but I wouldn't have any use for software modifications unless those modifications can reverse the prison sentence that put me in this place. That's my concern right now. That and my daughter. I've put my business ventures on hold."

Either Devereux was a convincing liar, or he was telling the truth. It might be a while before Luke figured out which, but for the time being, he was going to treat the man as he was treating Carrie and the others.

Like a suspect who wanted Elaina and him dead.

"How about your investment in the Brighton Birthing Center?" Luke questioned.

Devereux relaxed his shoulders. "Oh, that. The police were already here first thing this morning. I'll tell you what I told them. I make lots of investments, and I chose that one when my daughter informed me that she was interested in starting a family. I knew the former director at Brighton, I believed her to be an honest woman, and I learned the hard way that she wasn't. She was behind many of those illegal adoptions and even once tried to kill a police officer."

That meshed with the phone briefing Luke had gotten with San Antonio PD. There didn't appear to be anything sinister about Devereux's investment, but Luke would keep digging. If there was anything to find, he'd find it.

"Talk to me about my late wife," Luke insisted. He debated how to go with this and decided to take the direct approach. "Did you have anything to do with her death?"

"No. But I doubt you'll believe me." Devereux made a dismissal wave of his hand. "I'm a family man, Agent Buchanan. My problem is with you, not any member of your family."

"But you could have tried to get to me by going through my family," Luke quickly pointed out.

The man sighed dramatically. "That would create bad karma. And what purpose would it serve? It would only cause you to hound and harass me, and since I will almost certainly have my sentence reversed on appeal, why would I do anything to keep you on my tail?"

Luke could think of reasons. "For money, power or both."

"I already have those things in spades." But there was no smugness in his tone. Devereux had said merely as fact. "Has someone been trying to connect me to this software and your dead wife?"

"Me. I've been trying to do just that. She gave birth to a child at Brighton."

"I've never stepped foot in the place," Devereux insisted. "There is no connection between your wife and me."

"I hope, for your sake, there isn't."

"Investigate to your heart's desire, but you won't find my metaphorical fingerprints anywhere near your late wife."

Luke stared at the man, wondering if he'd get a different answer if he kept pushing, but Luke instinctively knew that he wouldn't. He didn't bother to say goodbye. Luke used the computer mouse to end the video call, and he clicked back to the agent who'd set up the connection.

The face of the agent reappeared on the screen. "Monitor all his visits," Luke insisted. "Report anything suspicious directly to me." Luke turned off the computer and looked at Elaina.

"Is Devereux a good liar?" she asked.

He stood, shook his head. "He's capable of lying, but I wouldn't say he's good at it."

Elaina huffed and clenched her hands into fists. "I just want answers. I want to know why someone is trying to kill us."

"We'll figure that out. In the meantime, Christopher is safe."

"But for how long?" But she didn't just say it; her voice trembled.

Luke walked closer.

"If it were just me at risk, it wouldn't hurt like this," she whispered. "But Christopher. God, Christopher could be in danger."

Oh, yeah. He understood that all too well. "I'm not going to let anything happen to him."

She looked up at him, and he could feel the attraction rear its head. The last time, though, that he'd acted on that attraction had been minutes before the shooting. If he hadn't been making out with Elaina in the hall, he might have spotted the gunman before he took aim.

And that was the reason Luke didn't go any closer.

"What's wrong?" she asked. But she lifted her hand, palm out in a *stop* gesture. "This is the conversation we were about to have after we nearly had sex. You backed away from me then, too. Not physically, but I could feel it." She paused. "Luke, that had nothing to do with me trying to keep custody of Christopher."

"I know it didn't." And it was time for him to apologize. His lust had nearly gotten her killed.

But the apology was put on hold when his phone rang. Since it could be an update on Rusty or the escaped prisoners, Luke quickly answered it.

"It's Sheriff Dawson. I have a problem. My wife was in a car accident. Nothing serious, but the doctor here wants to transfer her to the hospital in Luling for a CAT scan. I have to leave to be with her."

"How can I help?"

"Well, I have no one to cover my office, and I have a prisoner. A man I had to arrest this morning for taking a baseball bat to his brother. I can't leave him here alone, and I don't trust the security guard who let the other two escape."

Neither did Luke. "What about your deputy?"

"He's at Elaina's house still standing guard so no

one will get inside, but I've got to pull him from that duty and have him come here to the station. I've called the sheriff in a neighboring county, and he's planning to send some help, but it'd go easier for me if you could go to Elaina's house and stand guard until the federal agents show up to search the place."

The mental debate started, but it wasn't much of a debate. Those federal agents were likely tied up with apprehending the escaped prisoners. Plus, Elaina's house needed to be searched, and it needed to be guarded. He couldn't risk any of their suspects getting in to search for Kevin's software modifications—especially since they'd left critical items in the car in the garage when they'd made a mad dash to get out of there and come to safe house. Luke needed to find the modifications to discover the identity of T. They might be the key to making sure Elaina and Christopher were truly safe.

Luke checked his watch. "I'll be there in about two hours," he assured the sheriff.

Sheriff Dawson thanked him and hung up.

"Where are you going?" Elaina asked.

"To your house. The deputy guarding it is being pulled. I'll wait for backup to arrive, and while I'm doing that, I'll search the place."

"I could help you."

He was already shaking his head before she finished. "Too dangerous."

"It's broad daylight, and the search will go faster if there are two of us. Besides, I know what I brought to the house from San Antonio. You don't. For you, it'd be like a needle in a haystack."

"Those two men are on the loose," Luke quickly reminded her.

"Those two men have been on the loose for over a year," Elaina reminded him. "Christopher could stay here with Theresa, where they'll be safe. I could watch your back. You could watch mine."

She was right about one thing—the search would go a hell of a lot faster if she was there with him.

"It makes sense," she argued. "If we don't find anything in a couple of hours, then you can bring me back. Five hours," she said, obviously bargaining now.

Luke debated with himself some more. He weighted the consequences. And he finally nodded. "Five hours."

"I'll get my purse and tell Theresa."

Luke reached for his shoulder holster and gun. He prayed he wouldn't need it, and while he was praying, he added one more thing.

He hoped he wasn't leading Elaina right back into the path of a killer.

Chapter Fourteen

Elaina finished her call to Theresa and told Luke what she'd learned. "Christopher just finished eating his snack, and Theresa is about to put him down for his nap."

"How long will he sleep?" Luke asked.

"At least an hour, maybe longer. Don't worry. Christopher is used to being with Theresa all day. He won't be upset that I'm not there."

"Good. That's one less thing to worry about."

Yes, one less thing.

She checked her watch. What would have normally been a forty-five-minute drive to her house turned into nearly double that amount of time.

Before they'd even gotten in the car, Luke had told her that he would have to take a circuitous route to make sure they weren't being followed, and he was true to his word. One hour and fifty minutes after they'd kissed Christopher goodbye and drove away from the safe house, they finally pulled into her driveway.

"What now?" Luke mumbled when he saw the activity in front of them.

Elaina had expected to see yellow crime scene tape stretched around her property. And it was there, being assaulted by the winter wind. She'd also expected to see boarded up windows, and someone had indeed taken care of that chore. But her expectations hadn't stopped there. She'd expected to see a deputy or some other law enforcement official.

That, she didn't see.

But Gary was on her front porch, his hand poised in the air as if he were about to knock on the door.

Luke obviously didn't care for Gary's presence because he slammed on the brakes and came to a loud, screeching halt mere inches from the porch steps. That got Gary's attention. The man whirled around to face them, and he certainly looked guilty of something.

"Wait in the car," Luke told her. In the same motion, he drew his gun and got out. "This is crime scene, and you're trespassing."

Elaina lowered the window so she could hear everything they were saying.

"I, uh, know, but I saw the deputy leave, and I wanted to make sure Elaina wasn't here alone," Gary insisted.

"She's not."

"Oh. Okay." He peered into the car and waved at her. That was friendly enough, but the glare he turned on Luke wasn't so friendly. "You can put that gun away."

Luke didn't. "How long has the deputy been gone?"

"Fifteen, maybe twenty minutes. I was watching out the window, and when I saw him drive away, I got dressed and came over."

"To make sure Elaina wasn't here alone," Luke repeated, and he sounded totally skeptical.

"The crime scene guys have been here. They've already processed the house and the grounds," Gary continued.

"*Processed?*" More skepticism and a lot of suspicion from Luke.

"I watch a lot of cop shows," Gary explained. "That's the term they use."

"It's the right term," Luke verified. "But if you watch cop shows, then you know you should never step foot in a crime scene. Go home, Gary, and stay away until you hear otherwise from me."

Gary took a step toward Luke, and there was nothing submissive about it. Elaina noted the combative stance that was no doubt a result of his military training.

"I'm not sure why Elaina ever married you," Gary said, moving even closer to Luke.

"That's not your concern. Go. Home," Luke repeated.

The two men stood there, as if sizing each other up, but with Luke armed, Gary must have decided this wasn't a fight he could win. He lifted his hands in a suit-yourself gesture, cursed and stormed off the porch. Luke didn't take his eyes off him until Gary was back in his own house.

"You can get out now," Luke let Elaina know.

He carried that edgy, dangerous tone through to what he said to her. But once their eyes met, something inside him settled. Well, a little anyway. Luke lowered his gun a fraction, but he eased her behind him while they approached the front door.

"That deputy shouldn't have left until I got here," Luke mumbled. "Another minute or two and Gary would have probably been inside snooping around."

Luke tested the doorknob and cursed. "It's unlocked."

Elaina groaned. It was bad enough that the deputy had left early, but it was careless to leave the place unlocked. Of course, with all activity from the crime scene guys, it wouldn't have been difficult for someone to sneak in.

And then she heard the sound of someone talking.

Luke obviously did, as well. He pushed her to the side and threw open the door. Despite Luke's attempt to keep her out of the line of fire, Elaina could see inside her house.

Carrie was in her living room.

"What are you doing here?" Luke demanded.

Carrie turned toward them and froze. That's when Elaina saw that her assistant had the phone in her hand. Not her own personal phone but Elaina's house phone.

"Elaina," Carrie said, the breath all in her voice. She put down the phone and stared at Luke's gun. "I used the emergency key you gave me to let myself in."

Luke gave her a questioning glance, and Elaina nodded to verify that she had indeed given Carrie a key.

"I was trying to call you." Carrie hitched her shoulder toward the phone. "I can't find my cell phone."

And Elaina knew why. When Luke had first told her that the Justice Department had an interest in Carrie's phone, Elaina had totally dismissed it. But since the shooting, she wasn't feeling nearly as trusting, and she wasn't dismissing it now.

Carrie rushed to her and gave her a hard hug. "God, I heard about the shooting, but I had no idea it was this bad. There's glass everywhere in the kitchen and nursery. Are Christopher and you all right?"

"We're fine." Elaina pulled away so she could face Carrie. "But you shouldn't be here."

Carrie nodded. "I know, but I was so scared when I heard the news. I couldn't stay away." She looked around the room. "Maybe I can help you clean up the place."

"It can't be cleaned yet," Luke insisted. He reholstered his gun, but he kept his hand on it. "You really should go."

Carrie nodded, but she didn't look in total agreement. "Okay, but call me if you need anything."

"I will." But Elaina knew she wouldn't. Not unless her assistant was cleared as a suspect.

The moment that Carrie was out the door, Luke locked it and engaged the security system. He didn't stop there. He stormed through the house, checking each room. It wasn't a speedy process because he looked in every closet and beneath the beds. Apparently satisfied that no one else had let themselves in, he went to her phone. The one that Carrie had been using when they walked in.

Elaina watched as he pressed redial, and he held the phone between so both of them could hear. There were four rings before the answering machine kicked in. "Hi, you've reached Brenda. I'm not here right now, but leave a message at the beep."

Luke dropped the phone back into the cradle.

"Brenda," Elaina and he repeated in unison.

It was Elaina who continued. "Maybe Carrie thought Brenda would know how to get in touch with me."

"Or maybe she was giving Brenda an update of what she did or didn't find in the house. Maybe the women are working together for this T person."

Elaina's imagination began to run wild. She'd worked side by side with Carrie for a year, but did that mean anything? Carrie was being secretive about her application to Rice. Why wouldn't Carrie tell her something like that, especially since the woman discussed everything else with Elaina?

"But I don't know what Carrie would have found that I couldn't," Elaina commented.

"We left the box of files in the car in the garage," Luke reminded her. "She might have been trying to get another peek at them. Don't worry. That box won't be staying here. I'm taking it back with us to the safe house. We'll go over the files tonight."

"While we're here, I'll get some clothes and things. We didn't have much with us when we left."

Dreading what she knew she would see, Elaina went into the nursery. Carrie had been right. There was glass all over the floor and markings on the wall to indicate where bullets had been removed. It was sickening. Her baby's room was now a crime scene.

"I won't be able to live here again," Elaina said softly. But she obviously didn't say it nearly soft enough.

"I understand," Luke responded.

She looked over her shoulder at him. He was close. Very close. And he was watching her.

"I'll be okay," she insisted.

"Are you trying to convince me, or yourself?"

She frowned at his astute observation. Even though Luke hadn't known her long, he obviously *knew* her. Maybe all the danger and forced camaraderie could do that. Maybe that's why she felt so connected to him.

Luke reached out and pulled her into his arms. She felt stronger and weaker all at the same time. She also felt as if she owed him a gigantic thank-you.

"Despite the dramatic and crazy intrusion you made into my fake life, I'm glad you're here and on my side," Elaina confessed.

She would deal with the consequences of his presence after all of this was over. And she had no doubt that there would be consequences.

Since his arms were giving her a little too much comfort, and since the closeness was a reminder of how hotly attracted she was to him, Elaina eased back slightly. "I'll start going through the things in my bedroom."

He nodded and let her slip out of his embrace. Just like that, she felt the loss, and she cursed herself for it. She wasn't just getting close to Luke; she was falling hard for him.

And that couldn't happen.

Hadn't her disastrous relationship with Kevin taught her anything? She had lousy taste in men, and Luke might be good father material, but he'd made it clear that he wasn't looking for a personal involvement with her.

Well, at least he'd made it clear in the beginning. But maybe like her, he'd had a change of heart.

It was stupid, but that caused her to smile, and she carried that smile into her bedroom to begin the search. The smile soon faded. The room looked almost exactly the way they'd left it. The mattress was on the floor where Luke had left it. Pictures had been knocked off the dresser.

Elaina walked past all of that and went into her closet. She did a quick inventory to figure out if she'd brought any of the items with her when she fled her old life. She'd already given Luke the files and a few other things, but she went through each item of clothing and each pair of shoes. It didn't take her long to decide that all of her things were less than a year old. Because she'd been running for her life at the time, she hadn't brought much with her.

Giving up on the closet, she went into the bathroom to check her cosmetics. Again, this room was as they'd left it, with a bath towel draped across the edge of the sink. It was next to Luke's leather toiletry bag. Elaina started to stoop to look in the cabinet beneath the sink, but something in the unzipped toiletry bag caught her eye.

A small square-shaped gold-foil packet.

Elaina actually picked it up to verify what it was. Though it wasn't necessary. She knew it was a condom.

She felt as if someone had slapped her.

Her thought raced back to the night before, to the hot and heavy kissing session in the hall. Luke and she had nearly had sex. In fact, the only thing that had stopped him was there was no condom.

Or so he'd said.

But this proved otherwise.

Mercy, had he lied to her? Elaina didn't want to believe that. In fact, she refused to believe it. Luke had been just as aroused and ready as she'd been. If he'd known about the condom, he would have used it.

Wouldn't he?

Elaina didn't have time to ponder that particular question because there was a frantic knock at the door. She rushed out of the bathroom to find Luke already on his way to the front of the house. He had his gun drawn.

He motioned for Elaina to duck back in the bedroom, and she did. But she stayed near the door so she could see what was happening.

"Who's there?" Luke called out.

"Me, Brenda."

Elaina didn't know whether to groan or curse. Obviously, her friends, neighbors and possible enemies weren't concerned about traipsing onto a crime scene.

"Guys?" Brenda's pounding became louder and more insistent. "You really need to let me in *now*."

"Why?" Luke answered.

"Because there are two people sitting in a car just a half block up. I got a glimpse inside as I jogged past them, and both are armed. Elaina, I think your shooter is back."

Chapter Fifteen

Luke didn't open the door. Instead, he went to the window and looked out. There was indeed a dark green two-door car parked just up the block.

Because he didn't want to risk Brenda being shot, nor did he want to put Elaina at risk, he didn't lower his gun, but he went to the front door, disengaged the security system and opened it. Brenda was there, looking a little harried and sweaty despite the near freezing temperatures.

Brenda had her hand in the pocket of her jogging jacket, and Luke made an immediate assessment that there was something wrong with her body language and stance. He caught on to her arm, hauled her inside and reached into her pocket. He retrieved a small handgun.

"What are you doing with this?" he demanded.

"Isn't it obvious?" She pointed in the direction of the car. "There's a shooter on the loose, and I wasn't going to take any chances."

Neither was Luke. He kept her gun and didn't plan to return it until Brenda was on her way out. Even then, she might not get it back.

"Call the sheriff's office," Luke instructed Elaina. "Let them know we might have a problem."

However, before Elaina could pick up the phone, Luke's own cell phone rang. He handed Brenda's gun to Elaina and answered it. He was careful though not to use his name because as far as he knew, Brenda still thought he was Daniel Allen. Luke wanted to keep it that way for a while so it would save him from being asked too many questions.

"Agent Buchanan," the caller said. "This is Collena Drake. I saw your visitor and thought I should wait for her to leave before I come up to the house."

"You're in the two-door dark green car?" Luke asked.

"Yes. I came with a Justice Department agent. He's going to guard the place while Elaina and you are here."

Luke was relieved to hear those words. "I wouldn't say no to that." He paused. "Why'd you come to Crystal Creek?"

"We have something important to discuss."

No relieved feeling this time. He didn't like the sound of that. "I was just showing our guest out anyway. Give me a couple of minutes."

Brenda flinched. "What do you mean you're showing me out? I can't go out there. The gunman—"

"That's a federal agent and a former cop in the car. You'll be safe." He glanced at Elaina to let her know that the safety extended to her. "But, Brenda, I would like to know why you're here."

She squared her shoulders. "For Elaina, of course. I was worried about her."

"There's a lot of that going around," Luke mumbled.

Here, he'd thought Elaina and he were going to get some quality search time, and instead they'd been bombarded with people. The only one he wanted to see was Collena Drake. She wouldn't have come unless she had important information.

"I'll go," Brenda offered. "But just tell me where you're staying so I'll know how to get in touch with you."

"We'll be at my sister's in Arkansas," Luke readily answered.

It was obviously a lie, since he didn't even have a sister, but a lie was as good as Brenda was going to get.

"Okay." Brenda nodded. "So, you're not planning on staying here?"

"No," Elaina answered. "But there'll be someone guarding the place until the investigation is finished."

Another nod, this one was a little choppy. Brenda went to Elaina her and hugged her. She did the same to Luke, surprising him. And alarming him. He didn't like a suspect being so close to his gun.

And speaking of guns, he had to take care of the matter of what to do with Brenda's. Legally, he had no right to confiscate it. So, he walked Brenda to the door and handed her the weapon once they were outside on the porch.

"Who's out there in the car?" Elaina asked the moment Luke closed the door behind Brenda.

"An agent and Collena Drake."

The color drained from her face. "She's not here to take Christopher?"

"Nothing like that." But he couldn't say what this conversation would entail.

He walked to the front window and looked out. So did Elaina. She stood right beside him. "Collena will come in soon," Luke explained. "She just wants to make sure Brenda is gone first."

Elaina didn't say a word.

"Is anything wrong?" he asked. When the silence continued, he added another question. "Did you find anything in your bedroom?"

"Sort of. But it doesn't apply to the investigation. It's personal." She paused. "We can discuss it after you talk to Ms. Drake."

"That sounds ominous." Another glance out the window, and he confirmed that Collena still hadn't gotten out of the car. "It must really be bad."

She opened her mouth, closed it and she stayed that way several moments before she finally spoke. "When I was in the bathroom, I saw a condom in your toiletry bag."

It took him a moment to put two and two together. Hell.

Luke tried to explain but soon realized he didn't have a clue what to say. However, Elaina didn't have any problem in that area.

"You know, if you didn't want to have sex with me, that's all you had to say." She folded her arms over her chest and glared at him. "What I got from you was a pity orgasm, and I don't appreciate that."

"There was no pity. Not on my part anyway."

Oh, man. That was not the right thing to say. Her eyes narrowed, and her teeth came together. "It wasn't pity on my part, either. I wasn't playing a game while we were in the hall. Every emotion was real."

"I know."

"Do you?" she snapped. "Because I think you still believe that I'm trying to manipulate you into sharing custody of Christopher with me."

Now that riled him. "I don't think you'd use sex to do that, and trust me, I wouldn't have kissed you or touched you if I'd thought that was on your mind. I might be attracted to you, but I don't do all my thinking below the belt."

"Then why lie about the condom?" she asked.

Well, he couldn't just fire off an answer to that one. And it didn't matter how he said this, it wasn't going to sound good. Not to Elaina.

Probably not to himself, either.

"I didn't want to lose focus on the investigation," he told her. But that was only half the story, and judging from Elaina's expression, she knew that. She deserved better. She deserved to hear the truth. "I was a terrible husband to Taylor. I was never there when she needed me."

"And you thought…what—that I was looking for

a husband? I'm a grown woman, and not once did I think you'd owe a marriage proposal if we had sex."

Luke met her gaze. "But I thought maybe you'd think it was more than sex."

She threw her hands up in the air. "Mercy! You don't have much faith and trust in me. Don't answer that. I know. I know. You really don't know me well enough to have faith." Elaina shook her head. "Luke, it's all right if you don't want a sexual relationship or for that matter, any other kind of relationship with me. Heck, I'm not sure I want one with you. But please don't lie to me again. I've had enough of Kevin's lies to last me a lifetime."

"See? And that's the point. We both have so much baggage. That's why I didn't go get that condom."

She stayed quiet a moment. "I guess that's the bottom line. Neither of us might be able to get past our pasts. At least I know where I stand now."

No, she didn't. Heck, Luke didn't know where he stood. Or what he felt. He just knew that this wasn't the time or the place. They had to concentrate on finding the people who wanted them dead. That was it.

That was the real bottom line.

Luke saw some movement out of the corner of his eye, and he spotted Collena Drake making her way across the yard toward the house. The conversation would have to wait.

He glanced at Elaina to tell her that, but her attention was already on the tall, rail-thin blonde approaching the porch steps. Collena was dressed in black pants and a turtleneck. Her calf-length leather coat was black, too. Ditto for the dark sunglasses. She looked as if she could have been on her way to a funeral, but each time Luke had seen her, she'd worn a similar outfit.

"So this is the person...." But Elaina didn't finish that. Instead, she looked away.

Luke mentally finished the sentence for her. Elaina no doubt felt that Collena had ruined her life. Because Collena had helped him find his son, Luke had an entirely different opinion of the woman.

He opened the door to her, and they exchanged brief smiles as she entered. However, there was no joy in Collena Drake's smile. She introduced herself to Elaina and pulled off those sunglasses. There was no joy there, either. Luke was betting that a lot of heart-breaking sadness had put that emotion in her brown eyes.

"I won't stay long," Collena started. She shook her head, declining to sit on the sofa when Elaina motioned in that direction. "I'll tell you both what I've learned because it applies to this investigation." But her eyes landed on Luke when she continued. "You know that the police exhumed your late wife's body."

Luke nodded. "They're conducting another autopsy."

She brought out an envelope from her pocket. "The coroner is finished. He did me a favor and put a rush on it."

Luke took it and stared at it.

"I can give you the gist of it," Collena said when he didn't open it. "Taylor died from complications from a C-section. Basically, she got an infection, and her body didn't respond to antibiotics. The infection caused organ damage and then kidney failure."

Oh, man. That was hard to hear, but it also gave Luke some consolation. At least it didn't appear to be murder.

"So that lets George Devereux off the hook," Elaina concluded.

Collena nodded. "The coroner checked for negligence on the part of the hospital staff. In other words, they might have not taken full measures to stop the infection. His results are inconclusive. We might never know the answer."

Yeah. And somehow Luke would have to learn to live with that. At the moment, however, he wasn't even sure that was possible.

Since he had no choice, Luke sank down on the arm of the sofa. Elaina immediately went to him. She touched his arm and rubbed gently.

"Devereux might be off the hook," Elaina said. "But that doesn't explain who tried to kill us last night."

Collena nodded. "The SAPD have a theory for that, too. The day that Luke came to Crystal Creek, two men matching the description of the guy with the eye patch and his blond partner were seen near the Cryogen Lab in San Antonio."

Oh, this was not sounding good. "That's where I took Christopher's pacifier for the DNA test."

"Yes. The police reviewed surveillance tapes, and they spotted the men in the parking lot just minutes before you picked up the test results. It looks as if they were waiting for you and perhaps even followed you."

Luke shook his head. He was about to say that he would have noticed the men, especially if they'd followed him, but the truth was, he wasn't sure of that. Seeing those DNA results had felt like sucker punch. It'd confirmed his worst fears and his greatest wish.

"How would these men have known to follow Luke?" Elaina asked.

"Maybe through the information I was posting about the investigation on my Web site," Collena explained. "I have information there for parents who are still searching for their lost children. The two men could have realized that Luke was looking for you and his son, and they perhaps wanted to use Luke to get to you."

He pushed his thumb against his chest. "I'm responsible for those men finding Elaina and Christopher." He moved away when Elaina tried to continue to rub his arm. It was a loving gesture meant to soothe him, but he wasn't in the mood to be soothed. He damn sure didn't deserve any loving gestures from the very woman he'd nearly gotten killed.

"I'm sorry," Collena said. "I wish there'd been an easier way to tell you this."

She added a soft goodbye and quietly left.

Since Luke wasn't sure he could move yet, he was thankful when Elaina went to the door to lock it and re-arm the security system. With his state of mind, he needed all the help he could get.

"Well, at least we know Devereux's not the one who's after us," Elaina commented. She sounded hesitant as if she didn't know what else to say.

Luke was right there, on the same page with her.

She walked closer, also hesitantly, and stopped just a few inches away. She didn't reach out, didn't touch, she just stood there until he looked at her.

"Say it," Luke demanded. "Or slap me. Do something, anything, because I damn well deserve that and worse. I did this." He pointed toward the boarded windows in the kitchen. "I nearly got you killed."

"No. A gunman nearly got us killed."

Sympathy. Luke wasn't in the mood for it. "I brought them to your doorstep."

Elaina shrugged. "They would have found me eventually."

"You don't know that," he fired back.

"Oh, but I do. Remember, I lived with a criminal so I know how they think. Those software modifications are obviously worth a lot, and this T and his henchmen weren't going to give up their search."

Now, she touched him, putting her hand on his shoulder. "Look, I know you're beating yourself up, and I doubt I can say or do anything to convince you otherwise, so just listen. Those men would have found me. Now, what if that had happened after you'd taken Christopher and were no longer around? I seriously doubt the shooter would have been content to fire through the windows. No. The shooter would have waited for a clean shot and would have killed me so he or she could walk inside and search the place."

He wanted to refute that. Man, did he. He wanted to slap this blame right back in his own face. But he couldn't. Not about that particular point anyway. Because Elaina was right. These guys had taken massive risks with the shooting, and people like that usually did whatever it took to get the job done.

That put a fistlike grip around his heart. He could almost see it. Elaina alone under attack.

She put her other hand on his arm and curved her fingers around his bicep. "You know what I'm saying is true."

He didn't nod, didn't agree and he couldn't get those images of her out of his head.

"There are a lot worse things in life than having you here with me," Elaina said, her voice whispery and filled with breath.

He felt the same about her.

But Luke didn't dare say that to her. The air was already charged with the emotion of what they'd learned and with the argument they'd had moments before Collena's arrival. Added to that emotion was Elaina's attempt to make him feel better. She was being caring and sympathetic. Worse, Luke felt in need of some of that caring, even if he didn't deserve it. And there was no doubt about it—he didn't deserve anything but Elaina's wrath and anger.

She apparently didn't feel the same way.

Elaina leaned in and touched her lips to his. It barely qualified as a kiss, but it still packed a punch. Luke felt that punch in every inch of his body, and he knew it was time to move away and resume the search.

Then, she kissed him again.

It was more than a touch this time. Actually, it was more than a kiss. He could feel her hand trembling on his arm. Her mouth was trembling, too. He pulled back to see the tears in her eyes. Those tears cut him to the bone.

"I'm sorry," he told her. "I'm so sorry."

"So am I."

He shook his head, not understanding what she meant. "You have nothing to be sorry for."

"You've forgotten that I illegally have your son. True, it was Kevin who started the process, but once I saw Christopher, I didn't ask questions that I should have asked."

Luke was not going to let her go there. He stood and pulled her into his arms. "This is my blame-fest, and you've done nothing wrong. I know that now."

She looked up at him and blinked back the tears. One escaped though and slid down her cheek.

Luke couldn't bear to see it there, and he kissed it away.

And then for no reason that he could ever justify as logical, he kissed *her.*

The change in both of them was instant. Even if he hadn't been touching her, he would have noticed it. Whatever it was, it was intoxicating. His body shifted into a totally different gear, and everything inside him insisted that he continue to kiss Elaina.

So Luke went with that. He kissed her. It was slow and hungry. He took things from her that he hadn't even known he needed.

She pulled back slightly, looked at him and blinked. What she didn't do was stop or try to move away. She just seemed to be assessing the situation. Something was going to happen between them. Something that neither of them believed should happen. But it was as if they no longer had a say in it.

They stood there for heaven knows how long. Minutes, maybe longer. The rhythm of her heart seemed to fall into cadence with the pulse that throbbed in his wrist.

And the world seemed to just melt away.

"If we just do this fast," she whispered. "We won't have to think about it."

"True."

And it was tempting. Something wild and mindless. Sex against the wall. A frantic coupling that would leave them both exhausted and perhaps even sated.

But he knew it could be more than that. Much more. And maybe that was what they needed. A slow burn that would still leave them exhausted and satisfied, but would also keep her in his arms longer. For some reason that Luke didn't want to explore, that suddenly seemed like the most important thing that could happen between them.

"It won't be fast," he promised her. He drew her to him and kissed her forehead. Her cheek. Her jaw.

"Is that wise?" she asked.

"No."

But then, they were past the point of no return. So, Luke did the only thing he could do. He slid his arm around her waist, eased her closer and kissed her as if this would be the first and the last kiss they'd ever have.

WHAT WAS HAPPENING to her?

Elaina could barely think, but she could feel. Mercy, could she ever feel. It was so odd. The passion and need were there. She had no doubts about that. With just that kiss, Luke took her body from being interested to being desperate for him.

But there was something else.

Something simmering just beneath the surface that she couldn't identify. Maybe this was about the need to comfort each other, the need to try to heal the wound that had been ripped open all over again. It would have been so much easier if it'd been just sex. But Elaina needed to melt into his arms. She needed to feel that all would be right with them.

She needed Luke.

And he apparently needed her.

As if he had all the time in the world, he circled his arm around her waist. He touched his mouth to hers. Slow and lingering. Tender.

Elaina hadn't expected the tenderness.

She obviously hadn't expected a lot of things, including the slow, leisurely way that he lifted her shirt and eased it over her head. He dropped it on the sofa and began to lead her in the direction of her bedroom.

She went willingly.

Elaina tried to return the pleasure that he was giving her with his mouth, but Luke skimmed a finger down her bare skin, tracing her spine all the way down. That robbed her of her breath, and the heat rolled through her.

Did he know what this was doing to her?

Absolutely.

It was a slow, easy slide into the depths of passion.

He took that clever mouth to her neck. More kisses. He used his tongue and gently nipped her. Soon, Elaina was on fire. She wanted to touch him. She wanted to make love to him as he was doing to her.

She put her hands on his chest and slid her fingers over the taut muscles. He was solid. All man. Not that she needed to touch him to know that.

Because her body was already aching for him, she rubbed against him. He had an erection, and she rubbed against it, too, and had the thrill of hearing him suck in his breath.

He stopped them just short of the bed. He leaned down. No hurried motion, either. And he took off her pants. He kissed his way back up to her bra and removed it, as well.

Elaina reciprocated, but because the urgency and the heat were taking over her body, she didn't have

Luke's finesse. She practically ripped off his shoulder holster and shirt, and she heard him chuckle.

He was still smiling when he brushed a kiss on the top of her right breast. Then, on the left. He kept going down. Kissing. Her nipples. Her stomach. Her hip. The front of her lacy panties. He used his warm breath and more of those mind-blowing French kisses.

She couldn't catch her breath. And her heart was pounding so hard. The only coherent thought on her mind was for him to take her now. Now. Now. She didn't think she could wait another second.

But Luke made her wait.

He took off her panties with that maddeningly slow pace. He was seducing her, and she was totally helpless to do anything but let it all unfold.

His fingers moved over her. Exploring. Discovering. Pleasuring her. With those same slow strokes that matched an incredibly slow kiss, he eased his fingers inside her. And he found the right spot. Definitely.

The right pace.

And he even had the perfect pressure to make her forget all about the speed that she'd thought she wanted.

Because she could no longer stand, Elaina caught on to him and dropped back onto the bed. They landed in the perfect position, with him between her legs. But his jeans were in the way.

"I want you naked," she warned him.

Elaina found herself fumbling with his zipper. She certainly didn't feel as if she were doing her part to make this work. Then, he kissed her again. It was a reminder of what was waiting for her, and she forgot all about the fumbling. She got the zipper, and managed to rid him of his boots and jeans.

Luke left her for a moment to go get the condom from the bathroom. Each second he was gone seemed like an eternity. By the time he made it back to the bed, Elaina grabbed him and pulled him back down on top of her.

He slid his left hand around the back of her neck and eased his fingers through her hair. By now, she was frantic. Elaina struggled to get what she wanted, but Luke took his time entering her.

It was worth the wait.

Elaina stilled a moment just to savor the sensation of him being inside her. But the stillness didn't last when he began to move. There was no way she could not react to that. Those gentle, deep thrusts were exactly what she wanted.

She wrapped her legs around him to bring them even closer. Luke deepened the closeness with more kisses. It was perfect. But soon, it was no longer enough. Elaina knew this couldn't last. She didn't want it to last. She wanted one thing and that was release.

Luke obviously wanted the same thing. He quickened the pace. So did Elaina. They matched each other. Move for move. Frantic stroke for frantic stroke. Damp skin whispering against damp skin.

Until the pressure built to an unbearable level.

Until the only thing that Elaina could do was go over the edge.

And she took Luke with her.

Chapter Sixteen

Luke quickly came to his senses.

Of course, that didn't happen until he'd taken every bit of pleasure he could possibly take from Elaina.

That made him stupid.

Not because he regretted the sex. Nope. As good as it was, he could never regret that part of it. But he did regret putting her in danger again.

And that's exactly what he'd done.

He certainly hadn't been vigilant despite the fact that less than twenty-four hours earlier, someone had tried to kill them while they were in this very house.

"We need to get dressed," he told her.

He mentally groaned at his tone. It sounded clinical. A real contrast to what had just happened between them. There had been nothing clinical about that. He added a soft kiss on her mouth and hoped it would soften the order he'd just given her.

"We should gather up our things and get them

back to the safe house," he continued. He got up, made a quick trip to the bathroom and returned so he could dress.

Elaina was still on the bed. Naked, of course. She was staring at him as if trying to figure out what he was thinking. He considered reassuring her that all was well. But it would be a lie. All wasn't well. While he'd been having the best sex of his life, the shooter could have gotten past the agent outside and might be ready to go for another round.

And speaking of another round, despite Luke's sated body and urgency to get out of there, he still took the time to admire Elaina. She lay there, her body still damp with sweat. She smelled like sex. And him. It seemed like some kind of primal invitation for him to get back on that bed with her.

But he couldn't.

They'd gotten away with a lapse in judgment, but they might not be so lucky next time.

Elaina finally got up and gathered her clothes. She put on her bra as she went back into the living room to get her shirt. Luke used her absence to check the window to make sure no one was lurking outside. He didn't see anyone, but he still decided to hurry.

Elaina was dressed by the time he walked into the living room. Not only that, she'd gathered up some things—toys and papers—which she obviously wanted to take with her. He strapped on his shoulder holster, picked up his keys and put on his leather jacket.

"Since the other stuff is already in my car in the garage, is there any reason we can't just take it?" she asked.

Normally, the answer would be no since her car could be easily recognized, but since most of Crystal Creek had seen their loaner vehicle in front of the house, there probably was no such thing as a "safe car" for them to use.

"We'll use your car," he agreed.

Elaina walked to the table in the entry. She retrieved her keys, stopped and then fished out a six-inch long jeweler's box that had been shoved to the back of the drawer. "It's a charm bracelet that Kevin gave me. I'd forgotten about it."

Luke took it from her and flipped open the box. The bracelet appeared to be white gold and had six heart charms. He made a cursory examination and decided the hearts were large and thick enough to encase a miniature memory card. "I'll have the lab ultrasound it," he let her know.

She nodded, and they exited through the laundry room. Luke didn't use the remote clipped to her visor to open the garage door until he had the car engine turned on and was ready to drive away. He certainly didn't want to linger around in the open in case that shooter was in the area.

Once they were away from the house, Luke called headquarters to let them know there were en route to the safe house.

"Are we back on the condom issue?" she asked.

Of all the subjects he thought they'd discuss, that wasn't one of them. "Excuse me?"

"The condom that you originally lied about because you didn't want to risk a personal relationship with me. Is this silent, coplike attitude a way of keeping your distance?" But she didn't wait for him to answer. "Because it's not necessary. We can still be friendly—"

"This isn't about you," he interjected.

She studied him a moment, and then her eyes widened. "Oh, God. This is about your late wife, isn't it? I'm so sorry. You're feeling guilty—"

"Wrong again." Though he probably should be feeling guilty. "And *you* have no reason to apologize. I, on the other hand, owe you a huge apology. I should have been watching for the shooter. I should have been doing my job."

"Oh. That." Her look of relief only lasted a few moments before frustration replaced it. "I figured that would come up. The timing wasn't ideal. But we haven't exactly had a lot of opportunities to fall into bed, now have we?"

No. They hadn't. "It happened pretty damn fast."

"That wasn't fast," she muttered, and he could hear the sexual undertones in it.

Or maybe that was his overly active imagination. One thing was for certain, being with Elaina had been memorable.

And distracting.

Even now, he was thinking about her. Well, he was

thinking about having sex with her again, and that was the last thing that should be on his mind. What he should be doing was keeping a close watch on their surroundings.

Luke drove out of town and took the turn onto a rural highway. It definitely wasn't the fastest way to get back to the safe house, nor was it the route they'd used to come to town. He would have to drive well out of their way just to ensure that no one was following them.

His cell phone rang, and Luke fished it out of his jacket pocket. "Agent Buchanan," he answered.

"Agent Roark from headquarters."

Luke recognized the voice. Roark was a fellow agent. Someone he'd worked with on several assignments. He was a good man, and Luke trusted him.

"Are you ready for some good news?" Roark asked.

Luke had braced himself for the worst, but that had him relaxing a bit. "I'd love some."

"We've apprehended one of the escapees, and he's back in custody at Crystal Creek jail."

He experienced both joy and not so much joy. "I'm glad you caught him, but it's probably not a good idea to put him back in the very facility that he managed to escape from."

"It's temporary. We're transporting him to San Antonio this afternoon around two."

The timing was perfect. He could drop Elaina off at the safe house, have lunch with her and Christopher and then go and interrogate this guy.

"I'll see you at two," Luke told him.

"I figured you would."

"They caught the two guys?" Elaina asked the moment he ended the call.

"They caught one of them."

Elaina flattened her hand over her chest as if to steady her heart. "Well, that's one less maniac to worry about."

"It's better than that. During the interrogation, we'll play the one captured off against the one that's still free and make him think that he was sold out by his partner. By this afternoon we could know who these guys really are and who they're working for."

"You really believe that?" she asked.

"Of course. You would, too, if you'd ever seen me in an interrogation room. I'm not usually a screwup, Elaina. I usually do things the right way."

"I didn't mean that. I just didn't want to get my hopes up." She shrugged. "But then, hope is the one thing we have right now."

Unfortunately, it was. "I promise I'll do whatever it takes to end all of this so Christopher and you will be...."

Luke's words trailed off when he glanced in the rearview mirror. The entire time they'd been on country road, he hadn't seen any other vehicles, but there was an SUV coming over the hill behind them. And the driver was going fast.

"What's wrong?" she asked.

"Maybe nothing."

Elaina looked behind them and obviously spotted the SUV. "That driver's getting awfully close to use." Her gaze flew back to him. "What are you thinking?"

He didn't want to say, but this couldn't be good.

Luke drew his weapon so that he'd have easy access, and he sped up. According to the GPS, they had over twenty-eight miles to go before they reached a major intersection. Which meant they were out in the middle of nowhere with this fast-approaching vehicle bearing down on them.

The SUV sped up, as well, and came right up on Luke's bumper. Unfortunately, Luke had to slow down. There was a sharp curve in the road, and just on the other side was a narrow concrete bridge. He couldn't risk hitting that.

But the SUV didn't decrease speed.

"Brace yourself," Luke warned, just as the vehicle rammed them.

The jolt threw his body forward. Elaina's, too. He made a quick check to make sure she was all right, and pressed the emergency button on his phone. That would alert headquarters that he needed assistance, but he didn't want to consider just how long it would take for that assistance to arrive.

Basically, Elaina and he were on their own.

"Can you see the driver?" Elaina asked.

"No." The windows were heavily tinted, and the driver had obviously disengaged the airbag, or it would have popped up during that collision. Too bad it hadn't. It would have slowed him down.

Luke came through the deep curve and approached the bridge. Once he was on the other side, he could speed up.

But he didn't get a chance to do that.

The SUV slammed into them again. Harder this time. And even harder still the third and fourth times.

Luke fought to keep control of his vehicle, but it was a losing battle. The SUV was much bigger, and the driver apparently didn't care if he killed all of them in the process of running them off the road. He didn't have time to think beyond that. The fifth collision caved in the back of the car. He couldn't stop it from happening.

The car went into a skid and flew off the road.

There were no trees or shrubs in their path. Only dirt and rocks. That was the good news. The bad news was that meant there was nothing to break their forward momentum. And, unfortunately, their forward momentum was like an out-of-control roller coaster spearing them straight toward the river.

But it wasn't the river that was the problem.

Because of a drought, the water was hardly more than a stream, but the limestone and clay banks that ravined the river were at least twelve, maybe fifteen, feet high.

If he couldn't stop the car, they would almost certainly plunge to their deaths.

ELAINA SAW THE DEATH trap that lay ahead, and she yelled for Luke to hit the brakes.

But he already had.

Unfortunately, no amount of pressure on the brakes would do any good. The tires couldn't get traction on the silty layers of dirt and pebbles, and they were literally skidding toward that embankment.

She thought of Christopher, praying that she would get to see him again. And she thought of Luke. He was trying so hard to save them, but he might fail.

Elaina tried to brace herself for the inevitable. She didn't have to wait long.

It happened fast.

So fast.

Luke jerked the steering wheel to the right, and the car finally responded. It spun around and came to a stop. A precarious one. Elaina looked out the back window and saw that more than a third of the vehicle was dangling over the stony riverbank.

"Get out!" Luke shouted.

His shout and the wobbling car were all she needed to get moving.

"Hit the ground running," he added. "And head for that cluster of trees."

She spotted the trees. They were at least thirty yards away. And then she realized exactly what he'd said—why he'd told her to hit the ground running. The person responsible for this was up there on the road.

Still, if they stayed in the car, they'd die. The only chance they had was to get to cover.

"Go!" Luke shouted.

She did. Elaina threw open the door and checked to make sure she would land on solid ground. It was close. She barely had room to step out and maneuver around the door.

Her foot slipped, skipping off the winter-damp limestone, but she was determined to survive. She caught on to the door to steady herself.

Once she was certain she wasn't going to plunge to the water and rocks below, she started running. Her adrenaline level was already through the roof, but that sent it soaring even more. She didn't look back. She kept her focus on the trees. She had to get to safety.

Behind her, she heard the crash. The sound of metal crashing into the rock bed.

Her heart went to her knees.

"Luke!" she shouted.

God, had he gotten out of the car before it fell?

Terrified of what she might or might not see, she risked looking back, and Elaina saw him.

Relief flooded through her.

He was there, running toward her, but he also had his gun aimed. His gaze was firing all around them. Probably looking for their attacker. Elaina didn't see the person, but she spotted the SUV on the side of the road just above them.

"Run faster," Luke shouted.

Elaina tried, but the rocky ground beneath her feet didn't exactly cooperate. Just as their car hadn't been able to get traction, neither could she. The nearly freezing air didn't help, either. Her lungs were burning from the near panic and exhaustion, and she couldn't catch her breath. All of that made her feel as if she were moving in slow motion.

Luke remedied the situation. He caught up to her and latched on to her arm. His momentum thrust her forward, and he shoved her into the cover of the trees. He didn't stop there. He put her right against the rough bark of an oak and then sheltered her with his own body.

Elaina tried to level her breathing so she wouldn't make so much noise, but it was impossible. Her lungs were starved for air. Unlike Luke. His breathing was level, and even though he was vigilant, his muscles weren't knotted with tension.

"Do you see anyone?" she whispered in between gasps for breath.

He shook his head.

But someone was out there. The someone that rammed the SUV into their car and nearly gotten them killed.

Who had done this?

Who?

This had to be connected to Kevin and that damn software modification. His stupid antics had nearly gotten her killed—again.

That infuriated her.

For money and greed, he'd left Luke, Christopher and her a legacy of danger.

Luke put his mouth directly against her ear. "I hear footsteps."

She didn't, but then her pulse was pounding so hard that she could hardly hear anything.

He maneuvered her slightly and turned so that his back was to hers. Probably so he could get a better angle to see whom or what was making those footsteps.

But Luke shook his head, and she thought that meant the footsteps had stopped.

Where was this person, this would-be killer? Elaina didn't have to wait long to find out.

A bullet slammed into the tree next to her head.

Chapter Seventeen

Luke pulled Elaina to the ground and dragged her to the other side of the oak. The bullet splintered into the tree, sending debris flying, but he couldn't risk sheltering Elaina with his body.

Because he had to take aim and stop the shooter from firing again.

That bullet had come from behind them, and it'd landed within a fraction of an inch of Elaina's head. It had taken a dozen years off his life to see how close she'd come to dying.

Again, he could blame himself. He shouldn't have allowed this situation to happen. Yet, here they were trapped next to a deep ravine with a shooter behind them. They couldn't jump in the riverbed. That would be nothing short of suicide. Ditto for trying to make it back up the hill to the SUV. That would put them out in the open and in plain sight.

To put it mildly, things looked bad.

A glance down at Elaina confirmed that she knew

the severity of their situation. She looked scared but resolute. His glance confirmed something else that made him irate. There was blood on Elaina's forehead, just above her left eyebrow. It'd probably been caused by a splinter, and it riled him to the core to see her hurt by some cowardly SOB who'd ambushed them.

Luke thanked God that her injury wasn't any worse. At least she was alive. Plus, Elaina and he had one thing on their side. He'd pressed the emergency response button while he was still in the car. Backup was already on the way. Of course, they would have to hold off fire for at least twenty, maybe thirty minutes.

That would no doubt seem like a lifetime.

The next shot confirmed that. Hell. It hadn't come from behind them, but from the front. Specifically, from the side of the SUV.

Luke cursed, grabbed on to Elaina and scrambled for a new position. It was meager at best. The tree wasn't large enough to give them any real cover, and they weren't just dealing with one gunman but two.

The next sound he heard had Luke mentally cursing even more.

Footsteps.

They were crunching on the gravel easement just off the road. By the SUV. But not toward the back of it where the second shot had originated.

Mercy. There were three of them.

He lifted his gun and aimed in the direction of those footsteps. Luke waited.

"I wouldn't do that if were you," a man shouted.

Luke looked to his left, and he saw the guy with the eye patch, the very person who'd tried to kill Elaina and Christopher a year ago.

The anger raged through Luke, but the man was holding a high-powered rifle rigged with a scope. And he had that rifle aimed at Elaina. If Luke tried to shoot now, this bozo would fire right at her. With that scope, he likely wouldn't miss, either.

"Drop your gun," the man said.

"Why, so it'll make it easier for you to shoot us?" was Luke's answer.

"My orders are not to kill you. Yet."

Luke glanced around to make sure no one was sneaking up on them. He couldn't hear footsteps, but that didn't matter. If the trio were armed with rifles, they wouldn't have to get that close to be deadly.

"What do you want?" Elaina yelled.

She was obviously as angry as he was, and that anger came through in her voice. Of course, that anger was slightly diminished by that bloody gash on her forehead.

"You know what we want," the guy told them.

"If I did, I wouldn't have asked."

The man didn't answer immediately. "Your former fiancé was working on a little project. We need the memory disk."

It wasn't a surprise, but knowing the why didn't make it easier for him to figure out how they were going to get out of this alive.

"I don't know where the disk is," Elaina shouted. "If I did, I would have given it to the police."

"Maybe. Maybe not. Kevin had the disk with him when he was at the lawyer's office adopting your son. We know that because Kevin confirmed it."

"To whom?" Luke demanded.

"Me. He trusted me. Obviously that wasn't a wise decision on his part. Anyway, the only place he went after the lawyer's office was to the house in San Antonio that he shared with Elaina."

"And Kevin was killed early that evening when he left to get something from his office," Elaina quickly pointed. "As you well know, since you're the one who probably killed him, I left that night—after you tried to kill me."

He didn't deny it. He just stood there with that rifle pointed down at her. "But you took things with you when you ran. That memory disk had to be in those things because it wasn't in the house. We checked."

Elaina started to answer, but Luke nudged her to keep her quiet. He could go two ways with this. He could refuse to tell the man anything else, or he could tell him the truth and hope that it would disperse the three so that Luke would have a better chance at picking them off one by one.

Luke went with the second option.

"Those things that Elaina took with her from the house? Well, they're in the car," Luke informed him. "Thanks to you, those things are now in the river. If they haven't been destroyed by the crash or the water, they probably won't last long. In fact, they might be floating away at this very moment."

That got a reaction. The man lifted his head and looked in the direction of the SUV. He was probably waiting for his comrade or boss to tell him what to do. He must have gotten some kind of signal because he nodded toward the gunman who was behind Luke.

That minor distraction was all Luke needed. He shoved Elaina face-first onto the ground, he aimed, and he fired at the man with the eye patch. One shot to the head was all it took, and the man crumpled into a heap.

Luke didn't stop there. Staying low, he rotated his body and took aim at the gunman behind them.

But it was too late.

The man had already stood and had his rifle targeted right at them. He looked as if he knew what he was doing, and Luke didn't doubt that the guy was a pro. A hired gun. Dressed head to toe in winter camouflaged hunting clothes that explained why Luke hadn't been able to spot him earlier.

"My advice?" the guy snarled. "Don't move."

Luke didn't, mainly because he couldn't risk getting killed. If this goon eliminated him, then Elaina stood little to no chance of making it out of there. Worse, they might be able to drug her so that she'd tell them the location of the safe house. They might go there to search for the disk and create God knows what kind of dangerous havoc. Christopher could be in danger.

And that wasn't going to happen.

The gunman tilted his head slightly and mumbled something. Luke realized he wasn't speaking to them but to a tiny grape-size communicator on the collar of his hunting jacket.

"What's happening?" Elaina asked.

Luke knew she couldn't see since her face was practically right in the dirt, but he wasn't so sure it would do her any good to witness that big guy aiming another rifle at him. And the gunman seemed a little riled that Luke had killed his comrade.

"It's a standoff," Luke told Elaina.

"Not quite," the gunman countered.

Luke wasn't sure what he meant by that, but then he heard the footsteps again. They were coming from the direction of the SUV.

"The boss will keep an eye on you," the gunman explained in such a fake cheerful voice that Luke wanted to slug him for that alone. "While I search the car. For your sake, that disk had better be there."

"Why, so you can kill us anyway?" Luke challenged while he kept his ear tuned to those footsteps.

He needed to keep this situation under control until backup arrived. Control, in this case, likely meant being held at gunpoint by the "boss" while the goon went down into that ravine. Luke liked those odds—him against the idiot responsible for all of this.

Because Luke needed a back-up plan, he had to put Elaina in a position to evade and escape. He eased away from her. She immediately sat up and looked

around. From the corner of his eye, he could tell that
she was looking at him. Probably for answers about
what they were going to do next but he couldn't risk
taking his attention off the gunman. After all, the
man didn't need Elaina and him alive to do the search.

The footsteps stopped just a few yards away, and
the gunman hurried toward the creek.

Luke shifted toward the newcomer, knowing he
was about to come face-to-face with the person who'd
already attempted to kill them. There would likely be
another attempt within the next couple of minutes.

"Agent Buchanan, Elaina," the woman greeted
them. "I'd hoped it wouldn't come to this. Drop the
gun, or I'll shoot Elaina."

Elaina lifted her head. Luke did, as well, and he
speared the woman's gaze.

He found himself looking down the barrel of an
assault rifle.

And the woman behind the trigger was Brenda
McQueen.

ELAINA HADN'T KNOWN exactly whom she would see
holding that rifle on them, but she wasn't surprised
to see Brenda. After all, the woman was one of their
main suspects.

"Drop the gun," Brenda ordered Luke. "Or Elaina
dies, right here, right now. You might not be her real
husband, but I don't think you want her blood on
your hands."

Elaina held her breath. Waiting. Luke had probably

been trained not to surrender her weapon. Plus, if he was unarmed, it would make them both targets.

"If she kills me," Elaina said to him. "Then you'll just shoot her. That way, one of us will be around to raise Christopher."

"Oh, that's so touching," Brenda mocked. "But Agent Buchanan cares for you. He can't let you die. He's too honorable to do something like that."

"Let me die," Elaina whispered.

But he didn't. And Brenda was right—there was no way that Luke would stand there and watch her die.

Luke lowered the gun and eased it onto the ground in front of them. Brenda didn't waste any time, she kicked it out of his reach.

"You have to know where that disk is," Brenda challenged, and she directed that challenge at Elaina.

"Kevin kept a lot of things secret. The only thing he ever said about the project was that he was working for someone named T."

"That's old news," Brenda insisted. "I'm T. And I paid that weasel fiancé of yours a lot of money that investors had given me. Kevin didn't deliver, and now I've got those investors breathing down my neck."

"Don't expect us to feel sorry for you," Luke snarled.

"Well, you should. That memory disk is nothing to you, but I'm within a week of being murdered if I don't produce it. Believe me, my investors are not the sympathetic type, and I'm going to deliver that disk." She turned back to Elaina. "Think back to the night Kevin brought the baby home. What did he have with him?"

"You really expect me to help you?" Elaina asked.

"If you want to live, you will."

Elaina shrugged. "You're planning to kill us no matter what I say."

Brenda readjusted her aim. The rifle was no longer aimed at Elaina.

But Luke.

"Talk, cooperate," Brenda ordered. "Or I kill Agent Buchanan."

"Go ahead," Luke offered.

But Elaina knew from the moment Brenda had made her threat that the woman would indeed carry it out. And just as Luke couldn't let her die, Elaina couldn't let that happen to him.

"See what happens when you get involved with someone," Brenda commented. "You let your heart and other body parts do your thinking."

Elaina didn't necessarily consider that an insult.

"Well?" Brenda prompted. "What did dear ol' Kevin have with him that night?"

Elaina could either lie or tell the truth. She went with the truth because she hoped that if she named an item that might have the disk, then Brenda would have to go after it. She likely wouldn't attempt to kill them until she was sure she had what she wanted.

"Kevin brought home the baby and the adoption papers," Elaina answered. "Christopher was in a carrier seat, and he was wrapped in a blue blanket. He wore a gown with a drawstring at the bottom and a knit cap with a little pom-pom on top. All of that is in the car. He also had a pacifier, a bottle and some disposable diapers. They aren't in the car. I didn't keep them."

"Then you'd better hope that the memory disk is in one of the things you did keep. Because, you see, Elaina, I can make your deaths very quick and easy. Or I can decide not to do that."

Elaina looked at Luke to see how he was handling those threats, but he had a poker face. Well, except for the slight lift of his right eyebrow. She didn't know what it meant exactly, but Elaina figured he was about to do something. She only hoped that something didn't get him killed.

"Backup will be here soon," Luke informed Brenda.

"Yes. I assumed that you'd contacted them. We've got fifteen, maybe twenty minutes." She glanced down at her watch.

Luke moved so quickly that it was practically a blur. He launched himself at the woman.

Just as Brenda fired the rifle at Elaina.

Chapter Eighteen

Luke tried not to let Brenda's shot distract him. He tried to keep his attention aimed on tackling and disarming her. But he couldn't stayed totally focused.

Because that bullet could have hit Elaina.

Hell, it could have killed her.

He aimed all his fear, rage and adrenaline at Brenda. He plowed into her, all the while listening for any sound that Elaina had been hurt. But all he could hear was Brenda.

Yelling and screaming at him, Brenda fought him, hard, and she was much stronger than Luke had anticipated. Still, he outsized her, and he had a more powerful motive for winning—Elaina. He had to get to her in case she needed medical attention. The only way for that to happen was for him to neutralize Brenda.

Luke used his body weight and sheer strength to put Brenda in a chokehold. He kicked the rifle from her hands and rotated both their bodies so that he could see what was going on with Elaina.

She was still there, by the tree, but the sleeve of her jacket had been gashed open, and he could see the blood. His worst fear were confirmed.

Elaina had been shot.

Her injury didn't stop her from moving though. Wincing and holding her arm, she hurried to gather up both the rifle and his handgun. She managed to get the first but not the second when Luke heard the man's voice.

"Hold it right there."

It was the camouflaged gunman. He'd obviously climbed out of the riverbed when he heard his boss call for help. The man had dropped the boxes of items he'd taken from their car, and he was now holding a gun on Elaina.

"Don't," Luke warned her when Elaina started to aim the rifle at the man. It would be suicide. The guy was already cocked and loaded, and Luke figured a hired gun wouldn't miss. Elaina, however, had no experience with weapons.

"Let Brenda go," the man told Luke.

Hell. They were right back where they started, except this time it was worse because of Elaina's injury.

"How badly are you hurt?" he asked while he still kept a chokehold on Brenda.

"I'll live," she said. "I promise."

It was a promise that Luke knew she couldn't keep unless he could get her to a hospital right away. She was losing way too much blood.

"Let go of me!" Brenda yelled.

She rammed her elbow into Luke's stomach, and because of the rifle pointed at Elaina, he knew he'd have no choice but to let her go—eventually.

Still, he had to do something. The gunman had the things from the car. That was everything that Brenda and he needed, which meant they were likely going to be killed now.

Luke couldn't let that happen.

He came up with a quick plan. It wasn't a good one, and it had nearly as many risks as just standing there and facing down these SOBs. He took a deep breath, said a quick prayer and he let go of Brenda.

Cursing and hitting him, the woman struggled to get to her feet. Luke waited until Brenda stood before he made his next move.

"Drop to the ground!" he shouted to Elaina.

Thank God she listened. Elaina dove in the direction of his gun, and he hooked his leg around Brenda's. As he'd known it would do, it off-balanced her, and Brenda came crashing right back into his arms.

With the position of their bodies, the gunman wouldn't have a clean shot for either Elaina or him, unless the guy planned to risk hitting his boss.

Luke tried to move fast, and while he was doing it, he tried to gain control of the howling, fighting woman who obviously wasn't going to cooperate with his plan. He managed to put her back in a choke-hold, and he dragged her in front of him to act as a shield. He didn't stop there. He moved both of them in front of Elaina so he could protect her.

His plan had worked, but he figured it would work even better when he heard something he'd been praying to hear.

A siren.

Backup was about to arrive. Still, from the sound of it, help could be several minutes out.

Too much could still happen.

"I'm not going to jail," the gunman informed them. And the man did something that Luke had not anticipated.

He aimed his rifle at Brenda.

"What do you think you're doing?" Brenda yelled.

"Investing in my future. This way, if the memory disk is in these things, I'll find it and market it on my own."

Brenda cursed at him, and it wasn't mild. She continued to call him names while she struggled and kicked to get out of Luke's grip.

Luke faced a new dilemma. It was obvious the gunman would kill his boss if Luke continued to hold her in place. However, if he let Brenda go, then the guy would just shoot Elaina and him. What Luke needed was his gun. That would give him a chance to fight back.

The gunman made a sudden shift of motion. He angled his body away from Brenda.

And took aim at Elaina.

Luke looked down at her and saw that Elaina had not only moved out of cover to retrieve his gun, she'd pointed it at the man. Her hand was shaking, maybe because she was afraid, but he knew she could also be going into shock.

"Don't!" Luke yelled, hoping to draw the gunman's attention back to him.

When that didn't work, when it seemed as if they were seconds away from a shootout—a shootout that Elaina probably couldn't win—Luke had to take drastic action.

"Elaina, don't shoot," he whispered.

And he hoped like the devil that she'd heard him.

Luke shoved Brenda to the side, in front of Elaina, so that he could try to protect her. In the same motion, Luke snatched the gun from her hand. He took aim at the man.

He fired.

And fired.

And fired.

The man didn't go down. Even though Luke knew he'd delivered direct hits to the gunman's torso and chest. The seconds seemed to tick away, and the entire woods were quiet except their breathing and the howl of the approaching siren. Finally, the gunman fell to the ground.

Brenda immediately kicked Luke and went for her rifle. She might have succeeded if both Elaina and he hadn't dove at the woman. Both landed hard against Brenda, and all of them fell into a heap.

The impact knocked Luke's gun from his hands.

It was a race to see who would get it first, and while Luke fought to retrieve it, he was also mindful of Elaina. He didn't want to risk further injuring her, but he couldn't risk Brenda getting the gun, either. There was just enough time for her to kill them and try to escape.

Luke made sure that didn't happen.

He grabbed on to the back of Brenda's neck and shoved her against the ground. He anchored her in place with the upper half of his body and kicked the rifle toward Elaina. She grabbed it and then handed him his gun.

"Give me a reason to kill you," Luke snarled to Brenda as he put his gun against her head. "Any reason."

Just like that Brenda stopped struggling. But she didn't stop cursing. Luke didn't mind the profanity. He could handle anything as long as he knew Elaina was safe.

But was she safe?

She was pale and trembling, and her entire arm was now soaked with blood.

"I think I'm okay," Elaina assured him with her voice shaking as much as body.

It wasn't much of an assurance, and Luke knew she probably wouldn't stay conscious for long. He needed to get her to the hospital immediately.

A sheriff's car screeched to a halt right behind the SUV. Two men barreled out of the vehicle. Both were armed and ready. One was Sheriff Dawson, and Luke recognized the other as Agent Simon Roark.

"We're down here," Luke called out to them.

Luke didn't waste any time. As soon as the sheriff and Agent Roark got to them, he passed Brenda off to them, and he went to Elaina. Behind him, he heard the agent call for an ambulance. Good. Because they were going to need one.

He pulled Elaina to him so that he could keep her warm and because he desperately needed to hold her.

"I'm sorry about this," he whispered. He checked her wound, but there was so much blood, he couldn't tell just how bad it was.

"Why *are* you sorry?" she asked, blinking.

"Because I should be the one hurt and bleeding. Not you."

She managed a weak smile, but it faded as quickly as it came. "If I don't make it—"

"An ambulance is on the way," he said. He didn't want to hear this.

Elaina apparently thought he should hear it. "Yes. But if something goes wrong—"

"It won't."

She huffed, but it, too, was weak and filled with breath. "You need to let me finish."

"I know what you're going to say. That if something goes wrong, you want me to take care of Christopher. You know I will. But nothing will go wrong. It can't."

She shook her head, reached up and touched his face with her fingertips. Her hands were as cold as death.

"Things don't always work out for the best," Elaina muttered. Her eyelids eased down.

"Both of us have firsthand knowledge of that.

That's why it'll work this time," Luke promised. "It has to work. Because I won't lose you. Understand? I won't lose you."

But he was talking to himself.

Elaina was no longer conscious.

LUKE PACED. He sat down. Got up. And paced some more. None of that helped. He wasn't sure how much more he could take of this. He had to know what was going on in that E.R. procedure room where the doctor was with Elaina.

"These exams take time," Agent Roark commented. His fellow agent had followed the ambulance to the Luling Rehabilitation Hospital and was now sorting through the box of Elaina's items that they'd retrieved from the riverbank.

Luke glared at Roark for that totally unhelpful observation. Of course, these things took time. The doctor had already been in there a half hour.

It'd seemed like a decade.

Roark checked his watch. "The sitter and Christopher should be here soon."

Yes. Theresa and Christopher were indeed on their way from the safe house to the hospital. Luke prayed there'd be good news about Elaina before they arrived.

"You know, you could get your mind off things if you helped me go through these things," Roark continued.

Luke glanced at the items the agent had placed on the table of the private waiting room. The last thing he wanted to do was work, but if he didn't do something, *anything,* he might have to put his fist through the wall.

Once again, he'd nearly gotten Elaina killed.

He refused to believe that she could die. She couldn't. Somehow, she had to make it through this. Then he could tell her how sorry he was. Maybe, just maybe, she'd forgive him.

Or maybe she'd order him out of her life.

He couldn't blame her if she did.

"I don't see anything in this charm bracelet that could hold a disk," Roark informed him.

Luke was of the same opinion, but that miniature memory disk had to be somewhere. And he still needed to find it. Luke wanted Brenda and those investors out of Elaina and Christopher's lives. He darn sure didn't want these goons showing up in the near future to make a second attempt at finding the disk. So, that meant he had to find it and get it as far away from Elaina and Christopher as he could.

Drawing in a long breath, Luke sank down into the metal fold-up chair across the table from Roark. Luke stared at the items and tried to put himself in Kevin's place. Kevin, a sleazy liar on the verge of becoming a rich, big-time criminal. Yet, in the middle of that big software modification venture, he'd illegally adopted Christopher.

A coincidence?

Luke didn't believe in them, especially when it came to criminal behavior.

He picked up the clothes that his son had worn on

the trip from the lawyer's office to Elaina and Kevin's home. A soft knitted cap with a tiny pom-pom on top. A long gown with a drawstring. And a blanket rimmed with satin. All in varying shades of blue.

Luke moved those three items, the denim infant carrier seat and the adoption papers to one end of the table. He added the purple stuffed bear and yellow bunny. He remembered that Elaina had said that Kevin had called Christopher their little bunny. Kevin's pet name still didn't sit well with Luke. But unless the memory disk was in the items that Elaina had already discarded, like the pacifier and bottle, then it was likely here.

So, where would Kevin have hidden it?

Luke mentally went back to that night, and he tried to imagine what Kevin would have been feeling. The excitement mixed with a hefty dose of caution. Maybe even fear. Maybe he even knew that there were killers after him.

Where was the one place Kevin would hide the tiny disk? A disk that could cost him his life or else give him the life he'd always wanted?

And suddenly Luke knew the answer.

Chapter Nineteen

"I'm feeling great," Elaina insisted as the nurse wrapped her freshly stitched wound. She looked at the doctor to continue her plea for freedom. "Really great, considering everything that's happened. I'm ready to leave the hospital."

The doctor with the craggy face, Roman nose and sugar-white hair made a sound that could have meant anything or nothing, and he wrote something down on her chart. But Elaina knew the truth. Her arm had been wounded, and the adrenaline crash was making her feel bone-tired. The pain meds had made her a little woozy. But she wasn't critical. Heck, she wasn't even in serious condition.

But Luke didn't know that yet.

He was probably out in the waiting room blaming himself for all of this. She needed to set him straight before his guilt built to massive portions. And she also needed to feel his arms around her. While she was wishing and needing, she added Christopher to the list. She wanted to see her baby.

"You can't leave the hospital just yet," the doctor informed her. "You'll stay the night for observation, and then you'll have to come back to have those stitches checked."

Elaina barely heard him. She had only one thing on her mind. "I want to see Luke."

"So you've said at least a dozen times." The doctor examined the bandage when the nurse moved away. "He's asked at least that many times, too. Oh, and someone named Carrie keeps calling the nurses' station."

Elaina would talk to her later and tell her she wouldn't be returning to Crystal Creek. Once she'd recovered, she'd look for a place closer to Luke so that both of them would be able to see Christopher.

Well, she would do that if Luke approved. She had to get past that obstacle first.

"I want to see Luke," Elaina repeated.

He nodded. "Let me do something about fulfilling that request." The doctor left the room and walked across the hall. The nurse followed him.

Elaina couldn't hear what the doctor said, but she heard Luke. He came rushing into the room and came to a halt next to her bed. He looked rumpled, exhausted and worried. But he also looked incredibly hot. Of course, looking hot was the norm for Luke Buchanan.

"How are you?" he asked.

She told him what the doctor had told her when he made his initial examination. "I'll be all right.

The bullet went straight through and didn't damage any nerves."

Luke didn't take her word for it. He sank down onto the edge of the bed and examined her bandaged arm. And then her eyes. She examined his eyes, too. Yep, there was a hefty amount of guilt mixed with the fatigue.

Elaina decided to nip this in the bud. "You're not responsible for this."

He groaned. "Oh, yes, I am."

She shook her head and touched his hand. "Let's give ourselves a break and blame Brenda and Kevin."

Luke looked ready to argue with that, so Elaina leaned over and kissed him. He cooperated. Luke slipped his arms around her, eased her to him and returned the kiss.

It was heaven.

He was warm and solid, and he gave her exactly what she needed—*him*. But it didn't last nearly long enough.

Luke pulled back and met her gaze. "I do have some good news. I found the memory disk, and it's already on the way to crime lab."

Well, she certainly hadn't expected that news. But it, too, was like heaven. Hallelujah! They were free from Kevin's horrible legacy.

"Where did you find it?" Elaina asked.

"Behind the raised gold seal on the adoption papers. The seal was thick and nearly two inches wide, and I guess that's why no one noticed that anything was hidden beneath it. I figured that a fake adoption meant fake papers. Kevin wouldn't have wanted to put the tiny disk where it would be handled or crushed. He knew the papers would be kept in a file, waiting for him to retrieve it whenever he needed it."

Of course. She only wished she'd thought of that sooner. "Maybe the crime lab will be able to tell us why Brenda wanted that disk so badly."

"The lead investigators think they know. It appears Kevin was trying to implant complex computer viruses into commonly used antiviral software. These viruses would basically destroy a computer network's firewall and security measures. And it was aimed at banks and credit card institutions. Software like that could have made billons for anyone breaking into those cyber accounts."

Elaina had to take a moment to absorb that. "Billons," she whispered. No wonder Brenda had been willing to kill to get her hands on it.

"What about Carrie?" Elaina wanted to know. "She wasn't involved with this, was she?"

"No. It doesn't look like it."

"So, we're safe now?" Elaina asked.

Luke nodded. Then, shrugged. "Well, safe from bad guys. We still have some personal things to deal with. First of all, I want you to slap me for nearly getting you killed."

She huffed. She'd rather set her hair on fire than hit him. "I said we weren't going to do this. You're not to blame. Truth is, you saved me. Not just my life." She had to clear the lump in her throat before she could continue. "You saved *me*."

He didn't say anything. He sat there, staring at her. And that suddenly made Elaina feel uncomfortable. Had her confession of the heart been too much for him to handle?

"You still don't think I'm faking my feelings?" she asked hesitantly.

Luke blinked. "No. God, no."

Whew. That was something, but it didn't explain the change in mood. "Then why the glum face?"

He, too, cleared his throat. Not once. But twice. And he scratched his forehead. "Because I have something to say, to *suggest*," he corrected. "And I'm not sure how you're going to take it."

Oh. This was about Christopher's custody. That sapped what little energy she had left, and she eased her head back onto the pillow. "Go ahead," she prompted.

"You're exhausted. We can talk about this another time," Luke said. He started to stand, but she caught on to his arm.

"No. Let's get this out into the open."

He waited, looking at her, probably to make sure she was up to this.

"Go ahead," Elaina repeated. "Just please tell me that you'll give me visitation rights with Christopher."

Another blink, and he stared at her as if she'd lost her mind. "Visitation rights? That's what you want?" But he didn't wait for her to answer. "Because I want something more than that."

Since he wasn't smiling and since his intensity level was through the roof, Elaina had no idea where this was going.

"We could do this the safe way," he continued after clearing his throat. "We could spend the next year or so getting to know each other, to make sure that we're ready for a relationship."

She mentally repeated that and tried not to jump for joy. Her stitches couldn't handle that, even if that's what her heart begged her to do. "You want a relationship with me?"

He shook his head.

Her heart went into a nosedive. "The blood loss must have left me with a foggy head, because I'm confused."

He leaned in and kissed her, making her even more confused and foggy headed. He also left her breathless, incredibly warm and wanting more of him.

"Not just a relationship," he clarified. "I want to make love to you."

Oh, that remedied her nosediving heart. Elaina smiled and felt herself go all warm. "I think that can be arranged. Not now. Not here. But soon."

He smiled, too, and it made it all the way to his eyes. "I was thinking of lots of sex. On a regular basis. With us under the same roof."

Elaina was sure her smile widened to a ridiculous proportion. "I'd like that, to be under the same roof with you and Christopher."

But then, her smile faded.

She hated to say this. She truly did. But it had to be said. "I don't want a relationship of convenience."

He shrugged. "Trust me, being married to me will be anything but convenient. I'm pigheaded, moody and often a pain in the butt."

This time, her heart nearly stopped. "Married?"

Luke pulled away from her, went down on one knee and took her hand. "Let me back up a little. Will you marry me?"

She couldn't breathe. Couldn't answer. Couldn't move. Elaina just sat there with her mouth open.

"Please," Luke whispered. "Don't say no."

She tried to speak, but her mouth didn't cooperate. How had this happened? One day she was living a lie, and now she had the real possibility of living a real life. With Luke and Christopher.

"I love you," she heard Luke say. "I realized that when I nearly lost you."

Oh, mercy. That's when she'd realized she loved him. The tears came. Happy tears.

Luke stood. "Is that a no?"

She shook her head. "No."

He looked as if she'd slugged him.

"I don't mean no as in no to your proposal," she quickly clarified. "I mean no, I don't mean a no."

"Is, uh, that your way of saying yes, you'll marry me?" he asked.

Elaina didn't trust her mouth or her brain to answer him so she latched on to him and pulled her to him. Her injury protested the exertion, but she ignored the pain. She ignored everything but Luke. She kissed him, and she hoped that everything she felt for him came through in that kiss.

Luke turned the tables on her though. He kissed her, too. Mercy, he really did love her.

"I love you, too," she managed to say.

He nodded, and there were tears in his eyes. Elaina was past that point. Her tears were streaming down her cheeks. She'd never felt happier or more complete.

But it suddenly got a lot better.

She heard the babbling noises in the hall, and both Luke and she turned in that direction. A moment later, Theresa appeared in the doorway. She was holding Christopher in her arms.

"See," Theresa said pointing to Elaina and Luke. "I told you that Ma Ma and Da Da were here."

Christopher eyed them, especially the hospital bed and Elaina's bandaged arm. Then, he smiled and reached out for Luke to take him.

Luke did. He took Christopher, kissed his cheek and walked to Elaina so that she could kiss him, as well.

Elaina slid her arm around both of her guys. Christopher tolerated the hugs and kisses for a few moments and then wiggled out of her embrace. He babbled something that she couldn't distinguish. Something happy, no doubt, since he giggled and patted Luke on the cheek.

"Ma Ma, Da Da," Christopher said.

And this time, it was crystal clear.

Elaina's feelings were crystal clear, as well. In fact, she'd never been more certain.

"Yes," she told Luke.

He whipped around to face her. "Yes to what?"

"To everything. Yes, to being your wife. Yes, to us being a family."

He nodded. Kissed her until she couldn't breathe. Then, he gathered both Christopher and her into his arms and held on tight.

* * * * *

SECRET AGENT,
SECRET FATHER

DONNA
YOUNG

Donna Young, an incurable romantic, lives in beautiful Northern California with her husband and two children.

To Wendy and Jimmy,
I love you, Mom and Dad.

Chapter One

With the pain came consciousness.

It pierced the cataleptic depths with jagged teeth that gnawed through skull and skin.

The man lifted his head, testing. Blood coated his tongue, coppery and thick. He groaned as the nausea tightened his gut, pressed into his chest.

They're coming! The words screamed at him through the blanket of fog, adding a bite to the pain. His eyes fluttered open. Blurred lines altered, then cleared into comprehensible patterns.

Rain trickled in through the half-shattered windshield. The splatter of water mixed with his blood turning the air bag pink in the semidarkness. A light pole lay bent across the top of the sports coupé, its base uprooted from the cement.

How long had he been unconscious? He shifted, trying to relieve the pressing weight on his lungs, focusing on the half-deflated air bag wedged between the steering wheel and his chest.

A shaft of white heat impaled his right shoulder. He let out a slow hiss.

After a moment, he pulled his other arm in from the driver's side window, noting for the first time he held a pistol tight in his grip. The silver flashed in the night. The cold steel felt good in the palm of his hand. No, more than good, he thought. Familiar.

He fumbled with the safety belt, released the lock. Tightening his jaw, he shoved his good shoulder against the car door, stiffened at the new surge of pain, the wave of dizziness. Metal scraped, glass crackled. Another push and the door gave way. Slowly he slid through the opening and then stood, using the mangled roof for support.

Sirens wailed in the distance. Instinctively he turned. Bile rose, burned his throat. The ground tilted beneath him. Swearing, he fell to his knees and vomited.

They were coming for him. Cops. Rescue workers. It didn't matter which. Both filed reports.

Reports left paper trails.

With gun in hand, he waited a moment for his stomach to settle, using the time to get his bearings.

Rows of houses, dull with age and earth-toned brick, flanked the street. Each with covered porches that lay behind picket fences or scattered hedges. Each containing onlookers, mostly white-haired couples, their arms tightly wrapped over their chests, holding closed a variety of plaid and terry cloth robes.

Those who didn't brave the elements took protection from the rain behind the narrow bay windows of their homes. Their fingers held the curtains slightly apart, while eyes squinted with curiosity and fear, deepened the grooves of their features.

Enough fear to keep them away from the armed stranger who had invaded their quiet suburban neighborhood.

Carefully, he turned his head, his eyes searching the shadows of the road. How far was he from her?

A bent street post lay no more than five feet from the wrecked light pole. Proctor Avenue?

Too far, his mind whispered. Too far to help.

The sirens grew louder placing his rescuers no more than a few minutes out.

Hot needles pricked his eye sockets and images began to swim. A black fog seeped in, setting off another wave of dizziness. Struggling against the void, he rammed his injured shoulder into the car. Pain exploded through his arm, jarring his spine, driving consciousness forward, forcing the obscurity back.

Sheer willpower put him on his feet. He swayed, then stumbled. *Warn her,* his mind screamed. Before he passed out. Before his enemies found him.

Or worse, the whisper came. *Before they found her.*

Chapter Two

A storm swept over the outskirts of Annapolis. The air crackled and snapped, alive with the hum of lightning, the boom of thunder. Below, stinging sheets of rain pounded water and land with heavy fists, spurred by the fierce Chesapeake winds.

Grace Renne stood by her bay window holding one billowing curtain in her grip. When the bark of the storm reached her, a twinge of sadness worked up the back of her throat.

For the last several years she'd lived on the bay, admiring the city's fortitude, appreciating its history. It was a city born amidst the turmoil of the American Revolution. Time-honored traditions cemented every cobblestone, forged every piece of iron, framed every structure for more than three hundred years.

Grace caught a whiff of burning wood—fireplaces combating the early autumn chill. Underneath the smoke lingered the richer scent of the sea and sand. Slowly, she drew in a deeper breath, enjoyed the bite of salt on the back of her tongue.

She loosened her grip until the curtain fluttered against

her fingertips. Scents, textures…intuition were her tools to live by. Characteristics, her father insisted with irritation, she'd gotten from her mother.

She'd gotten her mother's looks, too. The pale, blond hair that hung in a long, straight curtain. The light brown eyes that softened with humor, narrowed in temper. Delicate features—until one looked close enough and saw the purpose, the character that shaped the high cheekbones and the feminine jaw.

She shut the window, smiling as Mother Nature beat at the framed glass. Any other time, any other mood, she would have let the storm have its way. Her eyes swept over the oak trim of her cottage, the barreled ceiling, the endless stacks of half-packed boxes. But the cottage was no longer hers, sold only days before to her friend and bar manager, Lawrence "Pusher" Davis. The reformed ex-con had bought her home as his first step to becoming a real-estate mogul. And she was sure he wouldn't appreciate water damage on his new hardwood floors.

"We won't have nor'easters in Arizona, baby," she murmured and patted her stomach, a habit begun to soothe the first trimester bouts of nausea.

And now? Grace stopped midmotion. What did her father say? A subconscious attempt to soothe a restless spirit?

Better than no spirit, she'd countered and brushed off the ache just beneath her heart.

With the window shut, the air grew thick with the sweet scent of baking cookies. A grin tugged at the corners of her mouth. "I'd say, handsome, that patting you is a self-defense mechanism to divert your constant cravings for warm milk and chocolate chip cookies."

Her oversized, navy sweatshirt fell to midthigh—its Annapolis insignia covered her midriff like a big yellow target. The shirt, combined with the thick cotton of her dark leggings, provided more than enough warmth to allow her to go barefooted.

Still, she threw another log onto the fireplace's burning embers. Its muted glow matched her melancholy mood.

Overstuffed furniture of glossy, dark oak and warm tweeds filled the room. She hadn't packed up the rich, brown chenille throws that draped the back of the couch. Putting it off had been a silly defiance, she thought. But even as she did, her hand ran over the nearest throw, her fingers curled reflexively into its thickness. After five years, she wasn't quite ready to give up the first true home she'd ever known.

The buzz of the oven timer broke through her thoughts, but the growl of her stomach prodded her into the kitchen. Tiles of white and cornflower-blue checked the six-foot counter—effectively separating the kitchen from the main room without diminishing the cottage's warmth.

For once, Charles Renne had agreed with her decision to move. In fact, her father encouraged her. Surprising, since he hadn't agreed with any of her choices in years. She'd been fourteen when her mother had died. But the war of wills had started long before.

She snapped off the oven and opened the door. The heat blasted her in the face. She hesitated over a long, drawn-out and downright decadent sniff.

The small flutter in her belly told her she'd gotten the baby's attention. She laughed, low and easy. "Okay, sport, one plate of cookies and glass of milk coming up." With an expertise born from cravings, she took the cookies from the oven and slid them onto a nearby cooling rack.

Lately, her battles with her father had flared to a whole new level. One that heightened after her refusal to reveal the baby's father.

The baby was hers. Only hers, she thought stubbornly.

That characteristic she inherited from her father. But it hadn't made the past pleasant for either father or daughter.

Four years ago, she'd stopped by a cigar bar called The Tens to meet a group of college friends.

The pungent smell of whiskey and the more earthy scent of imported cigars drew her in, but it was the low murmur of conversations and clink of glasses—a backbeat to the smoky jazz—that seduced her.

Two weeks later, she dropped out of premed and bought the bar with the rest of her trust fund. An emancipation of sorts, she thought in hindsight.

For the past several years, she'd indulged her passion for fast cars and jazz clubs and leaned ever more closely toward liberal ideas. And the more she indulged, the more distant her father grew. The more distant he grew, the more she hurt.

But over time, the freedom she'd gained became precious and the pain bearable.

The doorbell rang, startling her. She glanced at the mantel clock.

Almost midnight.

Unease caught at the base of her spine. She pushed it away, annoyed. "Who is it?" she asked, but heard no response. Only the wind whistling through the crack beneath, tickling her toes. She curled them against the floor. A look through the peephole proved useless.

"Hide." The command came low, splintered. Still, she recognized the underlining timbre, the slightly offbeat drawl that turned one syllable into two.

"Jacob?" She yanked open the door. He sat next to the door pane, his back propped against the side of the cottage. Blood coated him from top to chin, dripping off the slant of his jaw onto his torn shirt and his black dress slacks. "Oh my God. Jacob!" She fell to her knees beside him.

His eyes fluttered open, focused for a brief moment, one black pupil dilated to more than twice the size of its partner. Blood rimmed the iris until no white could be seen. "Hide, Grace." He rasped the order. "Before they kill you."

His head lolled back. Fear gripped her. Quickly, she placed her hand under his shirt. *Please, God.* The rhythmic beat of his heart remained steady beneath her palm. She closed her eyes briefly against the sting of tears.

The rain and wind spit at them. She raised his hand to her cheek, felt the ice-cold fingers against her skin. She glanced around and saw no car. How had he gotten here? Walked?

Her nearest neighbor was down the beach, too far to call for help. If she left him outside, he'd be worse off by the time the ambulance got there.

A few weeks ago, the doctor had said no heavy lifting. What would he say if he knew the father of the baby lay half-dead on her porch?

"Jacob!" She screamed his name, but he didn't stir.

She scrambled inside and grabbed her purse from the counter. She'd call the ambulance from the front porch—

Then she heard it, the familiar ring tone of her cell phone.

She dumped the contents of her handbag onto the counter, ignoring the lipstick and keys that fell to the floor. She snagged her phone, saw the displayed name and punched the button.

"Pusher?" She flipped the overhead switches on. Lights flooded the room, making her blink. A glance to the doorway told her Jacob hadn't moved. She ran back to his side, checked the pulse at his neck.

"Grace? Thank God." Pusher Davis paused on a shaky breath. "Are you okay?"

"I'm fine but I need you to—"

"Then you haven't talked to anyone?"

"Talked…" she said, momentarily off balance. Using the cuff of her sweatshirt she wiped the blood from Jacob's forehead, trying to get a good look at the injury beneath. "Pusher, I don't have time for this." His skin grayed in the porch light. She had enough experience to know he'd lost too much blood. "I need you to—"

"Helene's dead."

"Helene?" Tension fisted in her chest. "Dead?"

"Grace, I found her body outside The Tens. In the back alley."

Helene, dead? The fist tightened, catching her breath on a short choke of surprise. It couldn't be true. She'd just seen Helene earlier that day. They'd met at their favorite sidewalk bistro for a farewell lunch.

"It's Monday night. The bar should've been closed. She shouldn't have even been there this late. What happened?" The question slipped from her lips, but a prick at the nape of her neck told her the answer.

"She'd been shot," Pusher answered, then paused. "Grace, last time I saw her she was with Jacob Lomax."

She studied the wound in Jacob's shoulder, forced herself to inhale. *Hide, Grace, before they kill you.*

"Did you hear me?"

"Yes," she answered, then took another breath to steady herself. "Are the police there?"

"Not yet. But I've called them."

"Pusher, listen to me." She nearly screamed the words. "I need you to stall them when they get there. They're going to want to talk to me, but I can't right now."

"I don't think you understand, Grace. Helene has been murdered—"

"I understand." She cut him off, not trying to stop the urgency of her words. "Jacob Lomax collapsed on my porch a few minutes ago. He's been shot, too," she added, deciding to put her trust in Pusher. "And until I find out why, the police will only complicate things."

"But if Lomax is there—"

"I told you, he is."

"Then why the cloak-and-dagger, Grace? If Jacob has been shot, this could have been a robbery. A simple case of wrong place, wrong time. I've seen it before."

"I don't think it is and I need some time to make sure."

"Why? Do you think he shot Helene?" He said the words almost jokingly. But when she didn't respond, he swore. "You do, don't you?"

"No," she snapped. "I think his life is in danger."

When the manager didn't say anything, she added. "I can't explain right now. And I can't do this without your help, Pusher. Please," she whispered.

"Okay, okay. Lord knows, I owe you," he answered, the uncertainty thickening his Texas drawl. "I can probably stall them until morning. A little longer if they get ahold of my rap sheet. Will that work?"

She could trust Pusher to take care of the police. The ex-con had certainly sold her on hiring him a few years back, against Helene and her father's wishes.

"Yes, that will work," she said. "Thanks, Pusher."

"It's been a while since I've been in an interrogation room. Was feeling a little homesick, anyway," he mused before his tone turned serious. "Grace, watch your back. The cops aren't your only worry. I won't ask again why you think Jacob's in danger. But if you're right and he is a target, you could become collateral damage."

"I'll be careful."

She hung up the phone. Calling an ambulance was out of the question now. Not until she found out what was going on. She glanced at Jacob before hitting the speed dial.

The phone clicked on the fourth ring. "Hello."

"Dad, it's Grace."

"Grace. Do you realize what time—"

"Dad, I need your help." Jacob's wound couldn't wait for her father's lecture. "Your medical help."

Suddenly, his tone turned sharp. "Is something the matter? Is it the baby?"

"The baby?" She gripped the phone tighter. Deceit warred with desperation inside of her. "Yes, it's the baby."

"Are you spotting again?"

"No," she answered, not wanting to add that possibility to her father's worry. "But I can't explain over the phone. I need you to come over here now. And don't tell anyone where you are going. I want to keep this private."

"Don't tell… Grace Ann, maybe you had better explain—"

"Not now, Dad. Please," she added to soften her order. She moved her hand over Jacob's heart, took reassurance in its steady beat against her palm. "And bring your medical bag."

"I will, but I want to know what's going on when I get there."

"I promise full disclosure," she agreed. "And Dad, do one more thing for me?"

"What?"

"Hurry," she whispered.

Charles Renne hesitated for only a split second. They might not understand each other's views, but he was a father. One that understood fear. "I will."

Grace snapped the phone shut and shoved it into her sweatshirt pocket. Her father would take a good hour to reach her from Washington, D.C. Jacob couldn't wait that long.

"I can do this but you need to be easy with our baby, okay big guy?" It took some shifting, but she managed to maneuver herself behind him. Rain soaked her sweatshirt, plastered her hair to her forehead. Impatiently, she brushed the blond strands away, then slid her hands under his arms and around his chest.

Jacob was a good six inches over her own five-eight frame, and had well over fifty pounds on her. He was built lean, with the firm muscles and long limbs of a distance runner. Grateful her taste didn't run toward male bulk, she settled him back until he rested against her chest and shoulder.

The clatter of metal ricocheted in the night air. She glanced down. A pistol lay on the cement, its barrel inches from her feet.

His? Once again, her mind rejected the idea that Jacob had shot Helene. No matter what secrets he carried, he wasn't capable of murder. From the moment Helene had introduced Jacob to Grace, there was no doubt about the close friendship between the two.

Ignoring the weapon, she gripped him between her thighs. Slowly, she scooted him back through the doorway. Using the strength of her legs and arms, she tugged and pulled in short bursts of energy. The struggle took more than twenty minutes. Twenty minutes in which she pleaded, prayed, begged and swore. But she managed it.

Once inside, she scooted back toward the fireplace and lowered his shoulders gently to the floor. Quickly, she closed the door, grabbed a pillow and placed it under his head.

For months, she'd worried about him, raged at him—yearned, grieved, loved him—silently through the long, dark nights.

But not once had she been terrified for him.

Until now.

His face was pale, stark against his deep brown hair, now darker with rain, sticky with blood. His features cut in razor-thin angles. Sharper, leaner since the last time she'd seen him. A four-inch gash split the hairline above the middle of his forehead. Blood and bruises covered most of his features.

She knelt beside him, saw him shiver. Cursing herself, she threw a few more logs on the fire.

But it was his shoulder that worried her the most. Blood was everywhere. His face, neck and arm were coated with it. From his head, or shoulder, or both. She couldn't be sure which.

Her pulse thickened with fear, making her hands heavy, her fingers tremble. She shook them, trying to settle them and her nerves, then removed his suit jacket. A shoulder

holster crowded under his arm. Something she hadn't
noticed when dragging him in. Quickly, she unbelted the
holster and tossed it aside. Within minutes, she had him
stripped to his underwear and covered him to the waist with
her comforter.

The bullet had torn a hole through his right shoulder,
leaving an exit wound on the back side.

Fear and confusion warred within, but right now she had
time for neither. Instead, she crossed to the linen cupboard
and pulled out a clean, white hand towel.

After running the cloth under warm water, she returned
to his side with it and her biggest pan filled with hotter water.
She tucked the blanket around him, knowing she couldn't do
anything other than clean the wound until her father got
there.

With gentle fingers, she brushed a lock of hair from his
forehead, then systematically dabbed the blood away from
the gash.

"I'll give you one thing, Lomax," she whispered. She
rinsed the towel out in the water, watched it turn pink, before
she switched her attention to his shoulder. "You sure as hell
know how to make an entrance."

Chapter Three

"He's coming, Mr. Kragen."

Oliver Kragen sat on a park bench as dawn broke over the Chesapeake Bay. His enforcer, Frank Sweeney, stood no more then ten feet away, his bulky frame eclipsing the sun behind him. Dressed in an Armani suit, the man appeared more like a pro football player ready to renegotiate his contract than the mercenary he was.

And that's exactly why Oliver had hired him.

"I'll give you odds the bastard screwed up."

Oliver didn't acknowledge Sweeney's comment. Instead, he waited until the click of shoe soles sounded behind him. Rather than turn in greeting, Oliver tossed the remainder of his Danish to a nearby pigeon. After all, Boyd Webber wasn't a peer, he was an employee.

"She's dead."

Oliver glanced at Sweeney, a silent order to leave. Once the big man stepped away, Kragen spoke up, but his focus remained on the pigeons at their feet. "How?" The question was low, pleasant.

Boyd wasn't fooled. But he didn't care, either. The ex-marine had more than two dozen kills under his belt and had survived more horrors than the bloodiest special effects ever created. Nothing on this earth made him afraid of dying. Least of all a weasel like Kragen. "The Garrett woman had a gun. They both did. It forced my hand."

"They forced your hand because they were armed? They're government operatives. What did you expect, Webber?" Kragen's voice hardened. "If I remember right, I told you it was imperative that the Garrett woman was to be brought to me. Alive."

"It was a mistake. They killed one of my men, wounded another. The third man targeted Lomax, but somehow the woman took a stray bullet in the chest."

"And this third man?"

"I killed him."

"To save me the trouble? Or him the pain?"

"I was…angry." More than angry. Infuriated. Enough to lose his cool and shoot until the woman was dead. Enough to murder another man—one of his own—who had witnessed his transgression. "My man should have been more careful," he lied.

In Webber's opinion, Helene Garrett deserved no better than to die in a gutter. She had betrayed Senator D'Agostini. Slept with him, used him, stolen from him. End of her, end of story. Or it should have been. But the files were still missing.

"Did you clean up your mess?" Kragen's eyes shifted to his coffee cup. He took a sip, burned his tongue and swore.

"I thought it better to leave things." Resentment slithered down Webber's back, coiled deep within his belly. He studied Kragen's profile with derision. Kragen was the poster-boy politician. The meticulous, trimmed blond hair that enhanced the high slant of the cheekbones, the aristocratic forehead. A nose so straight that Webber would bet his last dime that Kragen had it cosmetically carved. All packaged in a five-figure topcoat and custom suit. All done to hide the trailer-park genes that ran through Poster Boy's veins.

"You killed your man without consulting me first." Oliver glanced up then. Twin metallic-gray eyes pinned, then dismissed the mercenary in one flicker.

"I consulted with the senator beforehand," Webber responded.

Oliver noted the verbal jab, but chose to ignore it for the moment. "Did you search the bar? Her apartment?"

"She'd moved out of her apartment days ago and left nothing behind. And we had no time to search the bar. Lomax was the priority."

"The woman had the files and the code," Oliver insisted. "I want the bar searched. And I want Lomax found."

"Shouldn't take long. We winged Lomax before he slipped away. We found his car wrapped around a light pole."

"Did you follow the blood?"

"Witnesses told the police he took off down the street but the rain washed away any bloody trail."

"And the police? What do they say?" Oliver prompted, his annoyance buried under a tone of civility. More than the Neanderthal deserved, in Oliver's opinion.

To say that Webber was ugly would have been polite. He had the face of a boxer, flat and scarred from too many alley fights, and a bulbous nose from too much booze. Like Sweeney, he wore a tailored suit, had no neck and too much muscle. Unlike Sweeney, he sported a butch cut so close it left the color of his hair in question.

"The police are questioning the bar manager. An ex-con by the name of Pusher Davis."

"If the man is an ex-con, they'll suspect him first," Oliver observed. "Tail him, just to be sure. I don't want any loose ends."

"There won't be. The police won't get anywhere. Helene Garrett will become just another statistic in a long line of unsolved homicides," Boyd explained.

For the moment, Oliver ignored the arrogance underlying Webber's words. "They have Lomax's blood on the scene."

Webber snorted. "Won't do them any good if they have no records to match it with. Right now, the cops don't have any information on either of them. Or the senator's connection to her."

Webber was right. Oliver had gone to great lengths to keep the senator's relationship with Helene Garrett private. A precaution he practiced with all the senator's mistresses. "That won't get us the Primoris files or the code. We need to find Lomax."

"My men are checking nearby hospitals and clinics."

"You actually expect him to show up on some grid? He's injured, not stupid, Webber," he snapped, annoyed over the fact that this wouldn't have happened if Helene hadn't slipped under their radar.

Oliver had investigated Helene months before the senator had started the affair. With his contacts, it took Oliver no more than a few calls to get everything from her finances to her elementary school records. False records, as it turned out.

"From the look of his car seat, he's lost a lot of blood. If he passed out, he'd have no choice. Someone might have taken him to the hospital."

"Find him."

"It would help if you could give me more than just his name."

"I gave you his name *and* the time and place of the meeting." Oliver paused, his eyes critical. "It should have been enough."

"I told you, they forced my hand. It couldn't be helped."

"Just find Lomax and keep him alive. I don't care what it takes," Oliver ordered, already making plans to advise the senator to call an emergency meeting. The others would have to be informed. "That bitch stole the Primoris file. I want it back. Do you understand?"

"I'll take care of it," Boyd responded automatically. "And the police?"

"I'll make a few calls. Jacob Lomax won't be on their data banks unless I arrange to put him there."

"Are you thinking of making the murder public?" Webber questioned.

"No." Any unwanted attention at this stage could sabotage their plans. "At least not for now." Not until the others met and reevaluated the situation. They were too close to their goal.

"How about her partner?" Webber asked. "Grace Renne?"

Oliver considered the possibility. "She might know something. Or at the very least, have seen something." Oliver remembered faces, names. It was vital in his world. He'd met Miss Renne once at some sort of political function—one of many. At the time, the association between Helene and Doctor Charles Renne's daughter seemed coincidental—and, in his mind, added to Helene's credibility. But now…

"They had lunch yesterday afternoon," Webber prompted.

"Then you should have already had someone talking to her this morning." Oliver stood, his gaze back on the horizon. He didn't like disloyalty within his ranks. And those who were foolish enough to betray him suffered. "I'm here in Washington, D.C., with the senator until after the fund-raising ball tomorrow night. You know how to get hold of me. And I mean me, Webber. The senator is too busy with the upcoming election to be bothered with this. Do you understand?"

Not waiting for an answer, Oliver turned to Sweeney. "Frank." He waited the moment it took for the enforcer to join them. "You're with Webber. Make sure he does his job this time."

"Now wait a minute—"

"Yes, sir." Sweeney stepped behind the mercenary, boxing the man in between Kragen and himself.

"One more thing." Oliver grabbed Webber's wrist. When Webber automatically jerked back, Sweeney clamped down on his shoulder, holding him in place with a viselike grip.

"I want to make sure they don't force your hand this time." Slowly, Oliver poured the cup of coffee into Webber's palm. Within moments, the hot liquid raised blisters. "Be diplomatic, Webber," he cautioned with noncommittal coolness.

Webber nodded, his jaw tightened against the pain until the skin turned white under his ruddy complexion. "And if the Renne woman doesn't want to cooperate?"

Oliver dropped the mercenary's wrist and tossed the cup to the ground. "Then be discreet."

Chapter Four

He wasn't dead. It took a moment for the thought to seep through. Another for the layers of fog to dissipate.

He surfaced gradually, registering the extent of his injuries. The throbbing at his temple, the ache over his brow. When his right arm refused to move when commanded, he shifted his shoulders no more than an inch. Pain rifled through him, setting off waves of nausea that rocked his belly, slapped at the back of his throat.

But his heart beat.

For a full minute, he concentrated on the rhythmic thumping, worked on breathing oxygen in and out of his lungs.

A keen sense of danger vibrated through him. But when his mind searched for details, he found nothing but the urge for caution. And an underlying edge of danger.

Slowly, he opened his eyes. The ceiling beams doubled, then danced before finally coming into focus. His gaze slid from the white ceiling to the white bandage on his shoulder.

With his good hand, he carefully searched the bed around him but found nothing. He let his arm fall back to his side. Molten heat blasted through his upper body, setting his shoulder and ribs on fire and telling him he'd been carelessly quick with the motion.

Cloth brushed leather, drawing his attention. Slowly, he turned his head. No more than four feet away, a woman straightened in the leather wingback chair. She uncurled her long legs in one slow, fluid movement. The morning light washed over her in soft pink rays, coating both her skin and pale blond hair in a hazy blush.

"You're awake." Her sleep-soaked voice reminded him of crushed velvet, rich and warm. But it was caramel-brown eyes that caught his attention. Carmel dusted with gold, he realized as she drew closer.

And edged with concern. Enough to tell him she'd spent the night in the chair.

"Is the pain bearable?" Her face was scrubbed clean, revealing a few freckles dotting her nose. With long, blond hair tied back into a ponytail and clad in jeans and a black, zipped hoodie two sizes too big, she looked no older than a first-year college student.

The back of her hand drifted over his cheek. Her cool, soft touch soothing. So much so that he felt a curious ache in his chest when it dropped away.

"No fever, thank goodness. How are you feeling?"

He caught her wrist with his good hand and jerked her closer. It was a mistake.

Skin pulled against stitching, bones ground against cartilage. A curse burst from his lips in a long, angry hiss.

"Where is it?" His question was barely a whisper. Dried bile coated his tongue in a thick paste, leaving his throat sandpaper-dry.

"Where is what?" she demanded. But a quick glance at

his shoulder kept her from tugging back. He didn't have to look because he felt it. Blood—thick and warm—seeped from his wound into the bandage, dampening the gauze against his skin.

"The 9 mm. Where is it?" he repeated, pushing his advantage. Whoever she was, she wasn't smart to let him see her concern.

"In the nightstand drawer. Both the gun and the two clips." Her temper surfaced, sharpening her tone.

He didn't take her word for it. Instead, he reached down with his bad arm—grunting at the shock of pain—then opened the drawer with his fingers.

But his actions took effort. Sweat beaded his forehead, his arm shook against her when he grabbed the pistol.

"Let go of my wrist." The fact she kept her words soft didn't diminish the anger behind them.

Or the concern.

Immediately, his hand dropped to the bed. More from weakness than her demand, he knew.

"Trust me, if I wanted you dead, I wouldn't have saved your butt last night." She rubbed her wrist.

Jacob resisted nodding, not wanting to set off another wave of dizziness. But he tightened his grip on his pistol. "What am I doing here?" His voice was no more than a croak.

She poured him a glass of water from a pitcher on the bedside stand and offered it to him. "Recovering."

When he didn't sit up, she lifted the glass to his lips. The cool water hit the back of his throat, immediately soothing the raw, burning heat. After he finished, she placed it back on the nightstand.

"What happened?" he murmured, resting his head back

against the pillow. The room tilted a little. That and the water made him queasy.

"You have a gunshot wound in your right shoulder, a forehead laceration and a concussion. You were lucky the bullet only caused minimal damage. We've stitched your wounds, but only rest will help the concussion," she explained, her voice softening once again with concern on the last few words.

First he digested her reaction, then her explanation. A bullet hole meant he'd lost a lot of blood. A hindrance, but not debilitating. "Who is we?"

"My father." She hesitated over the words, enough to obstruct any natural warmth in them. "He'll be back in a moment."

"How did I get shot?"

"I was hoping you could tell me."

The sunlight grew brighter, casting beams across the bed. When he grimaced, she crossed the room and pulled the curtains shut.

"And you are?"

She stopped midmotion, her eyes narrowing as they pinned him to the bed. "If you're trying to be funny, I suggest you work on your timing. Because whatever sense of humor I might have had, you destroyed it about five months ago."

What the hell was that supposed to mean? "Trust me, the only joke here is on me." His laugh was no more than a savage burst of air. "So why don't you tell me who you are and we'll go from there."

"Grace. Grace Renne."

Grace. He took in the serene features, the refined curves of her face that sloped into a slightly upturned nose, a dimpled chin and a mouth too wide to be considered movie-star perfect. But full enough to tempt a man, even a half-dead one like himself, to taste.

"You don't recognize me?" she asked. Disbelief—no, he corrected, distrust—lay under her question.

So she didn't trust him? Seemed fair enough, since he didn't trust her.

"Should I?" Vague images flickered, their edges too slippery to grasp. He focused beyond the disorientation, the fear that slithered from the dark void.

Again, he found nothing.

"Yes." She turned back to the curtain, took a moment to tuck the edges together until the sun disappeared. "We were friends. Once."

Her voice trailed in a husky murmur. A familiar bite caught him at the back of the spine. He swore under his breath.

"Once. We're not friends now?" He wasn't in the mood for cryptic answers or a prod from his libido. Obviously, his body needed no memories to react to its baser needs.

Sledgehammers beat at his temples, splitting his skull from ear to ear. He used the pain to block out her appeal.

"I'd like to think so," she responded. "What do you remember?"

"Not sure." Admitting he remembered nothing was out of the question. Clumsily, he shoved the thick, plaid comforter off him. Immediately the cool air took the heat and itch from his skin. She'd stripped him to his boxer briefs, he realized. Bruises tattooed most of his chest and stomach in dark hues of purple and brown.

He tried again, searching his mind until the headache

drove him back to the woman for answers. "A bullet didn't do all this damage," he remarked even as the void bore down on him with a suffocating darkness. He took a deep breath to clear his head, paid for it with a sharp slice of pain through his ribs.

"Feels like I've been hit by a train." Anger antagonized the helplessness, but something deeper, more innate, forced a whisper of caution through his mind.

"Someone tried to kill you last night." She spoke the words quickly, as if simple speed would blur the ugliness of them. "They almost succeeded."

Frustrated, he swung his legs over to the side of the bed before she could stop him. He fought through the vertigo and nausea. But the effort left him shaking.

"Where are my pants?" If he needed to move quickly, he didn't want to be naked doing it.

"You don't need them right now. You have a concussion." She glanced toward the door. "You need bed rest."

"What I need is my pants." He glanced up at her, saw the anxiety that tightened her lips, knit her brow. But once again, it was the fear dimming the light brown of her eyes that bothered him. He hardened himself against it.

The woman was definitely on edge. He tried a different tack. "Now," he ordered. For a moment, he was tempted to raise the gun, point it at her, but something inside stopped him.

As if she read his mind, she glanced from the weapon to his face, then surprised him by shaking her head. "You won't shoot me over a pair of pants."

"Don't bet on it," he growled. Right now, for two cents, he'd put a bullet through his own forehead just to relieve the pounding behind it.

"Then go ahead," she said before she swung around, leaving her back exposed. The movement cost her, he could see it in the rigid spine, the set of her shoulders. He'd scared the hell out of her but she didn't give an inch.

"Damn it." She had guts for calling his bluff, he gave her that. "All right, it seems I'm more civilized than I thought."

When she faced him, she didn't gloat.

She had smarts, too, he thought sarcastically.

He placed the gun on the nightstand beside him and ran his free hand over his face, ignoring the whiskers that scraped at his palm. "Look, for the time being, I'll accept the fact that you and I are…friends. But whoever did do this to me is still out there somewhere. And I assume they'll try again. Agreed?"

"Yes," she replied, if somewhat reluctantly.

"If I have to face them with no memory and very little strength, I'd at least like to have my pants on when I do it."

"Your pants and shirt were covered in blood. I burned them in the fireplace."

When he raised an eyebrow, she let out an exasperated breath. "Fine. There is a change of clothes for you in my closet."

She waved a hand toward the double doors beside a connecting bathroom. Another good idea, considering the state of his bladder.

But he'd be damned if he'd ask for help. He'd wait a moment for his legs to stop shaking. "Do I usually keep clothes in your closet?" he asked, knowing the answer would explain the pinch of desire he felt moments ago.

"You forgot them here," Grace explained and glanced toward the open bedroom door.

"And here is?"

"Annapolis." She paused for a moment, the small knit on her brow deepened. But when she brushed a stray hair from her cheek, the slight tremble of her fingers gave away her nervousness. She tucked her hands in her pockets. "You really don't remember, do you?"

"Right now, I don't even know what the hell my name is."

"Jacob Lomax."

He searched his mind for recognition. Found nothing that was familiar. His headache worsened, making it difficult to think. "How long have I been unconscious?"

"Since midnight last night." She glanced at the alarm clock on the nightstand. "Ten hours."

"Which makes today, what?"

"Tuesday. The twenty-third of September."

Slowly, he scanned the room, searching. The curtains and comforter, while a yellow plaid, were both trimmed with white lace. The latter was draped over a pine-slotted sleigh bed that sat more than three feet off the floor. Positioned across the room were its matching dresser and mirror.

Jacob studied his image. The blade-sharp cheekbones, the strong, not-quite-square jaw, covered with no more than a day's worth of whiskers. He rubbed his knuckles against the stubble on one cheek, hollowed more from fatigue he imagined than from pain. A bruise dominated the high forehead, spilled over in a tinge of purple by the deep set eyes of vivid blue.

No flashes of recognition. No threads of familiarity. Nothing more than the image of a stranger staring back.

His focus shifted down. Assorted lotions and powders cluttered the top of the dresser, along with a few scattered papers and a stack of books.

Packing boxes sat opened on the floor. Some were full, others half-empty, but most lay flat, their sides collapsed.

"You're moving?"

"Yes—"

"You're awake." A man entered the room, the black bag in his hand and the stethoscope around his neck identifying him as a doctor.

Grace met the older man halfway across the room. Jacob deliberately said nothing and waited. But his hand shifted closer to the gun beside him.

Her father was on the smaller side of sixty, with a leanness that came with time on a tennis court, not a golf course. His hair was white and well groomed, combed back from a furrowed brow.

After a few murmured words, he patted her shoulder, then approached the bed. "Jacob, my name is Doctor Renne. Grace tells me you don't remember what happened."

"That's right." Since the older man didn't ask Jacob if he remembered him, Jacob assumed they'd never met.

"How's the headache?" Doctor Renne pulled a penlight from his pocket and clicked it on. He shined the light in Jacob's eyes. First one, then the other. The bright flash set off another series of sledgehammers. He winced. "Bearable."

"Look up...now down." Another flash, another jolt of pain.

"How did I get here?"

"Since there was no car, we assumed you walked. Grace discovered you on her porch last night." The doctor clicked the light off and tucked it back into his inside pocket. "Stay focused on my finger without turning your head."

Jacob followed the doctor's finger, this time ignoring the pull of discomfort behind his eyes.

"There's definite improvement." The doctor waved his daughter over to the bed. "Grace, I'll need your help. I want to check his shoulder."

They eased Jacob back against the headboard. The doctor examined the bandage. "There's blood. You're moving around too much. I didn't spend hours stitching you up for you to take it apart in five minutes."

"Thanks, Doc. I'll remember that," Jacob commented wryly. "I'd tell you where to send the bill if I knew where I lived."

"Your driver's license says Los Angeles, California," Charles answered. "Seems you're a long way from home."

Home? Why did the address, even the word, sound so foreign?

Grace leaned over to adjust his pillow. A light floral scent drifted toward him. For a moment he tried to identify the flower, but came up with nothing. Still the fragrance was distinctive. Feminine. Clean.

"Do you remember a woman named Helene Garrett?" Grace asked without looking up.

Frames of shadow and light passed through Jacob's mind, but nothing he could zero in on, nothing to bring into focus. "No, but…" Suddenly, a snapshot—vivid but brief—flashed across his mind. A woman laughing. Her cheeks and nose pink from the falling snow. Her smile wide, her eyes brimming with…happiness?

No, he realized suddenly. Not happiness.

Love.

Chapter Five

"You." Jacob nodded slightly toward Grace, then frowned. "I see you."

"From last night or this morning?" The doctor asked, then took Jacob's wrist and checked the younger man's pulse against his watch.

"From a ski trip." Jacob closed his eyes, for a moment, trying to bring the image back. "I remember her hovering over me." When he opened them again, he caught the surprise in the doctor's features.

The doctor didn't know about me. Jacob decided not to mention how the scent of her shampoo triggered the memory. Not until he understood more.

"You were skiing? Where?"

Grace nearly groaned aloud at her father's questions. When she'd found out she was pregnant, she'd told him the father of the baby was no one he knew. Just someone she'd met skiing.

Lifting her chin, she met her father's glare head-on. "In Aspen. A few times."

When her father said nothing, her gaze shifted from him to Jacob. But her smile was forced, her teeth on edge. "You fell the first time we were there." What she didn't add is that he had faked the fall, pulled her into the snow and spent the next twenty minutes kissing her breathless.

She hugged her arms to her chest and walked over to the window.

She didn't want to see the anger—the disappointment—emanating from her father.

"Who's Helene Garrett?" Jacob's question snapped the thread of tension between father and daughter.

"A business associate of yours. And my partner. Ex-partner. She introduced us," Grace admitted reluctantly, but she continued to stare out the window. The bay's waves crashed against the sand and dock, not quite over its temper from the night before. She'd stayed awake all night helping her dad, jumping at every sound the wind and rain made. But no one came after her. No one pounded on the door or jumped from the shadows.

Hide, Grace. Before they kill you. The words floated through her mind for the thousandth time. But was the threat real or a side effect to his amnesia?

"Someone shot and killed Helene last night outside our bar." Grace could feel Jacob's eyes on her, studying her like some specimen in a jar. Something he'd done while they dated. Before his habit unnerved her, now it just annoyed her.

Amnesia. Her nerves endings snapped and crackled. She didn't believe him at first, but that lasted only a few moments. Admittedly, she had expected Jacob to clear up the confusion—the fear—that plagued her all night. How can you fight your enemies when you have no idea who they are? Or hadn't known they even existed until only hours before?

"And you assume because I took a bullet, I was there, too," Jacob said coolly.

He wasn't asking a question, but her father answered anyway. "It's a logical assumption."

"Did Helene have a gun on her?" Jacob asked, his tone flat.

"Yes, but you didn't shoot her. And she didn't put that bullet in your shoulder, either. The two of you were very close," Grace insisted, but she didn't face him. Not yet. Not when her emotions could be seen in her expression. The doubt, the fear. Everything in her being told her he wouldn't harm Helene. She had to believe that, for now. "You might not remember who you are, but I know what kind of man you are. And you aren't a murderer."

"Well, for all our sakes, I hope you're right," Jacob replied grimly.

"I am." Her chin lifted, defiant; she was under control again. She was betting her life on it. More importantly, their child's life. "How long do you think his memory loss will last, Dad?"

The doctor had remained quiet. She swung around, challenging. "Dad?"

"I can't give you a definitive answer, Grace. We're dealing with the brain. Anything can happen. The concussion, while it's nothing to dismiss, doesn't appear serious enough to have caused permanent damage. Of course, I would prefer to order him to undergo some tests and a day or more of observation to be sure." The words came out rigid, censured. "Without them, I believe we're dealing with more of a dissociative amnesia. A loss of memory due to a shock rather than an injury to the brain."

"Traumatic as in Helene's murder," Jacob replied. "So this is mental rather than physical."

"In my opinion, yes," Charles answered, but he prodded

Jacob's head wound, checking it. "If that's the case, my guess is that your memory will return in bits and pieces over the course of time." Her father took off his stethoscope and placed it in his bag.

"What span of time?"

"There is no telling how much will come back or how long it will take."

"He remembered his gun," Grace commented. "First thing when he woke up."

Dr. Renne glanced at Jacob, surprised. "You did?"

"Yes." He flexed his right hand, spreading his fingers. "I know I've been trained to use it. Even if I don't remember the when and the why." The confidence reverberated deep within him, hollow echoes from an empty void.

"That explains the other marks you're sporting. Two bullet scars on your back and a six-inch knife scar on your hip."

Charles Renne moved from the bed, his bag in hand. "Some traits—like combat training or studied languages—will surface instinctively. But most memories are triggered by emotions, reactions, physical evidence. A scent. A song. Any number of things. Experiencing them might eventually help your recollection, but there are no guarantees."

"He also remembered my name. Last night, before he passed out, he called me by my name," Grace inserted.

"If that's true, why don't I remember you now?" Jacob asked.

"Something must have happened while you were unconscious. Your brain could've just shut down from the emotional shock," Charles said. "If that's the case, your mind will decide if and when it's ready to remember."

"If?"

"There's always the chance you might not regain any of your memories," Charles indicated. "Especially those from last night."

Jacob considered the doctor's words. The sense of danger intensified after the mention of Helene Garrett. Could he have killed a woman he considered a friend? There was no doubt he had killed before. The certainty of it resonated through him.

Obviously, some things amnesia couldn't erase.

"I can make arrangements—"

"No, Dad. No arrangements. If he isn't wanted for murder, he soon will be."

"He carries a gun, Grace. One that might be a murder weapon. Do realize the implications of that?"

"Do you mean to your reputation or to my safety?"

"For once in your life, don't be irresponsible," Charles retorted impatiently. "So far this morning, we've been fortunate. It won't take long for the police to show up on your doorstep. Then what will you do?" Charles's gaze dropped to her stomach. "It's not just you I'm concerned for. You're not thinking about—"

"We agreed last night that it's not your decision."

"I'm required by law to report a gunshot wound," Charles snapped. "If I don't, I could lose my practice."

"Do what you have to do, Dad," she answered, the truth lying bitter against her tongue. It wasn't the first time she'd defied him. But a few moments earlier, when his eyes moved from her stomach back to her face, it was the first time she'd ever seen fear etched in his features.

"Damn it, Grace. I don't want to turn this into the same old argument. The man was shot. Your friend was killed.

This is not about the fact that once again I'm choosing my practice over—"

"Over what? Me?" Grace rubbed the back of her neck, trying to loosen the tension. Even she couldn't ask him to go against his oath. "You're right, Dad." She sighed. "I put you in this position with my phone call and I'm sorry." The words were sad, made so by their unending conflict. "But I'm not going to budge on my decision, either. He stays with me until we figure this out."

Jacob had been about to agree with the doctor. No matter who he was, hiding behind a woman wasn't acceptable. But the undercurrent of emotion in the room changed his mind. Something wasn't being said and Jacob wanted to know what it was. Better to wait and get the information from the daughter.

"I'm safer with Jacob. Trust me, Dad." When he said nothing, she added, "Please."

Finally, it was Charles who turned away. "The pain is going to get worse. You're going to need morphine in a short while, Jacob. Enough to take the edge off. I can give you some but I have to go get the prescription filled." He closed his bag and turned to his daughter. "I'll be back in an hour."

The threat was there, Jacob knew. He had less than an hour to find out what the hell was going on.

Chapter Six

"Why didn't you tell him?"

"Tell him what?" Jacob asked.

"That you won't take the morphine he's bringing back."

She was right, of course. He couldn't risk being doped up if trouble started. "For a person who doesn't know me, you understand me pretty well," he commented dryly.

"One doesn't discount the other," she countered. Her gazed drifted over his face. "You've lost weight."

"Really?" Jacob's mouth twisted derisively. "I wouldn't know."

"Yes, well—"

"I didn't tell him I didn't want the morphine because I thought you needed some breathing room," he lied. "But I agree with your father, Grace."

"A man you just met."

"Technically, I've just met you, too."

Her body grew rigid. "You remembered Aspen."

He'd hurt her with his comment. A vulnerability he could take advantage of, if needed. "I stand corrected."

"For the record, I agree with my father, too." At Jacob's raised eyebrow, she added, "To a certain point. But that doesn't mean I can do what he wants. We need to get you out of here before he gets back."

"We?"

"I have to find out what happened last night and you're my only lead to the answers."

"I thought I was to have bed rest."

"I couldn't risk his overhearing anything else," she said impatiently. "He would've stopped us. You're not safe here."

"What if I don't ever remember, Grace?" When she didn't answer, he continued, "Why not let the police handle it?"

"They can't be trusted. Not yet. Not until we find out who killed Helene. Don't you see?"

"If I remember right, the police are the ones who find murderers."

Her head snapped up, and what he saw was genuine fear. "Not if they've already decided on a suspect."

"Me." When he tried to maneuver his feet to the floor, she placed a hand against his good shoulder.

"Please, let me help you. If you move too fast, you could break open the stitching." Before he could stop them, her fingers drifted across his skin.

He caught her wrist, but this time with gentle fingers. His intent was to stop her, but the action brought her closer.

He caught her scent, breathed it in. Without thought, his thumb skimmed her pulse. When it jumped, his did, too. Slowly, he pulled her toward him until her hand rested against his chest. Her eyes met his and what he saw made him stop. The desire was there, but more than that, he saw panic.

He let her go. "I'm not so weak I can't put a pair of pants on."

Pink flushed her cheeks, but from embarrassment or temper, he wasn't sure.

She stepped back, letting her hands drop to her sides, but not before she made them into fists.

Temper, then.

When she walked to the closet, her actions were fluid, almost regal. And when she yanked open the door, he almost smiled.

She skimmed the hangers with her hand, pulled out a pair of slacks and a sweater. Judging from the high-end material of the charcoal V-neck sweater and the black chino slacks, he wasn't hurting for money.

"These should do."

"I guess they will." When he reached to take the hangers from her, pain exploded in his shoulder. He swore and grabbed at his arm, locking it to his side. "I'm going to need your car."

She tossed the clothes onto the corner of the bed. "Don't be stupid. You're not in any condition to drive."

He had to give the woman credit; she did snooty with a certain sex appeal.

"You're going to need someone to get you around."

Pointedly, he glanced at his gun. "I have a feeling I'm pretty self-sufficient."

But what he wasn't was flush. He needed cash.

Money, he knew, would open many more doors. "Did I have a wallet?"

She picked a slim, brown wallet from the dresser and handed it to him. "There's almost a thousand dollars, a few credit cards and your driver's license in there."

Instead of opening the billfold, Jacob laid it on the bed beside him. He'd search through it after she left the room.

"Now, do you want my help dressing?"

"No, I can handle it myself." He was in no mood to deal with the fluttery touch of her hands against him again.

"There's a brand-new toothbrush in the bathroom's medicine cabinet and fresh towels on the rack," she noted, then walked over and turned on the bathroom light for him. "You're not strong enough yet to take a shower. And even if you think you are, you can't risk getting your bandages wet."

"I'll manage." He leaned back against the headboard and studied her through half-closed eyes.

"You didn't take me to the hospital because I'd be vulnerable." The fear was back with his statement, tightening her features, only for a heartbeat but long enough for him to see. And understand.

"Running will only protect me for so long. And like your father said, puts you at risk whether you're with me or not."

"I told you I want answers. And once your memory returns I'll get them," she replied. "And I'm hoping neither of us will need protection."

"About my other scars." When her eyebrow lifted in question, he clarified. "You wouldn't know how I acquired them, would you?"

"No. We were never that close," she replied evenly. But at what cost, he thought.

"Then why is it that little bits I am remembering seem to revolve around you?" Even without her reaction to him a few minutes prior, his instincts were telling him they'd been intimate. The tightening of his groin, the itch at the base of his spine, told him that if he didn't watch himself, they just might be again.

"Maybe because I knew Helene."

"Maybe," he replied, but he didn't believe it. "Do you have a picture of her?"

"Yes." She went to her dresser and slid open the top drawer. After a moment of digging, she pulled out a newspaper photo. She crossed the room and gave it to Jacob. "This was taken the day we opened The Tens. Our bar. Her bar," she corrected, then sighed. "Actually, I have no idea whose bar it is now."

"We need to find out," he decided. "Could be the new owner wanted a premature switching of titles and I got in the way." He studied the picture. It was a waist-to-head shot. Even with that, Jacob could tell the woman was tall and on the athletic side but not enough to detract from her overall femininity. He glanced at the deep cut of the buttoned jacket with no blouse to ruin the sleek, cool effect of the navy business suit.

One of Helene's arms was casually looped around Grace's shoulders. Her hair was a deep red, spiked softly around the sharp angles of her cheeks, emphasizing a long nose, its feminine point.

"Do you recognize her?"

"No," he said, taking one last look before glancing up. "Can I keep this?"

When she nodded, he placed it by his wallet.

"Do you need help to the bathroom?"

He contemplated the wide span of hardwood floor between him and the bathroom door. "I can manage," he said and hoped he was right.

"Then I'll make you some toast. And some coffee." She turned to leave.

He waited until she reached the door. "Grace. Were you telling the truth earlier? Are you absolutely sure I didn't kill Helene?"

She hesitated for a moment, her hand clenched on the doorknob. "I'm not absolutely sure of anything. Least of all, you."

JACOB COULDN'T SAY he felt better, but he felt more human after cleaning up and putting on clean clothes. The itch was off his skin and his stomach had settled. His shoulder and head still throbbed, but he managed to find some aspirin in her cabinet. He'd found a razor and new blades also, but decided against a shave. No use causing more damage with a shaky hand.

Like the bedroom, the bath had a decidedly feminine appeal. The combination hardwood floor and bead-board paneling presented a casual coziness that was only emphasized by a pedestal sink, distressed vanity and an eclectic collection of candles.

Curious, Jacob grabbed the shampoo from the corner of the bathtub. He took a whiff, then read the bottle. Honeysuckle.

A small mystery solved.

For the first time, he simply focused on the facts of his situation and systematically sorted through what he'd learned over the last half hour.

In his mind, he saw flashes of pictures. From parks to fields to coliseums. He couldn't bring names to mind, or locations. He couldn't say if he'd been to these locations or merely seen them in photos or on television. They held no connection to him on any level.

The only thing, only person who seemed familiar to him was Grace.

A lead—his only instinctive lead. One he planned on pursuing.

The coffee aroma hit him as he stepped out of the bedroom. "Smells good."

The neutral colors, the rustic pine floors triggered no memories, but this time he hadn't expected them to. "How often have I been here?"

"Many times. Too many to count."

The walk to the kitchen caused his legs to shake. Enough that he was grateful for the stool when he slid onto it.

"Go ahead and have some while I get things together." She placed a travel mug in front of him, along with a plate with toast. "You liked your coffee black."

He lifted the mug. "Let's see if I still do." When he took a swig, the heat of it punched him in the belly. Enough to make him grunt and draw a slanted look from Grace. "It's good. Thanks."

"You're welcome." She grabbed two chocolate chip cookies from a nearby plate.

"So, do you and your father disagree often?"

"No more often than most fathers and daughters." She came around the counter and leaned a hip against the side. "I turned on the news while you were getting dressed and checked my computer. The shooting wasn't mentioned on either."

"You just changed the subject."

"You noticed." She took a bite of her cookie, chewed, then waved the remaining piece like a pointer. "Helene's death should have made the morning news."

"A murder would be hard to keep out of the press," he reasoned, even as a cookie crumb settled on her cheek, distracting him. "But the police have done it before."

Giving in to the urge, he leaned in and brushed the crumb away with the pad of his thumb. But instead of keeping the touch light, the gesture simple, he found himself cupping her face in his palm—told himself that he was only searching for memories. Answers.

"Jacob—"

"Shh." His thumb stopped her mouth, midmotion, leaving her lips slightly parted. He slipped between to the warm smooth touch of her teeth, felt her intake of breath rush over his skin—

The doorbell sounded, jolting them both apart.

Jacob swore, low and mean. His body went rigid, his hand already reaching for the gun in his back waistband. "Your father?"

"He wouldn't ring the bell," she answered, trying to get her heart back down from her throat. Not from the interruption but from the realization that in another minute, probably less if she were honest, she'd have been in Jacob's arms.

"Is your car out front?"

"Yes. It's parked under my carport."

"Then you'd better answer." Jacob's face turned cold, almost savage. The fact he reached for his gun only fed her trepidation.

"Leave my plate. It will look like you're eating breakfast alone. I'll wait in the bedroom," he whispered while he checked his clip. "But I'll be watching, so no worries." This time when he cupped her cheek, it was for reassurance. "You'll be okay. Just stay calm."

After Jacob disappeared into the bedroom, she walked slowly to the front door.

A second chime rang out just as she peered through the peephole. Two men stood on her front porch, both dressed in navy-blue suits, both holding badges in their hand. The law enforcement insignias glared in the sunlight.

"Who is it?"

"Annapolis Police, Miss Renne. We need to speak with you."

Her hand tightened reflexively on the knob. She glanced at the closed bedroom, unlocked the dead bolt and opened the front door. "Can I help you?"

"Miss Renne?" At her nod, the thinner of the two, a nearly bald man with a flat face and heavy eyelids, stepped forward.

"I'm Detective Webber." He pointed to his partner, a man with steroid-typical muscles packed into a tailored suit and crisp, white shirt. "This is Detective Sweeney. We're both with the Annapolis Police. Homicide Division."

"How are you, Miss Renne?" Sweeney's smile was a grim line but it was his gaze that drew her attention. Gray eyes studied her from under two rather thick eyebrows, before shifting past her shoulder to sweep the room behind her.

Grace resisted the urge to shut the door. "Fine, but uncertain how I can help you, Detective."

First one, then the other flipped his badge closed and pocketed it. "Can we talk to you about Helene Garrett?" Sweeney asked, his gaze back on hers.

"My bar manager called me earlier about her death and I'm really not up to answering any questions just now."

"You mean your ex-manager, don't you?" Sweeney placed his foot in the doorway. "It's either here or downtown, Miss Renne. Your choice," he advised. His tone, while professional, left her with no alternative but to believe him. "We have a murderer on the loose. What happened to your friend wasn't a robbery or an accident. And I'm sure you would want her killer caught as soon as possible."

"Of course, I do."

"The longer we wait, the less chance we have of catching him." Sweeney pushed against the door with his knee with just enough pressure to emphasize his point—if she wanted them to get physical, they would.

"All right, gentlemen." Grace released the door, allowing the two men to enter. She led them to the middle of the room, but didn't offer them a seat. "How can I help you?"

"You can start by telling us where you were last night at approximately eleven o'clock." Webber fished under his suit and pulled out a notebook and pen.

"I was here baking cookies." She gestured to the plate on the counter.

Neither man glanced over. "Was anyone here with you?" Webber continued.

"I'm afraid not."

"Did Helene Garrett have any enemies? Anyone who might have wanted her dead?" Sweeney asked. Once again those gray eyes skimmed the room, touching on the closed bedroom door before moving over to the window and back to Grace.

Grace shifted until she blocked his line of sight. "No one that I know of."

"How about her friends?" Webber remarked, his frustration breaking through. "Do you know anyone who was close enough to Miss Garrett to give some insight into the last few days of her life?"

"Helene didn't have friends, she had business acquaintances. Too many for me to know."

"You mean to tell us that after three years of being partners, you have no idea how Helene Garrett conducted her life? Who she associated with? Can't make a guess at who could have killed her?"

Grace hesitated.

Are you absolutely sure I didn't kill Helene?

No.

She put her hands in her sweatshirt pouch and pressed her palms against her stomach. She felt the weight of her baby against the burden of her decision.

The police would do their best to keep her safe. But she understood deep down that their best would not be good enough.

"I'm telling you exactly that, Detective Webber," she said. "Helene was a private person. She didn't share much about herself with anyone. And I wasn't her only partner. Her capital was tied into many business ventures."

"We're finding that out," Sweeney admitted wryly. "You recently sold your half of the club to her, right?"

"That's right."

"Did you know the new owner is Jacob Lomax? He was one of those business acquaintances you mentioned earlier." The shock of Sweeney's statement nearly shattered her rigid hold. But then Webber smiled with venom and Grace's nervousness gave way to anger.

"No, I didn't know Mr. Lomax was the new owner, but I'm not surprised."

"How well did you know him?"

"Not very well at all. In fact, I didn't remember him until you just mentioned his name. I met him briefly, about eight months ago, but shared no more than a handshake." Grace and Jacob had kept their affair private. But if the police dug deep enough, they would discover the truth.

"Even if I had known, it wouldn't have mattered." She nodded at the boxes in the living room. "As you can see, I'm moving. Out of state, actually. And I didn't want to manage a business long-distance. Helene understood that."

"Can I ask why you are moving?" Sweeney walked over to the nearest box and lifted the flap.

Grace swallowed a nasty comment about minding his own business. "A change of climate."

"When was last time you saw her?" Sweeney asked, before returning. He glanced over to the counter, took in the breakfast dishes.

Another lie was there on the tip of her tongue. But too many people could have known about their meeting the day before. "Yesterday at the bistro down on Main. We had lunch together. A farewell of sorts."

"Do you mind?" He nodded toward the cookies.

"Not at all."

"Thanks." Sweeney helped himself to a cookie, took a bite and nodded his approval. "You and Miss Garrett parted on good terms?"

"Yes, we did." The hair prickled at her nape. There was no doubt in her mind that Jacob was observing her conversation with the detectives. "Is that all, gentlemen?"

"For now." Sweeney finished his cookie in one more bite, then reached into his suit pocket and pulled out a business card. "If you think of anything else that might help us, please contact me."

Grace didn't take the card from him fast enough and it dropped between them. Sweeney bent down to retrieve it and paused, his eyes on the hardwood floor. "Miss Renne, did I mention that Helene Garrett managed to shoot her killer just before she died?"

"No, Detective. You didn't. But I don't see how that—"

"There are bloodstains on your floor."

Grace followed his line of vision. More than a few red streaks smeared the varnished cherrywood. Marks she'd missed in her hasty cleanup the night before. "Those are mine. I cut my foot yesterday on some broken glass. I must have missed a few spots when I cleaned up."

Sweeney automatically looked at her bare feet. "There's no bandage."

"It was a small cut." Her chin lifted. "I'm not going to show you the bottom of my feet, Detective."

"She's lying," Webber inserted, obviously pleased by the prospect. He shoved his notebook back into his pocket.

Indignation worked its way into her words. "You honestly cannot think that I'm somehow involved in Helene's death—"

"You're right, I don't." Sweeney stood, scuffed the stains with his foot. "Where is he?"

Webber took a threatening step toward Grace. Out of sheer willpower, she stood her ground.

"Where is who?"

The blow came from out of nowhere. Pain ripped through her cheek, burst behind her eyes. She staggered back, just managing to keep herself from hitting the floor.

"My partner is much more polite than I am," Webber warned. "Where is Jacob Lomax?"

Grace straightened, her legs shaking. She could taste blood on her lip, but her hand automatically went to her belly. "I told you I haven't seen the man in months."

When Webber raised his fist again, a gun exploded from behind Grace. Screaming, the big man doubled over, one meaty hand wrapped around the other. Blood oozed through his fingers and dripped to the floor.

"Move, Grace." The words came low and mean. Grace automatically stepped out of reach, giving Jacob an unobstructed view of the two men.

"Looking for me?" With one shoulder against the doorsill, Jacob shifted his 9 mm slightly until it pointed at Sweeney. Jacob's face hardened into savage lines.

Slowly, Sweeney raised his arms away from his sides, but shock flickered across his face before he masked it. "I am if you're Lomax."

"That's what I hear."

"You son of a bitch," Webber wheezed. He slumped to his knees and cradled his injured hand to his chest. "You just shot a police officer."

Jacob let out a derisive snort, ignoring Webber's gasps of pain. "Most cops don't hit potential female witnesses. Or wear suits that cost more than a year's salary."

Sweat broke out on Jacob's forehead. Grace could see the tremors in his left hand and understood he wouldn't stay standing very long.

He tilted his gun, just a bit to put Sweeney's chest in his crosshairs. "Want to try telling me who you both really are?"

"We work for a private investor that is extremely interested in your relationship with Helene Garrett," Sweeney answered, cautious.

"And this is how you get your information?" Jacob mocked. Out of his peripheral vision, he caught Grace wiping the blood from her lip. Rage strained against reason, pushing the limit of his control. "I think you boys need to work on your approach."

With a growl, Webber grabbed for his gun. Jacob fired and Webber stumbled back. Blood flooded from the man's neck.

He struggled, groping the wound with his hands even as he crumpled choking on his own blood.

Sweeney charged Grace. Reacting swiftly, she slid on her hip, taking out his legs and toppled Sweeney like a bowling pin.

Jacob slammed his pistol into Sweeney's head, knocking him out cold. "Let's see how you like headaches," he murmured, then dropped to his knees, shaking.

"Jacob!" Grace sat beside him. Immediately, she found herself drawn tight against his side. "I thought—"

"Are you all right?"

"Yes." Grace leaned into him, grasped his sweater in one hand to make sure he didn't pull away. Finding reassurance. Just for a moment, she buried her face against his chest. He smelled of soap. Basic. Clean. Reassuring against the heavy metallic scent of blood that already thickened the air.

"Do you need help?" she asked.

"Not yet." He blew air out through his mouth, trying to get a grip on his rolling stomach, his shaking limbs. "Who in the hell taught you how to take someone down like that?"

"You did." She tried to smile, but her lips wobbled. "That day in the snow."

Chapter Seven

"Looks like you were right." Jacob found handcuffs on Webber's belt and snapped them on Sweeney's wrists. "Do you have any cash?"

"About a hundred dollars."

"Make sure you grab it," he ordered. "And your keys."

The scent of blood grew to a sickening stench. Grace glanced down at Webber, his face now a contorted death mask of crimson. His expensive suit was no more than a soggy towel saturated with his blood.

With effort, she took a few deep breaths through her mouth to avoid the scent, drive away the nausea.

"Are you going to faint on me?"

"No." She dug her nails into her palm to prove it.

Swearing, he grabbed a throw from the couch and covered Webber's body. "That's the best I can do for you, Grace."

"Thank you." Her voice quivered, but with Webber covered, the queasiness started to fade. "Aren't we going to question Sweeney?"

"Questioning a prisoner takes stamina. I don't have any right now." He checked the two men's pockets, pulled out their wallets. "Let's see if they are who they said they were." He took out the badges. "Fake. Crafted well, though."

"How do you know?" Her panic faded under curiosity.

"Just do." Jacob shrugged, storing the information away for later. He was working on instinct and right now it was telling him to move. "But like my weapons training, I couldn't tell you how long I've had the knowledge or where I picked it up from."

He took the money from each of the wallets. "Whoever pays them pays them well. They're carrying over three thousand between the two of them." He handed her the cash. "We're going to need this. Credit cards put us out on the information grid."

"You were carrying almost as much in your wallet."

"Maybe we have the same boss," he answered derisively.

"Sweeney was in charge. If that's his real name. Anyone with this caliber of forgeries, probably works under a dozen different aliases." He patted a few more pockets until he found their keys and cell phones. He glanced at the phones. "All the numbers are deleted. These boys knew what they were doing. Still, if his boss decides to call, I want to be available." He pocketed Sweeney's cell phone, then handed Webber's phone to her.

"Crush it." Jacob's face paled to a sickly gray; his lips were bloodless. A sheen of perspiration covered his skin, dampened his hair. "I'd like to know what the hell they want from me."

Grace stomped on the phone, shattering it. If he was placing his life on the line, the least he deserved was the truth. "It's not you they want, Jacob."

"Say that again."

"It's not you," she repeated, grinding the last of the phone under her heel. "It's me."

He sat back. "Go on. I'm listening."

"Last night, you were still conscious when I found you. In fact, you knocked on the door, then collapsed on the porch."

She rubbed the back of her neck, suddenly feeling the weight of the world there. "You told me to hide. That someone wanted to kill me."

"I didn't say who."

"No. You didn't."

"Grace, Sweeney came looking for me. Not you."

Startled, she could only look at him. "You're right. He wasn't concerned with me at all. But that doesn't make sense."

"It does if we're dealing with two separate problems," he reasoned.

"You mean we're being chased by two different people?" She dropped to her knees, her hands braced on her legs. Her gaze was fixed on his. "But it still doesn't answer why whoever wants me came after you and Helene first. I can be found by anyone who has a phone book."

"Maybe someone chased me to your house and I was afraid you would get in the way," he reasoned. "Or maybe I was just delirious from my head injury."

"No, the threat was real," Grace argued. "I'm sure of it."

"And since I brought the message, you think you can trust me to help you?"

She looked pointedly at his shoulder. "That's what friends do," she whispered. "Besides, who else can I trust if it isn't the guy who warned me?"

After a moment, he nodded. "Okay, pal, grab whatever you can hold in your pockets. We don't have time for anything else." Jacob tossed Sweeney's keys under her couch. He was standing by the time she returned from the bedroom. "What kind of car do you drive?"

"A Jag," she shouted from the bedroom. "I filled the tank yesterday."

"Good. We might need something with some power."

She pushed her wallet into her sweatshirt pocket and phone into the back of her jeans. She grabbed her keys off the counter.

Before she could react, he opened the front door and fired a few bullets into Sweeney's tires. "How well can you drive?"

She glanced at the deflated tires and thought of Webber. "Better than you can shoot."

THE JAG WAS THE COLOR of hot salsa, with saber-chromed wheels and butter-cream leather seats. If a car could preen, this one would have a reason.

"Nice ride." Drained, Jacob shifted back into the passenger seat. The throb in his shoulder took on an edge of heat. He shifted using the armrest to brace his bad shoulder. What he needed was some time to regain strength and to sort through their situation.

"Thanks. That's what you said when you helped me pick it out."

"I did?"

"I wasn't lying to you," she replied. "We were friends." But like *father,* he noted, she infused no warmth into the word *friend.*

"Were we more than friends?" It seemed natural to cock his head, lift one eyebrow.

"No," she said, but with enough hesitation to feed his doubt.

"Am I gay?"

Her lips curled into a tolerant smile. "No."

"Are you?"

She laughed then. "No."

He decided he liked her laugh. It rolled through her, erupting in a slightly breathless chuckle. He realized he wanted to hear it again.

Her gaze turned to the road and he used the opportunity to take a long look. He took in the slope of her neck, the pulse at the base of her throat. A flush crept up over her cheeks, telling him she was aware of his scrutiny, but Jacob continued to study her nonetheless.

He'd distanced himself from his emotions, accepting the situation. Though, even at its best, it was nothing more than a maze of smoke and mirrors.

But something inside—an echo of what was, or what could've been—kept him from gaining that same emotional distance from her.

"You're sure we weren't more to each other?"

"Yes," she said, exasperated. The pulse quickened, the flush darkened. Her response was more than a little breathless, but this time there was no chuckle.

Did her reaction mean they had been involved and she was lying, or she'd thought about it and was embarrassed? Self-preservation either way, Jacob decided. And that he could understand.

"What happened?" This time the push wasn't for the truth, but for the reaction. Damn, he found her blush charming.

"Nothing really. You left."

He rested his head against the window, enjoyed the cool

glass against the pounding in his temple. "What do you mean? Did I leave the state? Or leave the country?"

"Both." *You left me,* Grace thought, keeping her pride intact but at the cost of another crack in her heart.

"So why did I leave?"

"I don't know." At least in that Grace could be truthful. She downshifted, taking a hairpin turn with the ease of a race car driver. She heard his reluctant grunt of approval. "You never explained. One day you were here, the next you weren't."

"Can't say I was a very good friend, then."

"You had no reason to be, really." She stopped the ache that threatened to harden the edges of her response. Just.

"How long had we known each other?"

"Not long," Grace hesitated, pretending to do the calculations. "Two months. Almost three." Eighty-one days.

Jacob realized she was choosing her words very carefully. A person only did that when they didn't want to offend or, more importantly, wanted to defend. From the white-knuckled grip she had on the steering wheel, he tended to believe her choice was the latter.

"I had accidentally interrupted a business meeting between you and Helene. I didn't know you were in our office and I burst through the door all excited about a jazz band I had just booked. One we'd been trying to get for months. She introduced us."

Helene again. Shooting Sweeney's partner had showed Jacob he was capable of killing. He'd felt no remorse, not even a twinge of regret. Webber needed killing. Period. But somehow Helene's murder didn't sit right. Almost as if murdering her didn't fit his sense of self.

"What you told Sweeney about Helene, was it true?"

"More or less," she acknowledged. "We had lunch together and she gave me the final copies of our sales contract. We ate. We laughed. We hugged. We cried a little, then said goodbye."

"What did you talk about?"

"Business details. Plans to meet again," Grace said, then glanced in his direction. "You."

"What about me?"

"She told me she was meeting you later that night and wanted to know if I had a message to pass on." Actually, Helene had threatened to tell Jacob about the baby. "I said no."

"I see." Grace's fingers flexed against the steering wheel. "Did anyone stop by your table?"

"Only the waiter," she said. "But he's been there forever."

"How about her demeanor? Did she seem angry? Afraid?"

"No—" She stopped. "Wait. When I came back from the bathroom after we ate, she seemed…" Grace thought for a moment. "Impatient."

"She could've been spooked."

"Or she could've had a hard time saying goodbye."

"Maybe. But if she kept herself distant, why would she be upset?"

"At least she said goodbye." The retort was out of her mouth before she could stop it. "I'm sorry, that was unfair."

"Why? Because I don't remember?"

Her lips smoothed out into a grin. "Well, it does put you at a disadvantage, doesn't it?"

"I suppose it does." Then seriously, he added, "I'd like to think I had a good reason, Grace. Maybe it even has something to do with what we're in now. But either way, if and when I do remember, I'll tell you everything."

Grace shook her head. "I don't expect you to—"

"I know," he said quietly. "Why would Helene leave me the bar?"

"She trusted you."

"But why didn't she leave it to you?"

"I told her I wasn't coming back to Maryland."

"Did Helene give you anything? Warn you about anything?"

"Nothing," she answered. "I told you, it was like every other lunch we've had together. Other than saying goodbye, of course."

"Did Helene ever talk about me? I mean, before the lunch?"

"No. Never. Her business was her business."

"Yet you trusted her."

"Implicitly," Grace said without hesitation.

"Why?"

"I don't know. Instinct, I guess."

"Is that why we became friends? Because you instinctively like me?"

"You could be charming when you wanted to be." Again there was no hesitation.

He watched the roadside for a moment. A few mailboxes, some scattered buildings. Remote, but not so remote a person had to travel far for food or fuel. "It's frustrating. I know this road, yet I'd swear to you that I've never seen it before."

Grace laid her hand on his thigh and squeezed. "It will come. We need to give it time."

"That's the problem, if Sweeney is any indication. We don't have time."

"So I'll tell you what I can and hope it prods your memories."

"That bothers me, too," he acknowledged. "After three months of being together, the only information I shared with you was my name? And that I'm a business associate of your ex-partner?"

"Yes." Sadness underlined her words, not resentment. "That's why I left, isn't it?" His eyes flitted over her, the blue in them flat and unreadable. "Because you pushed me to open up?"

"I told you I don't know why you left." More buildings loomed as they passed a sign welcoming them to Eastport. She glanced at the side mirror and changed lanes. "You didn't share that with me, either."

"Talk about irony." His laugh was harsh, tinged with self-deprecation. "If I had told you about myself, we both might have a better idea about the mess we're in. Even my driver's license is from out of state."

"Jacob, Helene had moved out of her place and into yours a few months ago. She told me she'd rather rent from a friend than a stranger. But she didn't advertise it. She told me she needed some peace and quiet away from work."

"Where?"

"You have a renovated boathouse. Down south off of the bay."

"And you were going to tell me this when?"

"Excuse me for being distracted," she muttered.

"Point taken." His sigh was long, ragged. "I guess that's where we're headed, then. If Helene left any clues behind, it would be either there or at the club."

"Shouldn't we go by the club first?

Jacob shook his head. "The police will be watching it. I'm not up for another confrontation."

"You might have spoken too soon." Grace glanced at her rearview mirror. "I think we're being followed."

Jacob studied the side mirror. "The black sedan?"

"Yes."

"Turn your blinker on like you're going to turn right. Then take the next left."

Grace gripped the steering wheel, taking the turn on a squeal of tires.

A few moments later, the black sedan skidded around the corner. The driver gunned its engine, picking up pursuit.

"Looks like I didn't smack our friend hard enough," Jacob commented dryly. He pulled out his gun and checked the clip.

Grace punched the gas.

"How DID HE GET a car so fast?" Grace demanded.

"Why don't you ask the guy in the passenger seat with the machine gun?"

Grace didn't take her eyes off the street. Instead, she swung the Jag into a sharp right. The back end fishtailed, but a second later Grace regained control.

The traffic light flashed red at the end of the block. "Run it," Jacob ordered.

"Hold on." Grace dodged a delivery truck with another twist of the wheel but didn't ease up on the accelerator. Pedestrians scattered, screaming as they dove for the curb.

Rubber squealed against cement. Bullets pinged off her side panel. "Are they crazy?"

"You don't have to be crazy to kill." His fist hit the window button before he released the safety belt and swung around in his seat. He thrust the gun out the window and fired at Sweeney.

"There's too many people, Jacob." Real fear caught hold of her. One slip, one bad reaction, and she could kill an innocent person.

A taxi cab skidded across the intersection. Grace slammed the brakes and wrenched the wheel, spinning the car into a one-eighty. People screamed and scattered, diving and ducking behind parked cars.

Jacob's shoulder slammed against the passenger door. Pain ripped through him from his elbow to his skull.

Swearing, Jacob righted himself and fired a few more shots. "Keep the car straight, damn it."

"You're kidding, right?" She shoved the stick into Reverse and hit the accelerator. Jacob's back crashed into the dash. Metal crunched metal as she hit the car behind her. She threw the Jag into gear, heard the whine of steel breaking loose from the back end.

"Was that straight enough for you? I just lost my bumper." Not waiting for a reply, Grace charged through the pattern of cars clogging the city streets, weaving when she could, cutting others off when she had to.

Grace hit her brakes, barely missing the back end of a bus.

Suddenly, their friends in the sedan skidded past them. Sweeney slammed the brakes, fishtailing against a corner mailbox.

Jacob's bullets pelted the sedan, doing very little damage to their windows. "The glass is bulletproof."

Sweeney reversed on a squeal of tires. Wide black stripes burned the pavement, smoked the air.

Grace floored the accelerator and shot forward, once again putting them into a two-vehicle race.

"Construction?" She nearly screamed the word. Orange barrels spotted the street in uneven lines, narrowing into a blockade across the highway on-ramp.

"We need that ramp, Grace. We can lose them on the stretch without traffic lights."

"You're out of your mind, Lomax." The back window exploded, shooting shards of glass into the air.

"Scoot down, damn it."

Grace couldn't get down far, not if she wanted to keep control of the car.

Jacob dropped his empty clip and shoved the second into his pistol. "They're using the machine guns. I can't hold them off very much longer."

"Damn!" She hit the steering wheel with one fist.

"Take the ramp." Jacob punctuated the statement with two shots from his gun through the back opening.

The sedan sped up, closing the distance between him and Grace's car. Close enough that Grace could see Sweeney in the driver's seat.

Grace waited a long few seconds, swerved toward the blockade of wood and barrels, her foot heavy against the accelerator.

The Jag hit the barrier, jolting them both. She gritted her teeth. "This car isn't even a year old."

"At the rate we're going, we'll probably be dead before the day's over. So I'm not too worried about it."

She pushed away thoughts of her baby. "Not if I can help it."

In the distance, she heard sirens. Felt the prickle at her

back. "Hold on." Grace took the car flying over the dirt and broken cement.

Police cars raced toward them, their red and blue lights flashing, their sirens screeching.

"We need to lose your car. It's too conspicuous."

"You think?" Grace commented as two more police cars joined the chase.

"You've got five cop cars on your ass."

"I saw. Now all we need is a chopper and we can have a party." Grace swerved, just missing a parked construction backhoe. One of the police cars wasn't so lucky. It bounced off the digger, spun and hit another cop car head-on. Air bags exploded. Grace said a small prayer hoping the bags did their job.

"Two down," Jacob said, his voice grim.

Wheels hit flat cement and Grace shoved the car into high gear. The Jag raced onto the expressway.

"Let's see what we can do with some elbow room." When she floored the accelerator this time, Jacob saw the needle shoot past one hundred.

Grace jerked the wheel sending the car onto the shoulder, creating her own lane as she passed cars one by one.

"Don't tell me. I taught you this on the mountain, too."

"No, we only had time for some light hand-to-hand combat," she said, and swerved two lanes to the right without touching the brake. "I learned this on my own."

The sirens behind them lessened, telling Grace the police cars were losing ground.

"Where are our friends?"

Jacob dropped his clip, checked the number of rounds left, shoved it back in. "Lost them when the police joined the party."

He glanced up and caught the sign for Chesapeake Bay. "Take this street."

"It leads to the harbor. Limits our options."

"Take it."

She saw the blood-soaked shirt, the gray-tinged skin. He'd ripped open his stitches and was losing blood. "Are you okay?"

"I'll manage."

The pier loomed ahead. Monday midmorning traffic had already congested the main path with tourists.

A barrage of bullets hit the car from the side. Suddenly, Sweeney was there again. This time close enough for Grace to see the grim slant of his features. "Where did he come from?"

"Look out!"

Grace swerved, barely missing a biker and his dog. But it cost them. The car slammed through the metal guard gate blocking the pedestrian's crossing and shot down the main pier. People screamed and scattered in mass panic. Grace slammed on the brakes, but there wasn't enough time.

The car skidded, the tires screeched. A heartbeat later, the car splintered the side railing and plunged into the water.

More screams shattered the air.

But this time, Grace realized, they were hers.

Chapter Eight

When the car hit the water, both air bags exploded, driving Grace back into her seat. Instinctively she struggled against the bags' suffocating weight. Water rushed in from the floor, a gush of icy liquid that sucked the oxygen out of the car, smothering what little gasps of air she managed.

Without warning, the car shifted nose up. Water gushed through the blown-out back window. Tossed backward, Grace stifled a scream. She clawed at the bag, trying to get leverage.

"Stop struggling, Grace." The order came in a short burst of air by her ear. Suddenly her safety belt broke free. "Hold your breath!"

The car submerged. Her breath backed up into her lungs. Out of nowhere, Jacob grabbed her hand and tugged her toward him. Blindly, she shoved the deflating air bag away.

Jacob pulled her through the back window behind him. The ragged steel scraped at her sweatshirt, snagging her like a fish on a line. Panic pressed in on her chest. She yanked on the material but it held tight. Quickly, she unzipped it and pulled free, leaving the jacket behind.

Her head broke the surface a few seconds before his. She

dragged oxygen into her lungs in huge swallowing gulps. The gritty water and air burned her throat and lungs.

The black sedan skidded to a stop by a small diving equipment rental shack. Both men jumped from the car, but Sweeney's passenger was faster. A machine gun appeared in his hands a split second later.

"Dive!" Jacob ordered. Gunshots peppered the water in front of them.

She gasped for breath and plunged below again. This time swimming deep as bullets whizzed past her.

Only when the blood pounded at her ears and the air slipped from her lungs did she kick to the surface.

Jacob reached for the semiautomatic in his waistband just as Sweeney grabbed the machine gun and smashed it into the other man's face.

Jacob heard Grace surface, coughing. "Stay behind me." With his feet he tread water, ignoring the pain that seared his back and shoulders. Instead, he scanned the rental shack. Racks of oxygen tanks lined one side of the front door. Pedestrians scattered, running away from the gunmen.

Jacob didn't hesitate. He fired into the rack of divers' oxygen tanks. An explosion ripped through the air. The gunmen hit the deck, but Sweeney's partner was too close. A fire stream shot from the ground behind him, the flames engulfed the man.

Jacob looked at Grace. "Are you okay?"

When she nodded, he said, "Follow me."

Jacob swam under the nearby fishing piers, looped out and followed an invisible line of water down south. Several minutes later, both he and Grace rode the waves onto the beach well away from the crowd of onlookers at the pier fire.

"This isn't good, Jacob." Grace stood and let the water lap

against her calves. Sand sucked at her feet. Her legs trembled, but with the effort from wading ashore or from sheer shock, she couldn't be sure.

"It's not done, either." He came abreast of her and stopped.

He was right, of course. She tried not to think about it. Instead, she pressed her hand to her belly, took comfort in the round swell of it, and then said a silent prayer that at least for now, they were all safe. "What's our next step?"

When Jacob didn't answer, Grace turned fully toward him. But his eyes weren't on her face.

Panic tripped down her spine as she followed his gaze to her stomach.

A thin cotton tank top stuck to her body, a second skin that outlined the fullness of her breasts, the more than slight roundness of her stomach. Her hand plucked at the material, pulling it away from the damp skin beneath.

But he barely noticed. His mind flashed back to Grace's house and her confrontation with Sweeney. He saw her hand dip to her belly when Webber hit her, saw her father's eyes drop to Grace's stomach during their argument.

"You're pregnant?" Suddenly, Jacob exploded with a string of curses.

"It seems you remembered some of your favorite words."

"You think this is a joke?" Pain ripped through his shoulder, down his arm. Bits of sand caught under his bandage, burned like acid in his wound. Sheer willpower kept him on his feet, fighting the waves that slammed against the back of his legs. "Since this morning, you've been shot at, punched and nearly drowned." He jabbed at the sky with his finger. "And the day isn't even half over yet." It wasn't a question, so he didn't expect an answer. But what he didn't expect was her chin to hitch, her eyes to narrow.

Her temper enraged his own. He grasped on to the anger with both hands, knowing if he didn't the thought of what could've happened—what might still happen—would make him shudder with fear. "How far along are you?"

"Almost five months."

He stood there for a moment, where the bay hugged the sandy shore, knowing that with her statement she'd just upped the risk. "Of all the idiotic—" He glanced at her, then stopped. Not because he'd gone too far. He was justified, damn it. But for the first time, he looked beyond her temper, beyond the stubbornness that kept her back rigid, her features tight. And he saw the hunted glaze of her eyes, the paleness of her skin.

The need to protect her rolled through him, knocking the breath from his chest. "Let's go." Annoyed, he shoved the pistol into his back waistband with his good hand and yanked his sweater over the handle. "Act normal."

Pregnant.

With a quick glance, he scanned their surroundings. The beach was fairly large with a parking lot that ran for more than a block. Just beyond lay a playground spotted with children and their parents.

"Stay down. Use the cars for cover."

Grace couldn't stop shivering. The brisk wind beat against her damp skin and jeans. "We're wet and you're bleeding." She nodded toward his shoulder. The sweater was more crimson than not across the shoulder and chest. "How normal do you think we can act?"

They walked briskly, cutting through several rows of cars, avoiding mingling families and other groups of people.

"Over here."

Farther down toward the back of the parking lot sat a truck with a camper shell attached to the bed. A classic, if you counted the early seventies, with more rust than paint across its hood and tailgate.

The driver's window stood half-open. Far enough for Jacob to reach in and unlock the door.

"Watch for trouble." Jacob opened the door, shoved over a baseball cap that lay on the seat. Shifting, he managed to squirm under the dashboard. He grabbed the wires from under the steering column and pulled them free.

"You're hot-wiring a car?" Grace scanned the surrounding area. She strained her ears for any signs of sirens but heard nothing but the wind whip through the cabin.

"It's better than walking." The engine revved, punctuating his remark. "Get in. You're driving."

Jacob maneuvered out from under the dash and let out a long hiss when his shoulder bumped the steering wheel.

She needed no other prodding and slid into the driver's seat. "Let's go," Jacob ordered. Then he grabbed the baseball cap and shoved it onto her head. "Can you drive?"

"It's an automatic," she said, throwing the car into gear. "If I run into trouble, I'll make sure you're the first to know."

"You do that." Gas fumes and stale vinyl filled the air. Her stomach rolled in protest but Grace resisted the urge to hold her breath.

Within seconds, she backed them out of the parking spot and drove away. "Are we safe?"

"For the time being." He noticed her shivering. He reached over and switched on the heat. "Where's my house?"

"If we go there, they might be there waiting."

"Doesn't matter. It's a chance we're going to have to take. Right now, that house might be the key to getting my memory back."

Grace tensed. Her home. Her father. "Jacob, I forgot about my dad." She groped at her pocket. "I need to warn him."

"Do you think you'll be doing him a favor?"

"What if he'd walked in on Sweeney?" She took her phone out of her pocket, biting back a curse when she flipped open the lid. The LED screen was cracked.

"Sweeney followed us too quickly." His eyes studied her for a moment. "Chances are that your father discovered Webber's body after Sweeney left. Which means he called the police. Which means he'll be questioned by the authorities— if he isn't being questioned already. He has no idea what happened. He can be honest with the police and tell them about me. Your father has no reason to trust me now. If you contact him, they'll know and realize you're not being kidnapped but a willing accomplice. We don't know who we're dealing and until we do, I'm not going to take a chance; it might be the police themselves."

"An informant?" She shook the water from the phone. When that didn't work, she used her teeth and popped open the back cover. Maybe if she dried off the battery and placed the phone to the heater vent…

"Let me do that."

"Not a chance. You'll throw it out the window." She glanced over at him. "My dad's better scared than dead? Is that what you're saying?" She balanced the phone across the steering wheel and used her finger nails to pry out the battery. "You think that my dad is involved with this?"

"Someone is holding Sweeney's leash. And until I discover who it is, the only person I'm sure didn't kill Helene is you."

"The only thing my father knows is that you are a friend of mine in trouble—"

The battery popped out and fell into her lap. Grace froze. "Jacob, there's a note."

"What?"

"A small note folded in half." She took out the thin strip of wet paper that clung to the underside of the battery and handed it to him.

Carefully he separated the back from the front. "It's a series of letters and numbers." Quickly, he counted them.

Grace shot him a side glance. "It's Helene's handwriting," she said. "Are they readable?"

"Yes. Only the edges are smeared a little," Jacob replied. "Did Helene have access to your phone yesterday?"

Did she? Grace went over the lunch yesterday in her mind. "I turned my phone off because I didn't want to be interrupted during lunch. We were sitting in a booth, so I set my keys and phone on the window ledge."

"Why not in your purse?"

She studied the road ahead, thinking. "It's a habit. Not one of my better ones. I'm constantly misplacing things."

"You said Helene became impatient at the end of lunch. Was it after you came back from the bathroom?"

"Yes," she replied, then remembered. "Actually, she had already paid for lunch and stood when I came to the table.

She handed me my keys and phone. Then jokingly she told me not to lose them." She jerked her gaze to his. "You don't think—"

"The hell I don't," he answered. "Where are your keys?"

"In the ignition of my car. At the bottom of the bay."

Chapter Nine

The Victorian mansion stood five levels high. Anything less would seem impoverished to a United States senator, Frank Sweeney thought derisively. And D'Agostini was anything but impoverished. A sophisticated blend of old and new, the mansion boasted an embassy-sized ballroom, an art gallery, a wine bistro and a media room with an adjoining twenty-seat cinema.

All with coffered ceilings and herringbone floors. All tastefully gilded, draped and cosseted by one man's wealth and affluence.

But Frank wasn't here to see D'Agostini. He ignored the bodyguards flanking the entryway and the nearby elevator. Instead, temper had him climbing the grand staircase. Each jarring step increased the tempo of the hammers that beat the inside of his skull and added to his sense of self-punishment.

He'd screwed up. He hadn't anticipated the kick from the girl. Whether he wanted to admit it or not, the sight of Lomax standing in the doorway caught him off guard.

The third floor opened into a wide lobby. With quick strides, Frank walked to the far end where two oversized mahogany doors stood. Not bothering to knock, he opened the doors quietly, already hearing the battle that went on from the other side and not wanting to disturb it.

At one time, the gymnasium stood as a ballroom, now renovated into a modern miniature health club. While the vaulted ceiling remained, the walls were covered with mirrors, the hardwood floor with mats. Weights and machines flanked one side, while a bar, sauna and hot tub stood opposite.

In the middle, he saw Kragen take a short jab to his mouth. His sweat-darkened hair plastered to his head. His teeth gleamed white as he wiped blood from his lip with the back of his knuckle.

"All right, Tomas." He taunted his opponent and waved the other man forward with his fingers. "Come on."

Frank knew the instructor—a wiry martial arts expert—was left no other choice. And he had to give the man credit for taking that step forward. Mistake or not, Tomas drew blood, setting the tone for the workout. No apologies would be accepted.

Both fighters were of equal height, and equal in build. A good match for workouts. Tomas attacked with a right round-house kick to Kragen's face. At the last moment, Kragen sidestepped, grabbed the man's ankle and slammed his elbow into his opponent's face. Frank heard the bone crunch against cartilage, saw the blood gush.

But Frank knew Kragen wasn't finished. A second later, Kragen twisted the leg. This time, the bone snapped and Tomas screamed. Kragen followed his opponent's momentum and slammed Tomas's head into the floor. "I think we're done for the day, don't you?"

When Tomas nodded, Kragen left the man rolling in agony on the mat.

Frank opened the door, waved the guards in and watched them carry Tomas out. A dislocated knee is a small price to pay for keeping one's life.

"You keep going through instructors like that, you won't have anyone to tear apart when you really get angry," Frank commented.

"I told him I had a meeting later with the senator. He failed to pull his punch." Oliver wiped his lip again, then grabbed a towel from the edge of the mat and patted his face.

After a moment, he studied Frank's bruised features. "It appears that I fared better than you, Frank." He threw the towel back onto the mat and walked over to the bar. "I see you found Lomax," he commented, smiling. "Or did Webber do that to you?"

Frank snorted, but took the insult. He deserved it after all. "Webber's dead."

"Really?" Oliver's smile thinned. He reached under the bar and pulled a bottle of juice from the refrigerator. "Did you finally get a stomachful or did Lomax kill him?"

"Lomax," Frank admitted. "But he only beat me by a few seconds."

"What happened?"

"I found blood on the woman's floor, suspected it was Lomax's. Before I could question the woman, Webber hit her. Pissed me off. Took my focus off of her and the situation just long enough for Lomax to catch me unaware. He burst into the room like some damn hero."

"It's not like you to blame others for your mistakes, Frank."

Frank's gaze drifted pointedly over the bar, searching.

"What are you looking for?" Kragen asked.

"Hot coffee," Frank answered, referring to Kragen's earlier meeting with Webber.

Oliver laughed and chugged some of his juice. "With your tough hide, I'd use acid," he said, but the underlying tone of truth raised the hair on the back of Frank's neck.

"The only mistake I made was not killing Webber before we even got to Grace Renne's place," Frank admitted, but the muscles in his back stayed tight. "The screwup at The Tens should have never happened."

"I agree. But then again, the senator handpicked Webber to take care of it, didn't he?" Oliver commented dryly. "Did you take care not to leave any evidence at the Renne woman's house?"

"I did, but it wouldn't hurt to make another phone call."

"It wouldn't hurt you," Oliver said noncommittally. "But the more I cover up, the more chance of exposure." He grabbed a nearby towel and hooked it around his neck. "What about Miss Renne? Is she involved?"

"Now? Definitely," Frank added, thinking of the small plastic case in his pocket.

"What about the father?"

"We're still uncertain. Webber said he'd shot Lomax. The blood I found was obviously from his wound," Sweeney said carefully. "But it couldn't have been serious. The Lomax I saw looked healthy enough. Although, his face is banged up a bit. If I had to guess, I'd say the father wasn't a problem. But he might be part of our solution."

"Webber is dead and Lomax is gone. Neither will please the senator," Kragen advised. "If we decide to pressure a prominent Washington physician, it had better be for a good reason."

"Show the senator this," Frank reached into his pocket, pulled out the miniature DVD case and handed it to Kragen. "I think you'll have your reason."

Chapter Ten

The sun had faded into the ember-orange blur of a cloudy Chesapeake dusk. In the distance, herons swooped and fed from the bay waters, their long, white bodies graceful, their eerie calls mournful.

The evening breeze picked up enough that the ends of her hair tickled her shoulders, touching off a chill that skittered down her spine. Grace stepped from the truck and hugged her arms to her chest to fight another bout of shivers.

The air was thick with the smell of pine and earth—and heavy enough with moisture that she could taste a hint of rain at the back of her throat.

Her jeans, damp and stiff, chafed against her skin with each step forward, but she ignored the discomfort.

"Not what I expected." Jacob observed from behind her, startling her.

"I think that's why you liked it," Grace admitted slowly, her heart still up in her throat.

Positioned out over the water, the four-story home stood on stilts of steel and cement. The design shouldn't have worked amongst four acres of wood, beach and bay. But it did.

The sleek, straight-lined style defined contemporary architecture with its square yet modern windows and a lone tower resting comfortably on the flat roof. Only the occasional right angle kept the design from being too boxy and gave the home enough class to be unique, not boring.

"Most homes around here are more traditional," she said, breaking through the silence that had settled between them. At one time, she'd foolishly dreamed of living here with Jacob. "Tell me again why we are here and not chasing down my keys?"

"We're going to wait until the city fishes the car out of the water. Let them do the hard work."

"How long do you think that will be?"

"Considering that we parked the car in the middle of a boat channel, I would say relatively soon," Jacob commented, slanting her a sardonic look. "And if we're lucky, they'll take the car to city impound."

"So we start making calls to find out where we go looking. Then we break in later tonight?" The shivers rippled through her. She hugged her arms to her chest to keep them contained.

"There's no we," Jacob acknowledged. "You're not going, Grace."

"Why?"

"You're pregnant," he snapped.

"And you've got a bum shoulder and no memory. That's more of a disadvantage than being pregnant if we run into a bad guy or two."

"If I don't think, my reflexes take over. Like they did at your house with Sweeney."

"That doesn't mean—"

"What happened with Sweeney and the car chase should tell you they're not going to stop. Hell, you're lucky that baby didn't get harmed when we took our dip in the bay."

"He's tougher than he looks. And so am I," she said, but she had thought the same thing and shivered once more. But this time it wasn't from the cold.

"Well, you scared the hell out of me," he replied, his voice tight. "Once we get to my place, you're going to stay put until I figure out what is going on."

"Jacob, I'd go insane waiting for some faceless predator to hunt me down in a dark corner."

"It wouldn't be a dark corner. It will be a whole different country if I have anything to say about it."

"You don't think they'd find me?"

"Not before I'd find them," he growled. "And that's a promise."

"No."

"You have no choice." His eyes snapped to hers.

"There's always a choice." Stubbornness set her jaw, but fury had her grinding her teeth.

"Why didn't you tell me you were pregnant?"

More than anything she had wanted to tell him. Had come here to his house looking to do just that and found it deserted. Her heart bled just enough to remind her she wasn't immune to the hurt yet. Better a baby without a father than a baby with a father who remained distant.

A lesson Grace learned from her own childhood.

"Because I was trying to avoid this argument," she snapped. "We have no idea who is behind this. At least with you, there's a chance you might remember."

"And the baby?" When she didn't answer, he continued, "Are you willing to put your baby at risk?"

"My baby is already at risk," she answered, pushing back the fear and doubts that threatened to suffocate her. She swiped at an annoying strand of hair that clung damply to her cheek. "Whoever gunned down Helene is still out there. I wouldn't be here right now if you had left me at my house. I'd be lying on the floor beaten and bloody from Webber's fists," she insisted, touching the sore spot on her lip with her tongue. "Even if I thought to hide at that point, he changed my mind. Nowhere is safe for me or my baby until we get to the bottom of this."

He was angry. She saw it in his features. But rather than scare her, it surprised her. The Jacob she knew never lost control, never gave anything away. This man wasn't covering up any of his emotions.

"Damn it." He pinched his nose between his thumb and forefinger. "Tell me, did I ever get the last word with you?"

"Yes. One time," she murmured. But he had to walk out on her to do it, she thought grimly. She turned her head away from him, stared out over the water until the tears stopped pricking her eyes.

"Well, the argument must have been pretty insignificant, then."

"You thought so."

"What the hell is that supposed to mean?"

"Nothing." Her tone was clipped, more out of annoyance with herself than him. "Look, I'm sorry. You don't deserve me taking shots at you."

"Just because I don't remember it doesn't mean I didn't

deserve it. Either tell me what I did or wait until I gain a point of reference for the hostility. All right?"

"Yes." She watched him for a moment, saw the set of his jaw hadn't relaxed. "But I want your word, Jacob, that you won't leave me behind."

He gave her a long, considering look. "You have it."

Until the old Jacob returned, she thought. "Fine," she said, but with much less conviction.

"How are we going to get in?" She followed him over the graveled driveway to the front porch.

"Don't suppose I keep a spare set of keys under a nearby flower pot?"

"You're not the type," she mused. His sense of humor hit her with a rush of pleasure. Enough that she almost forgot their reason for being there.

Almost.

"Can you pick the lock or something?"

"Actually, I'm doing the 'or something' part." He ran his hand down around the reinforced steel door until his fingers located the security trigger. "The mechanism is too sophisticated. I don't have the right tools. A problem I'm going to have to correct soon enough." He pulled out his gun, checked the clip before placing it back in his waistband. "We seem pretty isolated. How close is my nearest neighbor?"

"My best guess would be a mile in either direction. Why?"

"Because I have a pretty damn good security system, but not a linked one."

"You mean, no police are going to show up on your door step if you trigger the alarm."

"Exactly. And if I trigger it, you might have to cover your

ears. I don't expect an alarm to activate, but it's only a guess. Either way, you're not to move from the front door. No matter what. I don't want to shoot you by mistake. Got it?"

"Yes."

Without thinking, he leaned down and kissed her on the lips. A quick butterfly brush of the lips. "For luck."

Grace went still, paralyzed. Not from the touch of his mouth against hers, but from the longing the simple gesture invoked.

"I've done that before, haven't I?"

A simple gesture that gutted her from rib to belly. Grace tried to answer, tried to nod but managed neither.

He grabbed her arm, just above the elbow, shook it. "Tell me."

She managed a short nod then, but the words took another second to push past the tightening in her throat. "It was somewhat of a ritual you did when you left on one of your business trips."

She saw the shift, the laser sharpness that entered his gaze. Knew the rejection, the long-ago hurt showed in hers.

"Hell." He muttered the curse even as he dropped his hand. "Stay here. Don't move."

For a moment, she watched him melt into the semidarkness and almost laughed. Would have if she could have been sure hysteria didn't spur the urge.

Leave, he said? She took a deep, shuddering breath, realizing hysterics weren't so far-fetched.

Just where in the hell was she supposed to go?

FATIGUE RODE HIM HARD, making his movements slower, more sluggish than he would've liked. But it was the rage, the frustration over Grace's pain that drove him deeper into the shadows. That and the sweet taste of her still lingering on his lips.

Jacob worked his way around the perimeter of the house, stopping every few steps to listen, to wait. The wind rustled the trees, making the leaves dance and the branches whistle. In the background, the water rushed the beach, slapping foam and grit against the rocks in its path.

She'd stood her ground against Webber, he'd give her that. Held her own in a car chase, too. With five cops on her tail. Hell, she even managed to take down Sweeney without Jacob's help.

He played the last through his mind in slow motion. Damn, he thought he'd lost her that time. All it would've taken is one of Sweeney's meaty hands squeezing her neck.

His scowl brought a sharp tug of pain from the stitches in his forehead. He'd get her into the house, then he'd get some answers.

As darkness settled in, his eyes adjusted. He quickly discovered his night vision worked well enough for him to place most shadows into decipherable patterns.

From what he could see, there were no thermal or motion detectors. Considering the house sat on the edge of the woods, he wasn't surprised. Too many deer to hinder that kind of security.

Soundlessly, he worked his way to the back, noting the freestanding generator, two satellite dishes and a series of solar panels.

It seemed the house was set up to be independent of outside sources. The simplest way to maintain anonymity, if that was one's goal.

Considering they were two miles off the nearest main road, intentional isolation had been a distinct possibility.

Toward the back, he discovered the attached garage housing an SUV and a black Mercedes. Both locked up tight.

It wasn't until he investigated the boat dock, that he felt a deep pull of satisfaction in his belly. Wide enough to house two boats, the dock sat snuggly underneath the stilts of the house.

He sure as hell hit the jackpot.

The prize? A midnight-black Malibu speedboat moored to the steel posts—its keys still in the ignition.

ONE MINUTE STRETCHED to five, then ten. Agitation worked Grace's nerves until she was forced to pace back and forth to ease her anxiety. In the dark, the shadows seemed to grow and stretch. But it wasn't the shadows that left her on edge.

"Grace."

She screamed, swung around and realized too late that it was Jacob who stood in the doorway behind her.

He caught her fist with a smack against his palm.

"Damn it," she swore, more at herself for being jumpy. "Make some noise when you walk up behind me."

Inside the door, a security box buzzed. He dropped her hand, then reached over and broke open the box with the gun. He ripped out the inner wires.

The buzzing stopped.

"How did you get in?"

"Through a back window," he answered, tossing the lid onto the floor. "I broke the pane with the butt of my gun."

"It was that easy?"

"Not quite."

"But what if they come here?"

"There are other ways to protect us." He shot her a sardonic look. "Besides, if everything else fails—" the cold-blue of his eyes flickered to his weapon "—this seems to work well enough."

"Until it runs out of bullets," she retorted before following him through the doorway.

He shut the door behind them and turned the dead bolt. But made no other move. Instead, he leaned back against the door and folded his arms.

He glanced at the ceiling. "Lights on."

Track lights flipped on, hurting his eyes.

"Lights eighty percent capacity."

The relief was minimal, but acceptable. "How did you know to say that particular phrase?"

"I didn't think about it." The harshness of the light emphasized the unyielding lines of his features. "I think it's time you and I had a discussion."

"Jacob, I'm tired—"

"It's called, 'she said, he believed.' And it won't take long," he continued, ignoring her gasp of protest. "She said they were friends. He believed they were lovers."

"This is ridiculous," she replied, striving for nonchalance, but the small quiver in her voice and his raised eyebrow told her she'd failed.

"She said the baby she carried was another man's. He believed it was his."

Suddenly in two quick strides, he was in front of her. His hands gripped her shoulders, preventing her retreat. "She said he left with no goodbye. And for no reason."

Her head tilted back. "And?" she whispered, torn. "What did he believe?"

"There was no goodbye. But no reason?" he murmured as one hand slid up the back of her neck, cupping her head with enough pressure to bring her up against him. Her fingers curled into his sweater, holding her there suspended. "There had to be one hell of a reason for me to walk away from you."

His free arm slid around her, curving her body into his. Giving her only a second to adjust to the heat, to accept the primal intent that set his features into hard lines.

Then his mouth was on hers. But not with the fierceness she had expected. Certainly not with the same fierceness that her heart beat in her chest or the blood pounded through her veins.

His lips settled into a persuasive tempo that swept her up, rolled her under, left her trying to find her feet under their tender assault.

Caution tugged at her, urging her to step back. But the warmth of his body, the stroke of his hand up her spine blurred her thoughts, spiked her emotions until her arms slid up and around his neck.

With a groan, he deepened the kiss. He used his tongue to coax her mouth open. Then used it again to reward her, when her lips parted. Stroking, tasting.

A yearning broke free, snapping through her, catching her in a backlash of need. To be held, comforted. Cherished.

With a cry, she pushed away. Humiliation coursed through her, its ugly head rearing up, sniping at her soul, making her nauseous.

"Grace?"

Tears burned her eyes, but she blinked them back. She put out a hand, stopping him from grabbing her again.

"Please don't."

His arms dropped to his sides, but his hands became fists. The shadows cut edges into his already sharp features, turned his eyes into hard blue stones. "Tell me, damn it."

She understood what he was asking. First with his kiss, now with the words. Stricken with embarrassment, she clung to the one thing that straightened her spine, hitched her chin and locked her eyes on his. Self-preservation.

"This baby is not yours."

Chapter Eleven

"If I'm not the father, who is, Grace?"

"My baby doesn't have a father. Not in the sense you mean, anyway." Her eyes burned—from fatigue or the tears, she couldn't be sure. She rubbed them gently with her fingertips. "Besides, I met him after you left, so you never knew him."

"Did you tell him?"

"No," she said, using that part of the truth as her defense. "He isn't father material."

"Compared to whom?"

"I guess to my own." She sighed, suddenly so weary her bones ached with it. Lord, why couldn't he have forgotten his stubbornness along with his memory? "Look, Jacob. I don't want to be analyzed. Not tonight. Okay?"

"Fair enough," he bit out, exasperated.

She glanced around, striving for a lightness she didn't feel. "The house hasn't changed since I've been here."

"How long ago was that?"

"Four months," she answered, but didn't explain the reason. Jacob didn't push her. Instead, he studied his home. If you could call it that, he noted dryly.

Exceptionally renovated, the main floor was laid out in a

wide, airy space. The entranceway opened into a two-story living room with a loft and a black mahogany circular stairway that led from the boat dock beneath and to the third level above.

"Looks like I kept a pretty simple existence." Jacob looked around, trying to find something familiar.

Paintings covered the walls—expensive, judging from the vivid colors and the broad strokes. His tastes obviously ran toward abstract and modern, he thought, eyeing a particular flamboyant red and blue bust of a naked woman over the inset fireplace.

"The word is *impersonal,*" Grace commented quietly.

Quiet, he noted with growing admiration, not cowed.

"Do you realize that while you don't necessarily know my history, you really do seem to know me?"

"That's not true—"

"You know I like my coffee black," he pointed out. "What else do you know?"

"Nothing, really." She paused. "Maybe little things."

"So if you had to guess, what would be my favorite color?"

"Black," she answered, using her hand to sweep over the room. "Most things you own are black. Your cars. Your clothes. Your boat. Even your furniture."

"That's gloomy, isn't it?"

"You told me once it kept you from having to worry about coordinating problems."

"Seriously?"

"No, you winked at the time. But now that I think back on it, there might be some truth there."

"And my favorite music?"

For the first time she realized she did know many things about the man. Maybe not what he did for a living or about his background and family. But the man himself. Why hadn't she realized that before?

"Jazz. Blues. Rock—most of the vintage, less of the contemporary. And wine. You built a wine cellar to hold a pretty extensive and quite expensive collection."

"I'll have to try a little later," he mused. "Go on."

Grace shifted until she could see his profile, giving in to the sudden urge to study his expression while she gave him details. "You have a small addiction for a good cigar. One that you rarely indulge. A bigger addiction to fast cars—which you indulge frequently. You like five-star hotels, secluded tables in restaurants and are always willing to pay the money for good service."

"So I'm a big tipper."

"One of the biggest I've ever met," she teased. "*Huge* tips."

He gave her an exaggerated frown. "That's hard to believe."

"You don't play into the metrosexual trend and wouldn't be caught dead getting a manicure. But a good, deep massage by an attractive woman's another story. You'd keep it professional, but why turn down good eye candy while you're relaxing?"

Jacob got the distinct impression she was teasing him, but instinctively he knew better than to pursue it. For the first time, he'd gotten her to open up and he didn't want to spoil the mood. "Anything else?"

"You've told me details about countries that only someone well traveled would know. And as you said, you speak several different languages. I've heard French, Spanish and Mandarin."

"Sounds like I'm well rounded if you add in the weapons training." He stopped just short of sarcasm.

Her features softened into uncertain lines. "One time, you mentioned your mother."

"What was she like?"

"You didn't say," she replied, shrugging her shoulders. "You just told me that she would've liked me. But I don't think you meant to."

A pang of regret shot through Jacob, catching him off guard. He searched for an image or memory of his mom. A whispered word that would remind him of her voice, but it was a futile effort. "The one aspect of amnesia I never expected to deal with were the echoes of emotion."

"I don't understand."

"I had figured from the beginning that bits of my past would come back to me a little at a time or in one sweeping rush," he acknowledged. "But it's the emotions that are taking the jabs at me."

When Grace didn't say anything, Jacob glanced her way. But her face was turned from him. "What is it?'

When her eyes found his again, there was a sadness there. "It's just you've never said anything like that to me before. You never shared your thoughts."

"Maybe that will change," he said quietly before shifting his attention back to their surroundings. "I took a quick look around on my way to the front door. One bedroom. No office. If I'm a businessman, why wouldn't I have an office here? Or somewhere?"

"You told me once you never felt the need to have an office."

"No office. Sterile living quarters. Weapons and language expert. Doesn't seem I'm adding up to be an everyday Joe, does it?" Jacob glanced at the sleek black cabinets and hi-tech appliances. "Do I like to cook?"

"Not really. So I guess we can rule out chef," she answered and ran her hand over the granite top. "But you once told me you had an associate who loved to cook, so you kept your kitchen stocked for him."

"No name?"

"None."

Grace slid onto the bar stool next to the counter.

"Are you okay?"

Grace nodded. "Just tired." Exhausted really, but she didn't want to give him another reason to hold her. Comfort her. Not while her nerves were still snapping from their last encounter.

He studied her for a moment. "My fault," he murmured, the words more of a caress than an apology. The pleasure from them shot through her, an arrow to the belly. One that left her insides more than a little quivery.

"Why don't you get out of those clothes and take a shower. I want to check around the house some more, anyway. See if I can find anything that might prod my memory."

A shower sounded wonderful. Just what she needed to shake the chill from her bones, wash the feel of him from her skin. But she could wait. "Actually, I think we should change your bandage. See how much damage you've done."

"All right. But let's at least change our clothes. I'm sure we can find something warm to wear in the bedroom. Then you can change my bandage." He grabbed her hand and tugged her up the stairs behind him. When they reached the master bedroom, Jacob walked to the closet.

"Helene's?" He nodded to a row of dresses hanging on the rod.

"Yes." Startled, her eyes skimmed the pile of chiffon and sequins. "She moved in a few months back. About a month after you left."

Slowly, she picked out a black sarong evening gown. "I've seen her wear most of these dresses."

"Were she and I lovers?"

"Maybe at one time, but it would've been long before I met her or you." Grace frowned, trying to remember Helene over the last few weeks. "Actually, she was never involved with anyone seriously."

"Even lately?"

"I don't know. If there was, I never met him," she said. "Helene went through men pretty quickly." Grace studied Jacob. "She might have told you."

"Which doesn't help at all," he commented, then sorted through some of his clothes on the opposite side.

Moments later, Jacob scanned the bedroom. He took in the crisp, clean lines of the platform bed. With drapes and linens of tan and the sleeker base of black wood—nothing else was needed to highlight the masculine edge.

"Do you recognize anything?"

"No." His eyes followed the curved stairway in the corner. Of the whole house, this was his favorite feature. An exclusive access to the tower room on the roof.

"If I was hiding papers, I'd want them close and protected. I'd want to be able to grab and go." His eyes worked their way around the walls. "Something hidden in plain sight."

"Would it be small or big?"

"Small. Travel light." The disconnection gnawed at him. "But it wouldn't be in here. Too obvious."

Grace laid her hand on his forearm and squeezed. "Give it time."

"We don't have time." He tugged his hand free, not liking the empathy behind the words, not when somewhere deep inside he wanted more than that from her.

Fatigue paled her porcelain skin, left dark smudges beneath her eyes. "Look, why don't you get dressed first? I'm sure you can find something here. Meanwhile, I want to take another look at my boat."

A smile tugged at the corners of her mouth. "That boat was your baby."

"Might still be," he responded, a small grin of his own tugged at his mouth. "After, I'll take another turn around the perimeter before it gets dark."

"Perimeter?" Grace asked. "That's military, isn't it?"

"Goes with the weapons training, I imagine," he answered. "Go change. I'll be back before you know it."

Without thought, he went to gather her close. An automatic instinct to comfort. But just as quickly, she sidestepped him, placing more than a few feet of distance between them.

"Don't." The word wasn't a plea or an order. A hint of desperation underlined it. Enough that he couldn't even be sure she directed the statement solely at him. "All right?"

Jacob stiffened, finally understanding. The fear had never been of him or that he might harm her again. Although, in his mind, he must have certainly warranted it.

No, she feared herself—or her reaction, he corrected. She didn't trust herself.

He watched her leave the room, not waiting for his reply. A good thing, since he had no intention of answering her.

Not yet, anyway.

GRACE STEPPED OUT of the bathroom a half hour later feeling refreshed and in control once again. She'd found Helene's emerald-green velour jogging suit and decided it would be perfect for pajamas. Helene was one size larger than Grace, but that worked in Grace's favor. She rolled down the waist until it hung low on her hips and gave some relief on her stomach.

"You look comfortable."

Grace stopped midstride and glanced up. Jacob stood across the room wearing nothing more than a worn pair of jeans.

"So do you." He was barefooted and bare-chested. The dim glow of the bedroom light surrounded him, softening the harsh bruises and the white gauze of his bandage, shadowing the lean, hard form of his chest and the sleek, tight muscles of his arms.

Her gaze traveled down the masculine contours of his ribs, drawn like a moth to the flickering light that danced over the taut skin of his belly. Her mouth went dry as she followed the line of sable hair that started slightly below his navel and disappeared into the open vee of his unsnapped waistband.

"Are you ready?"

"I'm sorry?" Grace forced her eyes upward and caught the slight flexing of his jaw muscles, telling her he hadn't missed her perusal.

"I asked if you were ready to change my bandage," he

repeated, but each word was low, raspy. Each syllable ground against the next, sandpaper on sandpaper.

"Yes." She forced herself to take a long, steady breath.

"I found this in the boat." He grabbed a first aid kit from the bed and held it up. "Are you sure you're up for this? The wound isn't going to be pretty."

"It's nothing I haven't seen before," she managed, forcing her legs to walk toward him. "Who do you think took care of you before my father got to my house?" When Jacob raised his eyebrow, she added, "I was premed when I dropped out of college."

"Okay, Doc." Jacob nodded toward the bathroom. "I'm all yours."

She waited a moment to get her heartbeat under control, then followed him in.

Jacob sat on the bathroom counter, putting his shoulder eye level for Grace.

Grace murmured her apologies, concentrated on cutting away the bandage. Soon she was finished, and she took a deep breath.

"How does it look?"

"The wound is crusted with dried blood, but otherwise the sutures are still intact."

She dipped a clean washcloth into some water from the sink and started to wash away the blood.

"Tell me about your mom," Jacob said softly.

Because it kept her mind off their proximity, she obliged him. "Her name was Claire. She met my father during the Vietnam War. She worked for Senator Langdon, although he was a colonel then."

"And your father?"

"He was an army surgeon. The way my father tells the story, my mom came in to deliver some papers and it was love at first sight." She laid the wet towel down and used another to pat his wound dry. "They were married a little over twelve years when she died."

"How?"

"She was in a plane crash with Senator Langdon. He was seeking reelection."

Ignoring the slight trembling in her fingers, she applied some antibiotic cream.

"You must look like her."

She opened the package of square bandages, pulled one out and placed it against his wound. "Yes. Very much so." Carefully, she taped the bandage down.

Jacob's fingers played with a thick lock of her hair, testing its weight, the texture. The scent so familiar, something inside him strained to break free. "Honeysuckle," he murmured, reining the emotion back as her fingers fluttered and stroked him. Not with the heat of passion, but with the softness of concern.

"I'm sorry?" She shifted closer in order to start wrapping the gauze over his bicep first.

"Your shampoo is called Honeysuckle Sweet. When I remembered the trip to Aspen, it was because I recognized the scent of your hair. I looked in your bathroom when I couldn't remember the name of the flower."

"The fact that you noticed surprises me." Her gaze snapped to his. A moment later, she noticed how the dampness of the bay and wind clung to him. How the scent enticed her to lean in closer. "I didn't mean that in a rude way."

"I understand," he said, the truth of it saddening his words. "Maybe I didn't then. Who knows? But I'm noticing a lot of things now, Grace." He rubbed the strands of her hair between his thumb and forefinger. "Why is it I can remember the texture and scent of your hair, but nothing else?"

"Maybe because I was the last person you saw before you passed out." She saw the flash in his eyes, the desire that took the blue to slate. Her hand went to his chest to hold him off, but she ended up curling her fingers in the soft hair.

"My memories revolve around scents. Textures." His finger slid down her cheek, settled at the corner of her mouth. "Tastes."

Her body shuddered at the images his words invoked. "Stop, Jacob."

"I've tasted you before." His lips replaced his finger trailing down her cheek to the hollow beneath her ear. He nibbled, groaning softly when her body jerked in reaction. "Sweet." His mouth followed the line of her throat. Her head tilted back giving him more access. "Help me remember, Grace."

The heat of his mouth licked over her skin, seeped into her pores. Help him remember? She couldn't even think. Couldn't breathe.

The heat became dizzying. She reached out, tried to hold on. Suddenly, Jacob broke off the kiss. He swore. It wasn't until then she noticed her hand gripping his shoulder.

Fear made her drop her hand, but it was embarrassment that made her take a step back.

"Well, nothing like a little pain to kill the mood." Jacob strained for light humor, but couldn't get it past the rasp in his throat.

"No more," she whispered on a shaky breath. Her eyes darted to his. "I won't be seduced—"

"Again?" He shrugged and moved off the counter. "All right. We won't go there. For now."

When he stepped out of the bathroom, she found herself following him. "I mean it," she insisted, even if the words sounded lame to her own ears.

"All right." He tugged on a dress shirt, buttoned it half way up. "I could use something to eat. How about you?" When she didn't answer, he continued, "We only have a few hours before we go after your keys. I suggest you eat something, then take a nap." When he walked past her, he kissed her gently on the forehead. "You look like hell, Grace."

"I what?" But her words fell on an empty room. Annoyed, she followed him into the kitchen.

"There's milk, eggs, an assortment of take-out leftovers." Jacob straightened from inside the refrigerator.

"The house looks hardly lived in."

"You've always had a cleaning service—" Grace froze.

"What is it?"

"I've figured out a way to call my father."

"No," he declared. "The authorities will be watching your father."

"He has a housekeeper. Her name is Carol Reed. The police wouldn't have tapped into her cell phone, right?"

"Probably not, but that doesn't mean—"

"I can call her—"

"I said *probably,* Grace," he emphasized. "Even if the police overlooked her phone, would you trust her not to report back to them?"

"Yes. She's been with my father for years."

"It's too much of a risk," he said after a moment.

"If he's talked to the police, he might be able to help us," she pressed.

"It's still too risky. There's equipment out there. Laser microphones, for instance. A good one will pick up conversations from a hundred yards away."

"A what?"

"A microphone that…" He shoved his fingers through his hair. "Never mind."

"If I promise to not give out any information, we should be safe. Right?"

"What if Helene's murderers have a tap on your dad? What makes you think they won't use him to get to you? If you're not worried about your safety, worry about his."

"I am. That's why I want to warn him, Jacob." Her statement drifted between them. A hushed whisper filled with fear.

Jacob swore. "All right. Is his house fairly large? Bigger than this one?"

"Yes."

"Then have him walk into the closet or another room without windows."

"Why?"

"If they haven't bugged the house or the phones, they would have to use a laser microphone, which needs a window to record voice vibrations."

"These are big 'ifs.'"

Jacob handed her a disposable phone. "Make it short, simple. And no information. You can tell him you're safe. Even tell him not to worry. But don't tell him anything else. Then hang up."

"He might have information." She punched Carol's number into the phone.

"Then he better give it to you quickly. No more than a minute, Grace."

The phone picked up after the first ring.

"Hello?"

"Carol, it's Grace." She heard the housekeeper gasp, pictured her small, round face going slack with shock. "Please don't say my name out loud. And listen for a moment. I need you to go to the nearest room without window. A bathroom or a closet, okay?"

"Okay. One moment."

"Thank you, Carol." She waited until she heard a door shut. "Where are you?"

"In the pantry." Carol paused, seemingly shaking off her upset. "Grace. My god, where are you? Your father is sick with worry."

"I know," she replied, grateful the housekeeper had followed her instructions. "Tell me. Have the police been there?"

"Not the police. But someone from the government. FBI maybe," Carol answered, her voice lowered to a whisper. "They did not talk to me, so I can't be sure. But they spent over an hour in the library with your father."

"Is he there?"

"Yes. He hasn't left since he discovered you missing at your home."

"I'm going to hang up, Carol. I want you to get my dad and make sure he stays in the pantry with your phone. Tell him I'll ring him in five minutes. Okay?"

"Okay, Grace," the older woman acknowledged. "I don't know what you're involved in, but please take care of yourself."

"I will. Thank you." Grace hung up the phone before the housekeeper responded.

For the next five minutes, Grace paced the floor. Neither she nor Jacob spoke but the hard set of his features told her he wasn't happy.

Finally, Grace hit the phone's redial.

Her father answered on the first ring.

"Grace?"

"Hi, Dad." She paced back and forth, ignoring Jacob's frown.

"Thank God. Are you okay. Are you safe?"

"I'm safe," she answered. "Are you in the pantry, Dad?"

"Yes, yes," he said impatiently. "Where are you? When I got back to your house I found—"

"I know what you found. Look, I don't have much time," she said. "Have you been questioned by the police?"

"Of course. I walked right into their crime scene," he answered. "Why did you run away?"

"Dad, those two men tried to kill us. They broke into the house—"

"There were two?"

"Yes, Jacob knocked the second unconscious."

"Grace," Jacob warned, his hand reaching for the phone. She jerked away.

"Grace, where are you?"

"I told you, somewhere safe." She glanced at Jacob.

"Come home. The police can protect you."

"No. These men are dangerous, Dad. I think they have connections. Until I'm sure, I need you to be careful."

"The police think you're dead. Murdered by the same person who killed Helene," her father said, his tone low, suspicious. "They suspect it's Jacob."

"Did you tell them he was there?"

"No. But if they search hard enough, they'll probably turn up his DNA." Her father paused. "Is Jacob Lomax the baby's father?"

"Yes."

Her father swore. Something he never did. "Dad—"

"Never mind that, Grace. They questioned me about Helene's computer. Do you have it? They said it wasn't in the office or her home. They seem to think it holds the key to her murder."

"I don't have it. I thought it was at the bar."

"Grace," Jacob prompted.

"I've got to go, Dad. Please be careful. These men are dangerous," she whispered, blinking back tears. Words caught like shards of glass, shredding her throat until it burned like hellfire. She hung up the phone.

"I couldn't say it." Tears formed, then spilled. "I couldn't tell my own father that I love him."

Suddenly, Jacob's arms were around her. He led her to the couch and cradled her in his lap.

And she cried. Long, gut-wrenching sobs that set her body quaking. The problem was, she didn't know what she was crying over. Helene. The baby. Her father.

She cried because, at that moment, she had no more left in her. No more courage. No more strength.

Nothing left but the need to release.

For what seemed like hours, Jacob held her. Rocking her close to his chest. And when that didn't work, he whispered soothing words against her temple.

When the tears stopped and she settled, he kissed the wetness off her cheeks, rubbed her back until the shaking stopped.

"Feel better?"

She nodded into the hollow of his neck. "I don't suppose we can blame my hormones for that?"

His laugh rumbled deep within his chest. She tucked her hands between their chests, used his heartbeat to soothe.

"I'd probably blame exhaustion myself."

"I can see your point. A good cry is always draining." Her lips curved into a smile against his throat. "I'll tell you what. When it's your turn for a bout of hysteria, I'll hold you. Then after, we'll blame yours on the hormones."

"Deal." He shifted, reclining back on the couch. He pulled her down to him, tucking her head beneath his chin, her legs caught between his. "I think we both could use a nap."

She snuggled her cheek against the open vee of his shirt, enjoying the clean, masculine scent, the comforting rhythm of his heart beneath her cheek.

She'd missed this. The closeness with another human being. The simple act of holding someone, touching him, comforting him.

Loving him.

The crying, she understood now, had been the catalyst she needed to clear her head, help her mind catch up to what her heart already understood.

She'd never fallen out of love with Jacob.

Chapter Twelve

"We should have made the eleven o'clock news," Jacob commented while Grace cleared away their dinner dishes.

She'd woken up earlier to the sizzle of bacon and eggs frying.

"Guess the murder wasn't as big a deal as we thought," she said wryly.

"Or instead of the police covering up," Jacob answered, his brows lowered into a frown, "someone in the media is stopping it. Or both."

"You're saying that whoever is involved in Helene's murder owns the media in this area?"

"It's a definite possibility."

A chill went down Grace's spine.

"Tell me about Helene."

Grace wiped her hands on a nearby dish towel and leaned against the counter. "No-nonsense. Sexy in a cool, untouchable way. You were very much alike. You could have been formed from the same mold. A his and hers. I think I envied that about both of you."

"How did you meet?"

"At a political event. I was dating an up-and-coming lobbyist at the time."

"Was she political then?"

"Yes. Extremely so. Very much like my father. She enjoyed living amongst the Capitol Hill elite. Especially lately."

"Why do you say that?"

"The presidential election is only a few months away and she had been following the coverage very closely. She always seemed connected to everything. Politics, business, the world economy. She attended the right dinner parties, always escorted by the right people."

"You sound like you envied her."

"Only her decisiveness. She had the courage to back up her choices."

"From where I'm sitting, she has nothing on you."

"You wouldn't say that if you remembered her," she prodded mildly.

"Maybe she considered you her friend."

"She did. I think you and I were her closest, and still I didn't know much about her," Grace replied. "And now she's dead and I don't even know who to notify."

"Did she have a safe? Anything that she kept her personal papers in?"

"None that I knew." Grace stopped, slapped her hands on the counter in quick succession. "That's wrong. She kept most of her business records on her computer. One of those new, sleek laptops."

Grace swung to him. "Dad said the police were interested in finding her computer. At the time, it didn't register because I was overwhelmed emotionally. But he said the police couldn't find the laptop at the bar or her apartment."

"If she had always had it with her, it would have been at the bar, right?" Jacob glanced around. "Or here."

"Pusher." A slow smile slid across her face. "With everything going on, I forgot about Pusher."

"Who's Pusher?"

"Pusher Davis. My bar manager. Ex–bar manager." She straightened from the counter. "If I'm right, Helene had her computer with her. She never went anywhere without it."

"So it's at the bar."

"No, Pusher has Helene's computer."

"How can you be sure?"

"Because Pusher is an ex-con." She paced the floor, trying to sort through the steps the bar manager would have taken after discovering Helene's body.

"I'm not following."

"He's an ex-con who did time for cybercrimes. With a specialty or passion, I guess, for hacking into corporate and federal accounts. And my understanding is that he was the best."

"So, the first thing he would've noticed was—"

"Helene's computer." She sat on the couch, drew up her knees. "He would've taken it. Out of loyalty, if nothing else. Pusher hates cops. The only thing he hates more, he says, is dirty cops."

"First, we find Pusher," Jacob reasoned. "Then we get your keys from the impound."

LAWRENCE "PUSHER" DAVIS stepped off the apartment's elevator. The red carpet, well-lit hallway and pristine chandeliers spoke high-class in volumes.

Pusher lived on the trendy side of Washington, D.C.

Overblown, expensive but in the game he played, it was all about image.

The paper bag rattled a bit in his hand when he dug for his key. Because it played well to anyone happening by, he shifted the bag up into the crook of his arm like a sack of groceries.

For a moment, the irony struck him as funny. Pusher Davis carrying pretend groceries. It wasn't too long back that he'd been forced to go for days without food.

Pusher had grown up with a Baptist mother in South Texas. His father was nothing more than a temporary lover with enough cash to keep his mother in bourbon. Not that Pusher cared. His mom wasn't a mean drunk. On the contrary: the deeper into her stupors, the more genteel she became—spouting one slurred Bible verse after another until she passed out.

Until one day, she passed out and choked to death on her own vomit.

Barely ten years of age and homeless, Pusher took to the streets with only one valuable lesson—the need to survive superseded any laws of man and God.

At the age of twelve, he learned that cops held the same attitude.

And at the age of thirteen, he learned that information, of any kind, was power.

That's when he stole his first computer.

Now he was a grown man, one whom the ladies recognized as a charmer and a rogue. He kept trim, because it was expected, and his muscles were defined, not bulky, because that's what filled a tailored suit well.

He'd been born poor, but knew from the Bible that people

better than him had risen from dirt. A kid on the street, he watched people. He educated himself, studying only the people others stepped out of the way for. How they walked, how they styled themselves. Some he followed for days, studying their lives from the shadows of his own. Eventually, he'd embraced the best of their qualities and shed their worst like a snake's skin.

And when he dug deep and still couldn't find what he needed, he stole it—by mimicking those he'd watched or taking advantage of the poor souls he hadn't.

He had no doubts about who and what he was, but, more importantly, about what he'd done and had become.

The rest was God given. Six feet in height, ice-blue eyes and a boy-next-door grin. Add to the package sun-kissed blond hair—groomed on the short side, styled in the trend of messy chic—and a keen mind.

He held no ill will toward his mother. In fact, he'd always thank her and the sweet Lord for giving him a Texas accent and knowledge of the Bible. Both proved irreplaceable as tools for a hi-tech con man.

Now reformed.

He smiled at the word. As much as a con man could ever reform. His talent ran toward conversation and computers. To him, that made him just an everyday businessman. After all, in his opinion, some of the best cons were pulled by businessmen.

He set Helene's computer on his desk and started it up. The fact he was breaking his parole by just carrying the laptop didn't phase him a bit. The point was just not to get caught.

As predicted, the police had run his rap sheet. He'd been

dragged down to the station and questioned to all hours of the morning. Accusations were thrown back and forth between him and the cops.

He enjoyed the hell out of it. It was an enlightening meeting. Getting grilled gave Pusher a good opportunity to find out more about what was going on. Not by what was said, but more by what wasn't.

Pusher flipped on the lights and went directly to the kitchen. He grabbed a dark ale—his favorite import—from the refrigerator.

A few hours into the interrogation, it all suddenly stopped. They released him with no explanation. In fact, if he had to guess, the investigation was no longer a priority. If it made the local news, he'd be surprised.

The computer flashed on, its screen asking for the password. It would take time, but he would break it. And then he'd find what he was looking for.

Opportunity.

Chapter Thirteen

The meeting hadn't gone well. Richard D'Agostini hadn't
expected it to. These men and women were the elite one
percent of the world. Bankers, politicians, media moguls,
royalty. They were not accustomed to failing, and now they
were vulnerable. They had agreed, albeit reluctantly, to a
small window of time to let him deal with the situation.

And deal with it he would.

Tall, stoic and somewhat bald, he had the older, notable
features of a Harvard scholar. And he played the distin-
guished, upper-class role of Senate Majority Leader like one
who'd risen to royalty. He wore his pedigree like a tailored
suit—custom-made and fitted, with a well-honed charm and
a sense of diplomacy.

A quick knock on his suite door drew his attention.
"Come in."

Oliver Kragen loosened his tie as he shut the door behind
him.

"Oliver. Have a seat." Richard indicated one of the high-
back leather chairs. "Do you have a situation report?"

"Lomax killed Webber," Oliver said without preamble.
"Not that it was a loss."

"You mean because Webber was my man." It was a statement, not a question, but one Richard wanted answered nonetheless.

Oliver had been working for Richard for too many years not to understand his answer had better be an acceptable one.

"No, because Webber was an encumbrance. Lomax escaped from us twice because of him." Oliver sat in the chair and rested his ankle across one knee.

"He didn't allow Helene Garrett past his guard. You did." Richard paused, sensing rather than seeing Oliver's annoyance. Oliver was too good at what he did to show any reaction to Richard's baiting, but the senator couldn't help twisting the knife just a little bit more. Sometimes Oliver needed reminding of who pulled his strings. "And it seems the score now is three for Lomax, one for you." He walked over to his minibar and picked up the decanter of Scotch. "It appears Mr. Lomax is getting the better of you, Oliver."

He poured two glasses and brought one over to the younger man.

"Lomax is containable, Senator," Oliver commented, then took the glass and finished it in one swallow.

Something Richard would never consider doing. "Suppose you tell me how you plan on containing him." Richard took a drink from his glass.

"Once we have the Primoris files and the code back, he becomes less of a threat," Oliver reasoned.

"First we have to get them back."

Oliver pulled a disk from his pocket and walked over to the television. "Helene and Grace Renne had lunch together yesterday at a local bistro. Sweeney got his hands on the restaurant's security tapes. Seems the owner is somewhat of a techno nut and has a pretty decent security setup." He placed the DVD into the driver and hit the button. "Here's something you might want to see."

"You took a video from someone," the senator stated.

"Not me. Sweeney."

"At gunpoint?" Richard understood Oliver certainly wouldn't have hesitated to do the job himself. Something Richard never approved of really. As his top aide, Oliver needed to curb his tendencies toward violence.

Oliver shrugged. "Does it matter? I'm sure he was discreet."

A picture flashed across the television screen of Helene Garrett at a table, alone.

Oliver froze her image. "Take a look."

"What is she grabbing?" the senator asked as he watched, his drink held midair.

"Grace Renne's phone and keys."

"So what?" He took another swallow, then set the glass down.

"Watch." Oliver hit the slow motion button. Both men watched as Helene brought the phone and keys under the table into her lap. Two minutes later, she got up to leave.

"She kept her hands under the table," Oliver observed. "I think Helene made the drop to Grace Renne before she even met with Lomax last night."

"Looks like someone is keeping secrets from us," Richard mused. "So are we assuming Grace Renne now knows?"

"I think we must assume that, sir."

"Then take care of her. I want to see this over, Oliver," Richard ordered. "Now."

"It will be," Oliver agreed. "By the way, I had Lomax's DNA run through the government databases."

"And?"

"If he's an operative, the government buried him deep. One of my associates is working on it."

"It doesn't matter. Whoever he is, we'll find him," he murmured, and gazed out over the city. "And with him, we'll have the Renne woman and the Primoris file."

THE WIND PICKED UP pieces of garbage, whipped them around like confetti in front of the strip club. Its only neon light flashed its name, Chancellor's, in a hot-pink flare that drew more than the casual crowd off the street.

"Are you sure this is safe?" Grace asked.

"It's packed in here. Pusher made a good choice. Would be hard to find us in here."

"Good evening, sir." The dark eyes of the doorman—a guy on the younger side of thirty with more tattoos than hair—were curious but steady as they swept over Grace. "Club rules require that I search our guests. Do you mind?"

Grace tensed next to Jacob. He slid his arm around her and drew her close. "Not at all." Jacob smiled easily.

With a quiet efficiency, the bouncer patted Jacob down and checked Grace's purse.

"Thank you." The bouncer handed Grace back her purse and stepped to the side. "Enjoy your visit."

After walking through the door, Grace slipped the gun from under Helene's navy peacoat and gave it to Jacob. "How did you know he wouldn't search me?"

"Educated guess."

The music was loud, the air thick with cigars and perfumed oils.

A woman appeared, her black jacket and matching mini-skirt identifying her as one of the bartenders. "Mr. Lomax?"

"Yes," Jacob answered, his hand cupping Grace's elbow.

"Mr. Davis asked me to escort you to his table. This way, please."

They followed the woman to a semihidden booth in one of the far corners of the club.

"Pusher." Grace sighed in relief. She stepped away from Jacob to give her bar manager a hug. "I'm so glad to see you're okay."

Pusher pulled Grace into the curved booth beside him and kissed her cheek. "How are you doing?" His eyes darted down, just enough for her to get his meaning. She gave him another quick hug. "Fine. We're both fine."

"Lomax." Pusher rose slightly, reached across the table for a handshake. "Sure am glad to see you again."

"Glad to be seen," Jacob said noncommittally.

When Jacob didn't reach to shake, Pusher's hand dropped to his tie, smoothing it down. "Act like your having a good time. Otherwise, we're all in trouble." He waved a few fingers, signaling the waitress.

Within moments, a waitress dressed in a French maid's outfit appeared at their table. The woman was slight in build, teetering on the unhealthy side of one hundred pounds. A short cap of blond curls framed thin, delicate features, adding almost a comical edge to the slashes of red blush across each cheekbone and the matching crimson lipstick that slicked puffy lips. But it was her eyes that drew Grace's attention, caused her to settle uncomfortably in her seat. The big, sky-blue irises glittered with an unnatural intensity, rapidly shifting back and forth beneath long, mascara-laden lashes. "Hello. What can I get you all?"

Pusher smiled, revealing a perfect set of straight, white teeth. "A vodka martini for the gentleman, Maggie my darlin'. And another highball for me." Pusher glanced at Grace. "A glass of tonic water for the little lady."

"Sure thing, Mr. Davis." Maggie picked up Pusher's glass and set it on her tray. "The bar is really crowded tonight so I might be a few extra minutes."

"No problem, honey," Pusher responded with a slow wink. "We're in no hurry."

When Maggie left the table, Grace let impatience get the better of her.

"Since when do you hang out in strip bars?" She glanced pointedly beyond their table to the row of steel poles set on a long narrow stage. Half a dozen woman clad in a rainbow selection of G-strings worked their way around the poles in slow, seductive twirls and slides.

"I don't usually, but under the circumstances..." Pusher shrugged. "A few years back, I did the owner a few favors. That's why I asked you to meet me here. We're practically among friends. Besides, it's easier to keep my ear to the streets here. Fish out information on what happened to Helene."

"Did you find out anything?" Jacob asked.

"Word has it that Helene had hooked up with a major player in the city. Someone who foots big parties for even bigger clients."

"Who?" Jacob snapped out the question before Grace could.

"At this point, it can be anyone. But whoever it is has their fingers in every underground business in this district. Drugs, prostitutes, gambling. You name a sin, they've got the market cornered."

"Do you have Helene's computer?"

"Yes," he said. "I grabbed it before the police arrived. Trouble is, I've accessed most of the files and come up with nothing that might give us a clue why she was murdered."

"Did you bring it?"

"Under the table." Pusher took the stirrer from his glass and tossed it onto a nearby napkin.

"We need that computer, Pusher," Jacob said. "Whoever killed Helene might be after what's in her files."

"You can take it with you. I made a copy of the files to play with them a little more, just in case there is something encoded."

"What did you find on the computer?" Grace asked.

"That's the interesting part. Other than regular business files for the bar, like accounts and supplies, I discovered a couple of dozen dossiers on some pretty important people."

"Such as?" Jacob leaned forward.

"Articles and notes on the upcoming presidential election. The candidates, the voting, their supporters. A complete workup on Richard D'Agostini. From his college days."

"The Maryland senator?" Grace asked, puzzled.

"The one and the same." Pusher paused. "But he's much more than that. He's the Senate Majority Leader and a pretty powerful force on Capitol Hill."

"Here ya go folks," Maggie stepped up to the table and placed their drinks in front of them. "If you need anything else, just wave me down. Otherwise I'll check back with you in a little while."

"Thanks darlin'," Pusher said, then waited until Maggie left once again.

"If you were looking for Helene's major player, D'Agostini would be the one at the top of the list," Jacob commented.

"Sure would be." Pusher studied Grace for a second.

"What is it?"

"There was also a file on Alfred Langdon."

"Who is Langdon?" Jacob asked.

"He's the man my mother worked for." Grace frowned. "She was his top aide. He was running for reelection to the Senate. They died together in a plane crash right before the election that year. D'Agostini ran in Langdon's place and won the Senate seat."

"There's a coincidence."

"If you believe in them," Pusher acknowledged. "I don't."

"But why would Helene have that information?"

"She had more than that. She had a complete file on you, Grace."

"Me? Why?"

"Maybe she investigated you before she decided to become partners with you," Pusher commented. "She also had an extensive file on both your parents."

"Did she have anything on me?" Jacob asked.

"Some contact information. Phone numbers. Addresses," Pusher observed. "Didn't realize you were worth so much in worldwide real estate, Lomax. Otherwise I might have been nicer to you."

Jacob raised an eyebrow at that.

Pusher drained his drink. "It's all here." He reached under the table, pulled out the small laptop bag.

"All of it?" Jacob repeated, his tone sharp.

"I don't double-cross friends, Lomax," Pusher said, his own tone showing the same edge. "Not that you're my friend, but Grace is. I owe her my life. I don't pay my debts with betrayal."

Jacob studied him for a moment, then gave a quick nod.

"The file you want is listed under Primoris."

"Primoris?" Jacob frowned. "That's Latin for first or foremost. So the only good lead we have may be in one of those files."

"How did you figure out the password, Pusher?" Grace asked.

The bar manager shrugged. "I didn't. I bypassed the security and deciphered it afterward."

"You think one of those files will tell us who is behind this?" Grace asked.

"It didn't help me get any closer," Pusher responded. "But it's all we have at the moment. How are you two set for money and transportation?"

"We're fine for now. We're staying—"

"Out of sight," Jacob finished for Grace.

Pusher nodded, understanding.

"One other thing, Pusher. I need to go shopping for some equipment. Hi-tech stuff. Know anyone who doesn't ask questions?"

"Sure." Pusher pulled out a pen from his pocket and wrote an address on the napkin. "The dude who runs this place can hook you up. His name is on the napkin. Just tell him I sent you."

He handed Jacob the information. "If I get more information, where do you want me to contact you?"

"We'll contact you," Jacob said easily enough, then pocketed the napkin. "Soon."

Grace leaned down and kissed the bar manager's cheek. "Thanks, Pusher."

He caught her arm when she was about to turn away. "Be careful, darlin'."

"She will." Jacob cupped her elbow as they made their way through the tables. Suddenly Jacob stopped and swore. "We've got company.

A head above the crowd, it was easy to spot Frank Sweeney. Just then, the enforcer turned. His eyes caught Grace's and she gasped.

"Let's go!" Jacob yelled.

He snagged her hand and pulled. They shoved their way through the crowd, making little headway.

"They're coming." A quick glance told her Sweeney would catch them if she didn't think of something. She reached into her purse, grabbed a handful of cash and threw it up in the air behind them. A wall of people screamed. Strippers, bartenders, customers rushed the floor, diving for the money.

"Of all the—" Jacob swore. "I didn't give you half of our cash, so you could toss it away."

Quickly, they burst through the front doors, then ducked down the side street where they'd left the truck.

"It worked, didn't it?" Grace demanded, when they reached the truck. She automatically stepped to the driver's side. They were broke but safe. That's all Grace cared about.

"I'll drive." Jacob said, his voice barely containing the anger.

"What's the matter?"

"I'd like to know how Sweeney knew we'd be at Chancellor's."

"You don't think Pusher—"

"I won't if you can give me a better explanation."

Grace didn't say anything, simply because she couldn't.

Chapter Fourteen

Pusher threw money on the table and headed out the back. Since he didn't see Jacob and Grace in the throng of people, he'd just have to trust the man could take care of Grace.

He opened the door to the women's dressing room. A few of the girls screamed—mostly the half-naked ones—while others threw clothes and shoes.

"Sorry, ladies," Pusher said with a smile, dodging them and their sailing shoes. Quickly, he made his way to the back exit and stepped out into the alley behind the club.

He took a deep breath, clearing his head of the smoke and stale air. A slight shift in the shadows had him taking a step back and reaching for the pistol in his suit pocket.

"You look like a man with a problem, Pusher." Maggie, cigarette in her hand, stepped into the rim of light.

"Maggie, darlin'." Pusher let his hand fall back to his side. "You scared the hell out of me." He nodded toward the cigarette: "I thought you told me you'd quit those a few weeks ago."

She dropped the butt and smashed it under her heel. "I did, but today…" Maggie stopped. "Never mind."

Pusher liked Maggie. She'd pulled herself up from the gutter. Word had it that she had battled a drug problem for over a year and won. "Look, Magpie, I wish I could hang tonight. But I have important business to take care of. I'll catch you later, okay?"

"Sure, Pusher. I'll see you later."

He straightened his tie and stepped past her. Suddenly a hand gripped his shoulder from behind. Pain shot from his neck to his head. His knees buckled.

"Going somewhere, Pusher?"

The hand turned Pusher just far enough so he could see a man's face.

"Do I know you?"

"The name is Sweeney." The big man looked at his associate. "Pay the lady, Miller."

The second guy took a couple of hundred-dollar bills from his wallet. A big, bullish man with droopy lips and heavy eyelids, Miller wouldn't win any beauty contests, Pusher thought wryly.

"Sorry, Pusher." Maggie stuck the bills into her bra, her eyes meeting his with a quiet defiance even as they filled with tears. "I needed the money." With a sad smile, she turned back down the alley.

"I don't suppose we can talk about this, gents," he said, trying to ignore the death grip on his shoulder.

"Oh, you'll be talking. But to a man named Kragen," Sweeney commented. "He wants discuss a few things with you regarding Grace Renne and her new friend. I suggest you give the right answers, because your life will—" the smaller man grunted in pain as Sweeney squeezed his collarbone to emphasize his point "—depend on it."

"I guess I can spare a few minutes of my time." Pusher's struggle for nonchalance was lost in a painful rasp.

"Glad to hear it. Now I'd rather you walk to our car on your own two feet, but if you, say, get the urge to run, I have no problem throwing you in the car in a few broken pieces. Your choice."

Pusher didn't fight his way from the streets without learning a thing or two about survival.

"If I say okay, can I have my shoulder back?"

Sweeney let go and Pusher hit the ground. Pain exploded through his kneecaps, but he didn't cry out. He rolled his shoulder, helping the blood flow back into his muscles. "I'll have a chat with Kragen. But I'm not quite sure how I can help him."

"By having answers, Pusher. Because if you don't, I can guarantee you won't be able to help yourself."

"Lead the way, gentlemen," Pusher joked before he stood and dusted off his suit.

Sweeney shoved him forward. "You first."

Chapter Fifteen

The impound lot was located on the outskirts of town and hard to miss. As far as Grace knew, it was the only ten-foot-high chain-link fence topped with spirals of barbed wire in a fifty-mile radius of Annapolis.

"There's a good chance the perimeter is wired," Jacob muttered. He glanced down at his arm. "I'm going to cut through the fence. Which means I'm going to need your help."

Grace raised an eyebrow, wondering how much it cost him to make that confession. "Shouldn't we wait until midnight? Ten o'clock seems a little early."

"They shut down at six. The security guard is the only one we have to worry about." He handed her his Glock. "Ever shot a gun?"

"No." The steel was warm and smooth against her palm, surprising her. She expected the steel to be cold, the grip rough.

"Keep an eye out for the security guards. And for God's sake, don't shoot them."

"Then why give me a gun?"

"Because our friends might be out there, too. If you see one of them, aim for their chest and empty the clip."

He grabbed a small laser cutter from the backpack at his feet. "I'm going to keep the cuts low, so both my hands are going to be busy."

"I'll keep watch." Grace scanned the yard. More than a hundred parked cars lined the lot under the yellow glow of flood lights. It was like looking for the proverbial needle in a haystack.

As if he knew what she was thinking, Jacob said, "You're wasting your time. We don't need the car, we need the keys."

He nodded toward the trailer office to the left of their position. "I'm betting the keys are hanging in there."

The chain-link fencing broke free. Just as he lifted the bottom edge to slide under, dogs barked in the distance. "Figures. Cops' budget. Cheaper security and no pension plans."

Jacob cursed, then glanced at the gun.

Understanding, Grace whispered. "I'm not shooting the guard dogs."

He shrugged, letting the fence fall back into place. "Just a thought."

"Find another."

Suddenly, two German shepherds hit the fence at a dead run, their barks shattering the night air.

"How fast can you run?"

Grace watched the animals growl, their teeth bared back to their molars. "Not funny."

Jacob sat back on his heels. "Okay, let's go with plan B."

"What's plan B?"

"Back to the car."

Grace followed him to the truck and slid into the passenger seat. "We're just going to leave?"

He glanced at her. "Buckle up." Then he twisted wires together, starting the ignition. With suppressed annoyance, he shoved the truck into Reverse. "Hold on to something," he ordered, then punched the gas.

Too late, Grace realized his intention. The truck plowed through the locked gate of the lot.

"Are you crazy?" She screamed and grabbed for the dash-board.

He whipped the truck around and aimed for the wooden porch in front of the portable office trailer.

Within seconds, they plowed through, smashing the wood and scraping the side panel with a loud screech.

"Roll down your window and get ready to get us the hell out of here."

Within seconds, he crawled over her and climbed out the window and up on the roof of the truck's cab.

The dogs hit the truck, their teeth bared, their bodies trembling with anger as they jumped up against the driver's window.

Jacob kicked the trailer door in on the second try and slid from the roof in through the office doorway.

Immediately, Grace slid over to the driver's seat. "Come on," she murmured and gripped the wheel. In the distance, she could hear a set of sirens, certain they were heading in their direction.

A few minutes later, Jacob tossed a garbage bag full of keys in through the passenger window before climbing through himself.

"Go!"

Grace hit the gas and sped out of the parking lot, relieved when both dogs stopped their chase a block away from the impound.

She glanced over at Jacob. "Your shoulder is bleeding."

"I probably ripped open the stitches." He leaned his head against the back of the seat and closed his eyes. The wind washed over him, cooling the damp sweat on his skin. "But no dogs were hurt."

She nodded toward the bag. "You didn't know which keys were mine."

"Nope. So I grabbed them all."

"They'll know now that I helped you. There were cameras."

"Grace, there are always cameras."

In his mind's eye, he saw the flash. Helene was laughing at him—her face masked, her body sheethed in black spandex climbing gear. They were suspended from the side of building, hanging on ropes with pulleys.

Be careful, we've got cameras at two o'clock.

Darling, Helene laughed softly, there are always cameras.

The image faded into a frustrating void. He waited for more of the memory to break free. But no more came.

Earlier, when they left the house, Grace followed the truck with the SUV. "Time to ditch the truck. The front headlight is out, so be careful. We can't risk getting pulled over before we get it out of the way."

They left the truck parked on a deserted street and walked to Jacob's SUV two blocks away. "Do you have a key chain for your keys so I can find them easier?"

"It's a USB thumb drive in a black leather key chain." Grace stopped. "Do you think it would be that simple? She could've switched my USB with one of hers at the restaurant yesterday. I wouldn't have noticed."

"If she did, it won't be simple. Those keys sat at the bottom of the bay for a good three hours or more."

Once in the SUV, Grace drove while Jacob searched for her keys. It took a good fifteen minutes before he finally located them. "The leather case protected it to some extent but it's still wet."

"Does that mean it's ruined?"

"Possibly." He examined the small thumb drive. "But a USB memory stick has no moving parts and we're at the north end of the bay. With all the rains, that part of the bay is likely more fresh water than salt water right now. We could get lucky."

"We need a blow-dryer," Grace suggested.

"Blow-dryer might damage it. Our best bet is to let it dry naturally," Jacob reasoned. "But we might not have the time."

"Could the password code from my phone be for the files?"

"Hell, we don't even know if this holds the missing files. For all we know, it could be Helene's grocery list."

"I CAN APPRECIATE a man who wants to deal, Pusher." Oliver Kragen leaned against the bar in the gymnasium. "But some things I just don't haggle over."

Earlier, he ordered Sweeney to handcuff the bar manager to a chair. Not because he expected the younger man to escape but simply to keep him in the chair once the interrogation started taking its toll.

Which, in all honesty, the bar manager passed a good hour before the toll showed.

Pusher's head dropped forward against his chest. Blood dripped from the broken nose and split lips, soaking the shirt beneath.

Kragen nodded to Sweeney, who placed a bottle of ammonia under Pusher's nose to bring him around.

"Pusher, we need to establish some kind of rapport here."

He grabbed the younger man's hair and forced his head back until he was looking straight up into Oliver's eyes.

Pusher's face was no more than blood and ripped skin. Not surprising to Oliver, considering skin never held up well against leather-covered fists.

"Now, I'm going to ask you again where Helene Garrett's computer is."

"I told you Lomax has it," Pusher answered, his words slurred by his swollen lips.

"But you failed to tell me where Lomax is."

"I don't know. They were to get in touch with me."

"About what?"

"Updates on Helene's murder."

"And this disk I found in your pocket?" When Pusher's head lolled forward, Oliver slapped it back. "The disk!"

"I don't know. Haven't had a chance to look at it yet."

That earned Pusher another backhand across the face. Oliver nodded to Sweeney, who walked over to a nearby desk.

He slid the disk into the laptop computer.

"We need a password," said Sweeney after looking at the screen. "I could probably find someone to break it."

"That would take too much time. Besides," Oliver reflected, as he glanced down at Pusher, "I have the feeling the answer is right here on the tip of Pusher's tongue. We just need to convince Mr. Davis that giving us the password might just save that same tongue."

"Take a look at this, Jacob."

It was after two in the morning, but Grace wasn't willing to go to bed until they read Helene's computer files.

"Oliver Kragen. Top aide to Senator D'Agostini." She

rubbed the gritty fatigue from her eyes. Then looked again. "I've seen this guy before."

"With Helene?"

"I don't remember. Maybe at a political event."

"Pusher said she had detailed files on a lot of people."

"Including me, my father and mother. From the time my parents met in the military to my mother's death. And my father after."

"According to this," Jacob said, scrolling down, "your dad had top security clearance."

"What do you mean? He was a spy?"

"Not necessarily. He could have been in charge of a specific project, or even a specific part of the government or war department." Jacob pinched his nose between his forefinger and thumb. Without thinking, he walked to the kitchen cabinet, found the aspirin and took a few.

It wasn't until he finished swallowing the tablets dry that he realized what he'd done. Obviously, on some level he remembered where the pills were located.

"She's got complete files on several of her business acquaintances. And on Pusher and myself, too."

"But?" Jacob glanced at Grace, impatient.

"Pusher was right, she has nothing on you, Jacob." She paused, considering. "Other than a few addresses. Why?"

JACOB HEARD BRANCHES banging against the house. He tensed, and then relaxed. He blinked away the grit in his eyes and slowly flexed the stiffness from his bad shoulder.

He glanced over at Grace, gave in to the urge to smooth away the stray strand of hair on her cheek. Why had he walked away from her? She shifted closer, partially lying on him.

It took him a while to convince her to share the bed with him. But he did so on the pretense he didn't want to mistake her for an intruder.

She accepted his suggestion only after he agreed to sleep on top of the blankets. But in the end, it didn't matter. She moved restlessly in her sleep and kicked off her covers.

His hand automatically came up, drifted over her spine. She'd changed her clothes, finding a pair of black jogging pants to use for pajamas and a thin cotton T-shirt as her top.

The hem had worked its way up past her waist. Unable to stop himself, he placed his hand over her belly, just above her panty line. The pregnancy had hardened her stomach. Something in him shifted. Something he didn't look at too closely. Not yet.

He noticed a tattoo just inside the curve of her hip. His fingers slid over the delicate tracings of the butterfly wings.

Why a butterfly?

She smiled, running a hand up over his hip. Why the scar?

The memory stopped him. It wasn't the first. He'd been having bits and pieces all night since the one of Helene.

But the few he had after were all of Grace.

Her on a lounger beside a pool. Both of them sailing the bay. Romantic dinners. Evenings at the theater. Even more evenings at her home in front of the fire.

Each memory connected. Each ending with them kissing or making love.

But when? Five months ago? A year? He didn't know. Winter. Aspen. Long enough to have fathered the baby? He'd suspected all along, but suspecting and having proof were two different things.

Restless, he snagged a pair of jeans by the bed, slipped them up over his hips, only to pause before zipping.

It was there, just at the top point of his right hip. A jagged, raised mark six inches in length.

Why the scar? she'd asked.

Frustrated that he had no answer, he grabbed the phone off of the nightstand, then slowly climbed the stairs to the tower.

Once up at the top, he tried Pusher's number. But after letting it ring several times, he hung up.

Where in the hell was he?

He heard it then, the soft pad of her feet against the wood steps. "I didn't mean to wake you."

She sighed. "The baby decided to sleep on my bladder. But since you'd been gone so long, I wanted to make sure you were okay. What time is it?"

"After five in the morning," he said and sat on one of the window seats. He forced himself to look at her, study the delicate lines of her face, the soft waves of blond hair that settled on her shoulders. Beautiful, rumpled and decidedly feminine. Something moved inside him. The queer mixture of fear and vulnerability that came with the sense of inevitability. "You should go to bed, Grace. You need rest. If not for you, for the baby."

"The baby is fine," she murmured and stepped closer. He caught a new scent, the spicy scent of his soap she'd used earlier. A fist of desire tightened his gut, caused him to shift away.

Annoyed at his retreat, Jacob pushed the phone into his front pocket, drawing her attention.

"No answer still?"

"None. I think something happened to him."

"Something bad?"

"Something. I don't know what. He could have skipped town. Got thrown in jail again. Defected to the other side."

"I won't believe that. Not Pusher."

"Well, we aren't doing anything about it until tomorrow." Jacob looked out the window at predawn sky. "We'll start with the strip club and work our way from there," he said, then rubbed the back of his neck. "Look, Grace, I don't want you hurt—"

"Then I guess we better figure this all out soon," she responded softly. "Okay?"

The set of his jaw told her it wasn't okay. "Since we're both up anyway, let's see if we can prod your memory," she suggested, trying to distract him with a change of subject. Giving in to impulse, she brushed a stray lock of hair from his forehead.

"Tell me something I didn't know before when we were together," he insisted. He caught her hand, tugged on it until she sat in his lap.

"I was named after a prayer."

"Which one?"

"The Serenity Prayer," she said, her words lost against his neck as she rested her head against his good shoulder. She missed this, the closeness.

As if sensing her thoughts, his arms tightened around her, keeping her safe if only for that moment. "What were the words?" He whispered the question against her hair, making her smile.

"'God, give me grace to accept with serenity the things that cannot be changed, courage to change the things which should be changed, and the wisdom to understand the difference.'"

"Who wrote it?"

"No one knows for sure." After a moment, she added, "It was my mother's favorite, though."

"God, give me Grace," he repeated. She could feel his smile against her ear. "Honey, it's probably a good thing you're mother didn't name you Serenity."

Grace pulled back until her eyes met his. "That's exactly what she used to say." She winked, slow and deliberate. The surge of pleasure rolled through Jacob, catching him off guard. How could he forget a look like that?

"In fact, she swears that when they decided on my name, the earth trembled, just enough for her to know she was in trouble."

"You miss her, don't you?"

"Very much."

Jacob watched the moonlight halo her head, setting the golden highlights on fire. He gave in to the impulse and captured a few strands in his hand. Just then a second flash of memory hit him. "I kissed you here, before."

"Yes."

"It wasn't a friendly kiss, Grace."

"No, it wasn't."

He leaned in until his mouth hovered just above hers. "Anything you need to tell me?"

"Not if I can help it—"

He covered her mouth with his and breathed in her sigh, keeping the kiss light until a sexy purr rounded off the edge of her breath. It took him from comfort to desire in a millisecond.

What man wouldn't take the kiss deeper to hear that sound again, feel the roll from her throat to his gut?

His hand twisted in her hair, keeping her head still in case she wanted to pull away. He dove this time, swallowing her in one, long erotic gulp of sin and sex.

But Grace couldn't pull away. She couldn't think. She couldn't breathe. All she could do was leave herself open under the onslaught. Matching him stroke for stroke, taste for taste, texture upon delicious texture.

When that wasn't enough, when it didn't come close to enough, he brought her up against him, his body hard as much as hers was pliant. When her knees threatened to knock, she thought for a moment of sliding off his lap, giving herself some space, regaining some sanity.

But then he dove again and she managed not to think at all.

Jacob's hand cupped her thigh, keeping her in place. But she had no thought of moving. He squeezed gently, kneading the flesh beneath his fingers, letting his thumb stray in long lazy circles, tempting her to shift and then, moments later, to move against him when he upped the tempo.

When she trembled, Jacob slipped his hand over her belly, groaning when it quivered beneath his fingers.

He nuzzled her neck, followed the cord of it to her collarbone, suckled her nipple through the cotton of her tee. The tremors ripped through her as his fingers slid between her thighs, stroking her until her hips writhed, her muscles quivered.

"Let it go, let me see."

The warm, moist demand against her ear sent her over the edge. Grace erupted, clenching herself around his hand, riding the release, melting into him as it played out.

"I can't believe I've forgotten that," he whispered the

words against her neck. Visibly affected, he kissed her, soothed her trembling body with long, draining kisses until she quieted beneath his touch.

"You're shaking," Grace whispered against his chest. "You're whole body…you've never—"

He raised her chin with his hand, ignoring the slight tremor in his fingers. "Maybe you are finally seeing the real me. Maybe we both are. With no memories, I have nothing to guard against."

The truth of his statement hit her square in the chest. "A relationship with you is impossible, Jacob. You're still the same man. When all is said and done, those guards will go back up once the amnesia is gone." She softened the harsh words by kissing his neck. "You didn't want me then. What good would it do to become lovers again, after all this time?"

"Damn it, we never stopped being lovers, Grace."

"Yes, we did. The minute you walked away from us."

He stilled. "Us?"

"You and me," she snapped, using her finger to point back and forth between them.

For a moment, he'd thought she meant her and the baby. That he'd left her and the baby. "I really did a number on you, didn't I?"

Her silence gave him her answer.

"I'm sorry, honey. I think if I could take it back—" he murmured, then stiffened.

"What?"

"Shh." He instinctively placed his hand over her mouth. Then he heard it again. A car door shutting.

"We've got company." He looked out the tower window and saw two sedans parked outside. "Sweeney."

Grace tensed. "But how?"

"Ask Pusher," Jacob said grimly. "In fact, I'll ask him the next time I see him."

A trunk slammed shut. "They're not worried about surprising us."

"Why?"

"Probably because of all the guns their carrying."

Chapter Sixteen

Hugh Miller was the first to speak up. "Are they there?"

"Don't see them, but Lomax would be smarter than that," Sweeney answered, looking through infrared binoculars. "If I were a betting man, I'd say the odds are in our favor. This was the closest address of Lomax's on the list."

Sweeney took his pistol from his side holster. "If they are there, I want them taken alive. Got that?" Sweeney waved the other three men over. Miller checked his clip. "We need them breathing. Anyone who kills them by accident will be dead before Lomax or Renne hits the ground. Understand me?"

The other men nodded.

"Then let's go."

"GRAB YOUR JACKET and shoes! Now!"

They raced down the tower's stairs to the bedroom beneath. "The car?"

"No. It's too late for that. We're going to have to go across the bay."

Grace followed him down to the lowest level, her own sneakers in hand.

"Get down in the boat."

Within moments, she lay flat on her belly, curled at the bottom.

"No matter what, I don't want you sitting up." Jacob grabbed a nearby gas container and started pouring it over the dock.

The fumes caught in her throat, making her gag. "What are you doing?"

"Making sure they can't follow us."

He jumped into the boat and untied the rope from the post. It wasn't until then he noticed the anchor had been set overboard.

Quickly, he pulled it to the surface.

He swore. Grace glanced over and in the darkness she could see a large bag tied to the anchor weight.

Jacob tossed it into the boat. "What do you want to bet I've found my stash."

He left it and grabbed a life jacket. "Put this on." He took a lighter from his pocket, hit the switch and tossed it onto the dock. Flames immediately spread. "Hold your shirt over your nose."

"Your house, Jacob. You're burning—"

"If I'm as rich as you say, I'll have it rebuilt later."

He slammed the accelerator forward. Gunfire peppered their boat as Sweeney's men shot out from the dock, but none of the bullets hit close.

Grace peered over the side, saw headlights turned on in the distance. "They're following us," Grace yelled the words across the din of the motor.

"It will be hard to follow us without a boat." Jacob studied a bank of trees crowding the beach in the distance. He brought the boat around until it pointed directly toward woods rising over the crest of land.

"Hold on." He jerked the steering wheel until the boat headed straight for the beach. "This is going to get rough."

Chapter Seventeen

In the daylight the Chancellor's was nothing more than drab. Drab brown paint, drab gray cement. Even the neon light, blinking in the afternoon sun, lost the power to catch and hold the gaze of the few pedestrians who strolled past.

Jacob and Grace arrived at the strip club before its doors opened for the nooners escaping their jobs for a lunch hour of distraction and drinks.

"There she is," Jacob murmured, his gaze settling on the street about half a block down from their rented silver sedan.

It took over two hours to find a stretch of beach to ditch the boat, steal another car and head back into the city. And then another hour or so to secure the rented car and check Pusher's apartment.

"Let's go." They had been leaning against the car, waiting. Jacob cupped her elbow and guided her across the street until they intersected with Maggie at the alleyway entrance beside the club.

The blonde tossed her cigarette into the gutter just as they approached. Half expecting her to bolt, Grace braced herself, blocking the waitress's path.

"Hi, Maggie, do you remember us?" Jacob asked.

"Sure, you're Pusher's friends."

She folded her arms across her stomach. But it was her bloodshot eyes that drew Grace's attention.

"Actually, we're looking for Pusher and wondered if you'd seen him."

The waitress looked at Jacob. "You a cop?"

"No."

"You've got the smell of a cop."

"Pusher's my friend, Maggie," Grace said quietly.

"Well, hoorah for you."

"Last night, I got the impression Pusher was your friend, too," Grace added mildly.

"Then you got the wrong impression." Maggie tried to step past but Jacob grabbed her arm and held her in place.

"Let me go." She jerked her arm away, but Jacob gripped tighter. "I'll call a cop."

"You do that, Maggie, and you'll lose out. I'm willing to pay for information."

"How much?"

"Two hundred."

"Make it five and you have a deal."

"Okay, five."

Her eyes narrowed with suspicion. "Show me."

Jacob pulled out his wallet and took out five one-hundred-dollar bills. "They're yours if I get the answers I want."

Maggie stared at the money for a moment. "Okay. That guy who chased you last night? His name is Sweeney."

"We already know that."

"Well, what you don't know is that Sweeney and his goons went after Pusher a few minutes after you left," she said. "Yesterday, one of Sweeney's guys put the word on the

street that he wanted to talk to Pusher. He left his card at all
of Pusher's haunts. Rumor was that Sweeney was looking
for something Pusher had. Said he'd pay good money to just
talk to Pusher."

"So when Pusher showed up here yesterday—"

"I called Sweeney. I told him you two were with Pusher
and Sweeney went ballistic on the phone, ya know? He
started cussing a blue streak. I thought he was going to hang
up but then he told me if I saw you start to leave before he
arrived, I was to stall you if I could."

"Why didn't you?"

"Before I could think of something," she said, then
nodded at Grace, "your girlfriend threw all the money on the
floor." She shrugged. "I stopped and grabbed a few twenties
myself since I couldn't reach you anyway."

"You still haven't told me what Sweeney did with Pusher."

"Give me half first."

"Two hundred," Jacob said and handed over two of the
bills. She stuck them in her bra.

"Sweeney cornered Pusher in the alley last night. He forced
Pusher to go with him. Sweeney said some guy named Kragen
wanted to have a talk with Pusher." She glanced up the street.
"I don't know what about. I'd already gotten my money so I
left."

"Did you say Kragen? As in Oliver Kragen?"

"I don't know. I just heard the last name."

Jacob took the last three bills and stuffed them into her
bra himself. "Thanks. I'll make sure I pass along your story
to Pusher when I see him."

"You do that." Maggie tossed over her shoulder as she
walked toward the club. "If you need anything else, sugar,"

she added, deliberately adopting Pusher's accent, "you all don't forget to look me up."

For the first time, Grace noted Jacob's hands fisted in anger. "We need to find Pusher," he said. "I'm pretty sure I'm the type that would rather give an apology in person."

"Where do you think Sweeney took him?"

"I don't know, but I do know who does."

"Kragen," Grace stated.

"How would you like to attend a presidential election ball tonight?"

"I think I'd love to."

Chapter Eighteen

The Lakelear Grand Hotel stood on posh Connecticut Avenue. Labeled as more of a resort than hotel, Grace had to admit she'd never had the budget for a suite.

She glanced over at Jacob as he pulled up to the front entrance. "How much money was in that bag?" They had already used a good chunk, she thought, to shop for clothes, suitcases and other necessities.

"Enough not to worry about staying here for a while."

The valet opened the door. They had traded the sedan in earlier for a black Porsche. Grace swung her legs out, deliberately waiting to catch the valet's eye before stepping out of the rented Porsche.

"Welcome to the Lakelear."

"Thank you," she said, smoothing her carmel suede mid-thigh skirt back into place.

His smile slowly disappeared as Jacob rounded the hood of the Porsche. "Welcome to Lakelear Grand, sir."

Jacob just nodded, having already given his key to another valet. He cupped Grace's elbow. "Ready, darling?"

"Yes."

The hotel lobby lived up to the glamour and wealth of the D.C. elite, with its marble inlay floor and gold-trimmed reception desk.

"Welcome, sir. May I help you?" A man stood behind the cherrywood counter. His small mustache twitched only slightly.

"My name is John Eckert. My secretary made arrangements for a suite earlier today."

"Yes, Mr. Eckert we've been waiting for you. My name is William Fremont and I'm the assistant manager here at the Lakelear. All your arrangements have been taken care of." He nodded to include Grace, hesitating a long second.

Jacob pointedly ignored the silent request for an introduction. He didn't want to take any chances that her voice would be recognized as his secretary's.

The assistant manager shifted his gaze just over Grace's shoulder. "George will be happy to escort you to your suite." He handed the card to a young man in a bellboy uniform. "The Mayflower Suite, George."

"Follow me, sir."

"One moment." Jacob turned back to the assistant manager.

"Yes, sir."

"It seems one of our pieces of luggage has been forgotten and we'll need replacement clothes for our evening plans. I'll need to be measured for a tuxedo and have several gowns delivered to our room from your clothing boutiques. Have them call our room for the details."

"My pleasure, Mr. Eckert."

Jacob placed his hand at the small of Grace's back as they followed the bellboy.

"ROOM SERVICE work for you?"

It had already been a long afternoon. The boutique had sent up a selection of gowns and the men's shop had sent up their tailor. Both Jacob and Grace were ready for their appearance later that night.

"Maybe a vanilla shake, if you don't mind. My stomach is a little queasy," Grace added, thinking about Pusher. "The shake will help settle it."

As if reading her thoughts, Jacob walked over to her and pulled her to him, wrapping his arms around her. "No, I don't mind but I'm going to order some fruit and a sandwich with it. Try to eat what you can. Pusher will be fine. They won't do anything to him, for a while at least. They want what's on the USB thumb drive. Until they get it, they can't be sure what part he plays in this."

Grace knew Jacob was exaggerating, but there was an underlying truth to his words.

"I'm also worried that someone might recognize you," Grace reasoned. "Unlike me, you wouldn't have any idea who your friends or your enemies are at the ball."

"From what you've said, I don't have too many friends to worry about. That should narrow the playing field."

"That's not funny."

He sighed and placed his forehead against hers. "No, its not. And neither is this situation," he said apologetically. "Look, I've had time to think about the amnesia, Grace. There's nothing I can do about getting my memories back, so I'll just have to learn to punt. Seems that's second nature to me anyway."

"I can't disagree with that."

His hand cupped her jaw, then lifted her face up until she met his gaze. "But I don't think it's second nature to you. That's why I don't want you with me. It's too dangerous. For you and the baby."

"We're going to a swank ball at the Senate Majority Leader's mansion, not a drug dealer's lair."

"Bad guys don't have a dress code."

"I'll be fine," she said. "If there's trouble, I'll lose myself in the crowd like we agreed. Then leave after you've caused a diversion."

"I'll have to accept that, for now," Jacob said. "Why don't you go have a shower? The food will be here by the time you get out. Then after you eat, you can try and get some rest. It's going to be a long night."

"A shower sounds good." But they both noted she didn't comment on the rest of Jacob's statement.

"Most of this kind of work is a waiting game, Grace. We've got hours before the ball."

"What kind of work?"

"Government work," Jacob said automatically, then froze. He tried to follow that same train of thought, only to draw another blank. "Damn it."

"It's a start, Jacob," she said softly and kissed his cheek. "If you worked as an agent, you'd have to keep that from me, wouldn't you?"

"More than likely," he admitted. "But I wouldn't let me off the hook that easily, Grace. For all we know, I could be one of the bad guys."

"No way," she quipped, walking toward the bath. "You dress too nice."

His laughter followed her into the bathroom, making her smile. The old Jacob rarely laughed. So whenever she managed to get him chuckling, she counted it as a victory.

She stripped out of her clothes. On impulse, she studied her image in the mirror. Her breasts had gotten larger, the nipples much darker. A small hard bulge in her tummy told her the baby was growing. The small flutters she'd been feeling on and off told her he was getting more active. For precautionary reasons, she checked for spotting before folding her clothes and placing them on the vanity nearby.

It was hard for her to believe that less than forty hours earlier, she'd been in her house, taking it easy and baking cookies.

Alone.

Chapter Nineteen

On the Hill, there was a saying: Good politics require great staging.

Which made Senator D'Agostini's presidential campaign ball a full-blown Hollywood extravaganza.

Palladian windows were draped in patriotic blue, while diamond-infused chandeliers glittered and sparkled from twenty-foot coffered ceilings.

A sea of satin, silk and tailored tuxedos crowded thirty square yards of glossy herringbone wood, while a fifty-piece orchestra stood in the corner delivering a jaunty but sophisticated big-band sound.

"Dance with me."

Before Grace could react, Jacob's fingers skimmed over the small of her back, urging her forward into the crush of waltzing couples.

They made a striking pair. Jacob had opted for a basic black tuxedo. Severe in cut, the sleek but simple material complemented his broad shoulders, his lean hips. The arrogance of the cut went well with his predatory gaze, the dangerous slant of his chiseled features. A panther, she thought, stalking his prey.

He pulled her to him, holding her in the close intimate

circle of his arms. Making it apparent to anyone watching that they didn't want to be disturbed.

He bent his head close to hers. "Relax," he murmured.

"I am," she whispered back, hoping that saying the words out loud would make them true. Gaining access had been relatively simple. All one needed was to mingle, to laugh and part with a compliment or two about one's golf game or latest insider news on Wall Street. "My role is easy. I'm just the arm candy."

And for that purpose, she'd chosen a strapless gown of ivory silk chiffon. Feminine and alluring, the overlay material flowed from a bodice that hugged her breasts before falling gracefully into a cascaded drape of shirred layers.

She pinned her hair up high on her head, drawing more than one male gaze to the slope of her neck. And more than one female's glance to the diamond solitaires that winked at her earlobes.

"God, you're beautiful." His fingers drifted carelessly over the delicate point of her shoulder, sending ripples of pleasure down her spine.

His arm pressed her closer, until the heat of him seeped through the thin layers of her gown. Grace got lost in the sway of their bodies. She breathed in his warm, masculine scent. Caught the underlying hint of aftershave. She rested her head on his shoulder, promising herself only one song.

Suddenly, he went rigid against her. Her gaze snapped to his. The blue of his irises glittered with a fierceness, a cold savage fury that she'd never seen before. An air of violence suddenly surrounded them both like a tight leash.

A small flutter of panic worked its way up at the back of her throat. "Jacob?"

JACOB HEARD HIS NAME, the plea in Grace's voice through the static of sounds, the rush of images.

Suddenly, he was in an alley. It was dark. Pitch-black, he remembered. Glass crackled beneath his feet—the remnants of the alley's light, shattered by a bullet.

Gunfire spattered the Dumpster above Helene's head. *Get behind me*. But the warning came too late.

Pain exploded in his shoulder, but it was Helene who'd screamed, Helene who'd fallen. Frantic, Jacob reached for her, firing his pistol as he pulled her into his lap.

Blood covered her chest, rattled her lungs. *"Jacob...find Grace."*

The grief welled up inside, then seeped through his pores.

He grabbed her tight, willing her to live.

"Jacob. You're hurting me."

Relief poured through him. He blinked, refocusing.

"Jacob," Grace whispered, her voice harsh with worry or fear, he couldn't be sure.

"Grace." He glanced around the dance floor, satisfied no one really cared that they'd stopped dancing.

He automatically took up the rhythm of music.

"Are you okay?"

"Yes. Just had a flashback, but I'm fine now." He shifted, forcing the muscles in his back to relax.

"Kragen's here."

"Where?" The muscles snapped into tight rubber bands.

"Over your left shoulder."

He maneuvered her around in a slow, lazy circle. Oliver stopped across the room in front of an older gentleman. Jacob recognized the tall, thin, almost frail build. The gray ring of hair that circled a nearly bald head. "D'Agostini," Jacob commented.

Oliver leaned in to the senator, whispered something by the older man's ear, then stepped back again. The senator nodded. Within moments, the senator excused himself from the ball.

"Where are they going?"

"I don't know but we need to find out," Jacob said, realizing the need for revenge had been forgotten—until now. "He's our only lead to Pusher."

Jacob cupped Grace's elbow and led her off the floor.

OLIVER KRAGEN wasn't happy. There was nothing left to get out of Pusher Davis. The man had taken a beating without uttering one word of information. But for some reason, the senator wanted him kept alive.

"Going somewhere, Kragen?" Before Oliver could react, his arm was shoved up and behind his shoulder. Pain rushed up his back and exploded into his rotator cuff.

It would take very little pressure for Lomax to separate his shoulder. He felt a gun jab in his side. "How the hell did you get in here?"

"Doesn't seem your security is worth the money you pay," Jacob answered. He did a quick search of Kragen's pockets. "Although I have to say that you dress them well.

"Now unless you want to get intimately acquainted with a dialysis machine for the rest of your life, I suggest you do as I ask."

"And that is?" Oliver asked.

"Pusher Davis."

"Who?"

Kragen hissed with pain as Jacob applied pressure to his arm, moving it farther up his back. "I don't think you want me to snap your shoulder out of joint, do you?"

"Okay, say he is here. He's…incapacitated at the moment. You would never be able to get him out without notice."

"You let me worry about that, Oliver. All you need to do is take me to him," Jacob replied, his tone mild. "Agreeably. Pretend we're long lost friends." He punctuated his order with another jab of his pistol.

"And if we're seen?"

"You better hope we're not. Because you'll be the first person I'll want out of the way."

Kragen led them to a room on the third floor. In front stood a man, one of the personal bodyguards Jacob assumed.

He jabbed at Oliver's side.

"It's okay, Miller. These people are associates." The tone of Kragen's voice was smooth but firm.

"Grace."

Grace pulled out a small revolver, aimed it at Miller and fired. A dart imbedded itself in Miller's chest. No more than three seconds later, the giant crumpled to the floor.

Jacob shoved Oliver into the door. The senator's aide punched in the key code with his free hand.

Jacob opened the door. "Go, Grace."

Grace stepped through the door and stopped. Pusher lay unconscious on the bed, his wrists in handcuffs, his face nothing more than raw meat and blood.

Jacob stiffened at Grace's cry of alarm, turned slightly to make sure she was safe.

Without warning, Kragen rammed his elbow into Jacob's gut and twisted away. He grabbed for the gun, but Jacob let go of the grip, catching Oliver off guard. Instead, Jacob nailed the aide in the throat, then slammed his elbow into the man's face. He grunted in satisfaction when he felt the bone give beneath the impact.

Jacob snagged the pistol as Oliver went to his knees. He forced the man's head back by his hair and shoved the barrel under his chin.

Kragen gasped, trying to find his breath through the bruised larynx.

"Jacob. Don't."

Something in Jacob went cold. Grace's plea saved Kragen's life. He slammed the pistol against Oliver's temple and watched him crumple to the floor.

He turned to Grace, took in the fear on her ashen face.

"I didn't kill him."

The savagery of his features told her he could've killed him, would have, if she hadn't been there.

Quickly, Jacob went back to the doorway and dragged Miller into the room. "There's a chance he hadn't been spotted yet by the security cameras."

Grace barely heard. She was already at Pusher's side. "How are we going to get him out of here?" she asked.

Jacob didn't answer. Instead, he handed her the gun and lifted Pusher up and over his good shoulder. His features tightened with the effort, but he didn't waver.

"Let's go. I noticed a service elevator farther down," Jacob said, shifting Pusher slightly. "The only way to do this is make a dash for it."

They headed down the hallway, the thick carpet masking their footsteps. Grace's hand trembled against the gun. Nausea reared up in her stomach, swiped at the back of her throat. But she refused to give in to the queasiness. If they ran into one of D'Agostini's men, she wouldn't hesitate to shoot.

When they reached the elevator, Grace hit the button. Neither of them spoke. With the hall empty, their voices would carry. In the distance they heard a door slam, then muffled footsteps.

Suddenly, the chime sounded and the door slid open. The voices morphed into screams of rage.

"Go!" Jacob ordered, but Grace was already through the door. Panicked, Grace hit the basement floor first. Then punched the Close button with her fist.

"That won't make it shut any faster."

"I know, but it sure makes me feel better."

"We'll be fine, if we don't have to stop," Jacob said and took the gun from Grace. It wasn't until she looked down, she saw how badly her hands were shaking.

"It's all right, baby. You did good." He raised the gun, barrel up, ready to shoot when the doors slid open once again.

No one was waiting. Relief threatened to buckle her knees.

As if reading her mind, Jacob said, "We're not out of the woods, yet."

Suddenly, gunshots punctuated his statement.

"Move, Grace." They burst through the kitchen doors. Kragen followed less than a minute later. One of the cooks, a small man brandishing a knife, tried to stop them. Jacob laid him out cold with one punch.

"They'll have guards coming at us from both directions," Jacob said as they strode through the maze of ovens and counters. The kitchen staff yelled and cursed until they saw Jacob's gun. Then they screamed.

Suddenly, fire alarms exploded around them. The lights went out. The screams hit a higher pitch as people scrambled for exits.

"Jacob, here," Grace shouted. She stood in front of large garbage chute, holding its steel door open. "It should be big enough."

Quickly, he shoved Pusher down the garbage slide. He picked up Grace and tossed her in, ignoring her scream as she flew down the steel ramp.

Swearing, he dived in after her, a flurry of bullets exploding around him.

"Go!"

Grace jumped out of the Dumpster. Jacob grabbed Pusher and literally threw him into Grace's arms before jumping out himself. Once again, he slung Pusher over his shoulder. With gun in hand, Jacob joined Grace and they headed for the valet parking lot.

People poured from the mansion in a surge of chaos and indignation.

"What's going on?" A young kid, no more than twenty years of age, pulled up in a four-door sedan. His valet badge identified him as Peter. "Is it a fire or something?"

"Why don't you go check it out?" Jacob walked right up to the car and placed the gun in the young man's face. "Now."

"Yes, sir." The guy stumbled out of the car. "I don't want any trouble."

"Then go."

When the kid took off over the lawn, Jacob handed Grace his gun. "You're going to have to drive." He brought Pusher around to the back of the car. With difficulty, he laid the unconscious man in the backseat and then climbed into the passenger seat.

As soon as he was in the car, Grace hit the accelerator and took off through the gate and down the street.

"How are we doing so far?" She blew a stray lock of hair off her forehead.

Jacob checked the side mirror. "We're safe enough for now, but I think it's time to regroup back at the hotel."

"In a stolen car?"

"We'll ditch the car."

She glanced at Pusher through the rearview mirror. "We're going to look petty conspicuous walking into to a hotel like this."

"Who says we need to walk in?"

OLIVER SLAMMED OPEN his office door, nearly taking it off its hinges.

The bruise across his nose had turned purple, but the swelling was down. Oliver held a white kerchief up to the side of his head, stemming the stream of blood still oozing from the cut.

"Who set off the fire alarm?"

Unflustered, Frank Sweeney followed his boss into the office. "Still working on it. But Lomax and the woman got away."

"Of course they did." Kragen slammed his free hand against the desktop. "I want it on the news. Now! If we can't locate them, we'll market them as criminals and hang them out to dry. By tomorrow, I want their faces splashed across every channel in this country. Fugitives wanted for murders."

"I don't think that's the answer—"

"Did I ask your opinion?" Oliver sneered.

"You should. Your man is right, Oliver." D'Agostini walked into the office, his voice grim but the steel of his eyes unbendable. "I'm surprised at you. I don't think you've ever let your emotions rule your decisions. Can't say I like this side of you, Oliver, but I guess it's understandable. Lomax has certainly gotten the best of you over the last few days, hasn't he?" His eyes took in the bloody features. "In more ways than one, it seems."

Oliver forced himself to sit back in his chair.

"I'm going to tell you what we're going to do," Richard said. "Instead of flushing them out and bringing more unnecessary attention to this problem, we're going to do what we should have done in the first place. We're going to bring them to us."

"And how do you propose to do that?" Kragen said with sarcasm. "Call them up for tea?"

Richard D'Agostini's features subtly took on a hard edge. "Oliver, I'll excuse the impertinent behavior, simply because I know you're not at your best. But make no mistake. While I've found your services and devotion exceptional in the past, I will not tolerate insubordination among my people. Do you understand me?"

"Yes," the aide agreed, but inside he seethed.

"I have arranged a meeting tonight. A very important meeting." Richard said. "One that will take care of Jacob Lomax. You just make sure you're here to greet the couple when they show. Understand me?"

"Yes."

"Now, I think you've had a long day, Oliver," Richard observed. "I want you to get a good night's sleep. I'll take

Mr. Sweeney here for my meeting. He will inform you of what happens later."

Kragen fisted his hands. The senator was giving him a disciplinary slap by making him go through his own subordinate for information. Kragen looked at Frank, but the enforcer was smart enough to show no reaction over the change of plans.

"Of course," Oliver responded, his lips tight. "I'll be here, waiting."

Chapter Twenty

Pusher had made himself comfortable with a sandwich from room service. Although the man moved slowly and chewed even more slowly, Jacob was relieved he would suffer no permanent damage from his injuries.

Jacob showed the ex-con the paper from Grace's phone. "Try this."

Pusher took a look at the series of numbers. "It's not the right type of code for the USB. I don't know what this is for, but it's not the one I need."

"Is the thumb drive working?"

"So far so good. But I won't be really able to tell until I can access the information," Pusher explained. "How much time do I have to decrypt this?"

"Less than ten hours."

"I'll do my best."

Jacob arched an eyebrow.

"Ten it is."

Jacob placed a hand on the younger man's shoulder. "Thanks, Pusher."

"No problem." The younger man's smile went lopsided

under the swelling. He winced and touched his lips. "Besides, I owe them a little back."

Grace walked up to the men. "Will we be safe here?"

"Yes," Jacob lied, knowing they wouldn't be safe until he finished this. "At least until tomorrow. The senator is going to be dealing with the aftermath of the commotion tonight."

"Why don't you two get some rest," Pusher suggested. "If you want me to crack this, I'm going to need some quality time alone."

Grace smiled. "Okay, Pusher. I need to talk to Jacob, anyway."

Jacob followed Grace into the bedroom. During the ride home, emotions and memories stampeded through him, leaving his inside battered, his mind overloaded.

"Do you think the fire alarm was a coincidence?"

"Maybe." But neither of them truly believed it.

Suddenly, he heard the click of the lock before she crossed the floor to him. "All I could think when we were running over the lawn was what would have happened if we'd been caught."

With a gentle hand, she pushed him until he sat on the bed. "And I knew what they had done to Pusher wouldn't have even been close to what Kragen would've done to you."

"Grace—"

"I saw Kragen's eyes, Jacob. That man wanted to tear you apart."

Jacob felt the flutter of her fingers across his forehead as she brushed his hair back, then kissed his wound. "Grace."

"I decided then, at that moment, what I wanted."

"And what's that?"

"You," she said softly. "For tonight, tomorrow. For as long as we can have."

"You mean, for as long as my amnesia lasts," Jacob corrected. "And when my memory returns?"

"We'll have a decision to make."

When she stepped closer, he cupped the small of her back with his palms, brought her body in tight to his. "The baby is mine, isn't it?"

"Yes."

He had anticipated her answer. Still, his hands flexed against her in reaction.

"Jacob, I couldn't tell you before—"

Tears swelled in her caramel eyes, then spilled. He wiped the dampness with his thumb, tracing the bones of her cheek, the soft line of her jaw. "Shh. Tomorrow. We'll deal with it all tomorrow."

He studied her mouth, loving the soft curves, the slight tremble of anticipation.

"I've missed you," he murmured, then covered her lips with his own, catching the next quiver, soothing it with his tongue until she whimpered with pleasure.

His fingers moved to the back of her hair, releasing the pins, letting them drop—forgotten before they hit the floor.

The silky ends of her hair fell, then flowed over his hands.

One of them shuddered. He didn't know which one. He only knew he didn't care.

Her lips softened under his. She sighed, then shifted, trying to fit her body to his. He tasted the sweet curve of her shoulder while his fingers traced the bare skin of her back.

He caught her dress zipper between his thumb and forefinger and tugged, letting the side of his hand ride the bumps of her spine down to the small hollow above her hips.

"Wait," she murmured.

Slowly, he pulled back, but no more than a breath away. She reached up, took one end of his tie and slid it free. The silk whispered against his shirt in a long, seductive hiss. She dropped it to the ground.

Her fingers found the buttons of his shirt and slipped them free one by one. His heart picked up speed and he moved her hand to his bare chest. "See what you do to me, Grace?"

"What if I want to do more?" Loose, her dress slipped to the floor in a long, sexy sigh, leaving a puddle of chiffon at her feet.

She wore nothing now, except a wisp of white lace just under the round swell of her belly, a small scrap of material that provided no protection from his gaze. "How much more?" he rasped, as his eyes followed the long lean lines of her legs up to the gentle flare of her hips and back again to her belly.

A stab of possessiveness shot through him, on its heels a jolt of the need to protect her and his baby inside her.

"So much more," she murmured. She started to slip out of her heels, but a hand on her thigh, stopped her.

"Not yet."

Grace smiled, a wicked curve of the lips that thickened the blood in his veins.

Slowly, she stepped out of her dress, slid into his lap and straddled his waist. She guided his hand from the curve of her hip, down the length of her leg, stopping only when his palm flexed against the curve of her ankle and his fingers slipped under the strap of her sandal. "I never knew high heels turned you on."

Jacob shuddered, absorbing another punch of desire, before his hand gave in to the need to feel the silk of skin again. "I didn't, either," he admitted, while his fingers traveled back to her hip. "Let's find out what else I like."

His hand cupped the roundness of her belly—soft in tenderness, lingering with possessiveness.

Then he jerked back, his eyes wide.

The baby bumped his hand again.

Grace would've paid good money to be able to laugh. But the emotion caught at the back of her throat. She didn't think it was often that Jacob got caught off guard.

But he recovered quickly, she thought with delicious pleasure. His lips skimmed her shoulder, followed the delicate curve of her neck, tasted the hollow of her collarbone.

With a sigh, she leaned back. Just for a moment. Just for support. His mouth settled over one sensitive nipple, tugging, tasting. Little electric shocks exploded under his lips, setting her nerves humming.

He moved slowly, maddeningly so. Nibbling here, stroking there. She tugged off his shirt to show her impatience. When that didn't change his tempo, she fisted his hair, holding him still until her mouth found his. Hard, hot, impatient.

Suddenly, Grace was beneath him, the final barriers gone. The wisp of lace, torn and thrown. His pants peeled away and left beside her gown.

Jacob used his elbows for support, not wanting to crush the baby, but wanting—needing—it between them.

A double-edged sword of pain and pleasure sliced through skin, gut and bone. How could he have turned away from this, turned away from her?

He shifted back, bringing her hips to the edge of the bed. Her calves slid up over his shoulders. He absorbed the pleasure with the pain when one balanced over his wound.

His hands found the soft cheeks of her derriere. Because he could, he squeezed each, heard her gasp before he hitched her hips higher.

She felt open, exposed, balanced on the edge. Her heart beat, fluttering with fear. Of what, she didn't know. She gripped the covers in tight fists, trying to keep from falling.

At that moment, he slid into her.

They both groaned. "I'm a selfish bastard, honey, but I need to hear you say it."

Grace understood. His face was savage despite the endearment. The pain became unbearable, the words burned the back of her throat. Too much pain already, she thought. She looked into his eyes and stepped off the edge. "I love you, Jacob Lomax. I always have and I always will."

His muscles bunched reflexively against her, telling her what she needed to know.

The only way she needed to know.

He took her then, on a long, shuddered sigh—sweeping her into a rhythm that had her rising, cresting, tumbling into a free fall.

And for the first time in a long time, she wasn't afraid.

Chapter Twenty-One

I love you, Jacob Lomax.

Jacob watched Grace fall asleep in the crook of his arm. Lord, he hoped so. But even as she spoke the words, he understood they wouldn't get her through the next twenty-four hours.

The flashes of memories were coming at breakneck speed, tumbling over each other, battering the wall that had held them back for so long.

Jacob had parents, still living. Still together after almost forty years. Grace had been wrong. He had family, he had friends. No more than a handful, but friends he trusted.

He also had a past.

The memories of Helene remained just out of reach. But they were right there, lingering on the edge of the others. They would come soon, he knew. And then he'd be prepared.

Determined, he gathered Grace closer, closed his eyes and planned.

A SLIGHT TAP ON THE DOOR had Jacob up and out of bed. He reached for his gun on the nearby nightstand.

"Lomax." The bar manager let out a long, low whistle through the door. "We just opened Pandora's box."

Jacob opened the door, stepped through, then shut it quietly behind him. "Show me."

For the next hour, Jacob scanned the Primoris files. "Can this be copied?"

"With a little time," Pusher replied, concern deepening his accent. "I have to bypass more security codes."

"How long?"

"At least a few more hours," Pusher answered.

"We don't have a few hours." Jacob grabbed the USB from the side of the computer. Their escape from the party tonight had terrified him. Now that he understood what he was dealing with, he wasn't going to let her near the situation.

"I need you to watch over Grace." He handed Pusher his pistol. "See that door? No one gets through that door alive."

"Hey, man, my specialty is computers—" Pusher stopped. "Hell. All right. Why not."

"Thanks. I'll be back as soon as I can."

"She's going to want to know what happened to you."

"Tell her I'm taking care of some business," answered Jacob as he picked up the phone and punched in the number. When the other side clicked, he said. "It's me. I've got the files."

CHARLES RENNE PARKED his car in the parking garage on the west end of the city and waited.

When headlights flared in his back window, he opened the door and stepped out.

Sweeney approached him and quickly patted Charles down. "The senator would like to have a word with you, Doctor Renne."

Charles said nothing. Instead, he waited until Sweeney opened the limousine door.

When Charles slid onto the seat beside him, D'Agostini didn't bother with the usual pleasantries. "They showed up at the fund-raiser last night. They could have done serious damage to our plans."

"Who? Lomax?"

"With your daughter. They managed to escape with Pusher Davis. I need to know where they took him."

"And I told you, I need time."

"You've had time, Charles. More than I've allowed anyone else. Now I am out of patience. The election machines are waiting to be shipped from the warehouse. I need that source code."

Anger rose in Charles, burning hot until it threatened to spew from every pore in his body. "If Sweeney hadn't showed up at Grace's house, I would've contacted you and taken care of everything myself. But your man Kragen had to send in his enforcer. He put everything at risk. Not me."

"That was unfortunate," the senator said. "But you had assured me from the beginning that your daughter would not be a complication when you told me about Helene's deception. And here she is right in the middle of the problem."

From the first time Charles had met Helene, there had been something vaguely familiar about her. But it was only a few days ago that he placed her as Langdon's daughter. She was the identical image of her mother.

"I need you to contact Grace."

"I told you, I can't find her."

"I have a hard time believing that, Charles. What I need you to do is persuade her to meet with you. And have her bring the Primoris files and the code."

"And how am I supposed to do that?"

"Tell her you're in danger," D'Agostini suggested.

"You really think she'll believe me?"

"Yes, because if she doesn't, your being in danger will be the truth."

Fear, dark and ugly, slithered beneath Charles's skin. "I will do whatever is necessary. After all these years, there should be no question of my loyalty. Didn't I warn you that Helene was an imposter? Didn't I tell you about her meeting with Lomax? Once Grace mentioned she'd be at the club that night—"

"Your loyalty was bought and paid for, so it's always in question. What I'm concerned about is your devotion to your daughter. Will it become an obstacle?"

"None whatsoever," Charles argued. "You forget, she's never been my daughter."

Chapter Twenty-Two

I've missed you.

The memory nudged Grace from hazy edges of sleep. But it was the actual words that had her sitting straight up in Jacob's bed.

A glance around the bedroom told her he'd left. He wouldn't desert her. She knew him too well now. But he'd certainly protect her.

Even if it meant breaking his promise.

She drew her knees up under the sheet, then rested her forehead against them. He was putting his life at risk to save her and their baby.

Grace got up and slipped on Jacob's robe, hugging it close.

The scent of coffee drifted through the open door.

Her heart jumped. She smiled, chiding herself.

She rushed down the stairs, not caring if she wore her heart on her sleeve. "I thought you'd left."

Pusher stepped out from the kitchen. "He did."

He handed her some tea. "He gave me his gun and told me to protect you."

"Protect me." She nodded. So she had been right.

The phone rang, startling her. She automatically reached for it. Only Jacob knew where they were.

Carol's number. Her father.

"Dad."

"No, Miss Renne. This is Oliver Kragen. We met last night."

"How did you get this number? What have you done to Carol?"

"We have not harmed your housekeeper. In fact, she probably hasn't even realized her phone is gone."

"Then how—"

"Your father. Of course, he gave it to us somewhat reluctantly. Which is one of the reasons I'm calling."

"You better not have harmed him—"

"Or what?" Kragen laughed, a savage sound that chilled Grace to the bone. "You're going to send Jacob Lomax after me? Why don't you put him on the phone. I'd rather cut out the middle man anyway."

"He's in the shower."

"Please, Miss Renne, don't play—" Kragan stopped. "He's not there, is he?"

She could hear him smiling over the phone. "Well, well. Is he out hunting up the bad men for you?" Kragen asked. "Seems the father of your baby is an undercover government operative. Independent contractor, actually, which is why it made it difficult for us to find out information on him."

"He's not the father—"

"Please. I told you, I have been talking to your father." Kragen chided. "Not that it's important. What's important is that I have someone here who needs to speak to you."

"Grace, it's me."

His voice was harsh, ragged. As if he had run a marathon or was in pain. "Dad."

"They want the input code and the Primoris files, Grace. Helene stole both from them. Don't give—"

Kragen came back on the line. "In fact, Miss Renne, we want it back so much, that we're willing to kill for it. Starting with your father here. Now I know you're alone, so this should be relatively easy. I'm going to give you very specific directions on where to meet my car in fifteen minutes. I'll be waiting. If you're a second late, you'll be an orphan."

"I won't be. Just tell me where to meet you."

"In front of the Library of Congress."

"How do I know to trust you?"

"You don't."

The phone went dead.

"No, Grace. Don't do this. Let Jacob handle this one. He'll save your father."

"Pusher, I need you to stay here in case Jacob comes back."

"The hell with that. If he comes back and finds you gone and me still here, I'm worse than dead. No thanks, I'll take my chances with that psycho Kragen again."

"No."

"Yes," Pusher insisted. "They think you're going in alone. I'll just tag along at a distance. Watch your back until Jacob saves the day." He winked. "What do you think?"

KRAGEN PUSHED OPEN the double steel doors and motioned Grace in with his pistol. "The senator's waiting."

The warehouse smelled of cardboard and antiseptic. But, for a warehouse, it seemed unnaturally quiet. Only the squeak of her sneakers against cement echoed through the half-acre-large building.

Senator D'Agostini stepped out from behind a shelf filled with crates. "Were you followed, Oliver?"

"No. But we did pick up a hitchhiker." Miller stepped forward and shoved Pusher to the ground. "He tried to tail my car."

"Mr. Davis. This is a pleasant surprise," Richard said with a smile that didn't quite touch the cold, gray eyes.

"The pleasure's all mine."

"Really?" He nodded to Miller. The big man swung his foot, connecting hard with Pusher's ribs. The bar manager grunted, and rolled into a tight ball from the pain.

"Don't," Grace screamed and stepped forward.

"Shut up." Kragen jerked her back, his fingers digging hard into her skin.

"And Lomax?" Richard asked, his gaze on Grace. "Has he disappeared?"

"For now. But he'll show up soon enough once he realizes we have her." Kragen pulled Grace's phone from his pocket. "He'll call to check in and I'll make sure he knows where to find her."

"And Sweeney? Where is he?"

"Checking the perimeter with his men. I want to be ready when Lomax puts in an appearance."

"Well, let's get to it, then," Richard replied. "Do you have the code, Grace?"

"No. But I know where it is." She glanced at Pusher, caught the defiant anger in his eyes. "I can take you there, but first I want to see my father."

D'Agostini laughed. "You've watched too many movies,

Grace." He walked over to Oliver and nodded toward his pistol. "May I?"

Before Grace could react, the gun exploded next to her ear. Pusher cried out, grabbing his shoulder. Blood seeped through his fingers.

"Pusher." Grace would've run forward, but Kragen grabbed her arm and jerked, sending her to her knees.

"Now, I will start putting a bullet in your friend each minute you wait. And trust me, it will take several before he dies from loss of blood."

"Don't, Gracie," Pusher ordered. "Trust me. You tell them, you're dead. I'm dead, anyway."

Miller reached down and squeezed Pusher's shoulder until the younger man cried out again from the pain.

"Do you think you can stand here and watch us take your friend apart, Grace?" Richard's lips thinned over his teeth in a feral smile. "You would be amazed at how much pain the human body can take when the bullets are well placed."

D'Agostini took aim at one of Pusher's knees.

"I don't have it, damn you!" Fear cramped her belly, bile rose to the back of her throat. "I was bluffing. I don't have the code or the key."

"Then you'd better hope, Miss Renne, that your lover does," D'Agostini said. "Miller. Find out where Sweeney is. Inform him to watch for Jacob Lomax. If Miss Renne doesn't have what we are looking for, Lomax does. If he has the code and key on his person, you may kill him. If he doesn't, I want him brought to me."

Chapter Twenty-Three

A platform of crates stood in front of the machine, still hooked to the chains that lifted it from a nearby storage pit in the floor.

For a moment, Frank Sweeney toyed with the idea of climbing the stack to get a good look from overhead, but quickly discarded the idea. If he got spotted, he'd put himself in a bad position.

Lomax was one canny son of a bitch. There was no doubt in the enforcer's mind that Lomax would show up sooner rather than later.

But that was fine with Frank. He was more than ready to get the show on the road.

A series of low grunts drifted from across the warehouse. On its heels came the echo of scuffling feet, the thud of a body slammed against a nearby wall.

Frank grabbed the gun from his shoulder holster and circled toward the sounds.

Suddenly, Miller stepped from behind some crates and grinned at Frank. He waved his gun toward Lomax, who knelt on the floor in front of the big man's feet. "Look what I found, boss."

"Good work." His eyes swept over Lomax, taking in the

blood at his mouth, the look of disgust that hardened his features.

Frank raised his gun and fired. Miller grunted and fell to the floor dead, the back of his skull splattered the crates behind him.

"I've had it with you, Lomax. First you call me out of the blue and tell me you're on your way here," Frank snapped. "Then you let that idiot catch you by surprise. How in the hell did that happen?"

"He just caught me and we'll leave it at that," Jacob snarled out and wiped his mouth with the back of his hand.

"So you decided to trust me and not run away this time?" Frank snagged Jacob's gun from Miller's hand and gave it back to his partner.

"I wouldn't have run away from you the last time except I didn't know who the hell you were." Jacob dropped the clip, checked it and shoved it back into the pistol.

"What the hell does that mean? If you're trying to pull some crap because I owe you a crack on your skull—"

"It's the truth. I had amnesia. I'll fill you in later." Quickly, Jacob scanned the warehouse. "I have the files and the code. And I've already called in the cavalry. They should be here anytime now."

Frank swore. "Jacob, they've got Grace. The moment this place fills up with agents, she's dead."

"I left Grace at the hotel—"

"She came here to save her father."

"What? Her father?" Jacob scowled. "Did you find him with D'Agostini?"

"No. And she's not going to handle finding out he's a traitor."

"I'll deal with that."

"Pusher Davis is with her. The man needs to stick to bartending. D'Agostini's using him for bullet practice to make Grace give up the Primoris files. I had to choose you or him. I'm hoping Grace keeps him alive. Hate to see him die, especially after I helped save his butt the other night. He took a hell of a beating before you showed your ass up to save the day."

"You set off the fire alarms."

"You're damn right I did." Frank grinned. "Felt good, too. Didn't like watching that Pusher kid take a beating." Frank cocked his gun. "Let's go save your lady friend before the troops get here."

"No. You go stop the troops and anyone else who gets in the way. I'll get to her and keep her safe until everything's clear."

"Okay, man. But watch your back. Kragen's with D'Agostini and that man is no pushover." Frank turned to leave, then stopped. He placed a hand on Jacob's good shoulder. Gave it a gentle squeeze. "About Helene. I didn't know they made her, Jacob. I would've gotten a warning to you somehow. Webber handled the hit—"

"It's okay, Frank. We all know the score. Helene more than anyone. Just bring our friends in quietly until I give you the all clear. It's time D'Agostini got his payback."

"You got it. And when we're done, I'm taking a vacation."

"Me, too," Jacob murmured as he watched Frank slip back into the shadows. "But mine's going to be a honeymoon."

"I wouldn't count on it, Lomax." Kragen stepped from behind a nearby crate, his pistol pointed at Jacob's chest.

"WHERE'S Sweeney?" Kragen took Jacob's gun and tossed it across the floor.

Jacob shrugged, using the movement to loosen the tight muscles between his shoulders. "Around."

"How long has he been working for you?"

"He works with me," Jacob mused. "And we work for the good guys."

"Was Helene Garrett just one of the *guys,* then?" Kragen snorted. "It doesn't matter. Within a month, we'll be the good guys as far as the nation is concerned."

When Jacob didn't respond, Kragen said, "They won't believe him, you know. Too many people involved with too many connections. Frank doesn't stand a chance of convincing anyone without the disk."

"What makes you think he doesn't have it?"

"The fact that your girlfriend is just past those doors with the senator. You need the disk to save her. Not that it will help. She's probably dead already."

Fear slithered up Jacob's spine, coiled in his chest.

"I don't want the disk as much as the senator. You see, my name isn't on it. I made sure of that."

"And Frank Sweeney?"

"Once I kill you, there will be no one to protect him."

When Jacob didn't respond, Kragen waved his gun. "We could use these and have our own version of the shootout at the O.K. Corral. Or we can have our own little Tuesday night takedown. What do you say?"

Keeping his gun drawn, Kragen slipped out of his suit jacket, folded it in half and laid it over the nearest crate.

"I'm willing, considering my disadvantage right now."

Kragen laughed and tossed his own gun by Jacob's. "Now we're on equal ground."

Lomax waved his fingers, crooking them at Kragen. "Let's get it done then, Oliver. Why waste time?"

"That's right, you have the girl to save."

Kragen rushed Jacob, backing him up with a flurry of kicks and punches. Jacob blocked most with his forearms and absorbed others with his upper body before he dove underneath and rolled. He came up into a roundhouse kick that connected with Kragen's jaw.

Kragen stumbled back two steps. He rubbed his jaw. "Not bad."

"Want more?"

Kragen charged Jacob again. At the last minute he pivoted, catching Jacob off guard. His heel slammed into Jacob's forehead. Razor sharp stars burst behind Jacob's eyes.

He caught Kragen's leg, came up to jam a knee in his groin. Kragen immediately collapsed his other leg, sending both men to the floor.

Both men rolled, grappling for a death hold. Jacob grabbed Kragen from behind, his forearm wedged under Kragen's neck, squeezing.

Choking, Kragen reached behind, grabbed Jacob's shoulder and gouged. White-hot pain shot through Jacob's arm and up his back, forcing him to let go of Kragen.

Kragen flipped away, but remained on the floor. Both men blew the oxygen in and out of their lungs.

Blood trickled into Jacob's eye. He wiped it away with the back of his hand. "Come on," he growled, scrambling to his feet.

Kragen kicked, aiming for Jacob's wound again. Pain exploded, knocking the breath from him. But this time, Jacob was ready for the jolt. He staggered but stayed upright.

He heard it then, the sound of shots. Grace's scream.

With a savage cry, he fought past the pain, focusing his mind on the one obstacle between him and his family.

His family.

Jacob rammed Kragen in a football tackle, smashing them both into the crates on the nearby pallet. Oliver grunted, his hands grappling for a hold on Jacob's neck. "She's dead, Lomax. Can you feel it?"

Kragen forgot the neck and aimed a fist into Jacob's ribs, knocking himself free. "You think you can stop this? This is bigger than you or me. Bigger than the United States. We're talking world domination, Lomax. The most powerful men in the world have come together. World bankers, world leaders. Industrial giants. Do you really think you can stop that?"

"Maybe not, but I will stop you." Jacob got his feet under him. "Let's finish it."

Kragen moved, knocking Jacob back into the chains. Jacob grabbed hold of one chain for balance, kneed Kragen in the groin. Kragen fell backward onto the controls. Suddenly, the floor shifted beneath them.

Kragen tackled Jacob, rolling to the edge of the platform as they rose toward the warehouse rafters. His hands were around Jacob's neck squeezing the oxygen from his throat, forcing Jacob's head back. "Tell Helene hello from me when you see her."

Jacob's neck muscles corded, straining against Kragen's strength. At the last moment, he pivoted, bringing his good arm down on Kragen's hands, breaking the contact.

Jacob went to his knees. He wrapped his bad arm around a chain for balance as he heaved in bursts of oxygen.

Kragen charged, intending to knock Jacob off the platform.

Jacob grabbed Kragen's shirt and yanked, using the other man's momentum against his attack. The weight of both men flipped them off the platform. Jacob grunted in pain as the chain caught his bad arm, keeping him suspended midair.

"Go to hell," he rasped as he let go of Kragen's shirt.

Kragen screamed, his hands flying, grabbing at air as he fell. His body dropped into the pit. Jacob heard it bounce, once...twice with sickening thumps before hitting the floor. Jacob dangled for a moment, while his eyes searched the floor beneath. Kragen's head lay at an unnatural angle, his sightless eyes open and gazing up.

With his good arm, he maneuvered himself back up on the platform and hit the button. As soon as he could, he jumped to the floor, snagged his gun and ran. His mind was repeating the only word he could think of. *Please. Please. Please*.

D'AGOSTINI PLACED HIS GUN at Grace's belly. "Just think if I fire now, I will be killing two birds with one bullet, don't you think?" A thin line of madness underlay the senator's laugh.

"Why don't you join us, Mr. Lomax? I'm sure you'll want to hear what I have to say to the mother of your child."

Jacob approached, relief making his muscles shake. Grace was okay. Her cheek was bruised, her mouth was bleeding, but she was alive.

Pusher was another matter. The bar manager lay on the floor, bullet wounds in his shoulder and thigh.

"He's not dead yet. Only unconscious," Richard stated. "Like you, who should've died many times over. Maybe I should have hired you instead of trying to kill you."

"I'm particular about who I work for, Senator. Garbage, even the human kind, tends to come with a stench. One that I don't abide well."

Richard shrugged. "Charles Renne didn't seem to mind. Your father was easy to recruit, Grace."

"My father has nothing to do with this," she bit back.

"You are naive, aren't you? First your father, now your lover?"

"I have no idea what you're talking about."

"Betrayal. I'm talking about betrayal and how it does strange things to people.

"You see, once upon a time, your father suspected your mother was having an affair with Senator Langdon. So one night he drugged her. When he questioned her, she confessed everything.

"At the time, we suspected that Senator Langdon was gathering information on us. We had already decided he was a complication we needed to get rid of.

"What we didn't know was that your mother was privy to her lover's plans. She divulged many names, including mine. So when your father approached us, we took care of things for him."

"You caused the plane to crash?"

"I have to admit, he didn't expect us to kill your mother. But after, we convinced him that extreme actions are sometimes necessary. In this case, we saw his potential and needed something to guarantee his…loyalty.

"After her death it was easy enough to get him to drug

others, gather intelligence. He was already involved. Neck deep, so to speak. When his reputation grew here in Washington, D.C., so did his role in our organization. He became our truth serum expert. Allows us to keep others loyal or destroy them. Whatever we deem fit."

"I don't believe you. My father couldn't hate my mother that much. Not to stand by and let her—"

"Die with her lover?" D'Agostini laughed. "How about once he found out that you weren't really his daughter? That the affair had been going on for quite a long time. How old were you when she died? Ten?"

When Grace didn't answer, he shrugged. "I guess once you were conceived, your biological parents parted ways. Seems when Senator Langdon failed to divorce his wife, your mom slept with Charles on the rebound. Up to your birth, she didn't know who the father was. But as the years passed, and she hadn't conceived any more children, it became apparent that Charles wasn't your father."

"And you're telling me that Langdon and my mother reconnected and that was the ultimate betrayal."

"Washington, D.C., is no more than a small town that loves to gossip. Whether they did or not, your father was being laughed at behind his back."

"I don't believe you."

"But you see, Grace, that isn't even the best part of this story," D'Agostini taunted. "Senator Langdon had a family, too.

"A wife, who later committed suicide after falling into a depression." He paused. "And a daughter."

Grace froze, knowing what was coming. "Helene."

"And here I thought you weren't clever. Much quicker

than I was, actually," he added ruefully. "Helene was a few years older than you at the time. Old enough to suspect the plane crash had been deliberate. You see, her father was an excellent pilot. She knew it because she spent many hours up there with him. Bonding time, I guess."

Was it true? She glanced at Jacob, saw the answer in his eyes. Grace locked her knees to keep her legs under her.

"She must have panicked when her sister fell in love with her partner and got pregnant."

Grace jerked with surprise.

"Oh yes, don't you think your dad would've told me? He told me so much more," D'Agostini mocked. He reached into his pocket and pulled out a recorder.

Grace heard her father's—no she corrected, Charles Renne's—voice. *"You forget. She was never my daughter in the first place."*

Everything inside her turned cold.

"Grace Ann." The whisper was harsh from behind her. She turned to see Charles step forward with a gun in his hand.

Jacob recognized it as Kragen's pistol.

"I said what I needed to keep D'Agostini from suspecting." Charles tilted the pistol up, pointing it at the senator. "It's over Richard," he added.

"It's a little late to play the hero now, isn't it, Charles?" Richard responded derisively. But Jacob noticed the senator kept his gun pointed at Grace's belly.

Jacob could feel the cold steel of his own 9 mm dig into the small of his back, but he couldn't take the risk.

"Let go of my daughter or I will shoot you."

"Shoot and I will kill your daughter. Oh wait, she's not

your daughter," Richard said, snapping his fingers. "I keep forgetting."

"It's over, Senator. I have the code to the voting machines. I also have the files on your operation," Jacob said, his gaze flicking to Grace.

"And you think I won't get it from you?" The senator shook his head. "This is no mere operation, Lomax. An operation is run by two-bit criminals. Your small-mindedness is the reason you will fail."

"I haven't failed."

"You think what you have will bring Primoris to its knees?" His laugh was savage, the lines of his face distorted in his insanity. "All it will do is set back our timetable for a decade, maybe two at the most. There will be others. Primoris is a global power. It goes far beyond the banks and governments. We control the militaries, the sciences, technologies, economies and the law, whether it's martial or otherwise. Do not kid yourself. We control the very air you breathe, the food you eat, the ground you walk on. And like sheep, you exist because of our benevolence," D'Agostini spouted, his voice raging at Jacob. "We are the elite, the one percent. We have no sympathy for the weak." Suddenly, the senator swung his gun toward Charles and fired.

Startled, Charles fired a split second later. His bullet hit D'Agostini directly in the heart. The senator looked down at the blood as it gathered on his chest and slowly sank to his knees. Looking at Charles with astonishment, he fell forward, dead.

Grace turned to her father just as he crumpled to the ground. Hurrying to him, she turned him over onto his back and saw that the bullet had entered his chest. Charles looked up at Grace and tried to speak, only to cough up blood.

"Dad." Tears flooded her eyes. She gathered him close into her lap. "Hold on, please!" she whispered urgently. "Call an ambulance!" She screamed the words at Jacob, but when he didn't move, she whispered, "Please."

"It's too late, Grace," her father rasped, while a deep, moist rattle shook his lungs.

"I love you." Tears formed in her eyes, causing his face to blur. Angrily, she wiped them away with the back of her hand. "You have to hold on. Everything will be fine but you have to hold on!"

Charles reached up and cupped Grace's cheek in his hand, using his thumb to rub away a tear.

"Don't cry, honey. Not for me," he whispered. His hand dropped back to his chest. "It had to be this way, don't you see?" Blood bubbled at the corners of his mouth. "You're safe. That's all that matters."

"No, Daddy." Grace started crying in earnest now, her tears dripping unheeded onto her father's shirt. "Please, don't give up," she begged him. "Don't you dare die on me!"

Charles wrestled back another cough, but it cost him. "What I did to your mother, it was a mistake. I didn't…" He tried to inhale. "I love you…"

Grace shook her head, gripped him closer. "Don't. Don't, Dad. Stay with me."

But she knew Charles didn't hear her, didn't see her.

"Grace, I'm sor—" Jacob began.

"Don't say it. You remember, don't you?" she said dully, her eyes still on her father. Gently, she closed his eyes.

"Yes," Jacob answered, his tone flat with remorse.

"When?" She choked back the sob, the excruciating pain that sliced through her. Gently, she laid her father on the floor, then stood.

"Last night."

Her hands fisted before she could stop them. It took effort, but she forced them to relax. Anger wouldn't help, wouldn't make the facts any less harsh. "Before we—"

"Yes."

The word was a knife that severed an already damaged heart.

"Grace, its not—"

"Get away from me." She could've contained the rage, the slap of betrayal if he hadn't reached for her. Blindly, she struck at him when he tried to hold her. The second sob caught her off guard, then a sweep of them couldn't be stopped.

She cursed him, each word punctuated with the pounding of her fists against his chest. She didn't want to be touched, consoled. She wanted to grieve, to rage. She wanted to inflict the same pain that ripped her from chest to stomach.

Jacob took the hits, blocking them only when he thought she'd hurt herself. Eventually the screaming turned to guttural sobs, then desperate whimpers. Only then did he gather her close.

Drained, Grace couldn't, didn't resist. Minutes blurred together until Grace lost all sense of time.

Finally, when she gained some control, she moved away. "I'm okay now."

When he stepped to her again, she raised her hand. "Don't."

"Grace, we need to talk."

"You left me. You gave me your word. And at the first

moment you had to make a decision on whether to be truthful, you left. I thought I understood why, that you wanted to protect me and the baby. But this—" She waved her hand toward her father. "You had no right to protect me from this." Her stomach hurt, the insides twisting painfully with the betrayal. "Leave me alone, Jacob."

"I wasn't about to let you get killed, damn it."

"And as you can see, your plan worked out well." With gentle fingers, she reached down and brushed the hair away from her father's forehead. "I'm safe."

His sharp intake of breath told her she'd hit home. But she was already beyond caring. What he'd done, no matter the reason, wasn't forgivable.

"Grace, let me explain."

"No." She placed a hand to her stomach, willing the pain to stop. "You could've explained everything last night before you left me, damn you. We were in this together."

"I work for the government. Helene was an operative. One of my contacts."

"I don't care—"

"Listen!" He talked over her, almost believing that if he got the words out, she would understand. Maybe forgive. "She and I were meeting the other night because of the code. The one in your phone. It's the code that accesses the voting machines. Officials click on certain numbers and letters hidden on the touch screen and they can flip the vote to whatever party they want to win."

"I told you I don't care now," she said dully. "Last night, I might have cared. It might have made a difference. But you're too late."

Emotion, hurt, love, longing shot through him, catching

in his chest, catching him off guard. He stepped back, reeling as memories flooded. Pain-filled memories of the first time he'd left her.

"Grace. The senator was right. Primoris is worldwide. Helene managed to gather intelligence on over a hundred men and women working toward global domination. Prime ministers. Generals. Presidents."

"I told you, I don't—" A harder pain hit her this time, deep within her belly. She bent over, fighting against the next spasm.

"Grace!"

She realized the cramping hadn't been from fear or the pain of losing her father. She looked down, saw the blood spotting her pants.

"Jacob, the baby," she whispered, terrified. But the next spasm hit on another wave of gut-wrenching pain. "No, please—"

Jacob caught her before she hit the floor in a dead faint.

Chapter Twenty-Four

Two weeks later.

Mount Hope Cemetery was no more than a spot of grass and a grove of trees meshed between high-rises and skyscrapers on the streets of Washington, D.C.

But its history had long been established before the first historical monument had been erected. Long before the first war, even the first church. And Jacob had no doubt the cemetery would stand long after the last structure crumbled with age.

Gravestones dotted the small, rolling knoll. The cemetery was certainly more eclectic than the famed Arlington, but no less loved, if the flowers adorning most graves were any indication.

The newest of the gravestones was small, but so pristinely white it almost hurt the eyes. It lay by two others, no bigger, no more worn, but matching in a sallow-gray marble.

With a sigh, Jacob laid the pink roses against the white marble.

"Helene loved roses. She would buy them from the street vendor for our office."

He'd heard her, of course. Long before she spoke. The

scent of the honeysuckle hung in the air, had mingled with the roses.

"I remember," he said. "She preferred red, but for some reason...it didn't feel right."

His eyes swept over Grace from behind mirrored sunglasses. He hadn't seen her since the hospital. The day her father died.

"Isn't it too soon to be up on your feet?"

The concern in his voice warmed her heart.

"No." She shook her head when what she really wanted to do was take his hand, touch his face. Reassure him. "The doctor gave me her approval.

"She said I was to avoid stress, among other things." Her hand slid over her stomach, more pronounced than ever under the V-neck sweater, the loose cotton pants. But she wasn't surprised after a week of rest and spoiling from Carol.

"What other things?"

"Sex. Mainly," she teased and almost smiled at the growl that rumbled deep in his chest.

"I'm joking, Jacob.

When he didn't answer, her tone grew serious. "The pain had been from the stress, not the baby. And the blood—" even now, she had a hard time saying the words "—had been my father's."

She stepped closer to Helene's grave. Saw her parents' nearby. It had been her decision to bury them together. One she didn't regret. "A whole family destroyed because of power."

"I wish I could say it will never happen again," Jacob answered. "But corruption goes hand in hand with money and power."

She turned to him then, curious. "You know, you never explained why Helene went into business with me."

"I haven't seen you."

"Yes, you haven't explained that, either."

"I wanted to give you time. To heal. To adjust." He glanced at her, his gaze sharp and watchful. "To work through the anger so when I did see you, I wouldn't have to worry about injuries."

"And Helene?"

"Helene had government access to your whole life profile. It didn't take her long to discover you were her half sister. I think she just couldn't walk away from an opportunity to get to know you better. That outweighed any risk she might have been taking. But when you got pregnant, it changed everything."

"Why?"

"She wanted your baby to have a father. A good father, like she never had."

"And I never had," she added solemnly. "That's ironic if you think about it. I didn't want you to know because I didn't want the baby to have a father like I had. Emotionally removed. And Helene was going to tell you because she wanted the baby to have a real father. One who could love the baby. Helene had more faith in you than I did."

"Helene had an advantage. She knew my family background. Something I couldn't share with you. Not at the time. Not without risking your life."

Even now, it could hurt. The fact that he'd shared his life, his past with another woman so easily—trusted her so completely as a friend. "And now?"

"Now," he said, drawing out the word until it became two syllables, "I'd like to know what you're doing here."

"Pusher said you had left the bar with a bouquet of flowers. This was a logical conclusion. He says you've bought a bouquet every day."

"Not every day, but most days. I miss her, Grace."

"Me, too." Tears pricked the back of her eyes. She wasn't ready to talk about them yet. "How's the bar going?"

"I didn't realize when Helene left me the bar, she left me Pusher, too." He sent her a sexy, sidelong glance. "I don't suppose you'd come back as my partner?"

"I'm going to be really busy soon." She patted the flutter in her stomach, took a deep breath to settle the flutter in her heart. "Don't have any plans other than to get plenty of rest at my father's house."

"You're staying, then?"

"For a while. My father's being hailed a hero. His reputation is still intact. The only ones who know the truth now are you, me, Frank and Pusher," she said. "So I know his secret is safe."

"It is."

"What about you? I figured you'd leave Pusher in charge and head off on another mission."

"I'm retiring, actually. And thanks to Helene, I have a legitimate business to manage."

"What about your properties?"

"I can still manage them, too," Jacob said. "I'm staying at a hotel for right now, but I'm thinking about having the boathouse rebuilt. Make some improvements. Make it a real home."

"You mean, you're staying here for good?"

"I left that first time to complete some unfinished business. I had every intention of getting back with you after

I helped Helene bring down Primoris. Long before I found out you were pregnant."

She looked at him, startled.

"Helene told me the night she died. About you. About the baby. About the fact that she had to pass the information off to you. It frightened her, putting you in jeopardy like that, but she had no choice at the time. She had moved into the boathouse as an added precaution, but still suspected her cover had been blown. She thought someone had followed her to your lunch date. That's why she made the switch. When we were ambushed, I was on my way to you. The bullet that hit my shoulder went through me and caught Helene in the chest. She used her last breath to tell me she loved you."

Tears backed up in her throat. "I loved her, too. She was a sister to me in so many ways. I just never realized it until she was gone but she was my family."

"And Charles?"

"I still love him," Grace admitted. "He will always be my father. I haven't sorted it all out in my mind yet—or my heart—but I'm sure I will eventually."

"I guess that's it, then," Jacob said, his eyes resting for a last time on Helene's grave. "So you've told me how you found me, but you never told me why you came out here."

"We're having a baby girl. I found out this morning."

"We are?" The muscle in his jaw clenched and unclenched. "Grace, I don't have a right to ask your forgiveness—"

"Neither do I. But I'm going to ask you anyway. Will you forgive me, Jacob?"

"Forgive you?"

"What I said to you when my father died—"

"Was deserved." Jacob gathered her into his arms and kissed her softly. "I love you, Grace."

"I love you, too."

He hugged her to him for a moment, then pulled back. "I thought you wanted to be surprised with the baby's sex?"

She laughed. "I've had enough surprises for a while."

"Do you think you can handle one more?"

Her eyebrow rose, suspicious. "Depends on the kind of surprise."

"My dad is retired military. He and my mother own a bed-and-breakfast in Maine. I want you to meet my parents, Grace. I want you to look at my baby albums, see my old tree fort." Jacob buried his face in her neck, inhaled the sweet scent of honeysuckle. "While my parents are out playing bridge, I want to make love to you in my old bed, like a horny teenager. Then later whisper all my hopes and plans for our baby girl against your belly."

Love tightened her chest, squeezed a shimmer of tears from her eyes. Jacob was giving her more than his love, more than his trust. He was showing her his vulnerability. A precious gift from a man with so much control.

"I like Maine." Her arms circled his neck and for a minute she leaned into him, letting their hearts beat against each other. "But I don't go anywhere with strange men."

"Strange?"

Stiffening, he tried to pull away, only to relax when she chuckled, tickling the base of his throat.

"Frank told me Lomax wasn't your real name."

"He did? When did he tell you that?"

"When he called for my chocolate chip cookie recipe,"

she replied. "He's the friend you have that likes to cook, huh?"

"Yes, he is," Jacob admitted. "He's also my partner. And my uncle."

"Your what?"

"My uncle. He's the one that got me into government work, much to my mother's dismay. He's her younger brother."

"And you hit him on the head?" She gasped. "No wonder he looked so shocked when you walked through my bedroom door."

"Shocked is putting it mildly. I guess for a moment he was relieved, until I didn't lower the gun. That's why he grabbed for you. He knew he could buy some time using you as a bargaining chip until he could figure out what the hell was going on. I think at one point, he assumed your dad had used some kind of brainwashing drugs on me."

"You hit him really hard, Jacob." Her brow lifted. "He's not going to forgive you anytime soon, is he?"

"I'm already forgiven."

"That easily?"

"Hell, no. I didn't say it was easy," Jacob growled. "I had to give him my boat."

Grace laughed. She had a feeling Frank was going to be one of her favorite people. "So, Lomax, what is your real last name? Frank wouldn't tell me."

"Alexander."

"Jacob Alexander," she murmured, nodding. "I like it."

"Me, too," he joked. Then picked her up and twirled her in a circle. "But I like Grace Alexander more."

Epilogue

Four months later

Grace watched Jacob hold his daughter. The two-day-old lay comfortably in the cradle of her daddy's arm, her belly full, her eyes half-closed with sleep.

Jacob sat next to her on the bed, near enough for Grace to rest her head on his shoulder.

"You're asking for trouble if you go ahead with this," Grace insisted. But Jacob wasn't listening. He was too pre-occupied with the baby.

"I can't get over how thick her hair is," he whispered, running light fingers over the honey-brown locks, then tickled a tiny ear before brushing across the delicate cheek. "And how small she was. Remember?"

"Yes, she still is." And Grace was remembering other things. The slight shake of his hand when he held his daughter for the first time. The way his jaw clenched and unclenched to fight the emotion that overwhelmed him. The first time he kissed her small forehead, and held them both in his arms together.

Tears pricked at the back of her eyes, shuddered deep in her chest.

"Now, what were you saying about trouble?"

"You know exactly what I am saying. What you're planning on doing is worse than tempting fate, Jacob," Grace admonished, but the temper was no longer there. If anyone could take on fate and win, it was Jacob Alexander.

"I don't have the faintest idea what you're talking about, do you, honey?" he stage-whispered to their daughter, who was busy staring into the identical blue eyes of her father.

She bit her lip to keep the smile from getting the best of her. "You're spitting right in its face, and don't think I won't say 'I told you so'—"

"It's perfect. And you know that as well as I do." He held out his finger, smiling with pride when the baby grabbed it with her hand. "She's perfect."

How could you argue with a man who was driven by love?

A nurse walked in the door. The woman was young, with a short, bouncy bob of red hair and bottle-green eyes that took in Jacob in one long, feminine sweep.

"Are you ready for me to take her, Mr. Alexander?"

Grace glanced from father to daughter and felt her own heart quickening. "Not just yet," she answered for Jacob.

"All right. Call me if you need anything."

"I will. Thank you." The nurse started to leave, only to stop by the door. "By the way, the doctor wanted to know if you've decided on a name for your baby girl?"

Jacob glanced at his wife.

Grace didn't bother sighing. Instead, she took a deep breath, thought of her mother and waited for the ground to tremble. "All right," she agreed, resignedly. "But don't say I didn't warn you."

Jacob laughed and turned to the nurse. "Serenity. We're naming her Serenity."

* * * * *

A CONVENIENT
PROPOSITION

CINDY
GERARD

Since her first release in 1991 hit the National No.1 slot on the Waldenbooks bestseller list, **Cindy Gerard** has repeatedly made appearances on several bestseller lists, including *USA TODAY*. With numerous industry awards to her credit—among them the Romance Writers of America's RITA® Award and the National Reader's Choice Award—this former Golden Heart finalist and repeat *Romantic Times* BOOKclub nominee is the real deal. As one book reviewer put it, 'Cindy Gerard provides everything romance readers want in a love story—passion, gut-wrenching emotion, intriguing characters and a captivating plot. This storyteller extraordinaire delivers all of this and more!' Cindy and her husband, Tom, live in the Midwest on a minifarm with quarter horses, cats and two very spoiled dogs. When she's not writing, she enjoys reading, travelling and spending time at their cabin in northern Minnesota unwinding with family and friends. Cindy loves to hear from her readers and invites you to visit her website at www.cindygerard.com.

This book is dedicated to readers everywhere.
As a writer, I am so grateful for your passion and
enthusiasm and support of what I do.

One

A winter sky hung heavy over the Shadow range, spitting dime-size snowflakes like a white blanket shedding lint. As the rattletrap of a pickup slowly approached Sundown, Montana, Shallie Malone stared through the passenger side windshield, wishing she could shake the notion that maybe this snowstorm was an omen. Maybe coming back to Sundown was a huge mistake.

Imagine that. Her making another mistake. So what else was new?

She expelled a weary sigh as the old truck bounced along the snow-packed road. She'd made a lot of mistakes in her twenty-seven years. She hadn't wanted her return to Sundown to be one of them, though. She'd wanted it to be—well, she'd wanted it to feel like home again, not like another misstep on the very rocky road of life.

Face it, she thought, as a jagged line of mountain peaks disappeared behind a heavy clot of clouds; mistake or not, it wasn't like she'd really had many other choices.

She focused on the forest beyond the windshield as the wipers shoved wet flakes off the glass. The pine boughs bent like old shoulders under the weight of winter. She, too, felt very old today. And weighted down. Mr. Coleman, the elderly rancher who she vaguely remembered had been kind enough to give her a lift from the bus station in Bozeman. He had the heater going full blast. Even so, Shallie shivered beneath her lightweight jacket. And tried to ignore the queasy feeling in the pit of her stomach—the feeling that suggested the old adage might be true: You can't go home again.

A name on a mailbox at the end of what she knew was a long curving lane leading deep into the forest and halfway up the mountain caught her eye as they drove by.

She cranked her head around to catch another glimpse of black lettering partly covered with snow. "Did that say Brett McDonald?"

"Hum? Oh, yeah." Concentrating on keeping the truck from slipping off the slick road, Bob Coleman squinted through his bifocals after a cursory glance at his rearview mirror. "The boy bought the old Fremont place about the same time he bought the Dusk to Dawn."

Whoa. Mac? Her childhood buddy, Brett "Mac" McDonald, now owned the Fremont cabin? And she couldn't believe what else Bob Coleman had just said. "The Haskins sold the Dusk to Dawn?"

"Beats all, don't it?" Bob grimaced beneath the brim of a worn gray Stetson. "Never thought I'd see the day when Nadine and Chet would hang it up, but I guess they got a hankering to do some traveling and Mac had the cash to make it happen."

The Dusk to Dawn was Sundown, Montana's, local watering hole for the community and the ranchers surrounding town. It was bar, restaurant, coffee shop and minimart all wrapped up in one well-used, well-loved establishment. If someone got married, the reception was held at the Dusk to Dawn. If someone died, it was where the family had the wake. Birthday parties, graduations and regular Saturday-night party-hardy crowds had gathered under the green tin roof for as long as Sundown had been Sundown. And for as long as Shallie had known Sundown, the Haskins had run the Dusk to Dawn.

Finding out that they were no longer there—a major change to something so stable—made her a little sad. She'd been a long time coming home. She hadn't wanted to see changes. She'd wanted everything to be the same as when she'd left. There was security in the status quo, and that's what she needed most right now.

Foolish, yeah. But it had been comforting to think that in a world in constant evolution, Sundown with its slow pace and plain, honest folk would always remain pretty much what it had been.

"Seems Mac made quite a business for himself in Bozeman," Bob added, oblivious to Shallie's melancholy thoughts. "Got himself a fancy I-*tal*-ian restaurant folks flock to from all over. I've even taken the missus there a time or two when we could get a reser-

vation. Word is he decided he'd just as well branch out
a bit and bring some business back home."

Mac was a hometown boy. Thinking of him running,
as Bob Coleman put it, a fancy Italian restaurant made
Shallie grin.

Wild. Lord, had that boy been wild. Not mean wild.
Devilish, fun-loving wild. Whatever mischief he and
John Tyler couldn't think of to stir up when they were
kids wasn't worth talking about. More often than not,
she'd been in on making some of that trouble with them.

Shallie sobered. *Trouble.* Imagine that. Didn't take
long to come back around to the point that she was in
trouble again.

She placed a hand protectively over her flat tummy and
the budding new life sleeping there. Assured herself that
coming back was a good thing. The right thing. And when
the truck rounded the ridge and the tiny hamlet of
Sundown came into view, the little shiver of unease shifted
to anticipation and told her, yes. Yes, this *was* right.

How many times had she driven this road and seen
Sundown from this vantage point, nestled in the valley
like a multicolored and well-worn skirt at the base of
the Shadow range? That skirt was now blanketed in
white. Chimney smoke spiraled up in wispy drifts, like
steam rising from a bubbling kettle. How many times
had she taken this simple beauty for granted?

Way too many.

Well, she wouldn't make that particular mistake again.

She was almost home. At least she was as close to
home as she'd ever been. She might be coming back
with her head held low in shame, but she wouldn't let

her decision to return turn into another mistake. More to the point, she wasn't going to make the same mistakes her own mother had made.

Okay, she amended, absently touching her tummy again. She wasn't going to make *all* of the same mistakes. Joyce Malone had let down everyone who'd ever counted on her—including, Shallie figured, herself.

They'd no sooner rounded a switchback on a steep downhill grade when a sleek black pickup came roaring up the road and snapped her out of her thoughts. The club cab fishtailed on the slick skiff of new snow glazing the road's surface and headed straight toward them.

"Tarnation," Bob muttered.

He jerked the steering wheel hard right to avoid getting clipped by the big truck. "Hang on," he said, his jaw tight, his hands white on the wheel as he slammed on the brakes.

When Shallie saw the size of the tree directly ahead of them, she braced a hand against the dash and clamped her jaw together to keep from screaming.

Not that it worked. The sound that came out of her mouth was just this side of ear splitting. And the pain that knifed through her wrist when the truck crashed to a stop in a drift made her physically ill.

Swearing under his breath, Brett McDonald brought his truck to a skidding stop on the shoulder of the road. Damn. He hadn't seen that patch of ice. But he had seen Bob Coleman's pickup—and just in the nick of time. He'd risked rolling his truck to miss it. Thank God he *had* missed it—just barely.

Jamming the gearshift into park, he set the emergency brake and shoved open the door. Heart hammering like a piston, he jumped to the ground. Engine exhaust rose in white clouds as he sprinted toward Bob's truck, scared to death the old man had gotten hurt when he'd swerved to miss him.

The good news: the old Ford had stopped in a snowbank just short of a head-on with a huge white pine. Not a scratch on it. The bad news: the truck was sitting sideways on the narrow road; the front bumper buried deep into the drift the plow had left along the shoulder.

"You okay, Bob?" Mac yelled through the rancher's closed window.

"Yeah, I believe I'm of a piece." Bob turned his head toward the passenger seat. "What about you, Shallie? You okay over there?"

Shallie? Mac had only ever known one Shallie—but this couldn't be *his* Shallie.

He ducked his head so he could see across the cab. My God. His heart hit him a couple of good ones as old memories and old feelings tussled with the shock of seeing her.

Shallie. His Shallie Malone. He hadn't seen her since high school, when she'd lit out of Sundown like her tail was on fire. But he'd recognize those big brown eyes and that tangle of short brown curls anywhere.

And he'd recognize the mad scramble of his heartbeat and the catch in his breath as the reaction he'd always had around this woman. Okay. She'd been a girl last time he'd seen her. That hadn't made his feelings for her any less real. She didn't know it—he'd been too proud to ever spill his guts about how he felt about her—but Shallie Malone had been the one. The one that got away.

He scrambled around to the passenger side, waded through the knee-deep snow and jerked the door open with a grin on his face. Shallie was back—and unless she was married, engaged or otherwise taken, she wasn't getting away this time.

"Shallie! Darlin'. If you aren't a sight for sore eyes."

She'd been one fine-looking girl. She was beyond fine as a woman. His grin faded, though, when he searched her face and saw the unmistakable strain of pain in her eyes.

"Oh, damn." His heart sank as concern tangled with self-disgust. "You're hurt."

She shot him a valiant smile. "Leave it to you, McDonald. I travel almost two thousand miles without a scratch, then I'm one mile from home and you manage to break my wrist."

Two

"Okay, worrywart, you can wipe that death-door look off your face," Shallie assured Mac as she walked out of the emergency room three hours later. "I'm fine. It's hardly more than a sprain."

Mac's breath of relief when he finally saw her was tinged with the antiseptic scent of hospital. He rose from the hard, waiting-room chair and hurried toward her. Her brown eyes looked up at him from a face that was pale and weary. Dark smudges of fatigue painted violet bruises beneath her eyes.

Her left arm was supported by a sling. Inside the sling he could see what looked like a cast. *Sonofabitch.* He'd done this to her. "If it's just a sprain, why did they put it in a cast?"

She shrugged, as if the cast was of little importance.

"Okay," she finally conceded when he gave her a hard look. "So maybe it's a hairline fracture."

"Then it's *broken*," he pointed out with a sinking sensation in his gut as she tried, again, to minimize the damage. *Damn.* He'd broken her wrist.

Though pain pinched tight lines around the corners of her mouth, she still worked up a smile for him. "Well, if you're going to do something, just as well do it right."

"Damn, darlin'." He slung an arm over her shoulders when what he wanted to do was fold her into his arms and absorb all of her pain. Instead, feeling protective and responsible, and like a first-class ass, he pressed a kiss to the top of her head. "I am *so* sorry."

"Stop." She gave him a squeeze with her good arm, then pushed away from him. "I'm fine. Quit beating yourself up."

He needed more than a beating. He needed to be drawn and quartered for putting her in this fix. Once he'd bundled her into his truck, then made certain Bob Coleman and his pickup were okay and back on the road, he'd headed straight for Bozeman and the hospital.

She'd sputtered and tried to minimize the damage all the way. "I just *came* from Bozeman. And I don't need to see a doctor. I was joking about it being broken, for Pete's sake. It's just banged up a little."

It was just banged up a *lot.* Mac had suspected as much from the way she so very carefully cradled it against her ribs. He'd have given anything not to be right.

"They give you anything for the pain?" He snagged her jacket from the chair where he'd been holding on to it for her.

"I'll do fine with some Tylenol."

"You need something a helluva lot stronger than that," he insisted, helping her slip her good arm into the right sleeve. Carefully settling the jacket over her shoulders, he fought the urge to leave his hands there and pull her back against him. "What's the matter with that doctor?"

"I said no to a prescription, okay?" She glanced at him over her shoulder, then looked away, like there was more she had been about to tell him but changed her mind at the last second.

She'd said no to a lot of things since he'd found her in Bob's truck, Mac suddenly realized. Like medical care for starters. Mac had finally figured out why when they'd checked in at the E.R. desk. She didn't have health insurance.

The lightbulb finally went on. Which was probably why she'd refused the pain medication, Einstein. Maybe she can't afford it.

"Look, short-stack," Mac turned away to snag his own jacket, reverting to his old nickname for her because of her love for pancakes, "I already told you, I'm picking up the tab for this. It's my fault. That makes it my bill. Besides, my vehicle insurance will cover it, so it's nothing out of my pocket. Now…let's reconsider that prescription, okay?"

But she was already heading out the door.

On an exasperated breath, Mac stomped after her.

"Same ol' hardhead," he muttered. That was one of the things he'd loved about her. She was stubborn and strong and a survivor, in spite of what she'd had to endure growing up. She'd been a damn stubborn girl. Stood to reason that she'd grown into a damn stubborn woman. A damn beautiful woman. A woman who had set the bar for all others, none of whom had measured up.

"Okay," he conceded, catching up with her as he cleared the revolving door. "We do it your way—for now. But if I hear so much as a whimper of pain or see that you're suffering, we're going to have us a little talk."

"Let's talk anyway," she suggested as they walked side by side toward his truck. "How the heck are you, McDonald?"

Mac cupped the elbow of her right arm—telling himself it was to steady her and not because he couldn't resist touching her—as they picked their way carefully across the snow-covered parking lot.

"Hungry, that's how I am," he said hoping she wouldn't notice how aware he was of her.

The snow had started falling like it was going to get serious again by the time they reached his truck. With his hand still on her elbow, he punched the keyless remote and opened the passenger door. "How about we talk over a nice hot meal?"

That was one way to keep her with him a little longer.

"Works for me," she said as he helped her step up onto the running board then ease into the seat. "As long as it's not Italian."

His face must have fallen because she laughed and, making a gun with the thumb and forefinger of her right hand, fired at him. "Gotcha."

He grinned as he buckled her in then walked around and slid behind the wheel. "Har, har. It would be nice to think that news of my restaurant has spread far and wide." Just like it would be nice to think that maybe she'd kept track of him during the past several years and that's why she knew about his restaurant. But that amounted to ego and wishful thinking drawing the conclusions.

"If it makes you feel good, then you go right ahead and think it."

What would make him feel good was if she was pressed up against him on this cold winter night, but that was just crazy. So he grinned his good-ol'-boy grin instead of suggesting she slide on over close. "What I'm thinking is that Bob Coleman, as usual, must have done a lot of talking."

"No one would argue with you on that one," she said with a smile that looked like it zapped all of her energy.

She was dead beat, Mac realized as he cranked up the heat and headed out of the lot. And still beautiful and still turning him on like a strobe light.

Shallie. He still couldn't believe it. What stroke of luck had prompted her to return to Sundown after—what? Nine? Ten years?

He'd find out soon enough. In the meantime he didn't really care what had brought her back into his life. Or why she'd left and he'd never heard from her again. He was just damn glad she was here. He'd never stopped thinking about her—which was just plain dumb since he'd probably only crossed her mind in passing now and again in the past several years.

But still, despite the fact that he was responsible for breaking her wrist, he was happy as hell that he'd *almost* run into her today.

* * *

"I have to stop." Shallie reluctantly pushed away her plate of tortellini carbonara. She was too full to eat another bite. "I don't want to, but I have to. Good Lord, Mac, this food is amazing."

"That would be *good* amazing, right?"

Mac's lively blue eyes danced in his familiar, handsome face that still bore shades of a summer tan. She'd forgotten how blue his eyes were. Montana-sky blue. Still smiling. Still teasing. Still the eyes of a friend.

It was so good to see him. Not that Shallie was willing to simply come out and say so. That wasn't the way things had ever worked between them. She'd known. Even as a girl she'd known that, with a little encouragement, Mac would have taken their relationship past friendship into something more.

And it had been tempting. But tempting as it had been—as tempting as it might be now—she hadn't needed a boyfriend back then. She'd needed a friend. Just like she needed one now. Bottom line, she could not afford to screw things up between them. She'd never forgive herself if she did.

Besides, it would have been easy to fall in love with Mac. Looking at him now, it would still be easy. Too easy. She didn't trust easy. *Easy* wasn't a word that had ever been a part of her life experience. Especially where men were concerned. And when it had started to look easier to let her teenage emotions take over and fall that little bit of distance in love with Brett McDonald, she'd left Sundown. Running scared away from her emotions. It would have ended badly, and bad was something she couldn't bear when it came to Mac. That's why she hadn't kept in touch. She'd had to make the break clean. Final.

"Yeah. That would be good amazing," she said in response to his fishing expedition, then fell back into the safe pattern of gentle ribbing they'd established as kids. "Some things never change, I see. You're still trolling for compliments."

"What can I say? I've got a big ego. It needs lots of stroking."

That was so not true. He *should* have an ego; it was amazing that he didn't. Mac had always been the cutest, the most athletic, the smartest, the most macho, most sought after guy in school. Not by her, of course, because she *had* been very careful to always treat him like a brother. But he'd never taken himself—or his looks—seriously.

Speaking of serious, aside from the circumstances that had prompted her return to Sundown, and aside from her broken wrist, it had finally started to feel like she *had* done the right thing in coming home again. And sitting here with Mac smiling at her across the table in a quiet corner in his restaurant, Spaghetti Western, was reason enough to have come back.

Mac was her friend. She was mature enough now to keep him in that niche. One of the best she'd ever had. He'd been one of the few constants, the few comforts in a childhood where she'd lived a far cry from Mr. Rogers's neighborhood. In this moment he felt as comfortable as a warm blanket on this cold, end-of-December night. And comfortable was the extent of the feelings she could afford to let herself have for him.

"Damn it's good to see you," Mac said, shaking his head as if he couldn't believe she was really here. "So what brings you back to Montana, doll face?"

Logical question. The double trip of her heart was not, however, a logical response. Good friend or not, she wasn't quite ready to come clean with that little tidbit of information. Equal measures of guilt and shame kept her from telling him about the baby. At least for now.

"Just had a yearning to see the mountains again in the winter," she said evasively.

She glanced away when his eyes said they didn't quite buy her explanation. He'd always known her a little too well. But he didn't press, and for that she was grateful.

"And to see *you,* of course," she added, realizing how true it was. She really had missed him. Missed her friend, and she felt real bad, suddenly, that she'd allowed them to lose contact over the years.

"I'm sorry I haven't been much for staying in touch."

He lifted a shoulder in a throwaway shrug but she sensed, more than saw, the hurt behind his reaction. "Goes both ways. I'm just as guilty. It's a guy thing," he added with a grin.

"So catch me up," she prompted, smiling across a table draped in a charming red-and-white-checkered cloth. A white tapered candle burned between them, the flame flickering, making shadows dance across a masculine face that had matured with amazing grace. "How are your folks? Are they still in Sundown?"

"Dad is." He hesitated then added, "Mom's in L.A. They divorced several years ago."

If he had said they'd moved to the moon, she couldn't

have been more shocked. Tom and Carol McDonald had seemed like the perfect couple. Loving, caring, fun. They'd been the perfect family. Perfect parents. The ones she'd always wished she'd had. "Oh, Mac. I'm sorry."

"Yeah." His jaw hardened. "Me, too."

She wanted to ask what had happened. But she saw an uncharacteristic bleakness in Mac's eyes and understood that he didn't want to talk about it. That it was very painful for him.

"So what's happened to the old gang in the last nine years?" she asked brightly, determined not to put a damper on the evening. "Where's J.T.? And Peg and the rest of the crew?"

She listened with interest as he ran down the list. Many of the kids they used to pal around with, it seemed, had left the little pond for bigger ones.

"Peg's still in Sundown, though," Mac said as he toyed absently with the stem of his wineglass.

Candlelight glinted off his dark hair, cast his hard jaw in shadow. Handsome, she thought as she watched his mobile mouth. Devastatingly handsome.

"Married with two kids. Settled in raising bucking stock with Cutter Reno and Lee and Ellie Savage."

Shallie blinked, shocked out of an unexpected fantasy of the press of his beautiful mouth to hers. *What was wrong with her?* "Reno? Peg married that outlaw? He was chasing silver belt buckles and women on the PRCA rodeo circuit last I knew."

"Yeah, well, he's about as far from an outlaw as Preacher Davis now. I'm told a good woman can do that for a bad man. Same goes for J.T."

"J.T.? John Tyler is married?" They had been the three musketeers—Shallie and J.T. and Mac.

Times do change. And don't think about his mouth. Or the thickness of his biceps beneath his shirt. Or the breadth of his hands, the length of his fingers...

"Yep. Just this fall," Mac continued, his smile returning while she forced herself to take a sip of water. "He did a stint in the military after college. Ended up in Afghanistan. Messed him up a little—not that anyone but me knew it. Anyway, he took a liking to the new vet, and the feeling was mutual."

She chanced a look at his face, then surprised them both by laughing when she realized what she saw in his expression. "And the idea that J.T. tied the knot makes you nervous as heck, doesn't it?"

J.T. and Mac had sworn they'd never get married. There may have even been a blood oath involved. Of course, they'd been eleven years old at the time. The three of them had been big on blood oaths back then.

"Me? Nah."

"Liar, liar," she teased in a sing-song voice.

He ignored her taunting. "J.T. can't help it if he went soft in the head. I'm made of sterner stuff. You won't catch me settled in with a ring in my nose—I mean, on my finger."

She shook her head. "You're awful."

His eyes twinkled. "Just calling it like I see it."

"Hmm. Or did word about that sour disposition of yours finally get out and any woman with half a brain knows enough to stay away from you?"

"Hey—" He affected a wounded look. "Some of my

favorite dates only have half a brain, so don't go bad-mouthing my taste."

Shallie rolled her eyes and hoped her curiosity about the women he dated didn't show.

"What about you, Shallie Mae? Where've you been? Whatcha been doing?"

Yeah, well, she'd known they'd get around to this sooner or later. She laid her napkin on the table by her plate. "Not much of a story there."

"Somehow I find that hard to believe."

"Believe it," she assured him, feeling more than self-conscious about her lackluster career. "School and work pretty much tell the tale. It took me eight years to get my degree."

That was because she'd had to work to pay her way through college, and sometimes she'd have to drop classes altogether to stay on top of the frills like food and rent and electricity.

"But now I are a teacher," she said, adapting a goofy grin to go with her goofy grammar. Both made him smile.

He leaned back in his chair, considered her, then nodded. "A teacher. That's cool, Shall. Really cool."

"Yeah," she said reacting to his warm smile with one of her own, remembering why he had always been so special to her. He was proud of her. He always had been. Even when she hadn't been able to muster up a shred of self-pride. "It is cool. Kindergarten."

"So, you're on winter break?"

She *would* have been on winter break if she hadn't been asked to let go of her contract when the school board in the small town in southeast Georgia had found out about her pregnancy. Unwed kindergarten teachers, it seemed, did not make the popularity list in small town, rural South. She knew she could have fought it and won. The truth was, she hadn't had any fight left in her. And she'd wanted to get away from the mess she'd made.

"Yeah," she said, instead of leveling with him. "I'm on break."

Silence settled and with it another layer of guilt. Shallie had the feeling Mac saw right through her lie. If he did, he didn't quiz her on it, thankfully. He wouldn't be so proud of her now if he knew the whole truth.

"You sure you don't want some wine?" he asked instead. "I've got a nice red in the cooler."

She shook her head. "None for me. You go ahead, though."

He gave her another one of those considering looks, but let it drop. "That's okay. I've had enough. Besides, you have to be beat. And don't lie, I know your wrist has to hurt like hell."

She *was* tired. And her wrist *did* hurt. "It *has* been a long day," she admitted without acknowledging the pain. "I thought I'd be holed up in the Sundown Hotel tonight, but it's a little too late to head back now. So, kind sir, if you'll point me to a decent motel here in Bozeman, I'm ready to call it a day."

He snorted. "Yeah, like that's going to happen. You're not staying in any motel," he informed her as if that was the most ridiculous idea he'd ever heard. "You're staying at my place here in Bozeman."

She shook her head. "Mac—"

"No," he insisted, cutting her off. "I've got an extra bedroom, extra bath. Cripes, Shallie, it's the least I can do after banging up your wrist. And before you wind up for a fight, save what energy you've got left. This is not open for debate. You're staying with me. End of story."

She knew from experience that she was dealing with one stubborn Irishman. She should fight it a little harder, but the thought of not having to hassle with checking into a cold, generic motel room was just too appealing.

"And what will the woman in your life think about another woman staying over?" She hadn't planned on asking about his women. She hadn't planned on being this curious, either. And until he answered, she hadn't realized how relieved she would be with his response.

"There's no woman. So there's no problem."

Now there was a tidbit of information that she could happily dwell on if she let herself. She didn't let herself.

"Okay. Fine. I'll stay. Add *bully* to *insufferable*," she groused through a smile that acknowledged she knew she'd met up with a brick wall and was actually grateful.

"Don't forget *incredible cook*."

"And then some." Shallie stood when Mac did. "I'm not going to be able to eat for a week."

"So I shouldn't have the kitchen box up some tiramisu for a late night snack?"

"Tiramisu?" Oh my God. Tiramisu. Sweet. Chocolate. Heaven help her.

But she couldn't. Then her stomach growled.

He chuckled. "Thought that might perk you up. Still

got the same ol' sweet tooth, huh? Be right back." With
a nod toward the front door, he pointed her to a waiting
area and headed for the kitchen.

Shallie strolled over to the welcoming bench and sat,
aware that she was smiling. Interesting. Despite her
throbbing wrist, despite the fact that she had no idea
what she was going to do for money now that she'd been
given doctor's orders not to work for several weeks, she
was smiling.

She shook her head at her own lack of concern about
the direness of her circumstances. Then she cut herself
a little slack. There'd be time enough to worry about
money tomorrow. Tonight she was in the company of a
special man, a good friend; she was warm, and her
tummy was full.

And then there was the prospect of the tiramisu.

Just the tiramisu, she reminded herself when the delicious sight of Mac strolling toward her set a few
hormones zinging in a very dangerous direction.

"Whoa," Shallie said as Mac rounded the last turn
on a street on the outskirts of Bozeman and she got a
look at his house. "The restaurant business must be
very good."

Mac grinned as he punched the remote on his garage
door opener, pulled into his drive and eased his new
truck inside the triple-car garage. Yeah. The restaurant
business was damn good. He'd just moved into the
house he'd had built to his own specifications last
month.

"Who knew that a love of spaghetti, a beer major and

a business minor could translate into the American dream."

He killed the motor, jumped down out of the truck and pocketed his keys, thinking it was a damn good thing he finally had a chance to put a little distance between them. Riding in the dark truck with soft music playing on his CD changer and nothing but dim dash lights and streetlights illuminating the night had made it a little too intimate. He'd clamped both hands on the wheel, finding himself resisting the urge to reach out and cover her hand with his a little too often.

What would she think if he had, he wondered. What would she think if he'd just covered her slim thigh with his hand, squeezed gently and said, "I've missed you, Shall. I've missed you, and this time I'm not letting you go."

She'd have slapped him up alongside the head, that's what she'd have done, he thought as he walked around to the other side of the truck. And he'd have deserved it.

She was tired. She was hurting. And if he knew his Shallie, there was something else working behind those intelligent eyes of hers. Something big. Something that bothered. Something—other than him—that had brought her back to Sundown.

All in good time, McDonald, he thought as he opened her passenger door. She'd tell him what was bothering her all in good time.

"It's stuck," she said, trying to work the seat belt latch one-handed under the stark, bright light in his three-car garage.

"Here. I'll get you out of there." He reached across her

lap and gave the buckle a try. And met with resistance. Not to mention the solid heat of woman beneath her thin jacket.

This could be trouble.

And it was.

"Damn. It *is* stuck. Hold on."

He climbed up on the running board and leaned across her so he could get a better angle—and ended up pressed against more of her with more of him. And the front seat of his big club-cab truck suddenly shrank to roughly the size of a soup bowl.

"Ah…" He fumbled with the latch and made it worse. "Oh. Here's the problem. It's your jacket. It's caught in the latch."

And he was caught up in lust. She was so soft and full against his arm. Her skin so pale and flawless.

Because she's exhausted, jackass. For God's sake, get a grip.

"Just get me a blanket and a pillow," she said dropping her head back against the leather seat and closing her eyes. "I'll be fine right here for the night."

She looked so tired right then that Mac figured she was halfway serious. And he had to do something to jar himself out of his sexual haze.

"Okay. Have a little faith, will ya? I'm not the sharpest tack in the drawer but I'm smarter than this seat belt and I don't care how many people say otherwise."

That pried a weary smile out of her. She'd always had such a pretty smile. Sure hadn't changed. Pretty smile. Pretty eyes—cinnamon brown shot through with gold. And she smelled good, too.

His head was merely inches from hers. Their bodies

bumped as he worked to free the seat belt latch. Strike that. Her breast, *specifically,* brushed against his arm, *specifically,* while he worked away at the jammed buckle.

She felt soft and full against him. But this was Shallie, he reminded himself. The woman who had never wanted to be anything more than his friend.

A memory flashed. He'd been thirteen and in the process of discovering what all the fuss was about over the opposite sex. He'd tried to kiss her one night and cop a feel, randy little brat that he'd been then. Not that she'd let him get by with it. His tongue had been sore for a week where she'd bitten it. His thumb had been swollen for much longer after she'd bent it back to his wrist and beyond.

But he'd never gotten over the thrill of that first, tentative contact. That wild, gut-knotting kick he'd experienced when he'd touched her breast through her sweater.

"Don't you ever pull that crap with me again, McDonald," she'd warned and, trying not to whimper in pain, he'd promised that her mouth had seen the last of his tongue.

And that should have ended any "awareness" of Shallie Malone as a sex object.

It should have, but it hadn't. And he'd never felt the same thrill in a kiss since.

"Any luck?"

He'd been so wrapped up in getting a handle on his physical awareness that her question startled him. So did a sudden realization. If he moved his head, turned toward her just so, their mouths would be in perfect alignment. He'd be able to experience firsthand the scent and taste of the chocolate mint she'd tucked in her mouth after dinner. And to find out up close and personal if those lush, full lips were as soft as they looked. If they still tasted the same. Like wild sex and young love and the sweetest heat this side of the equator.

The urge to find out—the strength of it—blindsided him.

"Nope," he said, jerking his attention back to the latch and putting all he had in resisting that urge. "Not yet. But if I don't have you out by morning, we may be looking at a lifelong commitment."

He hoped his little joke came out *sounding* like a joke instead of the desperate bid to break the unsettling sexual tension that had suddenly shrunk the inside of the truck yet again—this time to the size of a soup *spoon*. Man. Between running SW and working on the Dusk to Dawn, he'd pretty much been out of circulation. All work and no play and all that, made Mac a horny boy.

If only. The truth was, it was her. Just her that put him in this state.

"Got it," he said when the buckle finally gave. He backed out of the truck, feeling way too much regret that the warmth of her breast no longer heated his arm and way too little relief that his sojourn into lust was suddenly over.

But it *was* over. Over. Done. Never happened.

This was Shallie. Short-stack. The woman who only wanted to be his buddy. She'd kick his sorry butt clear across Montana if she knew what he'd been thinking. At least she would tonight. It was too soon. And it was

too much for now. With a little time, though. A little
time and a little patient persuasion, maybe, just maybe
all these years of waiting will have been worth it.

And as he helped her down out of the cab, though,
and retrieved the box of tiramisu and her one piece of
luggage, all of a sudden it didn't seem like such a bright
idea to have her sleeping across the hall from his
bedroom. What if he couldn't control himself?

"Now you're just being stupid," he muttered under
his breath as he unlocked the door to the house and let
them into the kitchen.

He held the door open for her and stepped back so she
could go inside ahead of him. "Being stupid about what?"

Once he flicked on a light, he didn't have to figure
out a plausible answer. She got sidetracked when she
saw his kitchen.

"You have *got* to be kidding."

Her eyes were wide with surprise and admiration as
she took in his state-of-the-art kitchen with its gleaming
stainless steel restaurant-grade appliances, black granite
countertop and large, multipaned skylight that was currently laden with snow.

Mac tossed his keys on the counter and shrugged out
of his jacket. "It's not much, but it's home," he said then
added on a proud grin that he just couldn't dampen,
"and damn spectacular, huh?"

"In a *word*." She continued to inspect and admire as
he helped her carefully out of her jacket. "Little Brett
McDonald. My. My. You've come a long way."

"Got lucky," he said, shrugging off the compliment.
"Come on. I'll give you the fifty-cent tour, but let me

warn you right now, I just moved in a few weeks ago. I don't even know where all the light switches are yet. I think there might even be a room or two that I haven't found."

Turning on lights as he went, he led her down three marble-tiled steps to the great room. A flip of another switch and the fire flickered to life in the native stone fireplace dominating the south wall from the floor to the ceiling that was two stories high.

Beside the fireplace stood a holdover from the season. A very dry and ready-to-pitch fifteen-foot Christmas tree was losing needles like a white dog shedding hair on a black sweater.

"If I know you—and I think I do," she said, "that poor tree has probably been up since the first of the month."

What could he say. He'd always been like a kid about Christmas.

Brittle needles had fallen on a yellow pine floor that gleamed under the soft light. A multicolored area rug in muted tones of greens and blues and tan was soft underfoot in the seating area.

"Oh, Mac. This is all so lovely."

"Well that's a kick in the butt. It's *supposed* to be masculine," he pointed out, making a show of sounding insulted as she crossed the room to run her fingers across a polished mantel cut from a single slab of rose-beige granite.

"Lovely and *masculine*," she amended. "It's also you."

It was the nicest compliment she could have paid him. Yeah, he'd hired a decorator to help him but he'd dictated the colors—rich jade greens, slate blues and taupe. At least, that's what the decorator called it. He called it sand.

He'd chosen the textures, too—native stone for the fireplace, warm wood for the floor and supple leathers for the furniture. And the artwork reflected his feelings for the Bozeman area.

He'd purchased all the pieces from locals artists—colorful, vibrant oil paintings of the mountains on the walls, metal and stone sculptures on the tables and floor blended with gas-fired pottery pieces on the mantel and hearth.

"Oh, sweetie, I'm sorry," he said when he realized she was about to topple over from fatigue, "I was having one of those God-I-love-this-place moments. They tell me it will wear off when I get my first tax bill."

He held out a hand. "Come on. Let's get you settled in. We can catch up some more in the morning. Unless you've got to be someplace. Man—I didn't even think of that. Do you? Have to be someplace?"

She shook her head and besides the exhaustion and pain, he swore he saw a brief but palpable sadness fill her eyes before she looked away. "Nope. No place to be. Nothing specific to do. I'm sure you've got plenty on your plate, though, so don't think you have to enter-tain me tomorrow."

His heart did a dance at the news she was free for a while. "Entertain you? Honey, this is Bozeman. In the winter. You'll be entertaining me."

He met her halfway across the room and folded her carefully into his arms again. He couldn't help it. For all she knew, it was simply a fraternal hug. He was hugging his friend who he was simply glad to see after so many years and whose presence brought back memories of good times and cheap thrills—that unfortunately had jump-started his hormones into thinking they should be perking right up after an unseasonably long hiatus.

Well. There you go, he thought. There was part of the explanation for reacting to her so strongly. Seeing her made him feel like a kid again—and he'd always been a randy kid.

"Remember the time we—you and J.T. and I—took Jacque, the foreign-exchange student out cow tipping?" he asked, reining things back into perspective.

She wrapped her good arm around his waist as he walked her toward the guest bedroom. "We were so bad."

She was grinning when she glanced up at him and for more reasons he didn't want to analyze, he was happy to see her smiling. "To the bone," he agreed, and all felt right with his world again.

Three

The next morning Shallie lay flat on her back in Mac's big guest room bed and wondered if she dared to get up. It had been a week since she'd had a bout of morning sickness, but that didn't mean it was over.

To be on the safe side, she'd just lie here for a little while longer. Plus, it was as good an excuse as any to wallow in this huge bed with the smooth, expensive sheets and soft, down mattress topper.

Heaven. Mac's house was absolute heaven. This bed was cloud-nine quality. She'd been afraid that her wrist would keep her awake. Or that she'd be too wired to sleep when he'd shown her to the spacious guest bedroom done in rich earth colors with brick-red accents. She'd been wrong on both counts.

Even with thoughts of the big carry-out container of

tiramisu tucked neatly in his spotless refrigerator waiting for her, she hadn't been able to make herself leave the comfort and warmth of this bed for a little midnight snack. Once she'd given it an experimental pat to test its firmness and discovered the down mattress beneath a plush native print comforter, she'd taken care of her bathroom ritual, slathered on some lotion, tugged on her favorite sleep shirt and had sunk into decadent luxury. She'd propped her throbbing arm on an extra pillow, closed her eyes and that was all she wrote.

Now it was morning. And she really should get a move on. She glanced down at her arm. Lifted it experimentally—and gasped. Every raw nerve in her body seemed to congregate in her wrist and remind her that broken bones—even hairline fractures—hurt like the devil.

"So, Malone...now what?" she wondered aloud as the pain dulled to a throbbing ache. She had virtually no use of her arm, so what was she going to do to support herself? Teaching was out of the question for the moment. Even though she hadn't anticipated finding a vacancy midterm, she'd hoped to find some substitute teaching work in the area. Maybe supplement her income waiting tables somewhere until she found a full-time position. She'd done plenty of waitressing when she'd worked her way through college. Sure, she had a little savings to tide her over and she had one more paycheck coming. Neither would last long, not with student loan payments and basic living expenses to cover.

Thankfully, a soft tap on the door diverted her attention from her financial dilemma.

"Hey, short-stack. You awake in there?"

Mac.

How could she not smile?

"Awake. But barely." She scooted up a little, flinching when her wrist protested.

"Are you decent?"

She propped one of the extra pillows behind her back. "I have *always* been decent. *Your* respectability, on the other hand, has always been questionable."

The door cracked open, and Mac, with a gorgeous smile, popped into the room. He was dressed in a plaid flannel shirt and tight, worn jeans, and if he'd been any man but Mac, she'd have thought, wow, I could get used to starting my mornings this way. He was gorgeous.

"Not nice to tick off the cook—especially when he's bearing breakfast in bed."

"Oh, my gosh. You shouldn't have done that. I'm already imposing. I don't want you cooking for me."

"Hel-lo. Cooking is what I do, remember?" He walked over to the bed carrying a tray laden with juice and coffee and pancakes that smelled like heaven—for about five seconds.

Oh, Lord.

Shallie threw back the covers, jumped out of bed and ran for the bathroom. Where she promptly got sick as a dog.

"Was it something I cooked?" Mac asked in a really feeble attempt at humor, hoping to undercut his concern.

"Oh, please. Go away. This is gross. I don't want you to have to deal with this."

And what are you dealing with, sweet friend of mine, Mac wondered, but didn't ask.

"Comes with the deluxe package at McDonald Inn." He wet a washcloth for her. "Clean sheets. Breakfast in bed. Nursing skills. It's printed on the door along with the rates. You must have missed it."

Poor baby. She looked so miserable. He squatted down on his haunches beside his little short-stack, a comforting hand gently rubbing her back as she hunched over the toilet bowl.

He would like to ignore the conclusions he'd started to draw. He'd like to think she was dealing was a case of nerves or the flu. If he was right about what he suspected, however, he wondered how long it was going to take her to come clean.

Hell. Maybe he was jumping recklessly to conclusions. He hoped so. He hoped to hell he was wrong about what he was thinking. Because if he was right, there was a serious chance that he was going to get good and pissed off before this day was over. An even better chance that all those romantic thoughts he'd been thinking when he'd prepared her breakfast had all just gone up in smoke.

Her hand shook when she accepted the cool wet washcloth he offered her. "I'm figuring checkout time just got bumped up an hour or two."

"Don't be a goof." Thoughts grim, he watched with concern as she wiped her mouth. "So. What's up, kid?"

She started to shake her head, then thought better of it. "Don't know. I suppose I…could have picked up a flu bug on the bus."

Okay. Logical explanation, but somehow Mac didn't think they were dealing with a case of the flu.

But if she wanted to play that game, fine. He'd give her time to decide to level with him.

"You came here by bus? From where? Never mind." What was he thinking? She was dog sick. Now was not the time for twenty questions. "We can talk later when you're feeling better. Think you're tummy's settled some?"

She closed her eyes. Considered. "I think so."

"Then let's get you back into bed."

"I cannot tell you how sorry I am about this," she said as he helped her to her feet and walked her back to the bedroom.

"Like you never held my head when I tossed *my* cookies?"

They had not been angels during their teens. They'd never done drugs and had rarely drunk before they'd become legal. There had been occasions, however, when they'd experimented with some homemade wine or tapped the keg a little too often at any number of parties that always cropped up in the spring around graduation time. Mac and J.T. had always gotten sick. She never had.

"In you go." He covered her up and helped her to lie back on the pillows.

And that's when he saw how hard she was working to hold back tears. His Shallie, who used to come to him all quiet and sad eyes and sometimes have bruises on her face and tell him she was fine. That nothing had happened. That she'd fallen out of bed. Or run into a door in the dark.

He'd known damn well, even as a kid, he'd known, that what she'd run into was her mother's fist, or a backhand from one of Joyce Malone's transient boyfriends.

"Honey, what's wrong?"

"Don't...be so nice to me. I...I don't deserve to ha-have you b-be so nice to me."

"Hey, hey. What kind of talk is that?" He eased a hip onto the bed beside her, brushed the hair back from her forehead as a huge tear leaked from the corner of her eye. "You're my buddy. I love you. There's nothing you could do to ever change that."

He tugged a tissue from the table by the bed and handed it to her. "You ready to tell me what's going on?"

She closed her eyes, looked away from him to the far side of the room, and he could see that a huge measure of pride was in play for her.

For him it was pure disappointment.

"Maybe later," he suggested, knowing she'd tell him when she was ready.

Still not looking at him, she nodded.

He squeezed her arm. "See if you can get some more rest. Snow pretty much shut things down during the night, so I'm not going anywhere for a while—at least not until the city crew finds its way to this end of town."

Then he pressed a kiss on her forehead and left her.

Puzzled. Concerned. Afraid that he knew what her problem was—dejected by what that meant to the future he'd plotted out for the two of them in the wee hours of the morning when he'd lain alone in his bed and let himself think about the prospect of a future with Shallie Malone.

When she came looking for him later, Mac was sitting on the sofa by the fire with his laptop, where he'd spent the past hour glaring at his screen and reading about various stages of pregnancy.

"You took down the tree," Shallie said inanely. Somehow, it made her a little sad. There was something about a Christmas tree—even one that had shed most of its needles—that lit a warm little glow inside her.

Odd, since she didn't remember many merry Christmases in her childhood, or even her adulthood, for that matter.

And she was just plain pathetic to be thinking about that now.

"I think that tree was violating about fifty fire codes," Mac said, watching her carefully. "It was way past its prime. That's what I get for putting it up the day after Thanksgiving."

"Some things never change," she said, working up a smile as she walked to an oversize leather chair that faced the sofa and was close to the fire. She sank down into it. "You're still the little boy who loves Christmas."

"So," he said after a long, very silent moment, "how are you feeling?"

There was no avoiding this conversation. "Foolish."

She curled her stocking feet up under her, tugged her sloppy red sweater down over the knees of her jeans and propped her injured wrist on the arm of the chair. And damn, if she didn't feel tears well up again.

She was not a weeper. Never had been. Pregnancy-induced hormones had become the bane of her existence. She hated this constant surge of emotion that seemed to lie just below the surface.

How had she gotten herself in this fix? By being stupid. That's how. Damn Jared Morgan. She'd loved him. At least, she'd thought she had…just as she'd thought he loved her. Until he'd started losing his temper over nothing. At first he'd just shove her a little. Then it had been a slap. Then it had gotten to be a whole lot more. Even if she hadn't caught him with another woman—the last straw—she'd been going to leave him.

Oldest, saddest story in the book. She'd fallen for an abuser and a cheat—just like her mother had. It was a pattern as old as time. Grow up and move away from an abusive situation and land in another one.

Well, she'd gotten out of it. But then she'd made things worse. Still feeling low and undesirable and angry and hurt a month after she'd ended things between them, she'd let her friends talk her into going out with them one night to a singles bar.

Just to get back among the living again.

Just to remember what it felt like to have a man look at her and not want to hit her.

It had been a little Band-Aid for her ravaged pride when the first man who had smiled at her made her feel like a woman again.

She'd needed his lies so badly. To ease the hurt. To fill the void. To salvage her self-esteem.

One night. One stupid, stupid night. When she'd awakened the next morning and had to face what she'd done, it was the lowest point in her life.

And then it had gotten even lower.

Brad Bailey of the charming smile and winning ways was just another cheater. Only, he'd been cheating on his wife.

Which had made Shallie feel like the biggest slug on the face of the earth.

The apple didn't fall so far from the tree after all, did it, Mom? she thought now, as she'd thought many, many times since that night.

And just like her mother, who Shallie had vowed she'd never become, now she was pregnant by a man she abhorred—not only for lying to her, but for what he'd done to his wife and family.

Like Shallie, the baby growing inside her may not have been conceived under ideal circumstances, but Shallie was determined to do the right thing by her child. She would not ignore her baby. She would not desert it. She would never hit her child, never make it feel like a mistake. No. She would not do any of the things her own mother had done to her.

This child would be loved. And this child would know it. Every day of her life, Shallie would make certain of that.

Shaking her head, she fought for control when she realized that Mac's worried gaze was focused intently on her. She didn't deserve his concern. But he did deserve the truth. At least, as much of the truth that she could bear to tell him.

"I'm pregnant," she said, figuring she'd just as well blurt it out and get it over with. Her heart beat like crazy while she waited for his reaction. When it came, it was the last one she'd expected.

"I know. I'm thinking about three months along?"

Her gaze shot to his. "How did you *know?*"

He lifted the laptop. Shrugged, trying to hide his concern. She saw it anyway. Along with the merest thread of anger...and worse. Disappointment. "I've been reading. You should be out of the morning sickness stage soon."

"No. I mean, how did you know I was pregnant?"

"Lucky guess?"

Shallie was horrified. "Is it that obvious?"

"Only to someone who knows you. Shallie," he said gently, "you refused pain medication last night for one thing. I wondered about it then. I mean, I know you're tough, but that went a little beyond making sense to me. And you turned down my best wine. Nobody turns down my wine."

He was trying to make her smile, but she just didn't have it in her at the moment.

"As for this morning," he continued, "I remember that cast-iron stomach of yours. When we were kids, I'd be barfing my guts out with the flu and you wouldn't so much as burp. So you and a case of the flu at nine in the morning didn't really seem like a good bet."

She sat in silence, waiting for questions or recriminations or something. Instead he seemed to be waiting for her to talk. So she did.

"This is the part where you're supposed to say something like, how could you be so careless? For Pete's sake, Shallie. Ever heard of birth control? Or—"

He cut her off with a raised hand. Seemed to gather

himself. Shrugged. "Like I said. I'm your friend. Not your judge. Now what can I do to help?"

She should have known that he'd respond with generosity instead of giving her grief. But then, he didn't know the whole story. If he did, he might not feel so generous.

Because of that…and because he was who he was—solid, steady and true—she felt like crying and laughing at the same time. So she did that, too.

"You could get me some of that tiramisu," she said after she'd dried her eyes.

He rose with a forced grin. He paused by her chair for a moment, then gently ruffled her hair as he walked by her on his way to the kitchen. "One order of tiramisu comin' right up."

"Better?" Mac sat across his kitchen's island counter and watched Shallie clean up the rich chocolate and butter finger dessert.

"Much. Chocolate *always* works."

He scooted off his stool and retrieved a carton of milk from the fridge. "Then I'm your man because there's lots more where that came from. In the meantime, drink some more milk. Good for you and for the kid."

"Yeah," she agreed. "Good for me and for the kid."

"The baby…it's okay and everything, right? I mean, hitting that snowbank. It didn't jar something loose, or hurt the baby?"

"Oh, Mac."

She must have been able to tell from his voice how much he'd been worried about that possibility, because she looked sad for him.

"No. Don't worry about the baby. The doctor checked me out. Everything's fine."

"Thank God." He heaved a breath of relief. It was bad enough he'd been responsible for breaking her wrist. If he'd caused any harm to her baby, well, he didn't know if he could live with that, too.

Just like he didn't know how he was going to live with the idea that she was probably still in love with the baby's father. After all, she'd cared enough about the guy to sleep with him. The Shallie he knew would have to care—even love a man—to get that deeply involved. And yet, she was here—which meant the jerk wasn't the man she'd thought he was.

Poor kid. And poor him.

Pipe dreams. Last night had been one big pipe dream.

She lapsed into silence while he made a big show of wiping down the counter. He needed something to do with his hands. He was determined to wait for her to talk—about the baby, about the father, who he'd already decided was a lying, cheating lowlife or she wouldn't have had a need to come back to Montana.

Yeah, he'd wait and see if she needed to talk about it. Or, if she wanted to just be quiet, that would be okay, too.

His resolve lasted all of a minute. "Okay," he said, turning back to her with a scowl. "So, where's the father? Why isn't he here? With you? Taking care of you?"

Nothing. Unless you counted the fact that her shoulders stiffened. That told him the issue of the father was a lot more than nothing.

"Is there some jerk out there somewhere who needs his lights punched out? Because I'm just the man to do it."

Her brown eyes met his over the glass of milk. She smiled, but it was a sad smile and it made his chest feel all squishy. "Thanks for offering."

Which meant, yeah, there was some creep who'd broken her heart and left her in a bad way. But she wasn't ready to share that piece of information with him. Probably because she knew he wasn't blowing smoke. Seeing her this way—miserable and pregnant and on her own—he was pretty much in love with the idea of making the guy pay with a little blood loss for leaving her in this fix.

Her mother hadn't given her anything but pain when she was a little girl. She didn't deserve more of it. Not from some guy who wasn't smart enough to know what he was giving up.

"Know anyplace that would be willing to hire a one-armed, pregnant woman?"

Okay. So he'd let her change the subject. Even though he still wanted, in the worst way, to ask if she was in love with the bastard.

"You're not going back to your teaching job?"

She flashed a tight smile. "Yeah. Well. Here's the deal. I…I fudged a little on that. There's no job to go back to."

He frowned. "You wanna run that by me again?"

She raised a shoulder, looked toward the window where the sun was glinting off the foot or so of new snow. "I no longer have a job."

"You got fired?" Even as he asked, he couldn't believe that was possible.

"Kind of came down to that, yeah."

Now he was really ticked. "Because you're pregnant?"

"Because I'm not *married* and pregnant. It's okay," she added, evidently seeing just how ticked he was.

And he was ticked. And at the same time relieved.

She wasn't married to the jerk. She wasn't *married.* He shouldn't have felt so much relief. He felt guilty because he did. And confused. Most of all confused because the truth was, he didn't figure into her situation in any way other than a shoulder to lean on.

That's what she needed from him now. That's what he'd be.

"I know I could fight it. And I'd probably win. The truth is, I don't want to fight. I don't want to go back there."

Her gaze drifted to the window. "I need to start fresh, you know? Me and my baby."

She smiled again, plucky to the bone. "Hadn't planned on job hunting with only one good wing, though."

Yeah. There was that. Guilt settled on his shoulders, as heavy as last night's snowfall. "Thanks to me."

"Oh—I didn't mean that. It was just the luck of the draw. Don't worry about it. I've got a little savings stashed away. I'll get by until I can work again. It won't be *that* long."

Mac rose, poured himself a cup of coffee and thought about the idea that suddenly popped into his head. "Tell you what," he said, deciding it was the perfect solution. "I know where there's a place available. The rent should be cheap, too."

She perked right up. "Yeah? Where?"

"The old Fremont cabin," he said, figuring she didn't

need to know he owned it, because knowing Shallie she'd figure she would be taking advantage of him if she stayed there.

"Ah. You mean *your* cabin."

He scowled over his mug. So much for her not knowing he owned the cabin. "Bob Coleman really has got a big mouth."

"Your name is on the mailbox."

Oops. "Right. Forgot about that. Regardless, the only reason I bought it was so I'd have a place to sleep when I'm in Sundown, working on the Dusk to Dawn. You'd actually be doing me a favor if you stayed there. Keep an eye on things, you know? This way I won't have to worry if the electricity goes off or the furnace goes on the fritz."

"You're worried about the furnace?"

"Okay, well, no. I had a new one put in this fall, but winter is winter. You never know."

She shook her head. "You're fabricating excuses to make me feel like I'm not imposing. Look, Mac, this is very sweet—and so are you," she added, her eyes soft, "but I'm not going to take advantage of your friendship—"

"Take advantage…please," he pleaded giving up on the pretense of her doing him a favor. He wanted her close. He didn't want her so close, however—like in the bedroom across the hall—that he'd be tempted to…hell. What would he be tempted to do?

She was pregnant. And he was probably right—she was most likely still in love with the creep who was responsible—and if she was, Mac really didn't want to know.

The hell he didn't.

And that realization added a bone-deep ache, to go with the anger that was knotting his gut.

"Look," he said, just to keep things in perspective, "the cabin is just sitting there empty most of the time. I rarely use it, and if I need to stay there sometime, it's not like there isn't room for both of us."

"But it's your home."

He lifted a hand in a gesture that encompassed the kitchen. "*This* is my home. The cabin is a convenience. I only bought it because I knew I'd be splitting my time between Sundown and Bozeman until I got the Dusk to Dawn running the way I want it."

He expelled a patient breath. "Now at the risk of sounding redundant, you are my friend. Let me do this for you. Come on," he wheedled, flashing his most per-suasive smile. "Just say yes, for Pete's sake. I'm dying of guilt, here, for putting you in that cast."

She frowned into her glass of milk. But he could tell she was coming around.

"You have to let me pay you something."

Like hell. "Fine. Whatever. We'll work that out later."

"Okay," she said finally. "But just until I'm released to do some kind of work."

"We'll worry about that later, too."

She studied her fingers as she ran them up and down the glass of milk. "That's something I've gotten pretty good at—worrying about things later. One of these days, I'm going to have to figure something out."

Poor little short-stack, Mac thought. She really has had a lot on her plate to deal with.

"Well, that day isn't today," he said softly. "Today is all about you getting rested up and me making sure that you do."

One corner of her mouth tipped up. "Anyone ever tell you you've got a major mother complex?"

"Bite your tongue. I'm all man. And I've got the tools to prove it." He shook a finger at her when her burst of surprised laughter told him the direction her mind had taken on that one.

"*Hand* tools, Malone. They're in the drawer right next to my aprons."

She laughed again when he opened a drawer and pulled out a hammer and an apron with Kiss the Cook splashed across the front in bold red letters.

"God, I've missed you," she said in a voice that was warm with affection and a little sad with regret.

Yeah. He'd missed her, too. Just like it looked as if he'd missed his chance with her.

He pushed his little self-pity moment aside. She was the one with problems. He had the means to help her out. And making her smile was one of them. "You'll get over that soon enough. I'll make you sick of me in no time."

"Not likely."

No. It wasn't likely, Mac thought. He sure as hell knew he wasn't going to get sick of seeing her. Stressed over seeing her, he realized when, despite the disclosure of her pregnancy, she lifted her arms over her head and stretched, and her breasts pressed against that baggie red sweater. A sharp, direct tug of lust pulled straight from his chest to his groin.

That sweater. It was old and ratty and obviously well-worn and well loved. And until that uncalculated stretch, she looked about as shapeless as a sack of spuds in it.

But he knew that wasn't the case. He knew that her breasts were soft and full and warm underneath it. And as he watched her now, he had an in-your-face visual reminder.

"Mac?"

His name registered on a level that told him she might be repeating it.

"Yeah? Hmm? What?"

He dragged a hand over his face and avoided her questioning brown eyes.

Smooth, McDonald. Real smooth.

"Where'd you go?" she asked with a curious grin as she slipped off the stool that flanked the island.

"Maui," he said, deadpan. "Those quick trips do wonders for cabin fever. What did I miss while I was gone?"

Another smile. "I asked you how long you've had Spaghetti Western."

"Tell you what. You go sit by the fire. Since chocolate seems to settle, I'll make us some cocoa and be right with you. I'll tell you all about it."

And while she was in the living room, he'd putzed around making that cocoa until he had his head back on his shoulders where it belonged—instead of in his pants where it was giving him ten kinds of trouble.

Four

Half an hour later, Shallie hugged one arm around her waist and sipped her cocoa while she stood by Mac's huge picture window and watched him clean off his driveway. Snow flew in a big, high arc as the snow blower cut through the foot-deep snow and ate an ever-widening path on the concrete.

She couldn't help but smile. He was right about the all-man part. He was out there working in his jeans, a plaid flannel shirt and a black down vest. Boots and a pair of gloves were the only other concessions he'd made to the cold. Nothing on his head. No scarf around his neck. No jacket to cut the bitter winter cold.

His nose and cheeks were red with it. Frost puffed out of his mouth like smoke as he worked his way back and forth on the driveway. The women must still drool all over him, she thought, remembering the way the girls used to swarm around him in high school. Mac and J.T. both, with their rugged good looks and quick, teasing grins, had broken more hearts than Montana had mountain peaks.

He had that undeniable air of competent male about him. It was there in the way he carried himself. In the way he smiled. In the way he related to people. Competent, confident, in charge. And he had integrity to spare. He was a guy's guy. And he was a woman's dream man.

Why hadn't Jason been like Mac? Honest. Credible. Fun. True blue. And why had she had to meet Brad? Who cheated on his wife.

She always fell for the losers. And now she was one, too.

Mac was so much a winner. She'd bet he was still breaking hearts—then had the proof of her suspicions when his phone rang. She was about to open the door and tell him he had a call when the message on his answering machine kicked on.

"Hey, it's Mac. Leave a message."

"Hi, sexy man. It's Lana. I was hoping I'd catch you at home."

The voice was seductive and kitten soft and had Shallie rolling her eyes and feeling like an eavesdropper. Which she was. She was also very curious and—now here was an admission that shocked her—a little jealous.

She should leave the room, she thought, glancing over her shoulder at the phone. But she couldn't quite make herself move as the voice purred on.

"Anyway, you haven't called in ages," Lana continued, sounding a little pouty, "so I thought I'd see what you've been up to. We could do drinks sometime. I'm dying to see your new place."

Oh, I'll just bet you are, Shallie thought with a snort.

"Hey," Lana of the midnight-velvet voice continued, "here's a thought. New Year's Eve is just four days away. So, call me, baby. We could ring in the New Year together. I'll show you a real good time, I promise. Bye-ee."

"Bye-ee," Shallie mimicked, picturing Lana as a voluptuous, if slightly needy, blonde and wondering if she was one of Mac's half-a-brain dates.

That thought was funny for all of a moment.

Speaking of half-a-brain. Who was she to judge?

She was twenty-seven years old. She was broke. She was three months pregnant and on the run from a relationship that never should have been.

In short, she was not exactly living the lofty dream she'd had when she'd left Sundown ten years ago. She had been going to be somebody. She had been going to make a difference.

And look at her now.

Shallie looked down at her still-flat tummy and gently covered it with her good hand. "So, what do you think of your momma so far, little one?"

I'm guessing, not so much, she thought on a deep sigh.

"Don't you worry, baby mine," she promised in a soft whisper. "We've just hit a little bump in the road. It'll be okay. We'll be okay. I promise. I'm not going to let you down."

And that's how Mac found her.

She was standing in a shaft of light that angled in from his front window. The sun kissed the rim of her cheek-bones, cast glossy highlights on her soft-brown curls.

Her hand covered her tummy. Her voice was whisper soft and reassuring.

He must have cleared his throat or something because, startled, she turned her head abruptly to look at him. Her brown eyes were bright, her lips tipped up into a smile that said she was happy to see him.

And, damn, he thought, as his heart kicked him a couple of good ones in the chest, if she wasn't one of the prettiest sights he'd ever seen.

"Hey, hard-working man," she said, her eyes filling with a wicked light. "You got a phone call while you were outside."

He tucked his gloves into his hip pockets then shrugged out of his vest. "Who was it?"

"La-na," she said, drawing out the name on a breathy, theatrical sigh. "She left a message. Sounds like you're gonna get lucky. She promised you a reallll gooood time."

Mac snorted. "Lana promises everybody a real good time," he said, wishing he'd never gotten involved with her last year. You live. You learn.

"You up for a ride?" he asked, wanting to change the subject. Lana, like most of the women he'd dated, left a lot to be desired in the "real person" department. Why did women have to play so many games? Why couldn't they just be themselves? Be honest, for Pete's sake instead of devious to the point of deceitful? You couldn't trust one of them. Even his own mother, it turned out, had been a liar and a cheat.

Shallie. Now, there was a woman you could count on. Too bad she didn't want to count on him for anything more than friendship.

"Most of the main streets should be cleared by now," he said, damn grateful that the woman sharing his house at the moment didn't have a deceitful bone in her body. "I need to check on some things at the restaurant. We can have lunch while we're there."

"You can't go on feeding me."

"Why not? I feed half of Bozeman on a good weekend."

"Half of Bozeman *pays* for the pleasure."

"Half of Bozeman is not my good friend. What's the point of having a restaurant if I can't feed my friends?

"Look," he added when he could see she wasn't convinced, "if you were gainfully employed—which you aren't, thanks to yours truly—and you could pay your way, it would be different."

She walked into the kitchen and rinsed her cup in the sink. "Would it?"

"No, actually, it wouldn't," he admitted. "I'd still want to feed you for free, only you wouldn't think anything of it."

She glanced at him over her shoulder, then laughed. It was a great sound.

"Your logic totally escapes me," she said turning back to him.

"It's only when a person is unable to do something that they feel like they need to do it," he explained. "So, following that logic, if you were flush, and paying for dinner wasn't a problem, you wouldn't feel bad about accepting it free."

She opened her mouth. Shut it. Shook her head. "I'm not going to win this argument, am I?"

"Now you've got it," he said, and, acting on impulse, turned her around to face him and plopped a kiss on her forehead. She smelled fresh and warm and new. And sexy as ever-loving sin.

Pregnant, he reminded himself. The lady is pregnant.

"So…are you up for it?" he asked again. "And just so you know, the answer to that question is yes."

"Well then, yes," she said on a laugh.

"Cool," he said. "Whenever you're ready."

"Umm—" she made a gesture toward the phone "—what about La-na?"

He shrugged back into his vest. "What about her?"

"Aren't you going to call her back?"

"I'll get around to it…one of these days."

She grinned.

He'd like to think that maybe it was because Shallie was a little pleased that he wasn't going to call Lana back. Wishful thinking, McDonald.

"You're a bad man, Brett McDonald."

"I'm a *single* man," he stated with playful conviction. Shallie had spoiled him for any other woman. "And in spite of Lana's agenda, I plan to stay that way." Because the woman he wanted didn't have a clue that he loved her.

It hurt suddenly. Accepting that, after all these years, he still loved Shallie Malone, and the possibility of her loving him back was the same now as it had been back then. Zip.

"Besides, I'm going to be an uncle," he added, gently patting her tummy to project the illusion that all was fine and dandy in his world. "I'll have duties. No time for wild women because I'll be taking the little guy to the park, teaching him how to fish."

He could see in her eyes that she'd needed that small assurance that she wasn't going to be going through this alone. That he was going to be there for her and for her baby.

And he would be. He made that promise to himself as much as to her right then and there.

"Him?" she asked, her brown eyes glistening with speculation.

"Him. Her. Doesn't matter. Kid still needs to know how to fish. Now, come on. Grab your jacket and let's boogie. We'll talk about names on the way. I'm kind of partial to Heathcliff and Gertrude. Whadaya think?"

"Oh, man." Three nights later Mac sat back from his dining room table with a blissful look on his face. "Shallie, you give me the recipe for this cheesecake and not only will that running tab you insist on keeping, of what you think you owe me, be wiped clean, I'll end up owing *you* money."

Sitting at Mac's huge mission oak dining room table, three whole days after she'd arrived, Shallie grinned, watching him polish off the cheesecake she'd topped with a sugary raspberry sauce. "I'm thinking that means you like it."

"Like it? Honey, I'm crazy for it. What a proud moment. My little short-stack grew up and learned how to make something other than PBJs."

He was good at making her smile. He was just plain good for her, Shallie thought, not for the first time since she'd been staying with him.

And not for the first time she thought about what it would be like to be Brett McDonald's woman. The word *easy* came to mind. And just like that, the thought went away.

Don't trust *easy,* she mentally repeated the mantra that had proven itself true too many times in her life.

"I'm serious," he continued. "I'd kill for this recipe. How did you manage it, anyway—not just dessert but the entire dinner, which was awesome, by the way. How did you do it? I mean, with your arm and all?"

Grilling the salmon and making a salad hadn't been that difficult. And while it had been a bit of a trick to whip up the cheesecake with only one fully functional hand, Shallie had learned how to manage a lot of things in the past three days.

"It's all about leverage," she said. "And determination. Oh, yeah—and your state-of-the-art kitchen, gadgetman."

He leaned back in his chair, balancing on two of its legs, and waggled his eyebrows. "Like my toys, do ya?"

She laughed. "Oh, yeah. I like your *kitchen* toys." And she was happy that he'd enjoyed the meal she'd prepared for him. She'd been determined to make him something special after all he'd done for her.

"As to the recipe, it's all yours," she told him. "And small payment for such exceptional room and board."

He let his chair drop back down to all fours. Gave her a stern look. "Okay. Let's not spoil this kick-ass meal by forcing me to go into lecture mode. You owe me nothing. Nada. Zip. As a matter of fact, you just did me a huge favor. I was going to go back to the restaurant and work tonight, but now that I'm feeling full and lazy, I think I'll knock off for the night."

"You work too hard," she said.

"Damn straight," he agreed without any real conviction, unclipped his cell phone from his belt and punched in a number. "Cara. Hi. It's Mac. What's happening?"

Shallie watched while he nodded, answered some questions from Cara Brown, his night manager.

He did work too hard, whether he wanted to admit it or not. Mac, she'd discovered, was a very hands-on manager. Did everything from cooking to bartending to maintenance, if the need arose. He put in a lot of hours at the restaurant during the past three days she'd been staying with him.

Three days. Amazing. Shallie wasn't sure how it had happened, but the time had passed in a blur. She'd rested and was recovering from not only the broken wrist but from the past few months of stress and worry about her future.

Mac had a way of making everything but the moment seem to be in another realm. A realm that was not really part of the here and now. Like tonight, for instance.

He'd breezed in the door about six, after calling and telling her he'd come to pick her up and take her to the restaurant for dinner, as he had every night. When they'd gone grocery shopping that morning, she hadn't told him that she'd made certain to pick up the items for this surprise, special dinner.

"Sounds like you've got things well in hand," Shallie heard him say after he and his manager had apparently covered all the bases. "Listen. I'm going to call it a day. Give me a ring if something comes up. I can be there in five minutes. Yeah. Thanks. G'night.

"Done deal," he said after he'd hung up. "I'm yours for the night."

She shook her head at his big grin. And fought the urge to wish she really was his. He was so special, this man. Funny. Sexy. Tender, and yet as alpha as they came.

The question was out before she could stop it. "So why aren't you someone *else's* for the night? Someone like Lana?" she added with a teasing waggle of her eyebrows to hide how curious she really was.

"Don't you worry about Lana. The fact is, she's just not my type." He rose and started clearing up the table. And, if she didn't miss her guess, to run away from this line of questioning. Interesting.

"You cooked," he said, gathering dishes for the dishwasher, "I'll clean up."

Shallie stood, too, and followed him into the kitchen with her plate and silverware. And her seriously piqued curiosity. "So what kind of woman *is* your type?"

He shot a glance over his shoulder. "Anyone ever tell you that you're nosy, Ms. Malone?" He sounded more amused at her line of questioning than upset by it—and maybe he also sounded a little nervous. Interesting.

"More than one. You'd think I'd learn. So, why *isn't*

there a special woman in your life, *Mr.* McDonald?" She couldn't help it. Now that she'd opened up this channel, she wanted to know. "I mean, it's not like you're mud ugly or anything—"

"Aw shucks, thank you, ma'am." He winked at her as he opened the dishwasher and stacked their plates.

"And then there's that humble bumpkin thing you've got going for you," she added with a smile. "Plus, you're a nice guy. You're financially solvent—and then some—and unless you've switched teams while I've been gone, you're arrow straight."

"Same team," he assured her and made a show of flexing his bicep. "I jus' *luvs* the ladies."

She laughed. "And I'm sure the ladies jus *luvs* you. So, really—why haven't you gotten married? And don't give me that ring-in-the-nose bit because I'm not buying it."

He waited long enough that she was beginning to wonder if he was going to tell her to take a hike. Finally he turned back to her.

"Okay, here's the deal," he said, tossing a dish towel over his shoulder. Leaning back against the counter, he crossed his ankles then folded his arms over his broad chest. "I like my life. I like calling my own shots. I like doing what I want to do, when I want to do it. I like not having to be responsible for anyone but me. And most of the women I know, well, let's just say they leave a lot to be desired in many areas," he added, his eyes growing hard. "Besides, from my perspective, marriage, as an institution, isn't all it's cracked up to be."

She figured he was referring to his parents. Figured also—more from what he hadn't said than what he had said—that their divorce may have soured him. But the Mac she knew was also a cockeyed optimist. It was hard to believe he'd just written off marriage.

She eased a hip onto a bar stool, leaned her elbow on the granite countertop. "How do you know that, if you don't give it a chance?"

He considered, then pinned her with a look. "Did you? Did you give the institution of marriage a chance?"

Okay. Ouch. Not only had she not given marriage a chance, she'd almost been responsible for breaking up one. And that was something she would always have to live with.

A familiar sinking nausea accompanied that reality—and it had nothing to do with a biological reaction from her pregnant hormones. It was about shame. About being stupid and needy and so blinded by the humiliation Jared had caused her that she'd rushed headlong into a situation with Brad that added mortification to the mix.

She was not a home wrecker. And as soon as she'd found out she was pregnant, she'd made up her mind that Brad would never know about the baby. This baby was hers. She would raise it. Love it. Take care of it.

"Shallie? You okay?"

When she realized she'd been a couple of thousand miles and two months ago away, she pulled herself back to the moment. What was done was done. She couldn't undo it. But she could not bring herself to level with Mac about the truth surrounding her baby's conception. She knew that he assumed the father had abandoned her. She knew it was wrong the let him continue to think it. But she couldn't bear to see the disappointment in his eyes if he knew the whole story.

Which meant that she really needed to stop prying into his business since she hadn't confided the whole truth about hers to him.

"I'm fine—other than being a prying bore. Sorry. Your love life is none of my business."

An odd look that she couldn't read crossed his face.

"Tell you what," he said, tossing the dish towel over the edge of the sink and pushing away from the counter, "what do you say we let our relationship issues drop and see if we can find a movie on pay per view? I bought that monster of a flat screen when I moved in and I don't think I've watched it for more than an hour total—and that's been in fits and starts."

"Deal," she said, because she really did want him to just kick back and relax since that's what a night off should be about. "Just no blood-and-gore flick, okay?"

"You used to *love* blood and gore," he pointed out with a disappointed frown.

"And I will again—just not at this particular stage of my pregnancy."

"Ah. Got it. Does that mean we have to watch a chick flick?"

"Not my cuppa, either, at the moment."

In the end they compromised. They found an old Steve Martin comedy and, snuggled on the couch with a fire glowing in the hearth and a very light snow feathering down, laughed their way through it.

* * *

When Mac woke up several hours later, his arm was asleep. His neck had a crick in it. The TV droned softly, and a soft, warm and amazingly sexy woman was snuggled up against him.

Shallie.

For a long moment he just lay there, absorbing her heat, enjoying the moment. He didn't remember falling asleep. He sure didn't remember stretching out full length on the sofa and taking sleeping beauty with him for the ride.

But evidently he had, because he was flat on his back and Shallie was plastered against his side like a second skin, the weight of her cast lying heavily on his chest. The weight of her thigh, however slight, was settled with a much more pronounced effect across his lap. A lap that was suddenly reacting to all this soft woman heat sleeping by his side.

Perfect. Be a guy. Embarrass the hell out of both of us.

Or fix it. Fast, lunkhead.

So, as he'd sometimes had to make himself do the past three days when he found himself caught up in some unsolicited and inappropriate sexual fantasy about Shallie, he thought of anything but all that heat.

Tax audits. Quarterly payments. The waitress schedule. The reservation for the Simpsons' wedding rehearsal dinner that was going to be a nightmare to pull together. The leaky roof at the Dusk to Dawn that was going to cost a small fortune to fix.

And let's not forget, this is a pregnant woman you're holding in your arms.

Okay. That helped. Enough, at least, that he could draw another breath—but not an easy one.

Careful not to disturb her, he yawned hugely, then checked his watch. Holy cow. It was almost 2:00 a.m. He needed to get her to bed where she could get some quality rest. But then she stirred, and his arm automatically tightened around her back, sliding instinctively down her hip to hold her so she wouldn't tumble to the floor.

Lordy, she was small. Slight, fine bones. Slim, lean curves. But curves, just the same. Why had he never realized before how fragile she was?

Because of her grit, that's why. Tough. Shallie Malone had always been tough. She'd had to be.

He remembered the first time he'd ever seen her. She'd been all of eleven years old. She'd shown up at school near the end of the spring semester. Her clothes had been worn and patched and not all that clean. Her hair had been just as curly then as it was now, only it had stuck out around her face like a Raggedy Ann doll.

The Griener twins had cornered her on the playground at recess and had been giving her the new-kid-in-town third-degree.

"Where'd ya get them jeans? Looks like a clown wore 'em they've got so many patches," Billy Griener had said, acting superior and mean.

"Yeah," Willie had chimed in. "Got clown hair, too. Do a trick, clown."

"Yeah, clown, do a trick," Billie ordered on a mean laugh.

"I'll do a trick," the new girl had said. "See how you

like this one." Then she'd walked up to Willie and kneed him in the groin.

Mac smiled into the dark, remembering. Willie had howled like a scalded dog all the way to the teacher, who had promptly dragged Shallie to the principal's office.

Mac and J.T. had been waiting for her on the steps when school got out that day.

"What do you want?" she'd snarled, her little hands clenched into fists at her sides, the set of her mouth telling him she was ready to take on the world if she had to.

Mac had only been a kid himself, but he'd figured out then and there that Shallie Malone had probably taken on the world several times already in her short life. And if he hadn't already fallen in love with her, he did right then.

"I want to shake the hand of the girl who put wailing Willie to his knees," he'd said.

She'd looked suspicious at first, but then he'd grinned at her and stuck out his hand. "And I want to make sure I'm on your good side, 'cause I don't ever want to see your knee comin' at me the way it came at Willie."

Still uncertain, she drew back her shoulders but cautiously shook his hand.

"What about you?" She'd turned a dark look on J.T.

"You play baseball?" J.T. asked with a matching scowl.

"I can play circles around you," she'd said, her chin notching up, daring him to dispute her claim.

J.T. had grinned. "Cool. Let's go to the park and get us a game going. We'll whump the snot out of anyone who thinks they can beat us. You'll be our ringer."

That was all it had taken to melt her ice block of resistance. And aside from it being his first puppy love crush, the three of them had been fast friends from that day on.

If anyone ever needed a friend, it had been Shallie. Joyce Malone, Shallie's mom, had drifted into town, Mac had heard eavesdropping one day at the Dusk to Dawn, because she'd needed a place to hide out from a string of bad debts and bad relationships.

For whatever reason, Joyce had taken a liking to Sundown, and that's where she and Shallie had stayed, until Shallie had graduated from high school. Shortly after Shallie left, Joyce hooked up with a trucker and took off, too.

Mac had never liked Joyce Malone. Not just because of the physical bruises she sometimes put on Shallie. The emotional bruises were just as hard for his little short-stack to deal with. Both his mom and J.T.'s mom had always had time for the three of them underfoot. They'd always had cookies, too. And hugs when they'd needed them. Most likely they were the only hugs Shallie had ever gotten, Mac figured, because Shallie never took them home to see *her* mother. And she never had much to say about her.

"She's workin'," Shallie would say with a look that dared anyone to dispute it.

Truth was, Mac had figured out when he was old enough to learn the way it was with women like Shallie's mom, that in between her job at the dry cleaners,

Joyce Malone did a lot of work on her back. On more then one occasion, he or J.T. had had to wipe a smirk off one of their brainless buddies' faces when they'd suggested that maybe Shallie did a little back work herself for Mac and J.T.

She stirred again, and the warmth of her breath tickled his throat. His body reacted when her thigh slid across his lap. The sweet friction almost made him groan. And when the swell of her breast pressed oh, so sweetly against his chest, he thought he might dive right off the deep end.

Okay. Time to nip this little disaster-in-the-making in the bud.

Five

"Shallie." Mac whispered softly so he wouldn't startle her. "Sweetheart. Wake up. We need to hit the sack."

She sighed and nestled closer, her cheek resting on his shoulder. "Mmm. Okay. In a minute."

He lay rock still. Except for his heart, which was pounding so hard in reaction to her silky sigh and soft body that he was certain the reverberation would wake her up.

But she was asleep again. Or so said her deep, even breaths.

He was far from asleep. He'd dreamed about holding her like this for years. And now here she was. In his arms—yet just as unattainable as she had been all those years ago.

Lord help him.

"Shallie," he whispered, determined to do the right

thing. "Come on, sleepyhead. You're going to get all stiff and sore lying mashed against me like this."

"Comfy," she breathed, and shifted again and damned if all of her didn't somehow end up on top of all of him. "So…comfy."

Well, hell. Because the trouble was, it *was* comfy. Damn comfy. He could feel so much more of her now, and the weight was wonderful. Her breasts pressed firmly against his chest, and with a little imagination he could picture her nipples pressing against her bra. And of course that picture stirred up more and more pictures. Like the two of them skin on skin and him sinking deep inside of her.

He wasn't just rock still now, he was rock hard, too. And, Lord help him, she had to be able to notice.

She'd kill him. She'd flat-out kill him. Neuter him with that lethal knee if nothing else. And he'd deserve it.

He held his breath. Waited for her to lift her head, glare at him and tell him to grow up.

But she didn't. She did something else, instead. And he had to believe she was still half-asleep because never in a million years would a wide-awake and alert Shallie start moving her thigh back and forth along his erection as if she not only didn't hate that it had sprung up between them, but like she liked—more than liked—the way it felt against her.

Sweet heaven, he needed some of the blood that had shot to his groin to find its way north and fuel a little gray matter.

"Shallie," he groaned, feeling himself losing the battle with his better judgment.

She moved again with an answering little sigh, pushing herself higher, rubbing her breasts and her belly against him as she lifted her head and touched her mouth to his.

Mother.

He needed to push her away. Clearly, she didn't know what she was doing. Except she sure *acted* as if she knew, and she was doing it damn well. Maybe she was awake after all. Maybe…maybe she did feel something for him. Maybe she was as hot for him as he was for her.

Her lips were sure as hell hot, and so incredibly soft against his. And when that tentative contact of her closed mouth slowly transitioned to the sound of a yearning sigh and she opened for him, he ran out of reason and will to fight it.

He was only so strong. How could he not welcome her open kiss? Devour her questing tongue when she slid it along his teeth, then slipped inside.

Hunger. Yearning. Need. It was all there. And he fed it. His and hers. Catered to it. Built on it, wrapping her tightly against him and fusing his mouth to hers.

Heaven above, she tasted fine. Felt even better. The inside of her mouth was hot and slick. Her body was both lean and lush; her hair was like silk when he buried one hand in her tangled curls. And he was barely aware of his own actions as he slipped the other up and under her sweater.

More heat. Heat to the point of burn when skin met skin and she arched into his hand. Before he knew what he was doing, he slid his hand up along her ribs and higher to find the weight of a full, heavy breast. He swallowed her gasp of pleasure when he gently squeezed. And when he flicked his thumb over the lace that covered her nipple, she pressed into his touch, driving him deeper into her fire. So deep, he rolled her beneath him and settled his weight fully on top of her.

He wedged his knee between her thighs, simply had to get closer. He had to touch more. He had to... *Whoa.*

He had to stop. That's what he had to do.

This was insane.

This was Shallie. Half-asleep. Totally vulnerable. Completely off-limits.

Pregnant.

He didn't know where he found the strength, but he slowly dragged his hand out from under her sweater. Slower still, he pulled his mouth away from hers, fighting her kitten sounds of protest.

Fueled by guilt and desire, his heart was pulsing at about one hundred per when he pressed her face against his neck and held her. Just held her, groping for brotherly thoughts, praying she wouldn't hate him when she came fully awake and realized what had just happened.

Maybe he'd get lucky, he thought, gently stroking her hair. Maybe she'd slept through the entire thing and she wouldn't even remember.

But then he felt her stiffen beneath him. Felt the flutter of her eyelashes against his throat and knew he could kiss that notion goodbye.

"Well." Her voice sounded husky; her breath was kind of thready. "This is…awkward."

Awkward. Good word.

So was *incredible.*

Amazing.

Hot.

Oh, and here was a word: *suicidal.* At least it would be if he pulled that train of thought any further. Time for a little diversionary drivel to get the train back on the right track.

He lifted his head. Frowned down at her. "Okay, lady. Who are you? And what have you done with my friend, Shallie?"

Thank you, God, her mouth turned up in a smile.

"I'm going to start counting," she said in her best hypnotist's voice, gamely playing along, "and when I reach ten, you will wake up, no longer have the urge to quack like a duck, and you will forget this ever happened."

Not damn likely.

Still, he forced a grin. She was cool with this. They were cool. Well, technically he was still hot, but he'd deal with that later.

"Okay. Just one last quack. Maybe two," he said then pushed out two very anemic quacks that actually had her giggling. "Now that I got that out of my system…umm…damn, Shall. I am so, so sorry."

"You should be sorry. No self-respecting duck sounds like that."

He pushed out a snort. "I was referring to what happened between us just now."

Her eyes softened. "I know."

He watched her face, looking for anger, relieved when he saw none. "I really *am* sorry."

He would go to hell for lying, too, because the truth was, he couldn't muster up the necessary regret to be sorry about anything right now. The kiss had been incredible. "Guess we…uh, both fell asleep."

"And woke up next to a warm, snuggly body," she added with a nod.

"And naturally, instinct took over—"

"And what with our weakened mental capacity and all," she continued.

"The next thing you know…yada, yada, yada." He was doing his damnedest to keep this light, when the situation was anything but. It was explosive, but again she kept the fire from burning out of control when she smiled. "Or something like that."

She searched his eyes for the longest time. "For the record, McDonald, you yada very well when you're asleep."

Ah. So that was why she was being so forgiving. She thought *he'd* been sleeping when this started, too.

It was a straw and he grasped it.

"Right back atcha, kid," he said lamely, shoving back the guilt, and finally had the presence of mind to haul his sorry self off her.

Maybe it was because he was tired. Maybe it was because, like most men, he was born horny. Maybe he was just a jerk. Whatever the reason, as he stood there looking down on her, he was fresh out of reasons why he shouldn't just pile back on top of her sweet, soft body and finish what her sleepy, sexy eyes told him she wouldn't mind finishing. And that was probably just more wishful thinking on his part.

So he did what any self-respecting jerk would do in this situation. He bailed.

"Before this gets any weirder…I'm hitting the sack. You sure you're okay with…uh…you know?"

She nodded. "I'm okay."

"All right. Well. G'night, then, short-stack. See you tomorrow."

Then he hightailed it the hell away from her before yada, yada, yada turned into hotter, hotter, hotter and they both woke up naked and way more than embarrassed in the morning.

The next night was New Year's Eve. Spaghetti Western was standing-room only. Had been since about 6:00 p.m. when locals and out-of-towners had decided to start their evening early with a nice dinner before they either went on to parties or home to watch the crystal ball drop in Times Square on TV.

And finally, finally, Shallie was able to do something to help Mac out. His regular hostess was down with a bad sinus infection. His back-up was on a ski trip to Steamboat. And Mac had already pressed any additional staff into action to help cover the rush.

"I can do it," Shallie had said that morning, sitting at the island in the kitchen after she'd overheard Mac on the phone to his day manager. "I can fill in as hostess," she told him when he'd hung up.

"I can't ask you to do that," he'd insisted.

"Why? Because I'm pregnant? Sorry. That's a nonissue. Because of my wrist? Another nonissue. I don't need two hands to keep track of seating charts and to seat people."

He'd frowned, but she could tell he was considering the idea.

"If it's experience you're worried about," she'd continued, determined to do this for him, "I paid my way through college working in restaurants. I've done everything from cooking to waiting tables to busboy chores to playing hostess. And I've spent enough time around SW these past few days that I have a pretty good feel for how things flow there.

"Besides," she'd added, resorting to the big guns when he'd still looked dubious, "I'm bored. Let me help. It'll be fun."

"I don't know." He'd still hedged.

"Please," she'd wheedled in a really good imitation of a woman about to throw a little temper tantrum.

"Oh, for Pete's sake. If you're going to get all sulky about it."

She'd seen the grin through his grousing and rushed over to give him a one-armed hug. "Thanks. It'll be great. You'll see."

It was the first time they'd touched since the "nocturnal kissing" incident the night before. And since then, Mac had made it a point to keep his distance. Shallie had done the same. Which was silly, she thought now as, despite her cast, she felt festive and even a little pretty in her red velvet holiday dress, while she ushered an elderly couple to a table.

"Enjoy your meal," she said with a smile, and handed them their menus.

So they'd fallen asleep, woken up in each other's arms and let their bodies do the talking before their brains had engaged, she thought, walking back to the hostess station. It wasn't as if it had been planned.

And it was silly to be thinking about that kiss now, Shallie told herself as she caught a glimpse of Mac. He was currently dug in behind the bar helping the bartender who was overrun with orders.

Still, it was hard for her not to think about it. He was an amazing kisser, her friend, Brett McDonald. His lips were so soft and skilled. And his body—Lord. She'd known he was in great shape. One look was all it had taken to figure that out. Chest to chest, hip to hip, however…well, tactile contact was much more telling than visual.

Much more telling, she thought, and actually felt her face flame hot when she remembered the feel of his hand on her breast and his very impressive erection pressing against her belly.

"You okay?" Cara, Mac's assistant manager, asked making a point to check on Shallie as she hurried by on the way to the dining room.

"Fine. Great," Shallie said quickly.

"Okay," Cara said with a concerned look. "You look a little flushed."

"Has Mac been telling you to watch out for me?" Shallie asked, all of a sudden more concerned that he might have inadvertently spilled the beans about her pregnancy than she was alarmed by the turn of her thoughts.

"Mac? He hasn't told me anything. You have a broken wrist. Seems to me that's enough reason to be a little concerned about you. Thought maybe you might have bumped it or something."

"Oh. Sorry." Shallie forced a smile. "I'm fine. No problems, really." Unless you count the fact that she was having a sexual fantasy about her best friend, which was about as left field as waking up in his arms and thinking about kissing him every time she saw him. "I'm having a good time. Am I doing okay?"

"You're doing great. In fact, you've been a godsend. We'll have three tables bussed and ready in a couple of minutes."

As Cara took off at a fast walk, Shallie glanced at the crush by the door and in the waiting area. They were talking and laughing, enjoying the complimentary champagne Mac had made available. No one seemed to mind the wait. Probably because they all knew a meal at SW was worth waiting for.

The rest of the night flew by. Shallie only caught glimpses of Mac as he worked the dining room, making certain everyone was happy and well fed and covered whatever base needed covering to make certain everything went smoothly. Yet every time their eyes met she felt a sharp little zing of arousal flashing between them.

It was unsettling and pulse-altering and…well, exciting. And she was totally wrong to be thinking about the possibility of something more happening between them.

She'd made a big enough mess of her life. She wasn't

going to mess it up further—or mess his up in the process. She made it a point to avoid eye contact the rest of the night and finally, around ten-thirty, the crowd had thinned to a few tables and the kitchen was in the process of shutting down. Shallie had just bidden two couples good-night and happy New Year when she realized Mac had slipped up beside her.

"Hey," he said with a tired smile. "How you holding up?"

"I'm great. Okay," she confessed when he narrowed his eyes, "my feet hurt a little. But it's been fun. Really. I enjoyed myself tonight."

"We couldn't have made it through the crush without you."

"You're overstating, but thanks for that."

"What do you say I grab something from the kitchen and we take it home to ring in the New Year with a late dinner?"

It was her turn to question him—first with a look, then with an admonishment. "It's New Year's Eve," she pointed out. "You don't have to babysit me."

"What are you talking about?"

"Don't you have a party or something to go to? A date waiting with a bottle of wine and a come-hither smile?" She didn't much like the idea that a woman might be waiting for him, but the truth was, it would be better all around if one was.

He grunted. "I've got a date with my sofa, and that's about as much action as I want after taking care of this crowd tonight."

"Really?" She felt too much relief over that news, but

pushed gamely on. "Because I'm okay if you just drop me off at the house."

"I'm not dropping you anywhere," he assured her. "Sit tight. I'll go raid the kitchen and tell Cara we're out of here. Be right back."

Shallie's nerves zinged like the zephyrs of wind that whisked powdery snow into tall, swirling gusts beneath the streetlights as Mac drove through town on deserted, winter-cold streets.

Get a grip, she told herself mentally. Just because this was New Year's Eve, the date night of all date nights, and she and Mac were together, it didn't mean anything.

But there are implications, the suddenly insane side of her personality reminded her.

Okay, *normally* there would be implications when two single people decided to spend one of the biggest holidays of the year together. There shouldn't, however, be any of that stuff in the mix between them.

And there wouldn't have been—except that last night had happened. Last night when they'd more than kissed. That spelled *implications* with a capital *I*. At least, it did from her perspective. Mac, however, didn't seem to be affected by the kiss at all.

Shallie glanced at him across the darkened cab of his truck. Nope. He seemed oblivious to her thoughts. Thoughts that had her looking at him through new eyes. The eyes of a woman as opposed to the eyes of a friend. And with a new awareness and appreciation of just how much of a man he was.

Careful, she warned herself. You've forgotten about

the *easy* factor. *Easy* spelled disaster for her. No matter how appealing this amazing man was.

He drove, she realized now, the way he did everything else. With confidence and complete control. Just as he was in complete control of whatever awkwardness he could have shown around her.

He was still quick with his smiles. Still attentive to a fault. And she hadn't seen a flicker of a notion that he felt any discomfort left over from last night.

Which was good, Shallie assured herself. It was a very good thing that one of them had their wits about them, she thought and, indulging herself in a wistful look at his poster-boy profile, she told herself to give it a rest.

She chalked up her lingering fascination with Mac, the man, to haywire hormones. It was the only logical explanation. She normally didn't cry, and she normally didn't have attacks of the hots for her best friend—who very clearly had forgotten all about the kiss that she was going to do her darnedest to put out of *her* mind, too.

She had much more critical items on her agenda, anyway. Items like finding a job and taking care of herself and her baby. And she'd made enough mistakes lately. She wasn't going to make a mistake with Mac—and if she repeated that particular mantra often enough, she just might pull it off.

If he didn't get his act together, Mac thought as he set the table for their late New Year's Eve dinner, he was going to fool around and screw up their friendship.

He may have been acting like a fool but he *wasn't*

one—at least, not normally. Well, damn, that dress she had on tonight didn't help matters any.

It was bright-red velvet—a holiday dress—with long sleeves that covered her cast, a deep-vee neckline and a fitted and flirty short skirt. Man, he'd almost swallowed his tongue when she'd walked into the living room with a smile and an "Will this be dressy enough for the hostess at the hottest spot in Bozeman on New Year's Eve?"

Oh, yeah. It was dressy enough. The hottest spot in Bozeman that night, however had been anywhere she had been. Her full breasts pressed provocatively against the red velvet. Her tummy was still flat. And she had the most amazing legs, not to mention sweet, curvy hips that had had him salivating over the wet bar way too often for a man his age.

He shook off the wallop of seeing her that way. Good thing Shallie had her full wits about her. Half-wit was about the most he could lay claim to, because he'd been thinking about her in a totally man-woman way for the better part last night and today.

All because of that kiss, she hadn't even been aware that she'd initiated and then taken way beyond the initiation stage before he'd managed to put the skids on his wayward libido. And before things had gotten completely out of hand.

It was the out-of-hand part he hadn't been able to get out of his head. Another few minutes and he'd have had her sweater off her. And damn it all…he'd been thinking about that possibility way too much, also.

Well, it was clear that *she* wasn't thinking about it.

He was guessing the only thing she was thinking was that she was glad to be off her feet, that she was hungry as a bear and that it was way past time he fed her.

"You're stupid squared, that's what you are," he muttered while he debated—then against his better judgment—went ahead and lit the candles.

"Soup's on," he said as he walked into the great room where he'd ordered her to sit down in front of the fire with her feet up while he set out their meal.

"Smells like heaven," she said following him into the dining room. She stopped just inside the arched double doorway. "Oh. Oh, Mac. This looks wonderful."

"Let's hope it tastes good, too," he said, experiencing another one of those punches of lust when she smiled for him.

"For the lady." He made a grand gesture with a sweep of his hand and held her chair out for her. "Spinach salad, asparagus with cheese sauce and succulent Maine lobster. And for dessert, tiramisu. Oh," he added uncapping a bottle of sparkling white grape juice, "and a little nonalcoholic bubbly just for you to ring in the New Year."

Okay, he thought as he watched her face light up. Now he knew what it meant when someone said a woman looked radiant. Her eyes sparkled, her cheeks had turned a beautiful shade of carnation pink and, as tired as she had to be, there was a glow about her that made it appear she'd bathed in champagne.

And maybe he should have bitten the bullet and taken Lana up on her offer of a "really good time" because it was getting damn hot in here and he didn't have cooking privileges in Shallie's kitchen.

"This is all so special," Shallie said looking from her wineglass to the candles, then to him as he sat down across from her.

"It's New Year's Eve," he said with a brightness that he hoped to hell she didn't see through as his having a case of the hots for a woman he had no business being hot for. "And a special one at that when two old friends get together. So I figured we'd do it up right. Plus I thought you might be tired of eating Italian."

"I don't think I'd ever tire of the menu at SW," she said kindly. "You were so thoughtful to do this. As usual, it's too much."

"It's just right," he said, and snapped his napkin onto his lap. "Now, eat before it gets cold."

Cold. He should be so lucky.

"So," Mac said as they settled into the great room, him on the sofa, Shallie folded a safe distance away from him in a side chair, "my turn to play twenty questions."

She blinked, puzzled. "Your turn? When did I have *my* turn?"

"'What kind of woman is your type?' 'Why aren't you settled down?' 'Why aren't you married?'" he reminded her, mimicking her tone from the other day.

"Oh. *That* was my turn. I didn't know that. And I didn't know we were keeping track, but fair's fair." She grinned at him. "Okay. Shoot."

Oh, he planned to. During dinner he'd made some decisions. One: things had gotten just plain crazy from his perspective. So she was a gorgeous woman. So he'd always had a thing for her. Okay, more than a thing. So he'd always loved her. Still did, but that didn't really matter now. He had to cut it out. The overriding factor here was that all she needed him to be for her was a friend. So that's what he'd be. Period. Done deal.

Two: this sort of undercut the first issue, but he was now very interested in knowing what kind of man flipped her switch. And it wasn't a pride thing, he assured himself. He was curious, that was all. It wasn't as if his ego had taken a hit, knowing that the only time he had any male-female effect on her was when she was sleeping.

Okay. So maybe it *was* an ego thing. And maybe he didn't like knowing that he was jealous as hell of a man he didn't know. A man she was probably still in love with.

"You said something about a question?"

He looked up to see her waiting, with a curious and expectant look on her face.

"Why haven't you ever been married?" he asked finally, deciding to go for broke.

"Wow. Didn't see that one coming." Her feigned look of surprise made it clear she'd seen it a mile away.

Just that fast, however, she sobered. "Okay. The truth is, I came close. Well, at least I thought I was close. Turned out he wasn't close at all."

She fiddled with the sling supporting her wrist, and he had more thoughts of murder and mayhem when he saw the pain in her eyes.

"Only, he never made that little difference in life plans known to me. I still might not know if I hadn't caught him—" She paused, shot him a brittle smile.

"Well, if I hadn't *caught* him. In the interest of keeping this conversation civil, let's just leave it at that."

Bastard, Mac thought. So the guy had led her on, gotten her pregnant, then cheated on her. And Mac had the horrible feeling there might be more to this story than she was letting on.

"He's not only a jerk, he's a fool," Mac said. "I'm sorry. Really sorry he did that to you."

She raised a shoulder, as if it was no big deal, but he saw the hurt and something that even looked like shame in her eyes before she looked away. And, for making her feel that way about herself, Mac hated the guy even more.

"Yeah, well. It's all behind me now."

The plasma screen was on in the background. Times Square was packed as New Year's Rockin' Eve gave a minute-by-minute countdown to the stroke of midnight.

"Hey," she said, her attention suddenly caught by the music. "Remember that band? Oh, my gosh. I love that song."

Mac leaned over and snagged the remote, punching up the volume a couple notches. "Oh, man. I used to make out to that song with Wynona Gray."

She pushed out a laugh. "You used to make out to that song with everyone."

"Just the everyones who wore skirts," he corrected her, then on impulse stood and held out his hand. "Come on. Let's dance out the old year."

If there was hesitation on her part, it was as brief as her surprise. She laughed and took his hand. "Why not."

Oh, he could tell her why not, Mac realized the minute he pulled her into his arms.

Mistake.

Big, big mistake, he thought, liking far too much the way her heat nestled next to his. Hell. She wasn't even aware of what she was doing to him. But she'd know soon enough if he didn't do some serious maneuvering.

"We're going to take you to Times Square now, folks," the TV announcer said as the network cut away from the inside party and scanned the crowd gathered in the street. "The countdown to the new year is about to begin."

They stopped dancing and turned to watch the scene on the screen where the crystal ball had started to descend.

"Ten, nine, eight…"

Mac felt Shallie lean into him a little.

"Five, four, three…"

He turned away from the TV to look down at her…and realized she was looking up at him.

"Two, one! Happy New Year!"

A riot of noise erupted from the television as they stood in the suddenly close silence of his living room, eyes locked, smiles tentative.

"Happy New Year, Mac," she whispered.

"Happy New Year, Shall," Mac said just as softly, and knew, without a doubt that he absolutely should not kiss her.

But it was New Year's Eve.

It was tradition to kiss the one you were with at the stroke of midnight.

And he was just plain nuts. Because he lowered his head. Touched his mouth to hers and realized he wasn't really surprised that she'd lifted her face up to meet him.

It was soft, that kiss. It was sweet. And it was infused with a wary and tentative awareness. Awareness of the heat. Awareness of the little sparks of electricity arcing between them.

Awareness that they both knew what they were doing this time and where it could lead if they dared take it a little farther.

And oddly, Mac sensed the rightness of it all. In the gentleness in which their lips met. In the honesty of affection that passed between them.

The surprise came after. After he had slowly pulled away. After he'd searched her deep-brown eyes and had finally seen what all this awareness between them was really about.

It was one of those "it all became crystal clear" moments. One of those, "why hadn't he seen this before?" revelations.

What was going on here—it wasn't all about attraction. It wasn't all about need—although both were heavily seeded into the mix.

It was about being alone in the middle of a cold winter night when it appeared that the rest of the world was made of couples. It was about being lonely when both of them did their damnedest to never let that show.

Yeah, he realized as he lifted his hand and gently cupped her cheek. Both of them. He was lonely, too…only, he'd never really realized it until now.

For Shallie he suspected it was also more. It was about being afraid. His Shallie was afraid. Afraid of her future. Afraid of the mistakes of her past. Afraid that what she had now was all there was. And she was afraid she would accept and adjust and miss out on something special because of it.

He saw all of that in her eyes. And he saw it clearly because there wasn't a fear or an emotion that he didn't feel himself.

He was weary of the singles scene. Weary of the shallowness of it all, of the game playing and the sport so many made it. Did he expect to find lasting love? No. Not unless it was with Shallie.

That wasn't going to happen. She was still in pain from another relationship. Another man who had let her down. Left her pregnant and alone.

Alone. Like him. He didn't want to spend the rest of his life alone. And he didn't want mistakes he'd made or mistakes his parents had made to harden him and deprive him of something good.

Here was something good. Something like love. At least on his part. Oh, he knew she didn't love him the same way—not the earth-shattering, can't-live-without-you love. But she loved him just the same.

And he had always loved Shallie.

Would it be so bad, he wondered, to let her know that?

In this moment in time, alone together, could he share that with her? If for no other reason than to prove to her she wasn't alone. That she didn't have to be single in a world full of couples.

He kissed her again. And when she kissed him back, less tentatively now, more giving than guarded as she leaned into him and wrapped her arms around his neck, he knew that he was right on target.

There was power in her give, strength in his take. And there was understanding. Unspoken, unselfish and undeniable.

But most of all…most of all, he realized, there was vulnerability. She was so, so vulnerable.

And the real kicker? So was he—except he'd never realized it until right now.

Maybe he needed to think about this. Really think about whether he was willing to spill his guts and possibly settle for an "I love you but I'm not in love with you" apology.

From the look on her face when he pulled away, she needed some think time, too.

"That way lies trouble," he said with a smile meant to reassure yet make known that they were about to tread a potentially dangerous path if they continued doing what they were doing.

She searched his eyes, finally nodded with a tight, sad smile. "Yeah. That way lies trouble."

He expelled a heavy breath. It wasn't exactly relief he felt that she, too, saw the potential pitfalls if they took this further. It wasn't exactly regret. It was something in between. Enough of something that he knew he really had to think about what was happening here.

He pulled back, tipped her face to his with a finger under her chin. "Okay, then. Once again, we avert disaster."

She smiled, he suspected, because he did. "Once again."

He squeezed her arm. "Go to bed, short-stack. We might actually need to talk about this in the morning."

She nodded, turned to leave, then stopped and, stretching up on her toes, kissed his cheek. Her finger-tips trailed across his jaw as she left him.

Six

Morning came. And they didn't talk about it. *It* being what they'd both wanted to do last night. *It* being the fact that they'd both spent restless nights alone in their respective beds thinking about *it*.

Seems they were both big talkers after the sun went down and took a day's worth of inhibitions with it, Shallie thought as she sat in the front seat of Mac's truck as they headed down the highway toward Sundown. But in broad daylight, with a sleepless night behind them and the uncertainty of their relationship looming between them, it was easier not to talk about it at all.

Lord knows, they'd both done enough thinking about it. At least she had.

Mostly what she was thinking was, thank God Mac was the man he was or she might have made the biggest mistake of her life last night. Considering some of the mistakes she'd already made, that was saying something.

She didn't want to lose him. Not her friend. And friends and lovers…well, sooner or later you lost one or the other or both. He must have considered the same outcome because, like her, he didn't bring *it* up.

Instead when they'd gotten up, he'd asked her if she'd like to take a trip to Sundown, check out the cabin and if she liked it, move in.

And out of his hair, she thought as the miles flew by. Yeah. Maybe it was time she got out of his hair and out from under foot. She could use the distance, too. To figure out what she was going to do next. And what exactly she was feeling for Mac.

So, to keep their feelings firmly in check, they talked about the size of the snowdrifts along the highway. About the antelope bounding across the fields beside them. They talked about her broken wrist and about the plans he had for the Dusk to Dawn. They talked about anything but last night, like maybe if the subject didn't come up, it had never happened.

The games people play, she thought with a rueful smile.

"And there she is," Mac said as they descended into the valley and turned the final corner that led to town.

Sundown. Sleepy. Serene. Blanketed in white.

A peaceful stillness settled over her. And then she laughed.

"Oh, my gosh. I see progress has hit the great American West. Sundown's gone from a one-horse town to a one-stoplight town. When did they put the stop-light in?"

"This here ain't no Podunk Hicksville no more, missy," Mac said, launching into his best cowboy geezer voice. "Why, we even got us some o' them whatchacal-lits...some indoor outhouses." He pretended to spit tobacco out the window, wiped his mouth with his sleeve. "Yessiree, Bob. Up and comin'. That's what's happening here."

They were both grinning when he pulled the truck up in front of the Dusk to Dawn. It was a long building in the middle of the block on Main. The white clapboard siding was weathered but the sign above the double glass doors proclaiming it Dusk to Dawn in bold, sham-rock-green letters was crisp and new.

Shallie could see a light on and hear the muffled sound of voices and laughter coming from inside when Mac came around and helped her out of the truck.

"It's open today?"

"Yeah, I decided to open up at noon for anyone who wanted to watch a New Year's Day bowl game."

Judging by the trucks parked outside the bar and res-taurant, several people were doing just that.

"Hold on," Mac said when she couldn't figure out the best way get around the three-foot snowbank the plows had pushed up against the curb. "Here's how we'll handle this."

He picked her up, hefted her in his arms and scaled the drift with his long legs.

"He cooks, he does dishes—and he's got a white knight complex," she said batting her eyes at him when he set her down by the front door. "You're a handy man to have around, macaroon."

He laughed as he tugged open the door. "Macaroon. Haven't heard that in an age or two."

And she hadn't *ever* heard the chorus of, "Welcome home!" that greeted her when he set her down inside.

It had been the exact right thing to do, Mac thought, stepping back and watching Shallie become engulfed in a series of hugs and warm welcomes. After he'd made the call to J.T. a couple days ago suggesting they stage a surprise welcome-home party for Shallie, he'd started having second thoughts. Maybe she was a little too fragile right now. Maybe it would be rushing her.

But as he saw her smile of surprise and unqualified happiness as old friends surrounded her, he was glad he'd gone with his gut instinct. And he was glad he'd put J.T. in charge of contacting all the Sundown locals. J.T. was well liked and persuasive. Looked as if it was going to be a helluva party.

Besides the usual suspects who were always up for a party, J.T. and his wife, Ali, and Cutter and Peg Reno and their two kids, Shelby and little Dawson, were here. Among many others, Lee and Ellie Savage had driven in from Shiloh ranch to join the festivities. Crystal and Sam Perkins and their brood were here, too. Even old Snake Gibson, Joe Gilman and the Griener twins had shown up with their wives and kids.

Mac slipped behind the bar to help his manager, Colt Smith, mix another batch of punch for the kids and tap a keg for the adults who wanted something a little more celebratory to commemorate not only Shallie's return but the first day of the New Year.

"You are a sneaky snake," Shallie accused him an hour or so later as she wandered happily up to the bar and plopped on a stool.

"Guilty as charged." He slid a glass of punch across the bar to her as a whoop went up from across the room when someone's favorite team made a touchdown.

"You never said a word." She smiled over the top of her glass.

It was a good smile. A great smile. A smile that said she was happy as hell.

He wiped a bar rag over the worn and scarred oak surface, set a bowl of peanuts in front of her. "Wouldn't have been much of a surprise party if I had."

It had been fun watching her get reacquainted with her friends, Mac thought. But when her head went down—right after he swore he saw a tear, panic hit him like a brick.

"What? What's wrong?"

She shook her head and when she met his eyes again she was smiling and wiping tears at the same time. "This is the…the nicest thing anyone has ever done for me."

Relief was as sweet as the joy in her eyes.

"Thanks, Mac. I mean…really. Thanks for this. It's great."

While he was moved by her words, it was the look on her face that really got to him. He wanted to vault over the bar, gather up in his arms and tell her that if this was the nicest thing anyone had ever done for her, she'd been hanging with the wrong people.

And he might have done just that if J.T. hadn't shown up right then.

"I've been going to tell you that I know a good lawyer," J.T. said with an ornery grin as he slung an arm over Shallie's shoulders. "I figure you could take this no-count busboy to court and end up with everything but his shirt for breaking your arm. Probably get the shirt, too, if you wanted it, but ugly as it is, I'd take a pass."

"Hey, hey," Mac said affecting a wounded look, "don't be giving her any ideas. And you're in a helluva position to be insulting my taste in clothes. Although, now that Ali is picking yours out for you, there has been improvement."

"Just give me a beer, McDonald. I can do without the lip."

"*You* can do without the lip? See what I have to put up with?" Mac appealed to Shallie, who was grinning at the good-natured banter. "And in my own place."

"Yeah, well, you're just lucky we're a tolerant bunch of folks," J.T. continued, accepting his beer with a nod of thanks, "or we'd have run you out of town by now. Come on, Shall. They're about to crank up the karaoke machine."

"I don't care if you drink in here Tyler, but for God's sake, please don't sing."

"You ever see anyone so jealous of natural talent?" J.T. asked over his shoulder as he herded a giggling Shallie toward the stage.

God, it was good to see her smiling so much, Mac thought, resting both hands on the bar as he watched them walk away. Reminded him of when she was a girl and he and J.T. used to talk smack to each other just to make her laugh.

Hadn't seen all that much of her smile since she'd shown up a few days ago, Mac realized, grinning when J.T. dragged her reluctantly up onstage and shoved a mike in her hand to the enthusiastic cheers of the crowd.

No. He hadn't seen her smile all that much. At least not this kind of smile. Spontaneous, not forced. Truly happy, not an attempt to make him think she was happy. He was damn glad he'd had a hand in making her smile today.

And he'd decided he was also glad he'd put a skid on things between them last night and suggested she move into the cabin today. He'd had a moment of weakness. So had she. She was allowed; he wasn't.

She was pregnant, on her own and about as vulnerable as a body could be. She didn't need him sniffing around, putting on the moves and complicating her life even more.

She needed him to be solid and steady and supportive. End of story.

It was going to be hard, though, he thought as he watched her gamely sing along to an old Dolly Parton song. Her cheeks were flushed with embarrassment; her gaze sought him out in a "help me" plea. She looked so happy and so pretty it did all sorts of weird things to his heartbeat.

He made himself grin and gave her a thumb's-up. Then he went back to the kitchen where he could get a firmer grip on his equilibrium and left her in J.T.'s capable hands.

* * *

It was close to five and almost dark by the time Mac pulled his truck up in front of the weathered log cabin in the woods south of Sundown.

"Stay put," he ordered, jumping out from behind the wheel.

When he rounded the truck and opened her door, Shallie understood why. The snow was knee-deep. Only because his truck had four-wheel drive had they made it up the long lane after they'd left the main road.

"You're going to hurt your back hauling me around," she protested as he hefted her into his arms and carried her up the snow-laden steps to the front door.

"I expect insults from J.T. but not from you—not after I threw you a surprise party," he said, grinning.

"How was that an insult?"

"You obviously underestimate my virile manhood if you think that a lightweight like you could—oh. Ouch. Did I say lightweight? How much did you eat today, anyway?"

She cuffed him on the shoulder. "Okay. Okay. Point taken. I won't insult your supermacho ego, and you won't insult my new and piglike eating habits."

"There you go. Key's in my breast pocket," he said with a nod of his chin. "Fish it out, would ya?"

"Or you could just put me down now."

"I could, but the snow on the porch is ankle-deep so all this show of strength would have been for nothing. Now get the key, woman, and let's get out of the cold."

With a shake of her head, Shallie tugged off her glove and dug into his jacket pocket until she came up with the key. He angled her close to the door so she could slip it in the lock.

"Success," he said brightly, then shouldered open the door and deposited her on a bright, woven rug in the small entryway.

"Oh, Mac," she said when he'd flipped on a light switch. "This is charming."

"Okay, we're going to have that semantics problem again, I see. It's supposed to be rustic."

"Charming. Rustic. Whatever. Don't worry your tender sensibilities. It's very masculine. And very homey. I love it."

The cabin wasn't nearly as large as his new house in Bozeman but it was everything a mountain cabin should be. Lots of warm, aged pine covered the walls of a great room that was living, dining and kitchen all rolled into one. The tall peaked ceiling was crisscrossed with open beams of aged, native pine and hosted a loft at the far end with yet more natural pine railing. A massive stone fireplace commanded the center of the north wall, the fire well deep enough and tall enough to roast half a beef if need be. A wide, four-shelf bookcase loaded with paperbacks, CDs and DVDs filled the wall space between the living and the kitchen area.

"I know people who would kill to spend a single night in a place like this," she said, spotting more and more touches around the cabin that charmed her. Like the ancient webbed snowshoes crisscrossed above a mantel laden with thick, chunky candles. On the brick hearth sat an ornate iron fire-screen molded in the shape of a bear. Comfy mission oak furniture with cushions covered in Native American prints and colors flanked the fireplace.

Outside the cabin was a world of deep greens and winter whites and darkening sky as snow swirled, weighed down pine bows and drifted onto the corners of the multipaned windows. Inside, woven rugs in pallets of reds and blues and greens warmed the great room while Mac struck a match to a fire already laid out in the hearth.

The dry tinder caught quickly, and soon the licking flames of a toasty fire crackled to life, scenting the cabin of pine tinged with the pleasant aroma of wood smoke.

"Not that Sundown or even Bozeman are hubs of urban activity," Shallie said, forgoing a comfy-looking mission oak sofa and rocker to ease down on a soft rug in front of the fire so she could feel the warmth of it heat her cheeks, "but doesn't it feel a little like we passed through a time warp when we closed the cabin door behind us? I mean—I can almost get a feel for what it was like a hundred or so years ago."

"And what's your interpretation of how it felt?" he asked, walking over to a wall and turning up a thermostat that had obviously been set just warm enough to keep water pipes from freezing.

She raised both shoulders, held her hands out to the fire. "Isolated but cozy. Exciting and a little scary. And on a night like this…romantic," she said.

The minute that thought popped out, she wished she could snatch it back. *Romantic* was not a good thought to express at the moment. Not with the two of them alone again and all those unsettled feelings held over from last night.

And definitely not with her still trying to deal with the way it felt to be held in his arms when he'd carried her to the cabin. He made her feel small and feminine. Protected and cared for. And it made her ache—more than a little—to be held by him again, as he'd held her in his arms last night and kissed her.

She was swamped by a heavy wave of confusion. She didn't want to think of Mac in those terms. She had no business thinking of him that way. And yet…and yet he'd kissed her. Twice. How could she not think about it?

"Yeah," he said, snapping her out of her thoughts, "the prospect of ducking out of the cabin in the middle of a night like this to use the facility that, in those days, would have been twenty or so yards from the cabin, does have a romantic ring to it."

She turned to smile at him. Good thing one of them had things in perspective. Romance clearly wasn't on his mind. His next statement cinched it.

"But then, the prospect of hustling out in the cold again in the morning to hunt us up a possum for breakfast, now, that conjures all kinds of romantic thoughts."

She laughed. "Okay. So I may have glossed over a few of the hardships," she conceded. "Still, you have to admit, this place does take you back in time."

"Yeah," he finally agreed. "It's pretty cool. But speaking of possum," he snagged his jacket, "I'd better get those groceries out of the truck before they freeze or I *will* be hunting up our breakfast in the morning."

When he went outside Shallie rose and explored the

rest of the cabin. Besides the great room and the kitchen, there were two roomy bedrooms with a shared bath between them on the main level. Upstairs, in the loft, was a small sitting area and an open bedroom.

She heard the door open, then Mac's voice boom up the stairs. "Where'd you go?"

"I'm up here."

She started back down the stairs as Mac kicked the door shut behind him, stomped the snow off his shoes, then headed for the kitchen area with his arms full of groceries.

To the fire scents, he added the smell of winter— cool, crisp air and night. It clung to his jacket as she joined him and dug, one-handed, into a sack to help him put the groceries away.

It all felt very homey and domestic. As well as cozy and warm and…right. Just like it felt right to be standing beside him and feeling a warm and encompassing glow.

"Are you planning on feeding a football team?"

"A woman who's eating for two," he said, reaching behind her to open the refrigerator door and stow a carton of milk. "Can't have you going hungry just in case we get stranded out here."

She glanced out the window over the sink where the snow was still swirling. "You think that's a possibility?"

"Not in the next week or so. What you see moving around out there is the wind blowing snow off the trees— but you never know, so I wanted you to be well stocked."

He shoved a dozen eggs and some lunch meat into the fridge. "Before I leave for Bozeman tomorrow I'll put the blade on the truck and clear the lane. There's a four-wheel-drive Jeep in the garage you can use when you want to go into town. It's an automatic so you shouldn't have any trouble driving it."

She felt the tears before she even knew she was going to cry. They just welled up out of nowhere. And so fast, she couldn't hide them.

"Hey. Hey," Mac said so softly when he realized what was going on that it made her cry harder. "What's this? What's wrong? Is it your wrist? Are you hurting?"

Horrified by her outburst, she shook her head, then looked away from him, trying to hide her embarrassment over the sudden attack of waterworks. He wasn't having it.

"Come 'ere," he said gently and, tucking her under his broad shoulder, walked her into the living area and sat her down with him on the sofa. "Tell Daddy all about it."

She pushed out a weak laugh, then sniffed and buried her face in his neck. He still smelled of winter and a little like the Dusk to Dawn and a lot like Mac. Subtly spicy, warm male heat, comfort and strength.

"Come on," he coaxed when she couldn't find the words to express what she was feeling. He cupped her head in his big hand, lightly tapped a finger. "What's going on in there?"

And the dam broke. One moment she couldn't articulate a thing, the next, she was spilling out her feelings like water spilling over a broken dike.

"How did I get myself in this fix? How did I get to the point where I have to rely on the generosity of friends to feed me, to put a roof over my head? To shore up my bruised and battered ego by throwing me a party to take my mind off the fact that I'm without income, without prospects and without a father for this poor little child who never asked to be born to a woman who doesn't have the good sense to take care of herself?"

She stopped long enough to wipe her nose with the tissue he handed her. "I hate it. I hate taking advantage of you. I hate blubbering like a sissy every time my hormones get a little out of whack. I hate lying to Peg and J.T.—at least lying by omission—and not telling them about the baby. I hate thinking that all my life I was ashamed of my mother for relying on cheap men to make her happy, for not loving me enough to make her happy, for…for making such awful judgments in her life. And now…here I am. I'm just like her."

"You are nothing like your mother," he said, her white knight defending her honor. "You're kind and you're smart and I've already seen that you want and love this baby. And you'll love and care for your child. That's something your mother never did for you."

She sniffed again, snuggled closer into the sheltering warmth he offered and felt more hot tears track down her cheeks. "Why couldn't she love me, Mac? What was wrong with me that made it so hard for her to love me?"

His strong arms wrapped her even tighter. "Nothing was wrong with you. Nothing *is* wrong with you. Nothing, you got that?" he added adamantly. "The problem was with her.

"Who knows," he added after a moment. "Who knows what happens to some people to make them the way they are. Maybe she was abused when she was a kid. Maybe she was giving you the best she knew how to give. I don't know," he said quietly. "I don't know what made her tick. But I do know about you. I know what you're made of, short-stack. I knew it the first time I saw you standing up to the Griener boys."

She sniffed again, tipped her head back so she could see his face. "The Griener boys?"

He smiled, all sleepy and slow. "You don't remember?"

"I remember attempting to neuter one of them with my knee."

"I know. I saw it. And I was in awe."

His exaggerated, awestruck look made her grin. "You were afraid you were next, is more like it."

"That, too," he confessed, "but more than that, I saw someone who knew how to take care of herself. And I saw someone I admired. I still see someone I admire," he added before she could make a case for him thinking otherwise.

"You get up, Shallie," he said, tucking her head under his chin. "You take a hit and you get up. You always have. You always will. That's a lot to admire in a person. And that's one of the things I admire about you."

She didn't see much to admire. She saw a lot of mistakes, and they felt too heavy on her shoulders to move her out from under the sense of failure that had settled in for the night.

"You're tired," he said. "You've had a big day. Lots of emotions flowing, right?"

She sniffed. "Stop being so nice to me. I'll just get all blubbery again." She sat up and wiped her eyes. "God. I *hate* this. And don't look at me. I'm a mess."

"So's my shirt," he said, tugging the wet cloth away from his shoulder with such an exaggerated frown he made her laugh. Which, of course, is what he wanted her to do.

"Thanks," she said.

"For being a friend? Hey, you'd do the same for me."

"I don't know," she said, finally mustering up enough spunk to feel a little ornery, "if you threw a hissy fit like that, I'd probably tell you to take a pill."

"See, there's that respect thing again," he groused, even though his grin said he was glad to see her rallying. "I don't get any from J.T., and now I'm not getting any from you."

Shallie woke to the sound of silence. The sunshine slanting in through the cabin window was so brilliant and bright it was almost blinding. The plump down comforter covering her was warm and cocooning. She felt as if she was lying in a nest of feathers, all soft and snug and sheltering. And if it weren't for the demands of her bladder, she'd simply lie there for, oh, another decade or two, and wallow in all this homespun comfort.

The cabin was empty when she tiptoed out of the bathroom a few minutes later. She smelled coffee and followed her nose to the kitchen where, typical of Mac, he'd set food out for her. Chocolate-covered donuts, chocolate iced éclairs, and according to the note he'd set on the counter beside them, there was also tiramisu in the fridge.

She felt a smile crawl across her face. "That man would see me as plump as a Christmas goose if I'm not careful."

It was cute the way he coddled her. Took care of her. Made certain she had her daily chocolate hits. And if she wasn't careful in that area, she told herself as she filled a mug with coffee and wandered toward the big window in the living area that overlooked the forest, all this TLC could become addictive.

In particular, all this TLC from a *man* could become a habit. She'd never had a father to turn to while growing up. Jared had been her only steady relationship, and even before he'd gotten violent, he hadn't been the attentive or coddling kind. In fact, she realized now as she caught a glimpse of Mac behind the wheel of his big black truck, pushing snow with a blade attached to the front of the vehicle, Jared hadn't contributed much of anything in the TLC department. He'd been silent and stoic and, well, she could see now, he'd been a user.

Hmm. Funny how time and distance could add a little perspective. Too bad she hadn't had this kind of perspective when she'd gone "looking for love in all the wrong places" that night three months ago, she thought with a heavy sigh. She wouldn't be in this fix—depending on Mac. Living a lie.

She took a sip of her coffee; Mac made the best coffee.

As she watched him through the window, a fresh wave of guilt swamped her. She should tell him about the baby's conception.

She should tell him.

He looked up from his work about then, spotted her watching him and shot her a big sexy grin and a wave.

She waved back, and that wave of guilt gained weight and settled like a five-hundred-pound monkey on her back.

Yeah. She should tell him. But she just couldn't bear to see the look on his face when he found out the truth. At the moment he was the only stable, caring element in her life. In the short span of a few days, he had become everything to her. Provider. Friend. Family.

She'd always considered herself a strong person. She'd survived a childhood without a father, without the love of her mother. From the time she could remember, she felt as if she'd been on her own.

And now here was Mac. And now she couldn't imagine getting through this point in her life without him.

So no, she wouldn't tell him, because right now, this moment in time, as guilty as it made her feel, she needed him. Needed what he gave her. And of all the things he provided—food, shelter, transportation—it was his friendship, his unbridled affection for her that she needed most.

If she told him, she'd lose him.

"Oh, by the way this baby's father didn't leave me, like you think. No, this baby's father is a married man. Yeah. That's right. I slept with a married man. A man who has children of his own who need their daddy, rat-bastard that he is. He doesn't even know about the baby. He'll never know. At least, he wouldn't find out from me because he doesn't deserve to know."

And because I will not be responsible for breaking up a family, she vowed firmly. It was a little late to think about those particular consequences of her stupidity, but on that count she would not budge.

Mac waved at her again and shot her another big, goofy grin.

No. She would not tell him. Because she would not, could not, lose him.

Seven

"Shouldn't you be wearing your sling?" Mac came in from shoveling and pushing snow to find Shallie dressed and putting the finishing touches on toasted cheese sandwiches and tomato soup.

She was wearing a pair of worn jeans and a pretty pink sweater that made her cheeks look pink, too.

"Doctor said to use my own judgment. And right now it's in my way."

"You didn't have to do this," he said, slipping out of his vest and hanging it on a coat hook by the kitchen door.

"But I wanted to," she said with a smile. "A hard-working man's got to have something warm to eat when he comes in from the cold."

"Hardworking? I'll let you in on a little secret. Any

time I get to play with something with that much horse-power, I'm literally playing, not working."

"Boys and their power tools," she said with an exaggerated indulgent look.

He made a grunting, he-man sound and beat on his chest. "Me love horsepower and snow blades."

She laughed. He loved the sound.

"All right, tool man, take time out from the macho stuff and refuel, will ya? Eat while everything's hot."

"You shouldn't have any trouble getting out of the lane and into town now," he said, washing his hands at the sink. "I pushed snow all the way to the road, and the weather forecast calls for clear skies and light winds the next few days so there shouldn't be any drifting."

"I can't imagine that I'll need to go anywhere. There's enough food to last for a month, you've got a library that would take a speed reader a decade to plow through and enough movies to start a rental business. Besides. This cabin is like something out of a fairy tale. I don't think I ever want to leave it."

"Just the same, I'll feel better knowing that you can get out if you need or want to. Um. Good," he added, sitting down at the table and digging into his lunch.

"So, you're heading back to Bozeman?" she asked, oh, so casually as she sat down across from him at the small table.

Mac wasn't certain if he heard a little disappointment in her question. Wasn't certain if he was glad or concerned that she might miss him.

"Yeah," he said, "I need to get back to the restaurant.

I promised Cara a few days off this week, and I'll need to cover for her."

Then something else occurred to him. Maybe it wasn't the prospect of missing him that made her seem a little reluctant to see him go. "Hey, short-stack. In spite of all this talk of loving the cabin, are you worried about being out here all by yourself?"

"Absolutely not. And I do love the cabin."

"So, you're going to be okay on your own?"

"Mac. I've been on my own for a long time now. I'll be fine."

She'd been on her own too long, Mac thought when he left her an hour later as he drove down the highway toward Bozeman. Maybe that's why it had been hard for him to leave her there.

Maybe that's why he kept thinking about turning around, telling her to repack her bag and come back to Bozeman with him.

The truth was, he was going to miss her like hell. How could that be? Until last week he hadn't seen her for ten years. How could you miss someone who hadn't even been in your life for a decade?

How? Because he'd loved her all that time, that's how. And he'd missed her all that time, too.

He thought about her way too much during the next few days. Called her several times a day because he wanted to make sure she was doing okay.

And because he wondered what she was doing. If she was curled up with her nose in a book or doing something homey around the cabin.

He thought about how quiet his new house seemed

when he came home after a day at SW—which didn't make a lick of sense because he'd lived alone for almost ten years now, if you didn't count his college days when he'd lived first in a dorm, then in a frat house.

It wasn't as if he'd ever had a woman live with him, yet all of a sudden he missed the softness one could bring to a room. And the scent. Shallie definitely had a scent. In the middle of winter she smelled like spring flowers. Funny, he thought as he checked with his chef over the evening's specials. Funny how he thought of that now. With marinara sauce bubbling on the stove and garlic bread baking in the oven, he thought of spring flowers and Shallie.

"Phone call, Mac," his bookkeeper said, poking her head out of the office.

"Who is it?"

"Don't know. She's got a nice voice, though," she said with a grin.

His spirits dropped when it was a salesperson on the other end of the line instead of Shallie.

And it was then he decided he'd had enough of missing her. He was wired for sound when he pulled into the drive at the cabin and saw Shallie bundled up in her jacket and waving at him from the front porch.

It had been four days since he'd left her there. Since he'd scooped out the lane, shoveled the porch and left her with orders to call him if she needed anything. He'd also left J.T.'s and Peg's phone numbers with her in case she needed someone close and in a hurry.

Well, he'd come in a hurry—whether she needed him or not. And he'd be damned if he knew exactly what he had in mind now that he was here.

* * *

"What do you think?" Shallie asked, surveying her handiwork. Well, technically, it was her idea but Mac's work.

"I like it," he said, studying the new furniture arrangement with a critical eye. "Should have been this way all along. And I like that wreath over the mantel, too. What I don't like is thinking about how you managed to get it up there."

"No ladders involved, I promise," she said, plopping down on the sofa that now faced the fire and the TV, which sat on a stand to the left of the hearth. "I got it down with a hoe I found in the shed. Then I propped it on the mantel and used the hoe again to lift it from there and slid it on the hook."

"Very resourceful," Mac said, sitting down beside her. "Now hand over that popcorn."

It was funny, Shallie thought as they sat there and one of the DVDs began to play. He'd been gone four days.

She'd thought she would enjoy the solitude. And she had, but she'd also found herself waiting for the phone to ring, knowing when it did that it would be Mac. And it had rung. Often. And they would talk—sometimes for an hour or more. She couldn't remember now what they'd found to talk about. Nothing, mostly. But they'd laughed a lot and he'd fussed over whether she was taking care of herself, and she'd taken great pleasure in telling him that yes, she was being a good girl.

Silly banter. Necessary contact.

And now the contact was physical.

His thigh brushed hers as they sat side by side. She

tried really hard not to notice how strong that thigh was. How much heat his big body generated or how good he smelled. Just like she tried not to make a big deal of it when their fingers tangled, then dueled in the bowl of popcorn she'd popped for the "pseudo movie theater experience" as she'd told him.

"I can't believe these movies hold up after all these years."

They'd loved *Star Wars* when they were kids. They loved it now. Mostly she loved that Mac was back in Sundown and that he planned to spend the night at the cabin.

Truth was, she loved it a little too much.

Since he'd left her four days ago, she'd had a lot of time to think about that kiss New Year's Eve. A lot of time alone. A lot of time wishing they might have talked about it as they'd planned.

She wondered if he thought about it, too.

Beside her he smelled warm and wintry at the same time. She glanced sideways at him. The fire glow did incredible things to his profile as he slouched back on the sofa, his gaze locked on the TV.

Too much of a good thing. Now Shallie knew what that cliché meant. Mac was too much of everything. Too handsome. Too sexy. And tonight probably too close for comfort, given the haywire state of her hormones, which had chosen tonight to remind her she was a woman, with woman's needs.

She had to back away from that line of thought. She had to keep things on an even keel. So when he lifted his hand to dig into the popcorn bowl, she inched it away from him and prepared to shift into good-ol'-buddy sparring mode.

When he felt blindly around for the bowl, she moved it again until she had set it all the way to her left side. Since he was sitting on her right, it finally dawned on him that something was amiss.

"Hey," he squawked when he finally tore his gaze from the movie and discovered that she'd deliberately moved the popcorn out of his reach. "What's the deal?"

"No deal," she said with a shrug.

"Then give me some popcorn before you find yourself in some trouble."

"You want popcorn? Open your mouth."

He was on to her game but went along with it, anyway. "Bet you can't hit it," he challenged and opened wide.

She laughed and, taking aim, tossed one his way.

"That's the best you got?" he taunted, when she missed.

"I can do this," she insisted and tried again. And missed again, several times.

They were both laughing when he reached for the bowl. "A man could starve while you take potshots. Now gimme some of that popcorn."

"No problem." She pelted him with a handful.

He opened his mouth. Shut it. Narrowed his eyes.

"Okay. Now you've done it," he warned, and with a quick, deft move, managed to swipe the bowl away from her.

"Hey, give that back."

"My pleasure." Digging a big hand into the bowl, he fired a handful and hit her full in the face.

She fell back against the sofa cushions, laughing as popcorn cascaded over her head and shoulders. "I don't believe you did that."

"Believe it. You didn't really think you were going to get the best of me," he said, holding the bowl above his head and out of her reach.

"But I'm incapacitated," she wailed between giggles and plucked popcorn out of her hair. "You're supposed to let me win."

"You obviously have never read the bully's handbook. Now hold still," he said, swinging his leg over her lap, then straddling her with his knees dug into the cushions on either side of her hips. "You're about to get full payback for making me suffer through popcorn deprivation."

She shrieked and held up her cast to ward off the attack—not that it did any good.

He dumped the bowl over her head. Popcorn rained down all over her.

"You are crazy!"

"You started it."

So she had.

And as the room suddenly became very quiet, except for the war of spaceships going on in the background, she realized that Mac had become very quiet, too.

He wasn't laughing anymore, either.

Neither was she.

In fact, she was barely breathing...yet very aware of every breath. His as much as hers.

His chest was broad and hard beneath a thick navy-blue sweater. She could see the rise and fall of it so very close in front of her.

She chanced a glance up to meet his eyes, had to lean her head back on the sofa cushion to make eye contact as he stood on his knees poised over her.

He was watching her with eyes that had gone dark and searching. And testing. And asking the same thing she was thinking.

If he lowered his mouth, would she let him kiss her?

She heard a soft plunk, realized he'd tossed the empty bowl beside them on the sofa. Very slowly he lowered his hands to the cushion on either side of her head.

He searched her face, slowly shook his head. "You are one fine mess, Shallie Malone."

Oh, yeah. She was a mess all right. And not just from the popcorn. Her heart was knocking like an air hammer. Her breath was short and choppy. And if she got any hotter, she was going to have to take off some clothes.

Yikes. The look in his eyes told her he was thinking along the same lines.

"You…you made me this way," she managed on a faint, thready breath.

"Messy?" he asked, his voice whisper soft and spring-water deep.

She swallowed, slowly nodded. Messy. Yeah. And hot. And bothered and, man—

"Guess I'll just have to clean you up, then."

Before she could even gulp, he was doing an improvised pushup, lowering his upper body toward her and—oh, sweet heaven above—nibbling popcorn off her shoulders.

"I…um…"

"Shh. Hold still," he whispered, working his mouth along her collarbone, "this is man's work. I need to concentrate."

"Oh. Oh…okay," was the best she could do as he moved back and forth, his mouth gentle, his breath July hot against her throat, against her jaw…against the corner of her mouth.

"Umm. Salty," he murmured taking his time and licking her bottom lip. "And very, very sweet."

His lips felt incredible as they cruised over her face. She could feel the slight abrasive scrape of a day's growth of beard, smell the subtle scent of his after-shave. And, oh, my, she thought as the touch of his lips on the tender skin behind her earlobe made her shiver, she could very easily lose herself in the overwhelming sensuality of what he was doing to her.

Don't stop, she thought. Please, don't stop this time. To make certain he didn't, she lifted her right arm, buried her fingers in the coarse silk of his hair.

"Shallie." His voice sounded raspy, tightly reined. He closed his eyes. Pressed his forehead to hers. "We might be in a little trouble here again. We definitely should have that talk."

"Don't want to talk," she whispered, and lifted her mouth up to his, chasing it when he pulled away.

"Be sure," he said, more plea than warning, "Be very, very sure this is what you want."

She was sure. She was sure she was lost. So very,

very lost in the promise of his kisses, in the tenderness of his touch. And she trusted him. To make everything be all right between them. To make this one of the best experiences of her life.

"I want," she whispered and pulled him back down to her mouth for a long, hungry kiss.

And it was hunger she felt. Hunger to be held. Hunger to be loved. Hunger to believe that finally, finally, she was with a man—a good man—she could trust to always be honest with her.

Honest with his passion. Honest with his expectations. Honest with his love.

And Mac did love her. Just like she loved him. It was the best kind of love. The kind that came without complications. The kind that came from being friends. And this friend would take special care to make things good. To make things right.

She couldn't even call it surrender when he stood, lifted her in his arms and carried her to his bedroom. And she definitely couldn't call it defeat. What she could call it was wonderful as he laid her down on his big bed and then tugged his sweater up and over his head.

Mac knew he shouldn't be doing this. He knew he should be the one to stop it. And if she said the word, he would. In a heartbeat.

But she hadn't said stop. She'd said go. In the thick, rapid beat of her heart. In the long, burning look in her eyes.

He bent over her, kissed her long and deep. And felt one final tug of conscience.

"You sure you're up for this?"

She closed her eyes. And damned if all of her certainty didn't dissolve into a misty panic. "Am I making a fool of myself?"

Oh, God. "For making love with me?"

She swallowed. "For thinking...for wanting..." She hesitated. Looked away.

"For wanting something more for yourself?" he finished for her.

When she nodded, he cupped her jaw, gently turned her head back so she had to look at him. "Not a fool. You're just a little lonely. Just like me," he admitted, then smiled when he saw the disbelief in her eyes.

"Where's the harm, Shallie? We're both unattached, healthy adults who care deeply about each other. I trust you. You trust me. What could possibly be wrong with making each other feel good?"

"Nothing," she whispered. "Nothing at all."

"So we won't be sorry in the morning?"

All her hesitation had faded. She smiled for him. "I've been sorry for a lot of things in my life. I can't imagine that spending a night with you would be one of them."

He breathed a huge breath of relief. "Friends and lovers. Has a nice ring to it." He reached for the hem of her sweater.

"Who knew," he said when he'd helped her out of her clothes and she lay before him in nothing but a pair of lilac bikini panties. "Who knew my little short-stack was so...well...stacked," he finished, because he knew it would make her smile and because she was even more than he'd imagined beneath her jeans and sweaters.

Soft and full. Feminine and beautiful. He lowered his head, bussed his nose around a velvet-soft nipple.

"Are you sensitive?" he asked, remembering that he'd read a pregnant woman's nipples could be very sensitive and sore.

"A little," she admitted.

"Then you'll tell me if I'm too rough," he said just before he surrounded all that velvety softness with his mouth. He suckled her with special care, laved her budding nipple with his tongue and knew from the way she arched into his mouth that she liked it.

That was good. He liked it, too. Liked the way she tasted. Loved the texture and the heat and the plump fullness of her in his mouth. Loved it so much, his sex knotted tight when she moaned and sighed and urged him with the touch of her hand to the back of his head to take her deeper.

He did it gladly. Beneath his hands she felt like silk. All supple, graceful limbs, and skin as fluid as water, as hot as a winter fire.

Her hips were slim. Her tummy still flat, and while he'd seen her legs a hundred times when they'd been kids in the summer, he'd never touched her. The length of her calf. The inside of her knee. The tender flesh where her thighs joined, and a damp scrap of lilac lace—the only barrier between them.

"Okay?" he whispered against her breast when he slipped his fingers inside her panties and met with damp curls.

"Mmm."

He chuckled. "I'll take that as a yes."

"Mmm." She expelled a deep, restless breath when his finger found her wet and slick and swollen and open for him.

A very sensual woman was one Ms. Shallie Malone, Mac thought as he teased her with long strokes just so he could hear that delicious sigh, just so he could feel that quivering little eddy of shock ripple through her.

She was so special to him, he thought, pulling away from her long enough to shuck his jeans and briefs then skim her panties down her hips.

"Tell me what you like, Shall," he whispered, laving attention on her breast again when he'd lie back down beside her. Her skin burned his where they met, naked and needy for the very first time.

"Everything." She lifted her good arm and touched him, experimentally stroking his chest, the line of his hip, searching for his erection between them. Finding. Caressing. Making him moan. "I like everything you're doing to me."

"Oh, sweet woman. I haven't even got started."

"Seriously?" she asked with such a sober look that he laughed. Until she added, "In my experience, by this point in the process, anything to do with me as something other than a receptacle is pretty much over."

He scowled down at her. He didn't want to think about the guy who had cheated on her. He didn't want to bring him into this bed. But he was there just the same. And all Mac could think was the guy was not only a cheating bastard, he was a *selfish* cheating bastard.

"Well hang on, darlin'," he whispered, working his mouth along the fragile line of her rib cage, stopping to indulge in the delectable little dent of her navel. "Before I'm through with you, we're going to reinvent that process."

"I…um…we are?"

She hiked herself up on her elbows, looked down at him as he eased down the bed and made a comfy place for himself between her thighs.

"You…umm…really?" Her words came out on a quivering sigh when he lowered his mouth to her damp curls and kissed her there.

"Me. Umm. Yeah. Really."

And then he proceeded to really, really take her someplace she'd evidently never been before.

She tasted amazing. She made sounds of stunned wonder. And when she finally decided she could relax and let him have his way with her, she opened for him like a flower, came in his mouth with a shattered cry and collapsed back onto the mattress with a serrated gasp.

He was smiling when he crawled back up the bed and settled carefully over her slack and sated body.

"Well?" He nuzzled her neck, licked the salt of her sweat from her skin.

"I always thought," she said breathlessly as she raised a limp hand and cupped his face, "that *necessity* was the mother of invention. Here it was sex. Who knew?"

He chuckled and kissed her.

"Mac." She broke the kiss, made sure he was looking at her. "Thank you. That was…incredible."

"*You* are incredible," he said and, wedging his knee between her thighs, eased himself inside her giving warmth. "Now let's try for amazing."

It *was* amazing. The way she took him in. The way she gloved him, held him and became for him everything he needed her to be.

Supple strength. Sensual woman.

It touched him, the way she gave. Destroyed him, the way she clung then rode with him to a place they'd never been together.

Eight

This was the part where she should be feeling remorse, Shallie thought as Mac slept beside her. This is the part where she should be thinking, Oh my God. What have I done?

But as this big, gorgeous and sensitive man lay with his head on her breast, his arm slung over her waist and his muscled thigh thrown across hers, all she could do was smile.

Who knew? Who knew sex could be about more than giving? Not that giving to Mac wasn't wonderful, but, oh, wow. Taking was a whole new experience for her. And he made it so easy.

He made it so…amazing.

He made it so good, that for the first time she understood what all the fuss was about. Just like she understood she'd been looking for something with Jared that she was never going to find. He hadn't been capable of this kind of generosity.

"You're awfully quiet."

Mac's voice, deep and sleepy, roused her from her thoughts.

"That's because I'm very relaxed."

"Relaxed? Not regretful?"

"No." She lifted her hand and touched his hair. "I'm not regretful. What about you?"

He hiked himself up on an elbow, smiled down at her in the pale lamplight. "Does this face look like the face of a man feeling regret?"

She smiled back, stroked his hair. "Actually, it looks like the face of a very generous, very sensitive lover."

"We aim to please," he said capturing her hand in his, then pressing a kiss to her palm.

"You've got great aim there Mr....what did you say your name was again?"

He grinned up at her from beneath sinfully thick lashes. "Lucky. My friends call me Lucky. And what can I call you?"

"Satisfied," she said on a sigh, then stretched in contentment when he kissed his way down the length of her arm, lingering at her inner elbow.

She liked this. This peaceful, easy feeling. This playful sexy banter. But most of all she liked the way he made her feel.

She especially liked the way she felt right now. She was tired, sated and, thanks to the tender attention he was paying to the under side of her arm, which just happened to be in close proximity to her right breast, she was feeling very achy and anxious again.

"You have a beautiful body, short-stack," he murmured as he kissed a circle around her breast, his lips gentle, his breath warm, his tongue skilled, as he lapped at her nipple and brought it to a tight, aching peak.

"You're pretty gorgeous yourself," she said, running her hand down the lean, ropey muscles of his back.

"You do," he said, lifting his head, "have a problem," biting her gently on the chin, "with semantics."

She laughed when he rolled to his back and brought her with him. "Okay," she conceded as she straddled his lap, "not gorgeous. Handsome. Manly. Muy macho. And...oh," she gasped as he settled her over his heat and eased her down onto him.

"You were saying?" He was doing a little gasping, too, as his big hands grasped her hips and moved her slowly up and down.

"Hmm? Mmm. What?"

She couldn't think for the way he felt so deep inside of her. Could barely catch a breath and he expected her to talk?

Her breasts felt heavy. Her heart felt light. And the ache building low in her belly where they met and parted, met and parted, grew to a want so huge, a yearning so vast, it consumed her. Body. Soul. Spirit.

And if she wasn't careful, she thought moments later as she sprawled exhausted and sweaty and spent on his heaving chest, her heart was also going to take a fall.

But she wasn't going to think about that now. She

wasn't going to think about anything but the moment. This special, magical moment where she could give with total trust, take without inhibition. A moment that was hers.

She'd had too much taken away from her in her life. Nothing was going to take this away.

Mac was just debating about mixing up some pancake batter when Shallie, bundled from chin to shin in his navy-blue terry cloth bathrobe and wearing a pair of his wool socks, came padding into the kitchen.

Love hit him smack in the chest like a bullet. God, he loved this woman. It had taken every ounce of restraint not to tell her exactly that when he took her to bed. But he knew his Shallie. The *L* word would have scared her off.

Hell. It scared him and he was the one who wanted to say it.

"Your thermostat running a little on the cold side this morning?" he asked, leaning a hip against the kitchen counter and grinning at the house-frau picture she made.

Her hands were lost in the sleeves of the robe as she shuffled over to the counter and poured coffee into a mug he'd set out for her. "Seems I slept cuddled up to a furnace last night. I haven't acclimated to the loss of the heat source just yet."

"Hmm. How about I make the transition a little easier?" He walked up to her, wrapped his arms around her and pulled her close. "How's that?"

She nestled her head on his shoulder. "I'd say that's just about perfect."

Feeling more contentment that he figured he should

be feeling, Mac just held her that way for a while. She didn't seem to mind. And when he started to sway back and forth—just a little—she started humming. The next thing you knew, they were doing a little slow dance in place, her in his ratty robe, him in his bare feet and jeans.

And damn, if all didn't seem right with his world.

He needed to make sure, though, that things were truly okay in hers. "So, we're good, right?" He tucked his chin to look down at her.

"I'd say we're pretty damn spectacular," she said looking mighty pleased with herself.

"Yeah," he agreed with a final squeeze. "We are."

So. Everything was good. Everything was fine. They'd both scratched an itch. They'd given and received affection and pleasure. And they weren't going to make a big deal of it in the morning.

But later he planned to make a very big deal of it. Later, when she got used to the idea of him and her together. And during the night, when he wasn't making love to her or sleeping, he thought he'd come up with a way to make palatable for her the idea of the two of them together forever.

"How's that cast-iron stomach of yours doing? You up for some pancakes?"

"Don't you ever get tired of cooking for me?" She took her coffee to the table and sat down.

"I'm in the wrong business if cooking tires me out."

"That's what I mean. You shouldn't have to cook when you're away from the restaurant."

"Unless I want to," he pointed out. "And I want to."

"What can I do?"

"Just sit there and look hungry."

"Ha. I can do that without working up a sweat. Speaking of sweat," she unknotted the belt of his robe. "Thanks for warming me up."

"My pleasure."

And it truly had been. All night long.

They were snuggled up on the sofa later that afternoon, sipping hot chocolate, making stabs at reading, but mostly watching the fire and the falling snow. Mac's back was at one end of the sofa and Shallie's at the other; they'd been playing a hit-and-miss game of footsie beneath an old patchwork quilt when Shallie realized Mac was watching her.

She looked up over her open book. "What?"

His expression was thoughtful, searching. "We should get married."

She considered his statement, decided he was just being silly and went back to her mystery novel. "Sure. Okay. Whatever."

The silence from the other end of the sofa lasted a little too long, prompting her to look up again. Her heart kicked her a couple of good ones when she realized he was still watching her. And that he was serious.

"Think about it," he said as if he *had* been doing a lot of thinking about it. "We're not kids, Shall. We're not looking for storybook, fairy-tale love. We're not foolish enough to think that it even exists. Hell. Look at my parents. They were wild, crazy in love when they got married. Seems that ten years later, neither one of them remembered what the fuss was about. The next ten years they just stuck it out because they were too stubborn to fix it…or too mired in their own misery to do anything about it."

He leaned forward, all earnest eyes and handsome face. "I never knew. Never knew they weren't happy together. Never knew that Mom wanted to travel and Dad refused to go any farther than Bozeman. She wanted excitement. He wanted status quo. They were miserable.

"Anyway, Mom finally left him." He tried to sound casual, but his face had grown hard. "I understood that part. More or less, anyway. But it was how she did it that I'll never be able to forgive."

A sinking sensation swamped Shallie as she waited for him to explain. She had a horrible feeling that she didn't want to hear the rest. She was right.

"She had an affair. Some guy from Bozeman. A married man."

Shallie's heart dropped like a stone.

"How…uh, how are they doing…um, now, I mean, since the divorce?" she finally managed to ask, while his words rattled around in her head: an affair…with a married man…never be able to forgive.

He lifted a shoulder. "Dad's doing okay, I guess. It's been five years now. He more or less buries himself in work, lets the rest of the world go by."

"And your mom?" she asked softly while her heart pounded so loud it almost drowned out her question.

Another shrug. A disinterested look that didn't quite ring true. "No clue. Haven't seen or talked to her since she left him."

"Oh, Mac." Shallie could hear the hurt in his voice.

The disillusion. She ached for him. He'd loved his mother. Adored her. And Carol McDonald had adored her son. It broke her heart to hear they had lost contact.

She suspected that it broke his, too, because he quickly moved on.

"The point is, I've got a ton of friends in the same boat as they were. Either trapped in a marriage they no longer have a stomach for or divorced and looking to make the same mistake all over again."

She shot him a concerned look. "So now you want to join the ranks? Make your own mistake?" she asked, hoping to help him realize he was talking nonsense.

"See, that's the thing. We wouldn't be making the same mistakes they did. We know going in what we are to each other. You're my best friend."

"And you're mine," she agreed, "but—"

"No wait. What better foundation could you build a marriage on? Friendship. Respect. Trust. Most important, trust and honesty. We could make this work.

"Plus we've got this damn hot chemistry going on," he added with a grin. "And the baby. I don't want you raising this baby by yourself. It's not fair to you. It's not fair to little Heathcliff. Or little Gertrude," he added with another soft smile.

She studied his beautiful, sincere face. Yes, there was friendship. Yes, there was respect. And the chemistry was incredible. But trust? She trusted him, absolutely. But that coin didn't flip both ways. She didn't deserve *his* trust. She'd lied to him. And God help her, she would continue to lie to him about the baby's father because she just couldn't bear to see the look in his eyes if he knew the whole truth. Especially now that she knew how he felt about his mother.

"Unless," he said, a deep crease forming between his brows, "are you still in love with him, Shallie?"

Oh, it hurt to see that compassion in his eyes. And while it would have been her out—she could flat out lie to him and tell him that yes, she was in love with the father and he would probably back away—she just couldn't do it.

"No. I'm not in love with him. I don't think I ever was," she realized as she thought about Jared. "I just wanted to be."

"See," he scooted forward, looking unreasonably happy. He wrapped his arms around her raised knees and rested his chin on them, "that's what I mean. We all think we want something that doesn't exist. So why not take advantage of something that does?"

When she continued to frown at him, he let out a deep sigh, smiled. "Think about it, okay? Just think about it."

"Okay. I'll think about it. But you'd better think about it, too, friend of mine. Think about why you want to do this. Ask yourself if any of the reasons have anything to do with what *you* want or if they're all about this white knight thing you've got going on. I don't want you offering yourself up for a lifetime commitment for my sake. Not even for the baby's sake."

"Fair enough," he said after another long, searching look. "I'll give it some more thought—providing you seriously consider it, too."

"Do I have to be serious about it right now?" she felt an almost-panicky need to lighten the tension his suggestion had knotted tight in the room. "'Cause the only thing I'd like to get serious about is a nap."

One corner of his beautiful mouth turned up in a crooked grin. "I could go for a nap. Want some company?"

"Depends."

"On?"

"On whether we're going to take this nap with our clothes on or off."

His eyes flickered with fire. "I vote for off."

"Then it's unanimous," she said, and let him draw her into his arms for a long, hot kiss.

"Who knew we'd be so good at this together?" he said, after they'd done everything but nap.

"Yeah," she murmured on contented sigh, just before she nodded off. "Who knew."

She couldn't quite define the feeling. But she liked it, Shallie thought a few days later while she sat in a corner booth at the Dusk to Dawn watching Mac and J.T. give each other grief.

Maybe it was that sense of belonging she'd been looking for when she'd made the decision to return to Sundown. Maybe it was just being around these wonderful people who had welcomed her back—or in Ali's case, had accepted her as a friend.

She finally felt like she was a part of something. Something solid. Something good—which was a rare and special feeling for her.

"You'd think they would run out of insults after a while," Ali Tyler, J.T.'s wife and Sundown's veterinarian, said with a shake of her head as the guys chomped down burgers and the women shared a basket of fries. "I'll never understand that about men. The closer they are, the more smack they dish out."

"I read somewhere that it's a chromosome thing," Shallie said.

She'd liked Ali the first time she'd met her on New Year's day at her welcome-home party. Her opinion of the pretty blonde hadn't changed. It was a plus that she obviously made J.T. a happy man, but Ali's warm, open friendship didn't hurt, either.

"Really?" Ali gave Shallie a wide-eyed look.

"Well, no," Shallie admitted, "but I figure it's as good an explanation as any—and who knows. Someone might have done a study."

Ali laughed and nibbled on a French fry. "You're probably right. What a pair."

"You should have seen them when they were kids."

"Tell me," Ali begged, leaning over the booth top. "I could use some dirt on that man of mine."

"Oh, no," J.T. said with a waggle of his finger, suddenly tuning into the women's conversation. "Shallie. Remember our pact."

"Pact?" Ali grinned from J.T. to Shallie.

"They made me swear in blood," Shallie said.

Ali gasped. "You didn't."

"'Fraid so," Mac admitted, and winked at Shallie. "We've got enough dirt on each other that not one of us would dare open up that can of worms."

"You were kids," Ali protested. "How bad could it have been?"

J.T. glanced at Mac, who glanced at Shallie, who glanced at J.T. They all burst out laughing. Shallie figured they were thinking of the goat that disappeared from Clement Haskins's ranch and ended up in the town library. Or maybe the beautifully gift-wrapped boxful of horse manure that mysteriously showed up on Principal Cooper's desk. Or any one of a number of harmless, juvenile pranks that no one had ever owned up to but that the three of them were behind.

"I'll get it out of you," Ali promised J.T. with a wicked look.

J.T. made a show of looking worried. "She does have her ways," he admitted. "I may break under the plea-sure...I mean *pressure*."

"There are words for men like you," Mac sputtered.

"Yeah," J.T. said, caressing Ali with a very private look. "Happy." Then he leaned over and kissed his wife. "Should we tell them?" he asked, holding her gaze as he pulled away.

She nodded, then turned to Mac with a huge smile. "We're pregnant."

Shallie felt herself stiffen. She quickly recovered and gave them both a huge smile. "That's wonderful! Congratulations. When are you due?"

She heard all the animated and happy chatter as a blur of noise as Ali and J.T. filled them in on all the details. She made herself smile. She knew she was smiling because her face felt as if it was about to crack.

And she was aware of Mac watching her, his eyes filled with understanding and concern.

It should be this way for her, Shallie thought,

nodding her head, concentrating to keep her smile firmly in place. She should be able to announce to the world that she was pregnant, that she was thrilled about the prospect of having a baby to take care of and love and provide for.

But she couldn't. At least, she couldn't enjoy the sharing process the way Ali and J.T. deserved to enjoy it. Their baby would be raised in a warm and loving home. With a mother and a father to adore it and each other.

"You okay?" Mac asked quietly after Ali and J.T. had left for home.

"Sure." She flashed him a bright-eyed grin. "Great news for them, huh? They're so excited."

"Yeah. They are. I'm sorry, Shallie. I know that was hard on you."

"Don't be silly. I'm happy for them. They deserve to be excited."

"So do you," he said, wrapping an arm around her shoulders. "You deserve to be happy, too."

"I am," she insisted, and blinked hard and fast to hold back a waterfall of tears. Lord, she hated the way pregnant hormones messed with her emotions. "I am happy."

He pulled back. Cupped her shoulders between his big hands and gave her a little shake so she'd look up at him. "This guy. Whoever he is. He doesn't deserve your tears. And he doesn't deserve you. Or the baby."

And I don't deserve you, she thought when Mac hugged her again. But she was thankful, so thankful, for having him back in her life.

"I've got to go back to Bozeman tomorrow," he said after a moment. "Why don't you come with me? You need to have your cast checked about now, anyway. While you're there, we could find you an OB doc. And we could go to the courthouse. Pick up a marriage license."

He hadn't let the idea of getting married drop. He wasn't pushy about it. Just sneaky. He'd bring it up at the darnedest times. Like when she was feeling most vulnerable. Like now.

"You're kind of like a dog with a bone, aren't you?"

"Bow-wow."

She shook her head. "Mac." And took his hand. "What J.T. and Ali have…well, it's special. Peg and Cutter have it, too. It's proof, you know, that there is such a thing as over-the-moon in love. When two people have that, it's magical. You deserve that for yourself. You won't get that marrying me."

He looked down at their joined hands, absently rubbed his thumb back and forth across her knuckles. "Do you know the odds of two people finding that kind of connection? Approximately slim and none. Okay. Agreed. Our friends have it. But what that does is pretty much cut the possibility of it happening to either one of us down to nil."

"One of the things I've always loved about you is your optimism," she teased in reference to his gloom-and-doom prediction.

"I *am* an optimist, short-stack. But I'm also a realist. So let's be real here, okay?"

"Do we have to?" In the interest of trying to stall this conversation, she attempted to lighten the mood with a pout.

"Yes. I think we do."

He looked so serious suddenly that she sobered, too.

"Raising a baby on your own is not going to be easy. Sundown's a small town. Yeah. You've got good friends who will stand beside you...but do you really want to subject your little one to the small-town gossip?"

Her heart did a little stutter step. She hadn't wanted to think that far ahead. Most of all, she hadn't wanted to remember how it had been for her growing up. Kids were often unkind. And she'd been on the receiving end of snide remarks about more than her hair and her ragged clothes: "How come you don't have a dad? He get one look at that brillo pad hair of yours and hit the road? How come your momma has so many 'friends' comin' in and out of your house?"

"Shallie...honey?"

She looked up, realized she'd zoned out on Mac.

"I'm sorry," he said. "I didn't mean to hurt you."

"No. No, you didn't. You just said something that really hit home, is all. It just...really hit home."

She searched the face of this man who offered her the chance to save her own child from that kind of torment. Who offered her so much more than she really deserved.

And he looked so sweet. And so kind. And so determined that he had the right answer for both of them.

"You're really sure about this?" she asked, making it clear she was asking him if he was sure he really wanted to marry her and if he was sure he knew what he was giving up.

"Last I knew, life doesn't come with money-back guarantees, Shallie Mae. But I come with a few basic promises. I'll take care of you and the baby. I'll be your friend. I'll always be true. And you'll never have a reason not to trust me."

Trust. There was that word again. He promised that she could trust him. And she knew she could. Just like she knew she should trust him with the total truth surrounding her baby's conception.

Yet every time she screwed up her courage to tell him, something stopped her. Something like panic. Something like shame. Something that was too strong to make her do the one thing she knew was right.

So she said the one thing that made it easier, instead.

"Okay," she said, feeling like she was diving off a high board even though she knew that Mac would be there to catch her. "Let's go get that license."

He squinted, searched her eyes. "For real?"

She pushed out a laugh. "For as real as it gets, Brett McDonald, so you'd better be sure you're up for this."

When he smiled at her that way, she could almost believe he loved her. And when her chest filled with a sweet, aching joy, she could almost believe she loved him. Not just a best-friends-for-life-I'll-always-be-there-for-you kind of love.

The other kind. The kind that Ali and J.T. had. The kind the Peg and Cutter had.

Yeah. She could almost believe it. And if Mac hadn't been right about the odds of that happening being slim to none, she might have believed it. Lord knew, she wanted to.

Nine

"You dog, you!" J.T. railed at Mac a day later, even though he was grinning broadly. "I can't believe you didn't tell me.

"And you." J.T. turned an accusatory glare on Shallie now that he was done scolding Mac. "I'm your friend and you kept this a secret!"

Mac grinned from J.T. to Shallie, who was looking a little shell-shocked by J.T.'s reaction to the news that they were getting married.

The truth was, she'd looked a little dazed ever since they'd cut the deal. And he'd felt a little dazed himself. Okay. A lot dazed.

He had a shot. A real shot at making this work. She didn't love the guy. He'd been bouncing off the walls ever since that night he'd asked her, "Do you still love him, Shall?"

Not only did she not still love the creep, she was pretty certain she never had.

It was all he'd needed to charge full steam ahead. And he had—and done his damnedest to take it easy with her. They'd talked about the reality of getting married several times, and she'd insisted she was happy with her decision. And the closer the big day came, Mac realized he was more than happy. Yeah, the prospect of marrying Shallie made him grin. Made him feel mature. Settled. And it was time.

That's why he'd called J.T. and asked him to meet him and Shallie in Sundown. Since they'd wanted to talk with Ali, too, and she couldn't leave the office today because she was short-handed, they met at her vet practice instead of the Dusk to Dawn.

"I believe the correct response to our announcement is, congratulations," Mac said as, careful of her cast, J.T. wrapped Shallie in a big bear hug.

Ali did the same with Mac. "Congratulations!"

"You have my condolences, sweetheart," J.T. said, dropping a kiss on Shallie's cheek. "And I've got to tell you, I'm a little disappointed in you. I always thought you were so much smarter than to get hooked up with a no-account like this."

"Smartest woman in the world," Mac assured his buddy, who turned to him and extended a hand.

"Congratulations, man," J.T. said, serious now. "Really. This is great. Just damn great. I couldn't be happier for you."

"So, I'm in the market for a best man. Since the pickin's around here are pretty slim, what are you doing a week from Saturday?"

J.T. blinked. "No kidding? That soon?"

"Can't think of a reason to wait," Mac said. And he *couldn't* think of any good reason. Even Shallie seemed to want to make it official as soon as possible. Whether it was for fear that she'd back out or actual excitement, he didn't know.

All he knew was that his plan to play it loose and easy and slow had worked. She hadn't shied. She hadn't spooked. She'd said yes.

And he'd damn near blown a gasket.

She'd said yes. And he was determined that someday in the near future she'd say yes again to another question. One that went something like "Do you love me, Shallie?"

"Well, I'm your man, then," J.T. said, beaming. "Just tell me where and what time."

"Ali?" Shallie turned to her new friend. "I know we haven't known each other for long, but—"

Ali actually squealed. "I would be honored," she said, interrupting Shallie before she'd finished asking her to be matron of honor. "Oh, this is so exciting."

Mac loved the look that crossed Shallie's face when Ali responded with such excitement. He'd known she was hesitant to ask Ali to stand up with her, and on some level he understood the reason why.

He'd never had a doubt that Ali would be thrilled. Shallie had had doubts, though, and he figured it stemmed from the way she'd felt about herself from the time he could remember. Hell, when your own mother didn't want much to do with you, it was a leap of faith to think anyone else would. And Shallie didn't leap toward anything. She picked her way very carefully.

Ali's open and excited reaction was exactly what Shallie needed. It had been a major hurdle for her to let down her defenses enough to trust that someone might actually want to be a part of her life.

Yeah. It had been a major hurdle. And, judging by the look on Shallie's face, she was glad that she'd taken the chance on Ali.

The woman he saw right now was a happy one. And he liked it.

"Have you bought your dress yet?" Ali asked.

"My dress?" A look of minor panic replaced Shallie's smile. "I'm afraid I haven't gotten that far."

"Great. Then we can go shopping together."

God bless Ali Tyler, Mac thought later, as he and Shallie headed for the cabin. The two women had gotten their heads together to plan a shopping trip to Bozeman. Mac and J.T. had shot the breeze, occasionally warned the ladies with the bright eyes and excited smiles not to get too carried away and grinned because Mac knew he'd indulge Shallie in about anything she wanted to do to pull off her idea of the perfect wedding.

Well, not perfect, he realized. They couldn't do perfect in a week. But they could come pretty damn close, he'd decided and had already set the wheels in motion to make sure they threw one of the biggest, fanciest receptions the Dusk to Dawn had ever seen.

"You know," Shallie said, standing by the hearth one night after Mac had rebuilt the fire. "It would have been a lot easier if we'd just driven to Nevada and done this in a civil ceremony."

"Oh, boy. Here we go again. Haven't we had this discussion once or twice already and nixed the idea?"

"You nixed the idea," she pointed out.

"Come 'ere," he said and patted the sofa cushion beside him. "Let me explain this to you one more time."

With a self-conscious smile she eased down beside him, let her head fall back on his shoulder when he draped his arm around her.

"Comfy?"

She nodded and turned into him, snuggling close. He loved that she was so comfortable touching him now. Loved that they were so easy with each other.

"Now listen very carefully. We are not going to Nevada for a quickie civil ceremony. We're going to get married in the company of our good friends, and then we're going to throw the biggest reception Sundown has ever seen. Why? Because a woman deserves to have a special day to remember and tell her children and grand-children about."

He ran his hand up and down her arm in a slow caress. "And because a man wants to have a memory of his wife all dressed up and pretty for him when he thinks back on that day."

"I hate to break this to you McDonald, but in spite of your big talk to the contrary, you're a romantic, you know that? Even though you claim you don't believe in fairy-tale love."

Yeah. He was a romantic, all right. And someday he'd let her know exactly how romantic he was.

"What I am," he said choosing his words carefully, because for some reason he was suddenly having a hard time picking the right ones, "is a man who cares very much for a certain woman. I want to make you happy, Shall. And I want to start out by giving you a special day."

She tipped her head way back so she could look up at him. Her eyes were a misty, shimmering brown, and they were brimming with something that gave him a little lump, right in the center of his throat, and made it hard to swallow.

"You are such a good man," she whispered, touching his face with her fingertips, touching his heart with her smile.

They made love slow and easy, then. With the fire crackling in the hearth and the sun sinking low in the horizon.

"I'll do right by you, Shallie," he promised, moving in and out of her as she clung and arched and gave herself over to his loving.

"I'll do right by you and the baby."

"I know," she whispered back. "I...know."

When it was over she cried. His tough Shallie who never cried when someone hurt her. He held her close and stroked her hair and told himself it was all about those hormones she was always cussing. He pressed a soft kiss to the top of her head. Bless her, those hormones did give her fits.

She had to tell him, Shallie thought as she lay awake well into the night that night. He was so good.

So kind. And so trusting that she was the person he needed her to be.

She had to tell him. And in the morning she would. Maybe he'd understand. Maybe he'd forgive her.

Like he forgave his mother? she wondered, and snuggled closer to her future husband's side.

It didn't matter. Somehow, some way, she had to screw up the courage to tell him about her one night-stand with a married man.

She cringed, just thinking about it. Even so, even if he saw her for the horrible, deceitful person she was and he changed his mind about marrying her, she couldn't live with herself if she didn't come clean. And she had to do it before the wedding, which was only five days away.

He stirred in his sleep and pulled her closer to his side. And she realized, with a horrible ache in her heart, how much she was going to lose if she lost him.

She was going to lose the best thing that had ever happened to her. She was going to lose the one person who had ever really cared about making her happy. And, surprise, surprise, she *was* happy. Really happy.

With distance from her old life and the physical sur-roundings of her failures and with Mac's tender support, she was actually more happy than worried about the prospect of being a mother. She'd needed someone to love for so long. Someone to love her. She'd thought it would be just her and her baby. She'd thought she could make it enough.

But now there was Mac. And now she knew he truly did make her life complete.

That was the biggest revelation of all. She'd been determined to classify their relationship as friendship. She'd been determined they were marrying for convenience. For the sake of the child. And because Mac was ready for a family and had given up on love.

Well, guess what? She hadn't. She'd thought she had. She'd thought there wasn't a chance on earth that she'd ever fall in love again.

Turns out she was wrong. Turns out she'd never been in love at all. Not really.

Well, she was now. For the first time.

Mac. She loved him. Loved him for being there for her. Loved him for wanting to take care of her. Loved him for being the kind of man he was.

But most of all, over the course of the past week and a half, she'd fallen in love with him as she'd never loved another man.

It was more than love now. At least, it was more than any love she'd ever known. She couldn't wait to see him every morning. Couldn't imagine going to bed without him at night. Adored it when he touched her, kissed her, made love to her like she was the most special woman in the world. No one had ever given her that before. No one.

Her macaroon. Her white knight.

And because she loved him, she had to tell him in the morning, she reminded herself, sobering in the dark.

But when morning came, he was gone. She found a note tucked under a plate of chocolate-glazed long johns:

Hey, Shall,
You were sleeping so sound I didn't want to wake you. Cara's got a problem with the refrigeration

at SW so I had to head back to Bozeman. I'll call
you later, okay?
XOXOs, Mac.

Shallie slowly folded the note. And felt a relief too big
to be anything but cowardice. She'd been given a reprieve.
And she was grateful.

Tonight, she promised herself, walking over to the
kitchen window to watch a vibrant red cardinal eat
cracked corn from a feeder Mac had put up, for her as
much as for the birds. She would tell him tonight.

But he didn't make it back to Sundown that night.
The refrigeration problem had become a dilemma and
he'd had to drive to Helena for parts.

During the course of the week, a dozen things dis-
rupted their communication flow. Even when Shallie
and Ali spent a day in Bozeman shopping for their
dresses and they stopped into SW for lunch, Shallie
couldn't find the right time to talk to him.

The next thing she knew it was Saturday, their wedding
day, and, for a number of reasons, she still hadn't told him.

More to the point, she'd started to believe there might
be a valid reason that "life" kept interrupting her good
intentions.

Maybe fate was intervening on her behalf. Maybe it
was okay that he didn't know. Maybe it was okay to
leave her past in the past and start this new life with Mac
without the weight of her mistake hanging over them.

And maybe, just maybe, she deserved to have him
think of her the way he wanted to think of her, not the
way he would be forced to think of her if he knew.

Whatever the reason as she slipped into her wedding dress and put the final touches on her makeup, the only thing she was certain she was going to say to Brett McDonald this afternoon, was "I do."

Besides Mac and Shallie, only J.T. and Ali and Mac's dad, Alex, witnessed the vows as Preacher Davis performed the ceremony at the Sundown Congregational Church where they were pronounced man and wife.

The reception, however, was a different story. They wanted *all* of their friends at the reception.

The Dusk to Dawn was packed. From the bar to the eating area to the dance floor, it was party room only.

And for Sundown it was the party of the decade.

"How'd a couple of duds like us rate women like them?" J.T. asked Mac as they stood, beers in hand, watching Ali and Shallie dancing with the Griener twins.

Mac grinned and shook his head. "Beats the hell out of me. Sometimes it's best not to question good luck."

"Amen to that. Hey…there's Lee and Ellie Savage. I've got to go say hello. Be right back."

Mac was barely aware of J.T. leaving. Hadn't been aware of much of anything except Shallie since he'd caught sight of her walking down the aisle toward him at four o'clock this afternoon.

Shallie had always been a looker. She had that wholesome, girl-next-door-with-an-attitude look that had always made him think of a modern-day Annie Oakley. *Grit* was a word that always came to mind when he'd thought of her.

It wasn't the word that came to mind today. A lot of others did, though.

Beautiful, for one.

Special, for another.

Mine, however, topped the list.

As of today, Shallie Malone was Shallie McDonald. And she was his. To take care of. To share with. To have and to hold and to love and to cherish.

He'd meant every word when he'd said them. It wasn't that he hadn't expected their vows to have meaning. He just hadn't expected them to mean so much.

He grinned as Billie Griener twirled Shallie across the dance floor and she threw Mac a look that clearly cried, Help!

Setting his beer on the bar, he set off through the crowd to rescue his very own damsel in distress.

"I'll be taking my wife back now," he said, tapping Billie on the shoulder.

"Yeah, I saw the way you were watching us," Billie teased. "Figured you'd get to worrying 'bout me beating your time."

Mac grinned at Billie's receding hairline and to-bacco-stained teeth and pulled Shallie into his arms. "You read me right, man. Now give me some room to work here so I can make her forget all about you."

With a chuckle, Billie slapped him on the shoulder and headed for the bar.

"So," Mac said, slowing things down to an intimate, easy sway even though the band he'd hired was rocking to a Montgomery Gentry song, "you having a good time?"

"The best." When she looked up at him, her smile was so huge and bright it staggered him. "And even better now. Thanks for the rescue mission. I don't think my feet could have taken one more hit from Billie's boots."

"God, you're pretty," he said because he just couldn't hold it in. She'd done something special with her hair. Nothing too fancy. Nothing too much could be done with those short, springy curls, but she'd tamed them some and tucked a little sprig of flowers above her right ear, and damned if she didn't make him think of some kind of a forest nymph.

There was a little extra pink in her cheeks, a shimmery gloss on her lips—probably the dress had something to do with it, too. He didn't have a clue what it was. Silk maybe. And pale pink with long sleeves that covered the smaller cast the doctor had put on just yesterday. She looked sleek and slim and soft. Felt that way, too.

"You don't look so bad yourself, cowboy."

Just for her, because she'd remarked how sexy J.T. had looked at his and Ali's wedding—Ali had had them for dinner last night, and Shallie had spotted the picture on the wall—Mac had dressed in a black western-cut suit.

"Yeah, well. Told you I cleaned up pretty good."

"That you do," she agreed with the softest smile. The kind of smile that made him feel all full inside.

This was going to work, he told himself as the band changed gears and launched into a ballad. This marriage was going to work. Everything felt right about it.

More right, even, than he'd thought it would. He felt it

more and more every day. And seeing Shallie today, glowing and happy and knowing he was in part responsible for that happiness, he'd started to feel something else.

He could make her fall in love with him. He smiled to himself and lowered his head so he could nuzzle her ear and get a whiff of that amazing scent she was wearing.

Yeah. He could make her fall in love with him. This woman who was the antithesis of almost every woman he'd ever been involved with. A woman who didn't play games. Whose life didn't revolve around how she looked. A woman who wasn't after him for his money and wasn't overly impressed by his success.

She was fun and funny and sincere.

And she didn't have a deceitful bone in her body.

She was just Shallie. Honest. And real. And true. In short, she was perfect.

Any man would be lucky to have her. And as he held her in his arms and she snuggled up against him, he counted himself as one damn lucky man.

"What I'd like to know," Mac murmured as they cuddled under the big quilt on the floor in front of the fireplace later that night, "is what kind of woman prefers winter in an old cabin in the mountains to a condo on Maui for a honeymoon destination?"

Shallie snuggled closer, loving the feel of Mac's big naked body pressed against hers, sharing his heat with her. "I don't need Maui."

"I'm not talking about need. I'm talking about what you want."

"I want what I've got. And it's right here."

"Six-foot snowdrifts, Arctic winds, the possibility of power outages—"

She cut him off with a finger pressed to his lips. He promptly sucked it inside his mouth, gently latched on. "I want a home, Mac," she said, hearing her voice clog with emotion.

He heard it, too. Let go of her finger and looked into her eyes.

"I want a home," she repeated softly. "It's all I've ever wanted. You've given it to me." She searched his beautiful face, cupped his strong, hard jaw in her palm. "What more could a woman want?"

He was quiet for a long moment before he slowly shook his head. "You're one of a kind, short-stack."

"Broke the mold, all right," she agreed, giving him a smile.

"No. I mean it." He kissed her forehead, then her brow, then her cheeks. "I don't know anyone like you. Unassuming. Unspoiled. Honest."

She felt those damn tears well up again. Not just from the tender way he kissed her, not just from the sincerity of his words, but from the guilt over just how dishonest she had been with him.

"Mac," she began, overcome by an urge to blurt out the truth about the baby. Get it off her chest.

He shook his head. "No, wait. I'm not finished. There's something I need to say to you. Something I should have said before today but didn't have the guts."

She swallowed hard, her heart pounding, her nerves shredded as she waited him out. She'd let him have his say. Then she'd tell him.

"You know that notion of love and happily ever after I've been speaking out against?"

Heart in her throat, she nodded.

"Well, the deal is, I didn't know what I was talking about."

Her heart stopped then. Flat-out, still as stone, stopped.

"I want happily ever after with you, Shall. I want love with you. And I'm thinking maybe I'm going to get it."

"Mac—"

"There you go," he scolded, a smile in his voice, "Interrupting me again. I love you, Shallie. I've always loved you. Honest to God, head-over-heels, love you. There. I'm done. Now you can talk."

Like she could talk. Joy rolled over trepidation. Hope won out over guilt. She threw her arms around his neck, clunked him on the back of her head with her cast and made them both laugh. And then she just hung on. To this man. This beautiful, amazing man who thought he loved her.

"Hey. Hey, hey," he soothed. "Are you crying again?"

She laughed, pressing her face against his neck. "How do you think I'm going to react to a statement like that?" she sniffed.

"Oh, I don't know. I was kind of hoping you might tell me how *you* felt about the idea of love and happily ever after and stuff."

She sniffed again. "Stuff, huh?"

"Well, mostly about the love part."

She pulled back so she could look into his beautiful gentle eyes. "I really, really like the love part. In fact, I'm pretty much in love with the love part."

He smiled and her world went one hundred percent right again. "Pretty much?"

She nodded.

"How pretty much?"

And laughed. "Pretty much pretty sure that I pretty much love you, too."

He looked so happy. Not just the usual, good-natured, Mac-the-good-guy happy. But a-man-in-love happy.

"Lots of pretties in there."

"Yeah. Lots."

"So," he said, stroking a hand along her hip beneath the quilt. "This is like a good thing, right?"

"Yeah." She laughed again. "It's like a good thing."

He watched her face for the longest time, then turned serious as he slid his hand around and covered her stomach with his big palm.

It felt warm and gentle and protective against her.

"I want this to be *our* baby, Shallie. I want to raise this baby as mine. Yours and mine."

Her eyes blurred and burned and it felt like her heart was going to push its way out of her body through her throat. "Mac."

His big hand slowly caressed her there, where the baby slept and grew. "Our baby, Shallie. Okay?"

How could she say no to this gift he was giving her child? A gift that should be a birthright. A right she'd never had. How could she deny it to her child?

And how could she tell him the truth now and risk losing it all?

"Okay," she managed to whisper between trembling lips. "That is so very, very okay."

Ten

While the last of the women who had attended her baby shower said their goodbyes, Shallie bounced little six-month-old Jacob Savage on her knee. The baby drooled and grinned and made Shallie's heart swell with anticipation of her own baby's arrival in less than four months.

"He's such a sweetheart," she said to the baby's mother, Ellie Savage.

"He's our little miracle," Ellie agreed, beaming as she helped Peg Lathrop tidy up the Dusk to Dawn which had been closed today for the private shower.

Ali and Shallie started to show about the same time a couple of months ago. Shallie was sure people had wondered about the timing of her pregnancy but they were too kind to say anything. It was about that same time that Peg Reno and Ellie decided it would be a fine time for a joint baby shower.

They'd done it up right, too. Shallie was overwhelmed by the generosity of the Sundown women—some of them she barely knew. Judging from the look on Ali's face as she organized her gifts so J.T. could help her haul them home, Ali was pretty amazed, as well.

They were wonderful people, these new friends of hers. Shallie had gotten to know Lee and Ellie well during the past couple of months since she and Mac had gotten married. During that time, she'd grown to admire the young woman who struggled with epilepsy, yet didn't let it keep her from enjoying life to the fullest. Even if it had meant risking her own health to conceive and deliver this amazing child.

"Your momma thinks you're a miracle, baby boy," Shallie said, lifting Jacob to her shoulder and snuggling him close. "I have to agree. You're such a good baby," she murmured, rubbing his back and inhaling the wonderful scent of baby and powder and thinking that it wouldn't be long now until she held her own baby.

Hers and Mac's. And that's exactly how she thought of the life growing inside of her. Mac's child.

"I think that pretty much covers it," Peg said, looking around at the tidy room.

"You guys are too much," Ali said, her look encompassing both Peg and Ellie.

"Agreed," Shallie chimed in as Ali held her arms out so she could have a turn at cuddling Jacob before everyone headed for home.

"Any excuse for a party," Peg said with a grin just as the front door opened.

"Did someone say party?" J.T. beamed as he walked into the Dusk to Dawn followed by Mac, Cutter Reno and Lee Savage.

"Sorry, guys. It's all over but the heavy lifting." Ellie handed the diaper bag to Lee, then pried Jacob out of Ali's arms so she could bundle him into his little snowsuit.

"And what did you four troublemakers find to do to keep yourself busy for the last few hours?" Peg asked, grabbing her coat.

Cutter hurried over and helped her into it. "Just a friendly little card game."

"Friendly?" Mac snorted. "It was cutthroat."

Lee slapped him on the back and addressed the room in general as J.T. gathered up an armload of baby gifts and winked at Shallie. "Treat him with kid gloves tonight, Shallie. The man had a little string of bad luck."

"Card sharks, is what they are," Mac grumbled.

"Poker face is what he isn't," J.T. pointed out with a nod in Mac's direction. "But he *is* a sore loser."

"Har. Har." Mac walked over to Shallie, sat down in a huff.

"What's the matter, sweetie? Did those mean boys pick on you today?" She patted his hand with staged sympathy while the other guys looked anything but sympathetic.

"They beat me out of my lunch money, Mom," he whined, playing for a laugh—which he got along with a few more jabs from the guys before they all collected their women and headed out the door with a chorus of goodbyes.

"Thought they'd never leave," Mac said, urging her onto his lap. He kissed her. Smiled. "So, did you and Heathcliff rake in lots of loot?"

She laughed. "Me and *Gertrude* did pretty darn good. Wait until you see all this stuff."

"Had a good time, did you?"

She nodded. "Had a great time. These people…well, they're wonderful."

He kissed her again. "So are you. Now, what do you say we get this stuff loaded up and head for home?"

"Sounds good to me. I'm beat. Opening presents is very exhausting."

"Your wrist hurting?"

"No. Oh, no," she said quickly seeing the concern in his eyes. He'd been that way ever since she'd had the cast removed a month ago. "Will you quit worrying about my wrist? It's fine. Perfect. I was kidding, okay? Now, let's start loading up so we can go home."

"You will load nothing. I'll handle it. I don't want you lifting one thing."

That was another thing about Mac. He was a protector. If he had his way, he'd keep her in a glass cage where nothing could get at her. No germs, no possibility of accidents.

The independent side of her would complain, but he was so cute about it she couldn't bear to burst his bubble.

"Sit tight for a second," he said, sliding her off his lap. "I need to check on some things in the kitchen. Be back in about five minutes, and then I'll load this major haul into the truck."

"I'm not going anywhere," Shallie said, and watched him disappear into the kitchen.

Life, she decided, lifting a little yellow sleeper out of a box, just couldn't get any better. The past two months since they'd gotten married had been the best of her life. Mac was sweet and gentle and so much fun to be with. And he was an inventive and selfless lover. She got a little chill just thinking about the way he made her feel when he made love to her.

Yeah, she thought, holding the little sleeper to her breast. Life just couldn't get any better. For the first time in her life she had a home—a complete home. She had someone who loved her. Her. Just as she was, in the form of a man she still couldn't believe she'd been lucky enough to want to be a part of her life.

Yeah. Life was perfect.

And then the front door opened with a cool rush of mid-March air.

A man's silhouette filled the dark doorway.

"Hello, Shallie." He stepped into the light.

And Shallie felt her perfect world slip out from under her like a sinkhole.

"Jared."

Mac took a little longer than he'd thought, stocking the cooler for the bar action that the Dusk to Dawn was sure to see tonight when they opened back up to the public at six.

He was afraid Shallie might have given up on him when he finally shut the kitchen door behind him and headed for the main room.

"I told you to leave," he heard Shallie say before he saw her and every protective instinct in his body went on red alert.

She was standing and she looked agitated, and whoever was the cause of that agitation was some guy who looked about as determined to stay as she was for him to go.

"Damn it, Shallie, I didn't spend five months hunting you down, then drive two thousand miles to find you, just to turn around and go back to Georgia without you. I made a mistake, all right? I realize that. I said I was sorry. So quit talking nonsense and get in the car."

"I believe the lady said she wanted you to leave." Mac walked up behind Shallie, put his hands on her shoulders and gently set her behind him.

"Mac. It's okay. I can handle this," she said quickly.

The guy glared at Mac. "Who the hell are you?"

He was about Mac's height and weight. His eyes were a mean brown, his attitude superior as hell. And Mac didn't much care for the way his fists were clenched at his side.

He also didn't care for the implications. This had to be the guy. The guy who'd cheated on Shallie and left her pregnant.

Mac's gut clenched as he sized him up. He hated him on sight. Hated to think of this guy touching Shallie. Hated to think of him having anything to do with her. And rumbling through it all was a growing and consuming concern that he might be here to stake some claim on the baby. The baby Mac had come to think of as his own.

"I'm the guy," Mac ground out, "who's going to

invite you real nice-like to do as my wife says and get the hell off my property."

"Wife?" His dark gaze shifted from Mac to Shallie who had moved out from behind Mac and was trying to insinuate herself between them. He grunted, threw her a look of disgust. "Well, it didn't take you long to find another bed to crawl into, did it?"

"One more word," Mac ground out, pushing past Shallie and grabbing the guy's jacket in his fist and twisting, "and I'll kick your ass from here back to Georgia."

"Stop it!" Shallie reached for Mac's arm, tried to push him away. "Please. Stop. Mac. Don't. He's not worth it.

"Jared," she said, turning to the guy as Mac reluctantly let him go. "Leave. Now."

Jared gave a macho shrug of his shoulders, shot Shallie a glare. "This is what you want?" He lifted a hand toward Mac. "You want to be stuck out here in the boonies with cowboy Bob here?"

"Look, you're the one who screwed up, okay?" Mac was pissed now. Royally pissed. He shoved Jared hard in the middle of his chest, knocked him a step backward. "What kind of man makes promises to a woman then cheats on her? What kind of a man walks away from his own baby?"

Jared staggered when Mac shoved him, caught his balance and glared from Mac to Shallie. "Baby? What the hell are you talking about?"

"I'm talking about how you got her pregnant and then walked out on her."

"Whoa. Whoa." Jared lifted his hands beside his head

in a show of supplication. "I don't know anything about a baby. Is that what she told you? That I got her pregnant?"

"Figures you wouldn't own up," Mac said with a snarl.

"Own up? Hell, cowboy," Jared said with a cocky and ugly smile, "I'd own up if it was true, but the fact is, I'm shooting blanks, man."

Mac narrowed his eyes.

"Vasectomy," Jared supplied, looking smug. "Three years ago. I don't want any little bastards running around costing me money."

Mac glanced at Shallie. She'd gone statue still. Ghost white.

She closed her eyes. Swallowed. "You need to leave now, Jared," she said in a voice that sounded hollow and weary and empty of conviction.

Jared looked from Shallie to Mac then smiled a nasty smile. "Looks like maybe I do. My mistake, cowboy," he said, backing toward the door. "She's all yours. Her and the brat."

The silence that rang in the wake of his departure could have filled the Grand Canyon.

Mac was aware of Shallie suffering beside him. Aware but unable to do anything about it.

He felt as if he'd been gutted. He felt as if he'd been strung out, hung out, stripped of everything he thought he knew. About her. About them.

She'd lied. Shallie had lied to him.

It didn't compute. It didn't add up to what he knew about who she was and what she was.

And it left him feeling so fractured and confused he didn't know what to say. How to handle the sense of betrayal, the surge of anger that had him glued to the spot, his gaze stuck on the door that had shut behind the man who had just changed his life forever.

"Mac—"

He held up a hand. Shook his head. "Don't."

"Please." There were tears in her voice. No doubt, in her eyes as well. For once it didn't affect him. He didn't want to hear what she had to say. Didn't want to look at her.

"Let's get these things into the truck," he said, and started stacking boxes and grabbing sacks.

He walked around her where she stood in the middle of the room, looking helpless, looking hopeless.

"It was after I caught Jared cheating," she said and he stopped cold in his tracks. Back stiff. Shoulders back.

"He'd hurt me, you know? And I don't mean just hurt me because he cheated. He, um, he hit me."

All the muscles in Mac's body clenched tight. His gut knotted. And for a second, there, he thought he was going to be sick.

"That was it for me. I left him. And then I wallowed. If you can imagine, now that you've had the pleasure, I actually felt like I'd lost something other than my self-respect. For a month I threw one big pity party. Poor Shallie. Nobody loves me. Nobody wants me."

Mac swallowed. Lowered his head. And still he couldn't turn to her.

"Anyway," she said, sounding weary and resigned, "a couple of the girls I worked with dragged me with them to a bar one night. Just to make me get out. You know. Crawl out of my cave. This…this guy…"

She stopped, her voice trembling.

"This guy," she began again after she'd collected herself, "he was so…nice to me, you know? Made me feel worth something again. He was charming. And he charmed me."

Another pause, as if she was working up the courage to go on.

"Shallie," he finally said, needing to stop her. He didn't want to hear any more.

"It wasn't until the next time I saw him a week later that I found out he was married," she finished with a truckload of guilt weighing down her words.

Married. She'd slept with a married man.

Something inside of him went stone-cold dead.

"I didn't know. I swear I didn't know. And after… after that night, after I found out, he…he kept after me no matter how often and how vehemently I told him no. And when…when I found out I was pregnant. Well. I'm not a home wrecker, Mac. He has a wife. Kids."

"Anyway," she said after the moment it took her to compose herself, "I had to get away from there. And that's why I ended up here."

Mac drew a deep breath, let it out, thought of his mother who had cheated on his dad with a married man. And couldn't find it in himself to sort one situation from another.

"I meant to tell you."

"Then why didn't you?" he asked, finally finding his voice and with it the hard edge of anger.

"I…I tried. I really tried. But it was just so easy to let things get in the way of the truth. You…you made it so easy."

"Ah. So it's my fault."

"No. That's not what I meant. Mac—"

"Look. Let's just get out of here. I don't want to talk about it. I don't want to hear about it. It's over. It's done. Nothing's changed. You're still pregnant. We're still married. Let's just leave it at that."

Even as he said the words, he knew they were lies.

Everything had changed.

Everything.

Winter was almost over, but Shallie had never felt so cold. Cold outside. Cold inside.

A silence the size of a glacier radiated from Mac like an Arctic chill as they rode from Sundown to Bozeman.

She understood. She understood his anger. Understood his disappointment. In her. In who he'd thought she was.

And it was no one's fault but her own. She was the one who'd made the mistakes. She couldn't even blame Jared for showing up out of the blue and exposing her.

She still couldn't believe he'd tracked her down. No. She wasn't foolish enough to believe he'd taken the time and the trouble to find her out any sense of love or guilt. With Jared, it was about control. Possession. Evidently, he'd decided he missed that aspect of their relationship.

She didn't.

But she did miss what she'd just lost.

So much for happily-ever-after, she thought, as Mac

pulled into his garage and without a word and started unloading baby gifts.

So much for things finally being easy.

Three weeks passed in numbing, miserable silence. Shallie felt Mac pull farther and farther away from her. Farther and farther into himself.

He didn't act angry. If he had, maybe she could have handled it better. Instead, he acted indifferent. She was more than familiar with indifference. It's the best that she'd ever gotten from her mother. Indifference meant there would be no hitting, true, but the pain that lack of caring implied had almost been worse than a physical blow when she was a child. And the effect hung around much longer than a bruise.

It hurt as badly now.

So many times she wanted to ask him to say something. Anything. Curse. Belittle her. Berate her. Anything but this tepid, polite apathy. Anything but a cool good-night as he went to bed in the guest room and shut the door behind him.

No hugs. No kisses. No chocolate. She missed the chocolate most of all because it had become such a symbol of his love for her.

They were now husband and wife in name only. But he did his duty, this disillusioned husband of hers. He did what he had promised to do. He took care of her. He didn't have it in him to do anything else.

"Do you need anything from the supermarket?"

"When's your next doctor's appointment? Do you need me to take you?"

"I'll be at SW. Call me if you need anything."

That was about the extent of their conversation these days.

And it was slowly killing her right along with their marriage.

Tonight, when he came home from SW, was just another night in a string of nights where their communication consisted of short, guilty looks. He looked tired and haunted when he said a quiet, "Good night," and walked right past her without ever meeting her eyes.

That's probably the part that got to her most. She missed those smiling eyes. Missed the mischief. Missed the fun.

She'd done that to him. And it was this night that she'd finally had enough of dealing with the fallout.

With her heart in her throat she walked to the guest bedroom door. Knocked.

A few seconds passed before it opened.

Mac stood there in his bare feet, his shirt unbuttoned and tugged out of his pants.

"I give up," she said, before he could ask her what she wanted and make her feel even more of a pariah than she already felt.

He looked at her then. She'd given him little choice. All she saw was fatigue. Maybe a hint of anger.

It was the first real emotion she'd seen since that fateful day in March—and it spurred a surprising arch of anger in her.

"I'm sorry," she said. "It's too little. I know. But what else can I say? What else can I do?"

His jaw clenched and he looked away.

"Yeah. That's right. Look away. I'm sorry about that, too. That you can't even stand to look at me."

He scrubbed a weary hand over his jaw. "Look. I'm tired, okay? And I don't see what good this is doing."

"No. Of course you don't see. Your idea of dealing with what I've done to screw up *your* life is to ignore it.

"I've waited, Mac," she said, her voice rising in accusation. "I've waited. I've given you room. Hoped that with time you might talk to me. Might be able to forgive me. A lot to ask, I know. And why should you? I can't forgive myself. At least, I haven't been able to. But you know what? That stops right here. Right now. Tonight."

She was shaking now as almost a month of tightly wrapped emotions uncoiled like a spring inside her. She pushed past him, walked to the bed. Sat down on the edge of the mattress and braced her palms on either side of her hips.

"I made a mistake, okay? It was a horrible mistake. It wasn't my first. It probably won't be my last, but you know what, Mac? That doesn't make me a horrible person. A horrible person wouldn't have beat herself up over this. A horrible person wouldn't have left Georgia to avoid one mistake compounding into another."

"You're not a horrible person," he said with a grim reluctance that told her he wasn't one hundred percent convinced of that.

"Then why are you treating me like I am?" she implored, hearing the heartache, the humiliation, the disappointment in her voice and knowing he heard it, too.

He met her eyes, looked away. Again. Shook his

head. Again. "I don't know. Honest to God, Shallie. I don't know."

"I think you do," she said reacting to something she saw in that brief glimpse of his eyes. "I think you know exactly why. You just don't want to come to terms with it."

"Well. If you've got all the answers, by all means, enlighten me, then, will you?" There was just enough bite in his tone to let her know that the anger he'd bottled up all this time was near the bursting point.

Good. Because she was right there with him.

"I think the problem is that I'm not the same needy little girl who left here ten years ago. And you wanted me to be. You wanted me to be needy and perfect and a victim—just like I was back then."

"You let me think you were," he accused.

"Yeah," she said quietly. "Yeah. I did. I did because intuitively, I knew that's what you wanted me to be. I didn't want to let you down, Mac. From that first day we met when you were waiting for me on the school steps, I made it my mission to never let you down.

"And now I have," she said with her chin up. "And you reacted exactly the way I was always afraid you would. You turned away. You tuned me out."

"You lied to me," he said, a wealth of pain and defense in those four little words. "The last thing I expected from you was deceit."

"You think I don't know that? You think that wasn't a huge part of what stopped me from telling you the truth about the baby? I didn't want to disappoint you. You, the one person who always loved me.

"And now—" she lifted a hand, let it drop "—now I

have this chance for you to love not only me but my baby, too. Do you know what that means to me to know that my baby would actually have a father? A father like I never had? To have the *family* I never had?"

She felt tears push. She pushed back, determined not to give in to them now. "Did I lie? Yes. Was it wrong? Of course it was. Did I use you? Yes again. But I did something else, too, Mac. I loved you. There was nothing dishonest about that. It's all I had to give. It's all I've *ever* had to give anyone. And until you, it had never been enough."

She paused, met his eyes. "And you wonder why I lied? I lied because I was afraid of exactly what happened. I lied because I was afraid that like everyone else, my love wouldn't be enough for you, either. Turns out I had more than enough reason to be afraid."

When he said nothing, she knew it was over. She stood slowly, walked past him to the bedroom door. "Look…I got a response to the résumés I sent out a couple of weeks ago."

She stopped just inside the room, still hoping he'd say something, knowing in her heart that he wouldn't. "Actually got a job offer. So here's the deal. You won't have to worry about taking care of me anymore. But I would like a little time. A couple of weeks to find an apartment if that's okay. Then I'll be out of your hair."

She didn't expect him to follow her. And he didn't.

She walked to the bedroom they used to share, undressed in the dark and crawled under the covers. Tried not to remember the loving and the laughing they'd shared in this bed. Tried to reprogram, regroup and gear up for the next hurdle. Because that's what life was really all about. And that's what she always did to get by.

She'd be okay. She and her baby. They'd be fine. Just the two of them together.

Because that was the way it was going to be.

But she'd always be sorry. Always and forever be sorry that her love was never enough.

Eleven

Mac watched Shallie walk out the bedroom door. He had a lump in his throat the size of a football. Big enough anyway, that he blamed it for his silence.

Big enough that he blamed it for the burning going on behind his eyelids.

Feeling weary to the bone and as hollow as an empty well, he dragged his fingers through his hair. Flopped down on his back on the bed and stared at the ceiling.

What a mess. What a big, screwed-up mess.

Shallie's words kept replaying in his head, along with a litany of her sins.

He checked them off one by one, just as he'd been doing for days, rewinding and replaying and using them to distance himself from her emotionally.

She'd lied. She'd used. She'd deceived.

She'd slept with a married man.

Of all the transgressions he'd stacked up against her, the last one was the one that had been hanging him up the most. She'd committed adultery—just like his mother.

Yeah. He'd slogged around, knee-deep in those sins she'd committed against him for weeks now. Letting them build. Let them breed one on top of the other until he couldn't even look at her because that's all he saw. A liar. A cheater. A user.

But he had some new words to think about now. Words she'd delivered like a promise. A promise he knew she would keep.

Give me a couple of weeks. Then I'll be out of your hair.

Out of your hair…out of your hair…out of—

He sat up straight. Felt the kick of his heart. Felt the flood of panic spread through his chest.

She was leaving. She was letting him off the hook.

So, what did you think would happen, Einstein? Did you think she'd just hang around, like the ball and chain you'd decided she would always be? Just wear you down with the weight of her sins?

Out of your hair…out of your hair…

He swore into the darkness.

She'd do it, too. She'd leave him. For his sake. Because that was her true nature.

It all became so clear then. The accusation wheels stopped spinning in endless circles. What he hadn't been able to sort out in damn near a month slipped into place with the ease of the right combination on a safe lock.

All because her words made him realize what he'd be losing if he let her walk out that door.

God, he was a fool. The worst kind. The kind who couldn't see the beauty of a wildflower because his book of rules labeled it a noxious weed.

He rose, walked to the bedroom door. He had to fix this. He had to fix everything.

But it wouldn't be tonight, he realized when he carefully opened his master bedroom door and found her sleeping.

"Make it good," he told himself, and pulled on his shoes and socks. "Make it damn good."

And with that mission in mind, he slipped out of the house and started laying the groundwork for undoing the harm he'd done.

It was late the next morning when Shallie slipped out of the bedroom and ventured toward the kitchen. She hadn't slept well. She felt as rested as if she'd spent the night standing up in a corner—like a bad girl should, she thought morosely as she walked into the kitchen.

And stopped dead in her tracks.

Chocolate. There was chocolate everywhere.

Éclairs. Cake. Cookies. Candy. Tiramisu. Boxes and cartons and plates and trays of chocolate desserts of every size and description covered every inch of available counter space, some of it stacked layers deep.

"Thought you might have missed this, too."

Mac's voice startled her. She turned to see him standing just inside the kitchen, his fingers tucked in his back pockets, his hair a mess, his eyes blurry, as if he hadn't slept all night.

"I, um," She lifted a hand toward the mountains of chocolate. "I don't…understand."

But she hoped she did. She hoped with all her heart that the guilt she read in his eyes, the fact that he was looking at her, that he'd evidently bought the entire city of Bozeman out of chocolate by ten o'clock in the morning, meant that she understood perfectly what it meant.

Hope, it seemed, was stronger than despair. Because all he had to do was take a step toward her, hold out his hand and she was in his arms.

Clinging. Crying. Thanking God and her lucky stars and anything she could think of that she was in his arms again.

"I'm so sorry," he murmured into her hair. "So sorry for shutting you out."

"It's okay. It's okay," she whispered, beyond caring about how badly she'd hurt the past three weeks, only caring that he'd forgiven her.

"It's not okay," he said rocking her back and forth, holding her tight. "It's not okay at all.

"Come on," he said with a gentle squeeze. "Let's go into the living room. There are things I need to say to you."

She sniffed as, with his arm over her shoulders, he walked her to the sofa and sat her down.

"Nobody's perfect," he said, taking her hands in his and meeting her eyes. "And you were right. I wanted you to be. I expected you to be. And it wasn't until you pointed it out that I realized what a jerk I was."

"You weren't a jerk. I hurt you."

He shook his head. "I was a jerk," he restated emphatically. "Hell, Shall—I was a *perfect* jerk. Perfect life. Perfect business. Perfect woman for me to take care of and play perfect husband for."

He made a face that told of his self-disgust. "That's what happens when Peter Pan grows up to be a man. He expects the status quo. And he can't handle it when something happens that doesn't fit his standard, so he cuts it out of his life."

He wanted to talk, so she let him. Knew, instinctively that he was working his way through his thoughts very carefully.

"Well, life's not perfect. And you know what happens to a man who expects perfection? He loses out on some of the best things in his life." His gaze dropped to their joined hands before meeting her eyes again. "I don't want to lose you, Shallie. I don't want to lose what we had. I don't want to lose the most important thing that ever happened to me. Don't go. Please don't go."

Well, damn. She was crying again. "I'm not going anywhere," she managed to whisper between the tears. "You're stuck with me, Mac. You just try and shake me loose. See what happens."

"I love you, Shallie. I love you so much."

She wrapped herself around him. Held him close. "That's enough for me. That will always be enough."

And for the first time in her life she knew that what she had to offer—her love—was finally enough, too.

Epilogue

Ella Margaret McDonald came screaming and kicking into the world at 3:26 a.m. on June 9.

"Just like her momma," Mac whispered as he snuggled his baby daughter in his arms three hours later while Shallie dozed in her hospital bed.

"She's beautiful, Mac," his mother said with tears in her eyes and with a love he had missed for too many years.

Yeah, Mr. Perfect had learned a lot from his scrapper of a wife. He'd learned to forgive. And he'd learned that picking up the phone and calling his mother wasn't such a hard thing to do after all. In fact, next to marrying Shallie, it was one of the easiest and the best things he'd ever done.

Hearing the joy in his mother's voice when she'd realized he was letting her back in his life again took some of the bite out of the guilt he felt over turning away from her.

He'd told his dad first, of course. Told him that it was time for both of them to get on with life and learn to live with the truth of it. Yeah, it had hurt his dad at first, but he was a fair man. Of course, the fact that Widow Hammel had started making him pot roast on Sundays and keeping him company a couple of nights a week also helped.

"Hi, sleepyhead," Mac murmured when Shallie opened her eyes and blinked up at him.

"Hey. How's our girl?"

"Little Gertrude is doing just fine," he teased, knowing he'd get a grin out of her. "How's her momma?"

"Good," she said, shifting gingerly. "I'm good."

Mac leaned down and kissed her. "You're better than good, short-stack. In my book, you're *almost* perfect."

And that, Mac knew, was the best anyone could ever hope to be.

* * * * *